THE SUN ALSO RISES ON CTHULHU

THE SUN ALSO RISES ON CTHULHU

Ernest Hemingway
and Jorah Kai

Title: *The Sun Also Rises on Cthulhu*
Ebook ISBN: 978-1-95960-401-3
Paperback ISBN: 978-1-959604-19-8
Hardcover ISBN: 978-1-959604-18-1

SATIRICAL COLLABORATION DISCLAIMER:

The inclusion of dreamlike interactions with famous authors such as, but not limited to, Ernest Hemingway, Scott F. Fitzgerald, Zelda Fitzgerald, Oscar Wilde, Mark Twain, Edgar Allan Poe, H.P. Lovecraft, as well as gods of various pantheons and deep-sleeping ancient ones, is a fictional narrative device. These portrayals are not intended to be literal or to imply any actual communication, collaboration, or endorsement—spiritual or otherwise—on behalf of these figures or their estates.

The stylized signature attributed to Ernest Hemingway within this book is fictionalized and is not an authentic reproduction of any signature associated with Hemingway or his estate. Its inclusion is a satirical and creative element of the story and should not be interpreted as a factual representation.

Additionally, this book is not meant to be taken as an endorsement from Cthulhu or any other eldritch entity that they are, in fact, coming to destroy our universe. Such apocalyptic implications are purely speculative and should not be considered a given.

This book is a creative reimagining protected under United States Copyright Law, Title 17, USC. In the spirit of *Pride and Prejudice and Zombies*, this work merges a public domain classic with elements of horror and satire, honoring all original material and parties through an imaginative reinterpretation. The author and publisher maintain the utmost respect for the legacies of Ernest Hemingway, H. P. Lovecraft, and all other referenced creators, characters, and mythologies.

The portrayal of Garrett H. Jones as a "gibbering lunatic" in the narrative is an artistic device and not meant to imply that More Publishing is led by gibbering lunatics. The author is deeply grateful to More Publishing for their invaluable assistance in bringing this book to life.

For permissions, inquiries, or further information, please contact Garrett H. Jones at books@morepublishing.co.

BEFORE YOU READ

IMMERSE YOURSELF IN THE ABYSS
Welcome to a journey through transdimensional and metaphysical cosmic horror. To deepen your reading experience, we invite you to explore The Sun Also Rises on Cthulhu-verse, a specially curated collection of music designed to envelop you in the eerie and absurd atmosphere of the story:

- The Sun Also Rises on Cthulhu: Original Soundtrack (OST)
- Voidwalker by Jorah Kai and the Dark Beyond
- Sad Songs from an Old Goth in a Tree by Jorah Kai and the Dark Beyond

These albums create the perfect soundscape for delving into the depths of the narrative. Listen and download them for free at *https://jorahkai.com/cthulhu.*
May the music guide you through the shadows.

ABOUT THIS BOOK

Embark on a haunting odyssey with The Sun Also Rises on Cthulhu—a masterful reimagining of Ernest Hemingway's *The Sun Also Rises*. Co-authored by the Pulitzer Prize- and Nobel Prize-winning Hemingway and Jorah Kai, the modern minstrel of the macabre celebrated for the darkly psychedelic, internationally best-selling fairy tale *Amos the Amazing*, this narrative intertwines the existential desolation of Hemingway's iconic characters with the cosmic terror of Lovecraft, transforming a cherished classic into a realm of unimaginable nightmares and unfathomable dread.

Meet Jack Schitt, Ro'brt Ctholh'en, Brett Ashley, Creepy Bill, and their eclectic band as they traverse the enchanting landscapes of Europe. Amid their pursuit of love and freedom, an ancient, chilling horror begins to stir—a terror rising from the depths of time and intent on resurrecting elder gods. This malevolent force threatens not only their world but the fragile fabric of their very minds.

Reflecting the Lost Generation's struggle for meaning, this tale speaks to humanity's deepest fears and desires. It charts a path through relentless longing, weaving themes of identity, love, and despair against the backdrop of Cthulhu's unfathomable terror.

The Sun Also Rises on Cthulhu is a testament to why Hemingway remains one of the most emulated and respected writers in American literature, while Jorah Kai once again cements his place as a daring and imaginative voice in fiction. This is *one of the books of a generation.*

Credits:

Written by Ernest Hemingway and Jorah Kai

Edited by Rob Waller, Greg Jones, and Randy Green

Cover Illustrations by Jan Dornig

Cover Design by Shabana Awan

Interior Design by Mirko Fermani

Interior Illustrations by Benjamin Wang

Published in America by More Publishing, 2025

HOW THIS BOOK CAME TO BE

ERNEST HEMINGWAY IS ARGUABLY ONE of the most respected and aspirational writers in American literature. His distinctive style, characterized by concise, simple yet powerful writing, along with his renowned Iceberg Theory of subtext, has left an indelible mark on modern storytelling. Hemingway's ability to convey deep emotion and complex narratives through sparse prose makes his work not only accessible but also profoundly impactful.

This minimalist approach is surprisingly compatible with the genre of horror, particularly cosmic horror. As H.P. Lovecraft aptly stated, "The strongest human emotion is fear, and the greatest fear is fear of the unknown." The simplicity and precision of Hemingway's language can heighten the sense of unease and amplify the fear of the unseen, creating an atmosphere where the unknown becomes all the more terrifying.

One of Jorah Kai's literary heroes, Hunter S. Thompson, exemplified this admiration for Hemingway's craft. Thompson used to copy entire Hemingway novels on a typewriter, driven by a desire to internalize the power and economy of Hemingway's style. What began as a creative writing exercise evolved into a thorough and innovative reimagining of a literary classic, tailored for the modern reader. This dedication to mastering Hemingway's technique laid the foundation for what would become this novel.

Understanding the dynamics of public domain works further fueled this creative endeavor. As time passes, books enter the public domain, allowing contemporary authors to reinterpret and breathe new life into classic literature. Notably, Ernest Hemingway's own work *The Sun Also Rises* entered the global public domain in 2022, marking a significant milestone. Furthermore, 2026 will mark the one-hundredth anniversary of its publication, making this an exceptionally opportune time to publish a reimagining of such a revered classic.

A notable example of this phenomenon is *Pride and Prejudice and Zombies*, a unique retelling of Jane Austen's beloved novel co-authored by Jane Austen and Seth Grahame-Smith. This fusion blends traditional romance with horror elements, creating a fresh and engaging narrative that captivated readers worldwide. The book became an international bestseller and inspired a successful Hollywood movie adaptation, demonstrating the powerful synergy that can arise from reimagining public domain classics through modern collaborations.

This note serves to contextualize the genesis of our project—a modern reimagining rooted in the rich traditions of American literature and the transformative power of public domain works. By melding Hemingway's succinct prose with the evocative elements of cosmic horror and drawing inspiration from successful collaborative reinterpretations like *Pride and Prejudice and Zombies*, this book aims to offer a fresh and compelling experience for today's readers.

FORWARD TO THE READER

WHEN JORAH KAI FIRST CAME to me with his pitch, his scheme to weave tentacles and ancient horrors into the fabric of my Paris, I thought it was damn foolishness. A bastardization of what I'd penned with blood and sweat. But the kid was persistent and had that stubborn look in his eye I've seen in the mirror. He persisted, and eventually, I listened.

Slowly, I began to see—beneath the monstrous facade, the core was unaltered. It was still a tale of human folly and bravery, of love and loss, a story as old as time, just wearing a strange, new mask.

So, yes, Jorah Kai wore me down. It turns out we weren't so different after all. He with his eldritch gods and me with my matadors—we were both trying to tell a truth. He showed me that underneath the cosmic horror, it was still a story of people grasping for meaning in a world tipped sideways.

A century's turn is a hell of a long time, and words, like good whiskey, either mellow out or sour in the barrel. But if they're worth their salt, they endure. This homage, this 'reimagining'—it's taken a strange road from my old haunts to the wild runs of Thompson's fear, fun, and loathing, and landed in the lap of Kai. That lineage of raw, unfiltered honesty? It's there. If Hunter's spirit is gazing half stupefied over Kai's shoulder, I'd wager he's half-amused, half-proud.

Here's the unvarnished truth: Kai and I, we've wrestled with the sun, pinned it down long enough to say what we've got to say. We've looked the absurdity of life straight on and didn't blink, not once.

The times may change, the wars may differ, the loves may evolve, but the story, the raw, bleeding pulse of it—that's eternal. Collaborating with Kai? It's been like watching my own reflection trying to climb out of a bottle of Spanish wine. Unnerving, sure, but intriguing. The ride's been wilder than a Pamplona bull, and that's saying something. We've stayed true to the course, written what's true to us, and that's the only kind of writing there is.

So here's to you, the reader, and to Kai, the bearer of the torch. We're handing you a story that's heavy with history but dripping with new blood. Let the modern reader unearth the ancient truths, the stark realities, and the deep, dark pulse of the human beast. The pages turn, the stories unfold. But the dance—it's the same. It's always the same. – E.H.

Ernest Hemingway

ACKNOWLEDGEMENTS

To my typewriter, steadfast; to the sun, less so.

For the words, cheers to the muses.

For existence, a quiet nod to those who sleep.

To English teachers everywhere, and always.

And to publishers, without whom authors would have no place
to rest their weary heads.

Thank you for your service.

Dedicated the loving memory of Benjamin Wang — you were a
good boy.

To the city of Chongqing, where dreams come true.

To my dad, Bruce, my granddaughter, Naomi,
and to Azathoth, who still slumbers.

Epigraph

"One generation falls to darkness, and another rises from despair: but the earth remains, a silent sentinel. The sun also rises, cloaked in shadows, and sets into the abyss, hastening to its cryptic harbor."
— *Eldritch Ecclesiastes* 1:4–5

"The oldest and strongest emotion of mankind is fear, and the oldest and strongest kind of fear is fear of the unknown."
— H.P. Lovecraft

"A gem cannot be polished without friction, nor a man perfected without trials. It is not because things are difficult that we do not dare, it is because we do not dare that they are difficult. Sometimes even to live is an act of courage."
— Lucius Annaeus Seneca

"The task for young writers should be nothing less than saving the world."
— Ta-Nehisi Coates

TABLE OF CONTENTS

LIVRE UN

I

Paris, France

Winter, 1923

PROLOGUE

THE HAUNTING HOWL AT LES DEUX MAGOTS

T HE SOFT GLOW OF LES Deux Magots flickered, bathing the café in a golden haze. Charlie Walker stood amidst celebration, holding his latest accolade—a glass trophy depicting a philosopher with a pen raised high. It felt heavy in his hands. He shifted it awkwardly, glasses clinking and voices rising around him.

"To Charlie, master of words!" someone called, and the crowd roared.

A woman in a sleek black dress leaned close, her perfume sweet and sharp. Her voice cut through the noise.

"Wouldn't you prefer a quiet cab back, Mr. Walker?" Claire Dubois asked, her eyes showing concern.

Charlie chuckled, the scent of oak and smoke lingering on his breath with hints of sweet caramel. His cheeks flushed red. "Maybe tomorrow. Tonight, I want the open air." His grin was wide, but his eyes wandered, distant.

She kissed his cheek softly. "Au revoir," she whispered, her gaze holding an unspoken warning.

Stepping into the frigid night, Charlie pulled his coat tight, the trophy tucked under his arm. He felt ridiculous, like he was parading down the boulevard with his manhood on display. He smirked at the absurdity. "Always leave them wanting more," he muttered. The streets of Paris stretched before him, but tonight they felt unfamiliar—shadows shifting unnaturally, moonlight casting distorted shapes on the cobblestones.

A howl split the quiet, distant and strange, neither fully human nor animal. Charlie paused, the air hanging heavy, as if the night itself held its breath. His pulse quickened. He pressed on, each step echoing his growing unease.

The shadows along Rue de l'École de Médecine deepened, swallowing familiar landmarks in their inky grasp. He laughed nervously, but the night seemed to close in tighter.

Another howl—closer now, sharper—sent a jolt through him. The air carried the scent of whiskey and cognac, sweet and bitter, mingling with the cold. Charlie quickened his pace, breath misting in the air, but the sound followed, echoing off the stone walls. He turned onto Rue des Grands Augustins, his steps erratic as the singular howl multiplied into a chorus of guttural threats.

Panic surged. He bolted down an alley, feet pounding against cobblestones, but the narrow space felt like a trap. Memories of hunting deer in the Oklahoma woods flashed before him—now, the roles had reversed; once the hunter, now the prey.

Emerging onto a wider street, he stumbled against a shop window. The howls swirled around him, gnawing at his sanity. The stench of decay clung to the air, like damp earth disturbed by something foul.

He inhaled sharply, trying to steady himself, but the snarls warped his senses. Bitter irony tugged at him—a celebrated writer, now a trembling rabbit—but the dread tightening in his chest smothered any flicker of humor. He began to run.

He ran along the Quai de la Tournelle, lungs burning, legs aching, the Seine silent below. Gasping, he paused, seeking safety in the open, but the howling rose again—a chilling wail from the river itself.

Desperation drove him into a darker alley. A cold awareness settled over him—this was no mere panic. An ancient, malevolent force herded him, its sinister intent seeping from the city's stones to swallow him whole.

Two burning eyes cut through the darkness, watching—no, piercing him. They locked Charlie in place, stripping away his defenses. His limbs betrayed him, immobilized by an otherworldly force; those piercing eyes delved deep, rifling through the chambers of his soul.

He stood paralyzed, unable to move. Each step forward crunched softly through virgin snow on slick cobblestones, bringing the glowing eyes closer—a death sentence, their inhuman light suffocating as they filled his view.

A fleeting vision of Claire flashed through Charlie's mind—her warmth, her concern. The last tether to a world slipping from his grasp, dissolving into the abyss. Regret twisted deep within him—not for fame or fortune, but for the softness he had pushed away, the moments of tenderness squandered. The night had claimed him now; there was no escape.

The creature emerged from the shadows—a monstrous form defying comprehension. Its shape flickered, half-seen, as if darkness itself had woven it into existence. Tendrils of shadow coiled around it, writhing in anticipation. Eyes glowing with ancient malice locked onto him, piercing his thoughts, dragging him toward madness.

A growl emanated—not an animal sound, but a deep, resonant hum vibrating through his bones, the breath of the void itself. It echoed with knowing, mocking the terror twisting in his chest, as if it had awaited him all along.

Charlie's body locked up, frozen by fear. Then the adrenaline hit. He broke free, stumbled back, legs frantic—but the creature was faster. It knocked him to the cobblestones, its touch worse than claws. Something ancient and alien burrowed into him, not flesh but deeper. It twisted in his mind, unraveling thoughts, memories, and meaning itself. He felt the vast, pitiless void pressing down, and in its shadow, he began to disappear.

Pain exploded—crunching bone, ripping sinew—but the physical agony paled next to the creeping madness. The creature wasn't just killing him—it was erasing him, consuming the very essence of who he was.

As blood soaked the stones, his vision dimmed. Claire's image, once vivid, faded into the darkness, her warmth slipping away, swallowed by shadows.

The creature loomed above, its fetid breath washing over him as its jaws closed in.

And as it fed, tearing into his flesh with slow, deliberate cruelty, Charlie's mind shattered. The howl that rose from the beast was not one of triumph, but of despair—a final, broken cry for a soul lost to the endless dark.

CHAPTER 1

THE GLOAMING

R O'BRT CTHOLH'EN, THE GLOAMING SPECTER of Princeton, had once been its middleweight boxing champion—a title he earned through pain and perseverance. This accolade, meaningless to Jack Schitt, was everything to Ctholh'en. His gleaming head, intense eyes, and dark skin set him apart, fueling whispers of scandalous origins. In Ro'brt's eyes lay a wordless challenge, a depth of will that Jack respected despite the murmurs. His social graces couldn't mask the raw energy of a boxer's stance—a silent testament to his untapped dominance, a power he exercised only within the gym's eldritch shadows.

Under Spider Kelly's tutelage, Ro'brt mastered boxing with supernatural agility. Kelly's method emphasized lightness, irrespective of weight. An ill-fated match, however, left Ro'brt with a flattened nose, deepening his aversion to the sport. In his final year, his shadow seldom darkened the gym; instead, it lingered in the library's dim alcoves, keeping silent company with forbidden tomes. He began to sport a pair of spectacles, masking his squamous stare—a gaze as unnerving and alien as something dredged from the abyss—and rendering him more introspective, almost personable. Despite his enigmatic presence, Jack Schitt found few at Princeton who remembered Ctholh'en upon graduation; his boxing triumphs and unsettling rumors faded like twilight shadows, his looming presence dissolving like mist beneath the dawning sun.

Jack Schitt mistrusted all frank and simple people, especially when their stories held together. Doubts clouded his mind that Ro'brt Ctholh'en's claim to boxing fame might be a carefully crafted façade. Perhaps the real story was more macabre— perhaps it was a horse's hoof or esoteric rituals in the Hamptons. Jack, often receiving holiday invitations and without strong loyalties back home, found the Ctholh'en home a hub of eclectic social activity and esoteric hobnobbing. On one occasion, with the world teetering on the brink of global insanity, Jack attended an opulent wedding celebration. Under the gibbous moon, Ro'brt lured them from their youthful revelry into the hushed sanctum of his father's library. Amidst whispers and tenebrous secrets, Jack's fingers quivered nervously above the *Necronomicon*—the Book of the Dead. The cover pulsated grotesquely, a fearsome visage of human leather leering back at him. Ro'brt, his gaze awash with mischief yet abyssal in depth, handed the book to Jack.

It was locked tight, no visible keyhole, just an ominous oval recess on its cover. As Jack's gaze lingered, it felt as if the piercing obsidian eyes were drawing him into a world of dark, profane secrets.

Ro'brt, with his plastic smile, presented a fist-sized obsidian stone that seemed to swallow the light around it. Compelled by a force beyond his understanding, Jack placed the stone into the recess, feeling the book's binding give way as it clicked open.

Opening the tome, Jack was instantly overwhelmed by its allure, feeling a malevolent empowerment wash over him. Always clever with puzzles, his keen mind penetrated the esoteric glyphs on the pages, discerning their terrible meanings. They began to shift into tangible concepts that bled into his disturbed psyche, while a distant, sinister presence seemed to whisper back:

"That is not dead which can eternal lie, And with strange aeons even death may die."

A shiver ran down his spine, but he continued to turn the pages. The symbols writhed, each one drawing him closer to profoundly unsettling revelations about other dimensions and the unfathomable creatures that inhabited them. In that awful moment, he understood the hubris that had befallen Atlantis and why future civilizations would still be drawn like moths to a flame to this tome—both a relic of impossibly evil history and a guidebook for future apocalypse. The world around him faded; only the book's whispering voices and shifting glyphs remained. Shadows stretched from the darkness, beckoning him toward an abyss.

Amidst the engulfing shadows, a vision of his drowned, bloated mother surfaced in the icy waters. Her eyes snapped open—wide, empty, devoid of soul. Her crooked finger pointed at him as her lips parted. Her tongue writhed grotesquely from side to side, her head jerking violently as if seized by a seizure. Her features contorted, twisted by something truly evil animating her from within. She hissed, "You've... seen... too... much." From her gaping mouth, a torrent of rancid sludge spewed forth, flooding his eyes, nose, and throat.

Frantically trying to wipe away the acrid slime, a cold grip seized his limbs. The icy depths pulled at him, dragging him down into a hellish abyss.

A cacophony of alien voices rose in discordant harmony, accompanied by polyphonic soothing flute music, seeking to soothe the dreaming Azathoth upon whom reality hinged. Jack stood among endless slaves, twisted souls serving cruel, unfathomable gods. They toiled endlessly, building pyramids that clawed at a sky of seething darkness.

Time unraveled. He teetered on the brink of an abyss, the screams of the damned mingling with whispers of nameless entities. Shadowy overseers wielded whips of pure agony over the wretched masses.

The air reeked of despair and burning flesh. Flames licked the horizon but offered no light—only deeper shadows. Above, monstrous gods gazed down with cold indifference.

Jack's mind reeled. He witnessed ceaseless torment—no rest, only infinite toil under crushing hopelessness. The abyss beckoned, a maw ready to consume him. The alien chants grew louder, each note a razor slicing into his soul.

Amidst the unending torment, Jack's consciousness teetered on the brink of oblivion. The cacophony of alien chants and the weight of eternal despair pressed in from all sides. Then, faintly at first, he heard a voice cutting through the chaos.

"Count back from ten, Jack. Will yourself home."

It was Ro'brt's voice—steady, anchoring. Jack grasped at it like a lifeline.

"Ten," he whispered, his voice barely audible over the din. The shadows pressed closer, tendrils of darkness curling around his limbs.

"Nine," he continued, forcing the words out. The screams of the damned grew louder, trying to drown him.

"Eight." He closed his eyes, focusing inward, fighting against the pull of the abyss. The grotesque visions clawed at his mind, but Ro'brt's voice urged him on.

"Seven."

"Six."

Each number was a battle, his mind fraying at the edges, the fabric of reality threatening to unravel.

"Five."

"Four."

The infernal sounds began to fade, replaced by the faint rustling of pages and the scent of old books.

"Three."

"Two."

The weight lifted from his chest. The chilling cold gave way to a familiar warmth.

"One."

He opened his eyes. The hellish landscape was gone. Ro'brt stood before him, closing the ancient tome. The library's dim light cast gentle shadows, a stark contrast to the nightmare he had just escaped.

"Welcome back," Ro'brt said softly.

Jack's hands trembled. He struggled to cling to the fragments of esoteric lore that now haunted him, the potent necromancy slipping away, leaving only the echoes of infernal screams.

"Did you see?" Jack whispered.

Ro'brt met his gaze, eyes heavy with understanding. "Some things are not meant for us to know."

Burdened with forbidden knowledge, Jack began to seek refuge in the numbing embrace of alcohol, a warmth that dulled sanity's sharper edges. Not long after Princeton, Jack returned from the war cursed, impotent; forever changed. Ro'brt seemed to sense it, but they never spoke of it.

Still, Jack finally had someone verify Ro'brt's story from Spider Kelly. It turned out that Coach Kelly not only remembered Ctholh'en but also often wondered what had become of him. Through his father, Ro'brt Ctholh'en was a member of one of the wealthiest blueblood families in New York and, through his mother, one of the oldest. Growing up, he'd been untouchable until he went to Princeton. Despite enduring bullying there, his inherent kindness and timidity only deepened a contrast that brewed a quiet bitterness within him. Ro'brt took it out in boxing, and he came out of Princeton with painful self-consciousness and a flattened nose, quickly captivated by the first siren who seemed to see beyond his scars. Married five years, three children later, Ro'brt's fifty-thousand inheritance dwindled. He turned stony, like a bowl of left-out *pot-au-feu*, congealed under domestic unhappiness with a wealthy wife. Just when he had made up his mind to leave, she left him first for a gibbering miniature painter. As he had been thinking for months about leaving his wife and had not done it because it would be too cruel to deprive her of himself, her departure was a very healthy shock.

The divorce was arranged, and Ro'brt Ctholh'en was drawn toward the coast. In California, he fell among literary people and, as he still had a little of the fifty thousand left, he was backing an arts review in a short time. The review commenced publication in Carmel, California, and finished at Miskatonic University in Arkham, Massachusetts. By that time, Ctholh'en, who had been regarded purely as an angel and whose name had appeared on the editorial page merely as a member of the advisory board, had become the sole editor. It was his money, and he discovered he liked the authority of editing. He was sorry when the magazine became too expensive and had to give it up.

By that time, though, he had other things to worry about. He had been taken in hand by a lady who hoped to rise with the magazine. She was very forceful, and Ctholh'en never had a chance.

Also, he was sure that he loved her. When this lady saw that the magazine was not going to rise, she became a little disgusted with Ctholh'en. Grasping for an opportunity, she urged that they go to Europe, where Ctholh'en could write. They came to Europe, where she'd been educated, and stayed for three years. During these three years—the first spent in travel, the last two in Paris—Ro'brt Ctholh'en had two friends: Braddocks and Jack. Braddocks was his literary friend; Jack was his tennis friend.

The lady who had him, Frances, found toward the end of the second year that her looks were going. Her attitude toward Ro'brt changed from one of careless possession and exploitation to the absolute determination that he should marry her. During this time, Ro'brt's mother had settled an allowance on him, about three hundred dollars a month.

For two and a half years, Jack did not believe that Ro'brt Ctholh'en looked at another woman. He was fairly happy, except that, like many people living in Europe, he would rather have been in America and had discovered writing. He wrote a novel, and it was not as bad as the critics later called it, although it was a very poor one. He read many books, played bridge, played tennis, and boxed at a local gymnasium.

Jack first became aware of Frances' attitude toward him one night after the three of them had dined together. They dined at l'Avenue's and went to the Café de Versailles for coffee. They had several *clopes* after the coffee, and Jack said he must be going. Ctholh'en had been talking about the two of them going off somewhere on a weekend trip. He wanted to get out of town and get in a good walk by the sea. Jack suggested they fly to Strasbourg and walk up to Saint Odile, somewhere in Alsace.

"I know a girl in Strasbourg who can show us the town," Jack said.

Somebody kicked Jack under the table, but he thought it was accidental and went on: "She's been there two years and knows everything there is to know about the town. She's a swell girl."

Jack was kicked again under the table and, looking, saw Frances, Ro'brt's lady, her chin lifting and her face hardening.

"Hell," Jack said with a wry grin. "Why go to Strasbourg? We could go up to Bruges or to the Ardennes."

Ctholh'en looked relieved. Jack was not kicked again, and he said good night and went out. The cold December air bit as they stepped out of the café's warmth, festive anticipation hanging among the street vendors' garlands and the distant hum of preparations. Ctholh'en said he wanted to buy a paper and would walk to the corner with him.

"Why bring up the Strasbourg girl? Didn't you notice Frances?"

"No, why should I? If I know an American girl that lives in Strasbourg, what the hell is it to Frances?"

"It doesn't make any difference. Any girl would be a problem. I couldn't go. That would be all."

"Don't be silly."

"You don't know Frances. Didn't you catch her glare? Any girl would be a problem."

"Oh, well," Jack murmured, brushing away the first hesitant snowflakes. "Let's go to Senlis."

"Don't get sore."

"I'm not sore. Senlis is a good place. We can stay at the Grand Cerf, hike in the woods, and come home." His breath, a ghostly vapor, mingled briefly with the frosty air, a visible sign of life amidst the encroaching chill.

"Good, that will be fine," Ro'brt agreed, his words cutting through the frosty air. Yet, no mist betrayed his breath, a quiet peculiarity.

"Well, I'll see you tomorrow at the courts," Jack said.

"Good night, Jack," he said and started back to the café.

"You forgot to get your paper," Jack said.

"That's so." He walked with Jack up to the kiosque at the corner. "You are not sore, are you, Jack?" He turned with the paper in his hand, watching Jack carefully.

"No, why should I be?"

Ro'brt's penetrating gaze held Jack captive like a moth caught in the amber glow of a gas lamp. Then he nodded. "See you at tennis."

As Ro'brt melted into the gloaming, his form dissolved into the café's dim aura. The night air began to embroider itself with delicate flakes of snow, whispering through the air with a poet's quiet grace. Jack, a solitary figure, wandered a Paris transforming: an age-old labyrinth now becoming etched in electric glow, where snowflakes danced softly under the sharp, modern lights.

Jack halted as a bark echoed off the stone facades. He stood frozen, legends of Paris's spectral beasts clawing at the edges of his mind. His heart thrummed, dread pooling in his stomach. The shadows seemed alive, a presence waiting just out of sight. For a long moment, he didn't breathe, every sense straining in the silence.

Then, the soft, distinctly human whine of a stray terrier pierced the tension. Jack exhaled, the knot of fear loosening as he knelt to greet the quivering form emerging from the gloom. Relief, warm and soothing, washed over him, the curiously wagging tail grounding him in the reality of the moment.

Yet, as his gaze lifted, it caught on something unnatural—a sigil, chilling in its clarity, etched upon the wall. A shiver ran down his spine, not from the cold but from the recognition of something ancient and malevolent. The lamplights flickered, a prelude to horror, as shadows began to dance with a life of their own. Paris's familiar streets warped under the sigil's influence, revealing glimpses of a reality twisted and dark. Forms once human twisted into grotesque parodies under the stuttering light, the terrier's eyes reflecting a soulless void. The skeletal terrier skulked toward him through a dread panorama of Paris unmade. The air grew thick with the stench of decay, and the very fabric of existence seemed to tear, revealing glimpses of a dark, writhing chaos that lay beneath.

Panic surged, a visceral wave threatening to drag Jack into madness. His breaths came sharp and ragged, each one a battle against the encroaching dark. He closed his eyes, focusing on the steady rhythm of his heart, counting down from the edge of terror.

When he opened his eyes, the terrifying visions had dissipated, leaving only the cold, silent alley and the small, trembling form of the terrier by his side. The warmth of the dog's body against his hand was a lifeline, anchoring him to reality, a tangible connection to a world still governed by the familiar and the real.

Gathering himself, Jack wrapped his scarf around the small, shivering frame. The terrier looked up with a gaze piercing and profound—a silent communion in the frigid air. "Hungry?" he murmured, and soon returned with a *jambon-beurre*. The dog, now visibly less wary, tore into the offering with a fervor born of hunger. Then, with a look that seemed to plead for companionship, it moved to follow him. Jack shook his head gently—no, not this time—and stepped away, the promise of a nightcap calling him to the warm glow of a nearby bar. Behind him, the snow continued to fall, laying a gentle, purifying shroud over Paris's ancient scars.

CHAPTER 2

ELDRITCH ECHOES

THAT WINTER, RO'BRT CTHOLH'EN JOURNEYED to America with his novel, which a reputable publisher accepted. Jack heard whispers of Ro'brt's departure stirring their circles, suspecting that was when Frances lost her grip on him. Women in New York had been friendly, and upon his return, he was changed—a fervor in his eyes, an esoteric edge manifesting as newfound bluntness and detachment.

The publishers lauded his novel, praise that went to his head. Attention from women broadened his horizons. For years, his world was confined to his wife, Frances. Jack doubted Ro'brt had ever truly experienced love.

Then there was another factor: his reading of W. H. Hudson's *The Purple Land*. Innocent as it seemed, Ro'brt read and reread it. The book, perilous if embraced too late in life, depicts an English gentleman's romantic adventures in vivid landscapes. For a man of thirty-four to take it as life's guidebook is as risky as entering Wall Street straight from a convent with only Alger books in hand. Yet, this whimsical obsession paled beside the darker texts Ro'brt once perused in the shadowed corners of his family's Hamptons estate—ancient volumes whispering of worlds far from Hudson's idylls. In that light, *The Purple Land* was a less treacherous current in the dark sea of Ro'brt's mind. On the whole, the book seemed sound to him. That was all it took to set him off. Jack didn't realize how much it had set him off until Ro'brt came into his office one soggy spring day.

Jack looked up from his typewriter to find Ro'brt glaring frostily, lost in dusty, ponderous thoughts.

"Hello, Ro'brt," Jack said. "Come to cheer me up?"

Ro'brt stared in silence, the clock ticking several times as he considered. In the office, the world outside seemed distant—muted city sounds blending with the rhythmic ticking of the old clock, wrapping the room in hushed stillness.

"Want to go to South America, Jack?" Ro'brt asked.

"No."

"Why not?"

"Never wanted to. Too expensive. You can see all the South Americans you want in Paris."

"They're not the real South Americans."

"They look real enough to me."

Ro'brt leaned in, voice lowering. "There's something out there, Jack. Beyond the map's edge, where shadows swallow the sun. An artifact—ancient, powerful. They say it whispers in dreams, reveals secrets long buried."

Jack's smile was thin. "Sounds like a one-way ticket to hell. Chasing whispers comes with a price."

"Imagine the tale," Ro'brt pressed. "The truths we'd uncover, beyond mundane expectations."

"Chasing shadows won't fill the void, Ro'brt. It's not about escaping shadows but facing the darkness. Are you ready for that cost?"

Ro'brt's eyes held a mix of defiance and desperation. "You've got the language, Jack, and it'd be an adventure for both of us."

Jack was unmoved. "I find my adventures in Spain come summertime." He thought of the boat and train to catch and a week's mail stories, and only half were written. "Do you know any dirt?" Jack asked.

"No."

"None of your exalted connections getting divorces?"

"No."

"Put any stock in these wild animal attacks around town? Were you acquainted with that writer, Charlie Walker? What's your take on it? Zoo got a loose screw?"

"All my life, I've wanted to go on a trip like that," Ro'brt said. He sat down. "I'll be too old before I can ever do it."

"Don't be a fool," Jack said. "You can go anywhere you want. You've got plenty of money."

"I know. But I can't get started."

"Cheer up," Jack said. "All countries look just like the moving pictures." But Jack pitied him. He had it bad.

"I can't stand it to think my life is going so fast, and I'm not really living it."

"Nobody ever lives their life all the way up except bullfighters."

"I'm not interested in bullfighters. That's an abnormal life. I want to go back to the country in South America. We could have a great trip."

"Did you ever think about going to British East Africa to shoot?"

"No, I wouldn't like that."

"I'd go there with you."

"No, that doesn't interest me."

"That's because you never read a book about it. Go on and read a book full of love affairs with beautiful, shiny black princesses."

Ro'brt shook his head. "I want to go to South America."

"Come on downstairs and have a drink."

"Aren't you working?"

Any escape into a bottle was a solace from Jack's haunted reverie. "Yeah, but no." They went down the stairs to the café on the ground floor. Jack had discovered that was the best way to get rid of friends. Once you had a drink, all you had to say was,

"Well, I've got to get back and get off some cables," and it was done. It is very important to discover graceful exits like that in the newspaper business, where it is such an important part of ethics that you should never seem to be working.

They went downstairs to the bar and had whiskey and soda. Ctholh'en looked at the bottles in bins around the wall. "This is a good place," he said.

"There's a lot of liquor," Jack agreed.

"Listen, Jack," Ro'brt leaned in, voice low but insistent. "Ever feel like life's passing you by? That you're just a spectator? You've lived nearly half your life already, haven't you?" His gaze had a probing intensity, and Jack tightened, not in the mood for getting probed.

"Once in a while," Jack conceded.

"Do you realize, in about thirty-five years, we'll be nothing but memories?" Ro'brt pressed, his eyes never leaving Jack's face.

"What the hell, Ro'brt," Jack muttered, a mixture of irritation and resignation in his tone.

Ro'brt's unwavering, stygian gaze bore into Jack, threatening to dig up skeletons and secrets. Jack squirmed, and only when Ro'brt turned to look out the window did Jack feel he could breathe again.

"I'm serious, Jack." Ro'brt's voice was softer now but carried an undercurrent of concern. "Look at us, the old gang. Everyone's settling down, showing their years. Everyone except you, Jack, but you got to admit... well..." Ro'brt trailed off and turned back to gaze into Jack's deep sea-blue eyes. Jack could feel Ro'brt's perceptive probing niggling farther into murky depths.

Jack bristled, not thinking about the señorita, the Italians, certainly not a mirror. "I don't," he lied, his voice edged with irritation.

"You should, my friend," Ro'brt insisted gently, looking at the outside world beyond the glass. "Time is all we have."

"Let's drink," Jack said.

"Well, I want to go to South America."

"Listen, Ro'brt, going to another country doesn't make any difference. I've tried all that. You can't get away from yourself by moving from one place to another. There's nothing to that."

"But you've never been to South America."

"South America hell! If you went there the way you feel now, it would be exactly the same. This is a good town. Why don't you start living your life in Paris?"

"I'm sick of Paris, and I'm sick of the Quarter."

"Stay away from the Quarter. Cruise around by yourself and see what happens to you."

"Nothing happens to me. I walked alone all night once, and nothing happened except a bicycle cop stopped me and asked to see   my   papers."

"Wasn't the town nice at night?"

"I don't care for Paris."

"Well, there you have it," Jack thought, feeling sorry for him, but it was not a thing he could do anything about because right away, he ran up against the two stubbornnesses: that South

America could fix it, and he did not like Paris. He got the first idea out of a book, and Jack supposed the second came out of a book, too.

"Well," Jack said, "I've got to go upstairs and get off some cables."

"Do you really have to go?"

"Yes, I've got to get these cables off."

"Do you mind if I come up and sit around the office?"

"No, come on up."

In the outer chamber's silence, only the scratch of the editor and publisher's pen disturbed the air. Jack's unease grew, a pull toward the locked drawer of his desk inexplicable yet irresistible. The cool wood vibrated under his palm, a hum from within begging for release into the room's dimness. Jack settled into the humdrum of work.

From the next room came a cry—Ro'brt in the throes of a nightmare, sprawled across the chair, face twisted in agony.

Jack touched his shoulder to soothe him.

Ro'brt convulsed, muttering incoherently before his voice twisted into a guttural, polyphonic chant: *"Ph'nglui mglw'nafh Cthulhu R'lyeh wgah'nagl fhtagn!"*

The horrific, impossible utterance struck terror deep in Jack's core, stirring fragments of forbidden lore and the dark rituals they'd once whispered in secret. *In his house at R'lyeh dead Cthulhu waits dreaming.* Those words were a dark echo of the past and a key to something far more sinister bleeding into the present, wrapping Jack in an oppressive shroud of dread that constricted tighter with each syllable.

"Ro'brt!" Jack's shout was a mix of fear and desperation, an attempt to sever the connection to the nightmare.

When Ro'brt's eyes opened, the fear between them was palpable, a shared history of darkness momentarily bridging their current divide. "Did I... speak?" Ro'brt murmured, his voice heavy with the weight of his dream.

"Nothing," Jack lied.

Ro'brt's forced laughter did little to dispel the tension, the remnants of his dream lingering like a poison in the air.

Ro'brt's voice was a mere whisper. "Egypt held a key, in my dream."

"An enigma, indeed."

Ro'brt's gaze, lost to the amber depths of his whiskey, found little comfort in its embrace. "The night's silence was my only company," he finally admitted, the weight of unslept hours heavy in his eyes.

"Did the typewriter put you to sleep?"

"Guess so. I didn't sleep all last night."

"What was the matter?"

"Talking," he said, about to say more but stopped.

Jack could picture it. He had a rotten habit of picturing the bedroom scenes of his friends.

Abruptly, Ro'brt shook off the remnants of his haunted rest. "Let's grab something to eat, shall we? I'm famished."

Together, they drifted into the welcoming embrace of Paris, where light and shadow intertwined like lovers beneath the moon's gaze. At Café des Rêves, they found sanctuary in the intimacy of wine and murmured dreams. Paris breathed with life—a symphony of shadows and whispers beneath the Eiffel Tower, its spires catching the first blush of dawn, casting ethereal shadows that swayed with the promise of a new day.

CHAPTER 3

OBSCURA

ON A MIDSUMMER'S NIGHT AT the Napolitain, Jack Schitt sat alone. The electric signs eventually came on, offering fleeting comfort in that liminal space between worlds. In Paris, if Jack could be said to have had any goals, it was finding a precarious balance—using the deceptive warmth of drink to ward off the encroaching gloom and unnamed horrors skulking on the periphery. The traffic signal blinked red and green, punctuating the flow of the crowd. Horse cabs clippety-clopped along the edge of the solid taxi traffic as the *poules* went by, singly and in pairs, shrouded by an air of mystery and looking for the evening meal.

Jack watched a good-looking girl walk past his table, then saw another, and then the first one coming back again. She went by once more, and he caught her eye. Drawn together as if by invisible magnets, she sat down at the table. The waiter approached.

"Well, what will you drink?" Jack asked.

"*Pernod.*"

"That's not good for little girls."

"Little girl yourself. Dites, garçon, un *pernod*. T'as une *clope*?"

"A *pernod* for me, too," Jack said. He lit the *clope* with a match and delicately pressed it between her cherry lips.

"What's the matter?" she asked. "Down to party?"

"Sure. Aren't you?"

"I don't know. You never know in this town."

"Don't you like Paris?"

"No."

"Why don't you go somewhere else?"

"Isn't anywhere else."

"You're happy, all right."

"Happy, hell!"

Pernod, a greenish mimic of absinthe, turned milky with water—sweet as licorice at first, then plunging one into depths as it waned. Sitting together, they drank. Her mood mirrored the *pernod's* bitterness, eyes clouding over like the tempestuous Parisian sky.

"Well," Jack said, "are you going to buy me dinner?"

She grinned, lost in the cerulean blue of his eyes, and Jack saw why she made a point of not laughing. With her mouth closed, she was a rather pretty girl.

The bustling ambiance of the Napolitain was abruptly pierced as a man in a plum suit barged in, his bulky camera swinging like an albatross around his neck. His laughter, grating and out of place, shattered the evening's calm. Then came the camera's flash—sudden, blinding—thrusting Jack into a realm of mud and distant thunder, where echoes of shells mingled with wraith-like silhouettes of the past.

"Caught in zee act, Jack Schitt!" the photographer boomed with a thick French accent, the twist of his mustache betraying his amusement. "Right in zee obscura," he slurred, a smug grin plastered on his face. "Forever."

Jack blinked, the sudden light leaving afterimages dancing before his eyes, cracking open the door to his past, allowing shadows to seep through. "Do I know you?" he snapped, the intrusion stirring a deep-seated rage.

The man, already turning to leave, paused. "Remember, zat soirée last spring?" he teased. *"Je m'appelle Paul."*

Jack's reply was terse, his patience thinning. "I don't remember, and I didn't ask for a portrait."

Paul's attempt at humor fell flat. "Ah, well, zee obscura never forgets," his voice fading as he retreated into the night.

Turning to the girl, Jack muttered, "Let's get out of here," the café's walls now suffocating, tainted by the resurgence of unwelcome memories. He settled their tab and guided them out into the street, where the night air offered a welcome reprieve from the pooling dread.

As they hailed a horse cab, the driver greeted Jack by name with a friendly wave. Settling into the cab, she asked, "Are you famous?"

Jack smiled, replying, "No, I'm just tight."

The rhythmic clop-clop wove a soothing melody against the backdrop of the Parisian night. As they nestled into the cab's embrace, it moved up the Avenue de l'Opéra, its grandeur highlighted by the glow from locked shops casting pools of light onto the deserted avenue. The cab rolled past the New York Herald bureau, where a mosaic of clocks from across the globe adorned its window.

"What are all the clocks for?" she asked.

"They show the time across all of America."

"Don't kid me," she said, laughing.

Jack leaned in, his whisper thick with mystery. "See that solitary clock? That's the Clock of Lost Time. It's rumored to whisper one's final hour if you listen beneath its face."

Her laughter faded into a tense silence as the cab decelerated, bringing the ominous clock into clearer view, its hands ominously still. She grew still, tense as a caged rabbit.

Jack playfully pounced upon her, and she shrieked as he nipped at her neck in mock ferocity. The driver chuckled knowingly. She laughed, her initial fright melting away as she swatted at him. "You're terrible," she declared, amusement sparkling in her eyes.

Jack's smile was mischievous. "Just a taste of Parisian enchantment."

They turned off the avenue onto Rue des Pyramides, navigated the Rue de Rivoli traffic, and entered the dark gate to the Tuileries. She leaned into Jack, seeking warmth. Her eyes, inviting a kiss, met his. Her touch sparked a fleeting blaze within him, but it twisted into discomfort. Jack shuddered, gently moving her hand away. "Never mind."

"What's the matter? You sick?"

"Yes."

"*Boire d'une traite! Quel dommage.* Everybody's sick. I'm sick, too."

They shared a lingering glance, and Jack sighed. They came out of the Tuileries into the light, crossed the Seine, and then turned up the Rue des Saints-Pères.

"You oughtn't to drink *pernod* if you're sick."

"You neither."

"It doesn't make any difference to me. It doesn't make any difference with a woman."

"What are you called?"

"Georgette. You're Jake?"

"Schitt. Jack Schitt."

"You look like a Jake to me."

"It's Jack. Schitt."

"That's a Prussian name."

"American too."

"You're not Prussian?"

"No, American."

"Good. *Je déteste les Prussiens.*"

By this time, they had reached the restaurant. Jack called to the *cocher* to stop. They got out, but Georgette didn't like the look of the place.

"*Ceci, ce n'est pas un grand restaurant.*"

"Don't call me Ceci," Jack said. "Maybe you would rather go to Foyot's. Why don't you keep the cab and go on?"

Jack had picked her up because of a vague sentimental idea that it would be nice to eat with someone. It had been a long time since he had dined with a *poule*, and he had forgotten how dull it could be. They entered the restaurant, passed Madame Lavigne at the desk, and were seated in a little room. Georgette cheered up a little at the sight of food. Jack, on the other hand, battled nausea. Since the flash—not right in the head. As they dined, shadows in the room's corners writhed, transforming beneath the electric glow into phantoms of latent fear. The atmosphere, laden with the aroma of decay, hung as heavily as soil over shallow graves.

"It isn't bad here," she said. "*C'est pas chic*, but the food is all right."

"Better than you eat in Liège."

"Brussels, you mean."

Over another bottle, Georgette's jokes cut through the heavy penumbra suffocating Jack. She smiled and showed all her bad teeth, and they touched glasses. The sound of the *trinquer* made him tense.

"You're not a bad type," she said. "It's a shame you're sick. We get on well. What's eating you?" she pressed.

"War wounds," Jack muttered, eyes squeezed shut. He tried to think of anything but her and failed, the scent of old perfume filling his nose until he gasped.

"Oh, that dirty war."

They would probably have gone on and discussed the war and agreed that it was, in reality, a calamity for civilization and perhaps would have been better avoided. Jack would have said anything to get his mind off her. Just then, from the other room, someone called: "Schitt! Hey Schitt! It's you! Jack Schitt!"

"It's a friend calling me," Jack explained and went out.

There was Braddocks at a big table with a party: Ctholh'en, Frances Clyne, Mrs. Braddocks, and several people Jack did not know.

"You're coming to the dance, aren't you?" Braddocks asked.

"What dance?"

"Why, the dance. Don't you know we've revived them?" Mrs. Braddocks put in.

"You must come, Jack. We're all going," Frances said from the end of the table. She was tall and had a smile.

"Of course he's coming," Braddocks said. "Come in and have coffee with us, Schitt."

"Right."

"And bring your friend," said Mrs. Braddocks, laughing. She was a Canadian and had all their easy social graces.

"Thanks, we'll be in," Jack said and excused himself back to the small room.

"Who are your friends?" Georgette asked.

"Writers and artists."

"There are lots of those on this side of the river."

"Too many."

"I think so. Still, some of them make money."

"Oh, yes."

They finished the meal and the wine. "Come on," Jack said. "We're going to have coffee with the others."

Georgette opened her bag and made a few passes at her face as she looked in a little mirror. Jack was drawn into her gaze as she redefined her lips with the lipstick and straightened her hat.

"Good," she said, watching him watching her, and winked at him.

They entered the room full of people, and Braddocks and the men at his table stood up. Their smiles were warm, but Jack's unease lingered. Laughter sounded too loud, chatter too fervent, shadows in the corners unnaturally deep.

"I wish to present my fiancée, Mademoiselle Georgette Leblanc," Jack said, leaning into it. Georgette smiled that wonderful smile, and they shook hands all around.

"Are you related to Georgette Leblanc, the singer?" Mrs. Braddocks asked.

"*Connais pas*," Georgette shrugged.

"But you have the same name," Mrs. Braddocks insisted cordially.

"No," said Georgette. "Not at all. My name is Hobin."

"But Mr. Schitt introduced you as Mademoiselle Leblanc. Surely he did," insisted Mrs. Braddocks, who, in the excitement of speaking French, was liable to have no idea what she was saying.

"He's a fool," Georgette said.

"Oh, it was a joke, then," Mrs. Braddocks said.

"Yes," said Georgette. "To laugh at."

"Did you hear that, Henry?" Mrs. Braddocks called down the table to Braddocks. "Mr. Schitt introduced his fiancée as Mademoiselle Leblanc, and her name is actually Hobin."

"Of course, darling. Mademoiselle Hobin, I've known her for a very long time."

"Oh, Mademoiselle Hobin," Frances Clyne called, speaking French very rapidly and not seeming so proud and astonished as Mrs. Braddocks at its coming out really French. "Have you been in Paris long? Do you like it here? You love Paris, do you not?"

"Who's she?" Georgette turned to Jack. "Do I have to talk to her?"

In the bar's dim light, shadows thickened as the bulbs flickered, casting the room into a fractured dance of light and dark. Jack's pulse quickened, each flicker tightening the knot of dread in his chest. Frances and Georgette's laughter felt distant, muted like voices through a fog, as though muffled by an unseen weight pressing down.

Without warning, the room plunged into darkness. The world seemed to stop breathing. Jack's skin prickled, the air around him thick with a familiar, suffocating tension—too familiar. His chest constricted, the sensation pulling him back to places he had long since tried to bury. The lights sputtered on, erratic bursts tearing through the dark, each flash pulling nightmare images from the recesses of his mind.

In those jagged flickers, the bar warped. Faces sagged into grotesque masks, frozen mid-laugh as flesh melted away, leaving hollowed eyes and slack jaws. Georgette's face twisted into a skeletal grin, worms writhing where her eyes should have been. The walls pulsed, as if alive with the same dread that gnawed at Jack, the same pulse he'd felt in the trenches.

Jack couldn't move. His body locked in place, the way it had so many times before when fear tightened its grip. His mind groped for something real, something tangible to hold on to, but the horror unraveled in front of him, pulling him under.

Desperate, Jack squeezed his eyes shut, forcing himself to count backward from ten, the way he'd trained himself to in the thick of nightmares—real or imagined. Breath by breath, he tried to pull himself back. By the time he reached one, the lights had steadied, and the visions receded like smoke on the edge of memory.

He opened his eyes. The bar was the same. The laughter, the clinking glasses, Frances' voice cutting through the hum—it was all normal. But the weight in Jack's chest hadn't lifted. His heart still pounded, a lone drumbeat of unease. He had seen the veil lift—just for a moment—and it left behind the unmistakable chill of a darkness that lingered, watching.

Mrs. Braddocks turned to Frances, sitting smiling, her hands folded, her head poised on her long neck, her lips pursed, ready to start talking again.

"No, I don't like Paris. It's expensive and dirty," Georgette said.

"Really? I find it so extraordinarily clean. One of the cleanest cities in all Europe."

"I find it dirty."

"How strange! But perhaps you have not been here very long."

"I've been here long enough."

"But it does have nice people in it. One must grant that."

Georgette turned to Jack. "You have nice friends."

Jack grunted and ordered a couple of shots of whiskey.

Frances was a little drunk and would have liked to have kept it up, but then the coffee came and Lavigne with the liqueurs. After that, they all went out and started for Braddocks's dancing club.

The dancing club was a *bal musette* in the Rue de la Montagne Sainte Geneviève. Five nights a week, the working people of the Pantheon quarter danced there. One night a week, it was the dancing club. On Monday nights, it was closed. When they arrived, it was quite empty except for a policeman sitting near the door, the wife of the proprietor behind the *zinc bar*, and the proprietor himself. The daughter of the house came downstairs as they went in. Long benches and tables ran across the room, and at the far end, a dance floor.

Jack tried to shake his unease as they danced, but the shadows made him unreliable, and the room seemed to shift and twist. A shiver coursed through him, sensing unseen, lurking presences. For a brief moment, dance offered an escape into ecstasy before the liminal air thickened once more. The music, though lively, began to grate on his nerves.

"I wish people would come earlier," Braddocks said. The daughter came up and wanted to know what they would drink. The proprietor got up on a high stool beside the dance floor and began to play the accordion. He had a string of bells around one ankle and beat time with his foot as he played. The room, sweltering, throbbed with dance; even the ceiling wept drops of their collective fervor.

"My God," Georgette said. "What a box to sweat in!"

"It's hot."

"*Chaud, mon Dieu!*"

"Take off your hat."

"That's a good idea."

Someone asked Georgette to dance, and Jack went over to the bar. The sweltering heat contrasted with the accordion's soothing strains in the balmy night. He chugged a beer and then ordered two more, standing in the doorway and catching the cool breath of wind from the street. Two taxis were coming down the steep street; they both stopped in front of the *bal*. A crowd of young men, some in jerseys and some in their shirt sleeves, got out. Jack could see their hands and newly washed, wavy hair in the light from the door. The policeman standing

45

by the door looked at him and smiled. They came in. As they went in under the light, Jack saw white hands, wavy hair, white faces—grimacing, gesturing, talking. With them was Brett. Jack gasped, and the rest of the world melted away like mist under the morning sun. She looked very lovely, and she was very much with them.

One of them saw Georgette and said, "I do declare. There is an actual harlot."

Jack clenched his fists for a moment, feeling the heat wash over him again, but he got up and walked toward the dance floor. Mrs. Braddocks followed him. "Don't be cross with Albert," she said. "He's still only a child, you know."

"I wasn't cross," Jack replied. "I just thought I might throw up."

"Your fiancée is having great success," Mrs. Braddocks observed, looking at Georgette dancing with the tall, dark man called Lett.

"Isn't she?" Jack agreed.

"Rather," said Mrs. Braddocks.

Ctholh'en approached. "Come on, Jack," he said, "have a drink." They walked over to the bar. "What's the matter with you? You seem all worked up over something."

"Nothing. This whole show just makes me sick."

Brett joined them at the bar. "Hello, you chaps."

"Hello, Brett," Jack greeted her. "Why aren't you drunk?"

"Never going to get drunk again. I say, give a chap a brandy and soda."

She stood holding the glass, and Jack noticed Ro'brt Ctholh'en watching her intently. Ctholh'en's expression reminded him of someone who had just glimpsed the promised land. Ctholh'en, of course, was much younger, but he had that look of eager, deserving expectation.

Brett was undeniably attractive. She wore a slipover jersey sweater and a tweed skirt, with her hair brushed back like a boy's. She had started that trend. She was built with curves like the hull of a racing yacht, and her form-fitting wool jersey left little to the imagination.

"It's a fine crowd you're with, Brett," Jack remarked.

"Aren't they lovely? And you, my dear, where did you find her?"

"At the Napolitain."

"And have you had a lovely evening?"

"Oh, priceless," Jack replied sarcastically.

Brett laughed. "It's wrong of you, Jack. It's an insult to all of us. Look at Frances there and Jo." This was for Ctholh'en's benefit. "It's in restraint of trade," Brett said, laughing again.

"You're surprisingly sober," Jack commented.

"Yes, aren't I? And when I'm with the crowd I'm with, I can drink in such safety, too."

As the music started, Ro'brt Ctholh'en bit his lip and asked, "Will you dance this with me, Lady Brett?"

Brett's smile widened as she spoke to Ro'brt. "I've promised this dance to Jack," she said with a laugh, her eyes twinkling with mirth. "You know, Jack, you've got quite the biblical name.

And I must say, tonight, you haven't aged a day since our first encounter. Not like the rest of us." With a soft, graceful touch, she reached up, her fingers cool and delicate, brushing away a smudge of lipstick from his cheek. Jack held his breath, and the moment hung in the air between them.

"How about the next?" Ctholh'en asked, deflecting Brett's attention back toward his wide hazel eyes.

"We're going," Brett informed him. "We've got a date up in Montmartre." As they danced, Jack glanced over Brett's shoulder to see Ctholh'en still watching her from the bar.

"You've made a new admirer there," Jack told her.

"Don't talk about it. Poor chap. I never knew it until just now."

"Oh, well," Jack conceded. "I suppose you like to add them up."

"Don't talk like a fool."

"You do."

"Oh, well. What if I do?"

"Nothing," Jack replied as they danced to the accordion and banjo. The heat surrounded them, and a sense of happiness enveloped him. They swirled near Georgette, now dancing with another man.

"What possessed you to bring her?"

"I don't know. I just brought her."

"You're getting damned romantic."

"No, bored."

"Now?"

"No, not now."

"Let's get out of here. She's well taken care of."

"Do you want to?"

"Would I ask you if I didn't want to?"

They left the dance floor, and Jack took his coat from a hanger on the wall and put it on. Brett stood by the bar with Ctholh'en, talking to him. Jack stopped at the bar and asked for an envelope. The *patronne* found one. Jack put a fifty-franc note inside, sealed it, and handed it to her.

"If the girl I came with asks for me, will you give her this?" Jack said. "If she goes out with one of those gentlemen, will you save this for me?"

"*C'est entendu*, Monsieur," the *patronne* agreed. "You're leaving now? So early?"

"Yes," Jack confirmed.

They started for the door, with Ctholh'en still talking to Brett. She said good night and took Jack's arm. "Good night, Ctholh'en," Jack said. Outside in the street, they looked for a taxi.

"You're going to lose your fifty francs," Brett predicted.

"Oh, yes."

"No taxis."

"We could walk up to the Pantheon and find one."

"Come on, let's get a drink in the pub next door and send for one."

"You wouldn't walk across the street."

"Not if I could help it."

They went into the neighboring bar, and Jack sent a waiter for a taxi.

"Well," Jack said, "we're away from them now."

At the *zinc bar*, Jack and Brett exchanged silent, knowing looks. The waiter's arrival with news of a taxi broke their trance. Brett's grip tightened on Jack's hand as they left, Jack tossing a franc to the waiter.

"Where should I tell him?" Jack asked.

"Oh, tell him to drive around."

Jack instructed the driver to go to Parc Montsouris, got in, and slammed the door. Brett was leaning back in the corner, her eyes closed. Jack joined her, sitting beside her as the cab started with a jerk.

"Oh, darling, I've been so miserable," Brett confessed.

CHAPTER 4

WHISPERING ON MONTPARNASSE

THE TAXI CLIMBED THE HILL, passing the illuminated square before continuing into the darkness. It ascended briefly before leveling onto the dim street behind St. Étienne-du-Mont. They rolled down the asphalt past tall, furrowed horse chestnut trees and the motionless bus at Place de la Contrescarpe before turning onto the cobbled Rue Mouffetard.

Amid the hum of lively bars and shops, they jolted together and apart in the taxi, navigating the old cobbled street. Brett's hat was off; her head tilted back. Jack glimpsed her face in the lights from the open shops; then darkness enveloped them again. Her face reappeared, clear as day, as they emerged onto Avenue des Gobelins. Men worked on the torn-up street, their figures cast in sharp relief by the acetylene flares.

Brett's face was pale, and the long line of her neck was visible in the bright light of the flares. The street darkened once more, and Jack kissed her. Their lips pressed firmly together, but she turned away, pressing against the corner of the seat, as far from him as possible. Her head hung low.

"Don't," she whispered, a faint echo in the void between them. "Not now."

"What's the matter?"

"I can't stand it."

"Oh, Brett."

"You mustn't. You must know. I can't stand it, that's all. Oh, darling, please understand!"

"Don't you love me?"

"Love you? I simply turn to jelly when you touch me."

"Isn't there anything we can do about it?"

She sat up. Jack's arm encircled her, and she leaned back against him, completely calm. In her eyes, he saw something vast and deep, like looking into the sea or the night sky. There was a calmness there, louder than any words, holding the world and all its mysteries. For a moment, Jack saw a vastness, a reflection not of him but a flicker from a mirror's clouded surface, revealing shadows of smoke and forgotten regret.

"And there's not a damn thing we could do," Jack admitted.

"I don't know," her words brushed the surface of a shared past, mirroring his pain in the silence that followed.

"We'd better keep away from each other."

"But, darling, I have to see you. It isn't all that, you know."

"No, but it always gets to be."

She had been gazing into Jack's eyes the entire time. Her eyes possessed different depths. Sometimes, they seemed entirely flat. Now, it was as if one could see all the way into them.

"When I think of the hell I've put chaps through," Brett mused, "I'm paying for it all now."

"Don't talk like a fool," Jack retorted. "Besides, what happened to me is supposed to be funny. I never think about it." Humor was a pitiful mask—thin as gaslight whispers holding back the endless, uncaring sky.

"Oh, no. I'll bet you don't."

"Well, let's shut up about it." Silence, their uneasy truce, spoke volumes. She watched the moon high above them, almost full.

After a time, Brett looked back to him. "I laughed about it too, myself, once." She wasn't looking at him. "A friend of my brother's came home that way from Mons. It seemed like a hell of a joke. Chaps never know anything, do they?"

"No."

His restraint, thin as ice over a deep winter lake, bore the cracks of smoldering battles fought in silence, where despair and rage lurked unseen but ever present just beneath the frozen surface. Jack had mulled over his situation many times, understanding that certain scars or flaws might be a source of humor for others but carried a profound weight for those who bore them. In the silence, a stoic whisper, "We suffer more in imagination," barely a balm to the searing memories and desires bubbling up like lava beneath his calm exterior.

"It's ironic," Jack mused. "Being in love is supposed to be marvelous."

"Do you actually believe that?" Brett's gaze seemed distant.

"Not in the typical sense. It's a peculiar sort of joy."

"No," she said. "I think it's hell on earth."

"It's good to see each other."

"No. I don't think it is."

"Don't you want to?"

"I have to."

They sat like two strangers. On their right was Parc Montsouris. The restaurant, where they kept the pool of live trout and where patrons could sit and gaze out over the park, was closed and dark. The driver leaned his head around.

"Where do you want to go?" Jack inquired. Brett averted her gaze.

"Oh, go to the Select."

"Café Select," Jack told the driver. "Boulevard Montparnasse."

They drove straight down, circling the Lion de Belfort that guarded the passing Montrouge trams. Brett stared straight ahead. On Boulevard Raspail, with the lights of Montparnasse in sight, Brett said, "Would you mind very much if I asked you to do something?"

"Don't be silly."

"Kiss me just once more before we get there."

When the taxi stopped, Jack exited and paid. Brett emerged, putting on her hat. She offered him her hand as she stepped down, and it trembled. "I say, do I look too much of a mess?" She adjusted her man's felt hat and headed for the bar. Inside, against the bar and at tables, were most of the crowd who had attended the dance.

"Hello, you chaps," Brett greeted. "I'm going to have a drink."

"Oh, Brett! Brett!" the little Greek portrait painter, who called himself a duke and whom everyone called Zizi, approached her. "I got something fine to tell you."

"Hello, Zizi," Brett acknowledged.

"I want you to meet a friend," Zizi said. A rotund man approached. Jack disliked his pomposity.

"Count Mippipopolous, meet my friend Lady Ashley."

"How do you do?" Brett asked.

"Well, does your Ladyship have a good time here in Paris?" inquired Count Mippipopolous, who wore an elk's tooth on his watch chain.

"Rather," Brett replied.

"Paris is a fine town, all right," the Count declared. "Always has been. But I guess you have pretty big doings yourself over in London."

"Oh, yes," Brett agreed. "Enormous."

Braddocks waved to Jack from a table. "Schitt, have a drink. Your girl got into a terrible argument."

"What about?"

"Something the *patronne's* daughter said. A huge argument. She was quite impressive, you know. Showed her yellow card and demanded the *patronne's* daughter's too. I say it was a row."

"What finally happened?"

"Oh, someone took her home. Not a bad-looking girl. Wonderful command of the language. Do stay and have a drink."

"No," Jack said. "I must leave. Seen Ctholh'en?"

"He went home with Frances," Mrs. Braddock chimed in.

"Poor fellow, he looks terribly down," Braddocks said.

"I dare say he is," Mrs. Braddock agreed.

"I have to leave," Jack said. "Good night."

Jack said good night to Brett at the bar. The Count was buying champagne.

"Will you have a glass of wine with us, sir?" he asked.

"No. Thanks, but I must go."

"Really leaving?" Brett asked.

"Yes," Jack said. "I have a terrible headache."

"Will I see you tomorrow?"

"Come by the office."

"Hardly."

"Well, where will I see you?"

"Anywhere around five o'clock."

"Make it the other side of town, then."

"Good. I'll be at the Crillon at five."

"Try and be there," Jack said.

"Don't worry," Brett said. "I've never let you down, have I?" Brett's tone carried a hint of irony, a subtle smirk.

"Heard from Mike?" Jack countered.

"Letter today."

"Good night, sir," said the Count.

Jack's departure was halted by a murmur, a whispered warning that slowed his stride:

"Montparnasse after midnight is no place to tread. *Les ombres là-bas, elles respirent, Marie. Merde.*"

A skeptical laugh. *"De telles histoires pour me tenir compagnie?"* she teased, pulling away while stroking his beard.

But the man's insistence pierced her skepticism. *"Je l'ai vu, je l'ai senti. Those shadows... they're not empty. Elles sont... des horreurs. Stay here with me instead. J'insiste."*

Jack passed the young couple and slipped outside.

Jack's walk into the Parisian night plunged him into palpable fear. Shadows stretched into sinister shapes, the city's vibrant pulse fading into darkness. Each step on ancient stones echoed in oppressive silence, a lone heartbeat lost in the void.

The Boulevard Saint-Michel, once a beacon of nocturnal energy, now lay desolate, whispering secrets through the gaps in its dimmed lights and abandoned tables. The play of shadows against the faint moonlight conjured phantoms at the corner of Jack's vision, urging him to hasten his pace toward Montparnasse.

Here, the streets twisted into a narrative of dread penned by the unseen. The flicker of streetlamps, now agents of a darker will, cast elongated shadows that danced with Jack's every move—a macabre ballet choreographed by the night itself. His pulse quickened, a symphony of fear conducted by the whispering wind and the ghostly caress of unseen hands.

Then, from the heart of this darkness, a shadow emerged—vast, threatening, a creature born from the abyss of Jack's own fears. He steeled himself against this demon of the night, only to watch, incredulous, as the looming horror dissolved under the moon's fickle gaze into nothing more than a tree branch, swaying gently. A laugh, brittle and short, broke the silence, a feeble shield against the encroaching dread.

In the dimly lit alleys of Montparnasse, Jack's solitude was shattered by the haunting click of high heels following close behind, a spectral pursuer invisible to the eye. He spun, heart leaping to his throat, to face an empty street—a theater of shadows mocking his terror.

An intoxicating perfume enveloped Jack. A sultry, spectral voice whispered, "Jack, *mi niño bonito.*" The words caressed him. "*¿Por qué me abandonaste, mi amor? Ven a mí...*" Distant cries echoed, "Why did you leave us, Jack?"

A chill swept over him. "Jack, *mi corazón*, you cannot escape me..." His pulse raced.

The scent intensified. Memories of forbidden nights shadowed by horror. Her breath on his neck. "*Mi amor, te he esperado en la oscuridad. Regresa a mí...*"

"Leave me alone!" he shouted.

A haunting laugh. *"Nunca podrás olvidarme, Jack. Somos uno, por siempre..."* The words pulled him toward darkness.

He stumbled as shadows twisted, reaching out. *"Mi alma perdida, mi dulce amor, ven conmigo..."*

He ran, her voice pursuing. *"Jack, no huyas de mí..."*

Breathless, Jack lurched into a halo of lamplight. Her haunting whispers faded, but dread clung to him, and now the echoes of his fallen comrades washed over his mind, weaving a grim tapestry: "Why did you leave us, Jack? Leave our spirits to wander alone?"

His heart, ensnared by the night's malevolence, pounded a frantic rhythm—a dirge for his slipping sanity. The streets of Montparnasse, familiar by day, contorted into a labyrinth of shadows, each corner twisting deeper into his personal hell. Streetlamps, once beacons of safety, flickered and died, leaving Jack adrift in a sea of darkness.

He fled down a forsaken alley, the cold air biting—a cruel reminder of his isolation. Each shivering breath mingled with the fog of his fears. Ahead, pools of lamplight throbbed ominously, shadows writhing at their edges, forming the sigil— a symbol of dread that vanished as swiftly as it appeared.

Then, darkness absolute. The world collapsed, smothering him in a silence so profound it roared in his ears. He fell, crying out, the cobblestones a harsh reminder of reality as imagined battle cacophonies erupted around him. The horrors of his past, born from muck and mist, reached with phantom fingers, dragging him back to wars long ended.

A cannon's blast beside him—or perhaps the sudden, jarring sound of a motor-car backfiring—shattered the spell, scattering the phantoms of his mind like smoke in the wind. Jack rose and sought the sanctuary of light, each step a testament to his defiance of the darkness that had sought to claim him.

He made it to his apartment. The concierge looked him over, seeing a madman or a tramp—caked in mud and filth, breathless, soaked through. Passing by, he offered a tale of a carriage accident, a quick word to excuse his state. The door shut behind him, a sound that for a moment seemed to chase away the dark.

Inside, basking in the warm gaslight glow, the mundane task of sorting through his mail was a stark contrast to the terror he'd just escaped. Yet, as he sifted through letters and bills, the normalcy was a thin veil over the night's haunting experience. He washed the grime away.

In the silence, Jack found no escape from his tormented mind, despite the flicker of candles and lamps. The night's stillness enveloped him like a watchful presence. The distant chug of a night train, a solitary sound in the quiet, served as his tether to reality. Yet, it wasn't enough to prevent his thoughts from wandering to terrible places.

There was a pull, a dreadful magnetism emanating from his desk, where the locked drawer lay like a sealed crypt. It called to him, not through sound but a deep, visceral longing that threaded through the darkness—a siren's call that was both terrifying and irresistible. Jack fought against it, the effort to remain still in his bed a battle of wills against the unseen force.

He pondered the peculiar cruelty of night, how it stripped away the distractions of daylight and laid bare the soul's darker currents. At night, the struggle to maintain one's goodness, to ward off the seductive whisper of one's baser impulses, became a herculean task. The darkness seemed to amplify every whisper of doubt, every shadow and past misdeed, into a full-blown chorus—a symphony of temptation.

As the phantom heartbeat from the drawer grew more insistent, a physical manifestation of his inner turmoil, Jack's resolve began to fray. The room, once a sanctuary, became a stage for a macabre drama in which he was both audience and actor, powerless to escape the unfolding narrative.

Extinguishing the gas, Jack's actions were mechanical. The act of undressing, a mundane end to the day, did little to quiet the insidious beat that throbbed like a warning in the back of his mind—a reminder of the vast darkness that lay just beneath the surface of his carefully curated existence.

Settling into bed, the room's stillness was a stark contrast to the turmoil within. The night, once a canvas of infinite possibilities, now stretched around him with an oppressive density, its silence punctuated only by the distant, haunting pulse that seemed to echo with the ghosts of what might have been. In these hours, devoid of distraction, the heartbeat grew louder—a cursed cadence that spoke of desires unfulfilled and paths untaken, a stage for the whispered voices of regret and longing that danced just beyond the reach of understanding, their murmurs a sinister lullaby that accompanied him into the uneasy embrace of sleep.

CHAPTER 5

THE FLOWING CRIMSON

JACK JOLTED AWAKE, SUBMERGED IN the cold embrace of the bathtub, his senses ensnared in a fog of disorientation. Sunlight sliced through the blinds, casting shadows that danced with malevolent intent. Draped over him, a plum-colored suit bore a patchwork of crimson stains.

Around the tub's edge, symbols drawn in the unmistakable rusty hue of dried blood pulsed with an alien life. These markings—twisting sigils spiraling into labyrinths, interlocking geometries watched by omnipresent eyes—dragged Jack's mind to the brink of comprehension and revulsion. The room seemed to tilt in a nauseating dance under their gaze, the symbols blurring into a vortex that threatened to swallow him whole.

Jack stripped off the suit, its fabric stiff with blood. Under the harsh bathroom light, he frantically scrubbed away the night's grime, but the water reddened with guilt, unable to cleanse the deeper stain on his soul.

He caught his reflection—subtly wrong, features skewed in ways that defied logic. As he watched, the image contorted further, taking on a dizzying, monstrous aspect. In the mirror's harsh revelation, Jack witnessed two selves: one walking in the Parisian light, the other lurking in shadows, each step a betrayal of the man he once was. A bitter chuckle escaped him. Shaking his head, Jack exhaled through his nose telling himself it was nothing that an early night wouldn't fix. He looked back to find the horror gone, replaced by his own pale, haunted face.

As he hid the bloody clothes, his heart pounded a frantic rhythm, each beat echoing the night's horrors and the whispered call of cursed objects left behind. The suit, hastily wrapped and weighted with the gravity of his deeds, was a shroud destined for the Seine's indifferent depths. Navigating the waking streets of Paris, the judgment in strangers' eyes weighed upon him, their glances cutting through the façade he struggled to maintain.

Jack's paranoia grew as he walked Rue des Écoles and Rue Saint-Jacques, each step amplifying his dread. He stalled as a young couple strolled arm in arm, gazing at his watch, hat pulled low, attempting to appear nonchalant and unmemorable.

Finally, confident he wasn't being watched, he gifted the Seine, a grim confidant, his dark secrets, and the river seemed eager to swallow the plum-colored suit, pulling it into its depths. As the fabric submerged, the water's surface rippled, and for a fleeting second, Jack saw faces in the water, twisted in agony, reaching out to him. Then they were gone, swallowed by the river. A whisper, barely audible above the lapping water, slithered into his ear—a voice not heard but felt, emanating from that cursed object locked away in his office. It spoke a single, chilling word: "Deeper."

The city itself appeared to watch him, the statues in Luxembourg Gardens ominously turning their heads as he passed, whispers of condemnation following him like a curse. The judgment of strangers felt unnervingly telepathic, their thoughts a chorus of accusations gnawing at his frayed nerves. Paris, once vibrant, now seemed a stage for a macabre play with Jack as the unwilling lead.

At the office, Jack sought refuge in work, trying to drown out whispers of the night's horrors. The cursed object in his drawer pulsed like a jealous lover's heart, yet he did not submit to his desire to answer the call. Later, he joined colleagues at the Quai d'Orsay, sharing a taxi with Woolsey and Krum.

"What do you do nights, Jack?" Krum inquired.

"Oh, I'm over in the Quarter," Jack replied casually.

The conversation meandered to mundane topics—tennis, work, life in the country. Jack's thoughts, however, lingered on the previous night's events and Brett Ashley's captivating presence.

Jack returned to the office to find Ro'brt Ctholh'en standing motionless by the window. The usual poise was gone, replaced by an eerie stillness. His large, bulging eyes stared unblinkingly into the distance, and his stoic visage bore an unsettling resemblance to a gargoyle perched atop some ancient cathedral. As Jack approached, a shiver crawled down his spine; Ro'brt's presence felt almost otherworldly, an unsettling mythical creature gazing expectantly at him.

"Bad news, Ro'brt?" Jack inquired, his voice barely masking the unease that gnawed at him. He noted the uncharacteristic shadow swirling in his friend's abyssal eyes.

"A telegram from the Hamptons," Ro'brt murmured, his gaze distant and unfathomable. "A fire in the library. My parents are. .. it's a mess. They suspect it was a robbery."

A heavy, oppressive silence descended upon them, thick as the mists of some forgotten moor. Jack felt the weight of unspoken dread pressing in. Their shared knowledge of what truly resided within that library hung in the air like an unspeakable secret, a lurking horror neither dared to name. The moment stretched taut between them, fraught with the unsaid, each man grappling with the existential implications.

"Lunch, then?" Jack suggested, keen to break the somber spell.

Ro'brt managed a faint smile. "Yes, lunch. Let's go somewhere... new."

"Wetzel's?" Jack offered, the name a welcome distraction. "Heard they've got a new chef."

A subtle shift in Ro'brt's demeanor hinted at gratefulness. "Wetzel's it is."

As they weaved through the Parisian streets toward Wetzel's, Jack's gaze inadvertently met his own reflection in a shop window. For a moment, his face seemed grotesquely twisted, features contorted in a silent snarl. A cold chill ran down his spine, like icy fingers tracing his vertebrae. He jerked back, stunned.

Beside him, Ro'brt's eyes, sharp and probing, missed nothing. "You alright?" His voice was laced with an unnerving blend of concern and curiosity. "You look like you've seen a ghost."

Jack forced a nod, pushing the disturbing image away. "Yeah, just thought I saw... Never mind," he muttered, the echo of distant laughter ringing faintly in his ears. He quickened his pace.

At Wetzel's, the lively clatter and the aroma of freshly baked bread mingled with rich spices, momentarily displacing the weight of the morning's news. The sommelier's expertise was evident in each dish's presentation and the beer's crisp coolness.

"How was your night?" Jack probed, casually sipping his beer.

"Not great, really," Ro'brt confessed.

"And your writing? How's it coming along?"

"Terrible. I can't get my second book started."

"That happens to everyone," Jack reassured him.

"I know, but it still worries me."

"Thought any more about going to South America?"

"I have, actually."

"Well, why don't you go?"

"Frances."

"Take her with you."

"She wouldn't enjoy it. She prefers having many people around."

"Tell her to go to hell," Jack remarked with a note of firmness.

"I can't. I have obligations to her." Ro'brt pushed aside a plate of cucumbers, reaching for a pickled herring instead.

The conversation shifted when Ro'brt asked about Lady Brett Ashley. "What do you know about Lady Brett Ashley, Jack?"

"Her title is Lady Ashley. Brett's her given name. She's lovely," Jack said. "She's getting a divorce and plans to marry Mike Hawk. Why?"

Ro'brt's disbelief was almost comical, and he spat out his drink. Around them, other patrons glanced over at the commotion.

Ro'brt clucked disapprovingly at Jack. "I don't believe you."

Several patrons murmured about the scene they'd made, but Jack didn't care. If anything, he was amused and engaged. Jack smiled. "Why not?"

"I don't know. I just don't believe it. Have you known her long?"

"Yes," Jack said. "She was a V.A.D. in a hospital where I stayed during the war."

"She must have been young then."

"She's thirty-four now."

"When did she marry Ashley?"

"During the war. Her first love had just passed away from dysentery."

"You sound bitter."

"Sorry, I didn't mean to. I was merely providing facts."

"I don't think she'd marry anyone she didn't love."

"Well," Jack said, "she's done it twice."

"I don't believe it."

"Look," Jack said, "don't ask me foolish questions if you dislike the answers."

"I didn't ask you that."

"You asked what I knew about Brett Ashley."

"I didn't ask you to insult her."

"Oh, go to hell."

Ro'brt glowered at Jack, that unblinking stygian stare, and rose from the table, his face tight and furious, looming over the small plates of hors d'œuvres like a shark upon the reef bed.

"Sit down," Jack urged. "Don't be foolish."

"You have to take that back," Ro'brt clucked.

"Enough with the childish behavior."

"Take it back."

"Fine. Anything. I've never heard of Brett Ashley. How's that?"

"No, not that. About me going to hell."

"Well, don't go to hell," Jack said. "Stay here. We've just begun lunch."

Ro'brt smiled and sat down, relieved. What would he have done if he hadn't sat down? "You say such terribly insulting things, Jack."

"I apologize. I have a sharp tongue," which was true, and often due to his irritability, but today was purely for sport. "I never mean the nasty things I say."

"I know," Ro'brt admitted. "You're truly one of my best friends, Jack."

God help you, Jack thought. "Forget what I said," he spoke aloud. "I'm sorry."

"It's okay. It's fine. I was just upset for a moment."

"Good. Let's order something else to eat."

The tension dissolved, and they agreed to order more food. Post-lunch, they strolled to Café de la Paix for coffee. Sensing Ro'brt wanted to revisit Brett, Jack steered the conversation elsewhere. Eventually, Jack excused himself to return to the office, leaving Ro'brt amidst the buzz of the café.

Stepping into the bustling streets, a magnetic pull tugged at Jack, urging him back to the office. It was as if the fate he tried to outrun beckoned—a silent call from the throbbing, evil force locked away in his desk drawer, whispering of unfinished business. Each step strengthened the pull—a siren's call that steered him, like a devilish lighthouse, toward an inevitable confrontation with his shadows.

Chapter 6

Murmurs À (la) Plumb

AT FIVE O'CLOCK, JACK WAS in the Hotel Crillon waiting for Brett. She was not there, so he sat down and wrote some letters. They weren't very good letters, but he hoped their being on Crillon stationery would help them. Brett didn't show, so around a quarter to six, he went down to the bar and had a Jack Rose with George the barman. Brett hadn't been in the bar either, so he looked for her upstairs on his way out and took a taxi to the Café Select.

Crossing the Seine, the sight of barges drifting like specters struck a dissonant chord within him. The river's waters were unusually low, casting a pall over the journey's charm. Paris, with its timeworn bridges that once promised adventure, threatened to expose ancient secrets and reveal Jack's growing disillusionment.

The taxi meandered through Boulevard Raspail—a monotonous stretch shadowed by looming buildings—and arrived at the Rotonde. Harvey, ensconced in the café's dimness, beckoned Jack to join him.

"Sit," Harvey's voice was low and heavy.

"What's new?"

"Paul's gone." Harvey's words sent a jolt through Jack.

"Disappeared?" The word echoed in Jack's racing heart, a maelstrom of fear and suspicion awakening.

"He left photos... disturbing ones." Harvey's fleeting, wary glance unsettled Jack.

"How so?" Jack swallowed hard.

"I went by his studio... it had been ransacked. His favorite camera, smashed on the floor. I salvaged the film—curiosity, you know? Jack... there's one of you." Harvey's stare, now unflinching, bordered on an indictment. The acrid scent of stale whiskey emanated from Harvey's breath; he'd been here awhile.

Jack's laugh rang thin and unnatural, a weak defense against the surge of paranoia. The mention of a photograph sent a shiver down his spine. "I don't recall."

Jack's fear swelled, a silent scream clawing at his mind until crimson shadows edged his vision; only then did he realize he'd been holding his breath. When Harvey pulled a manila envelope out of his coat pocket and unfolded it to produce a set of photos, it was just him and Georgette, lost in the simplicity of a moment, glasses of Pernod between them. Relief washed over Jack. What was he worried about anyway?

Then, Harvey flipped through the rest of the collection: eerie snapshots of Paris by night, its streets haunted by the painted faces of *poules* under the moon's indifferent gaze and the aimless drift of drunken silhouettes. Each photo whispered of loneliness, of lives momentarily caught in the camera's eye, yet infinitely distant.

The tension between them tightened as Harvey hesitated, then displayed the penultimate photo—a pair of glowing eyes nestled in the dark, a silent watcher. Jack's heart stalled, his breath caught in the cold grip of recognition. Amid the gloom, the sigil hovered—an eye surrounded by chaotic lines, an esoteric curse scrawled in the night.

"Do you see that?" Jack's voice was barely a whisper, a thread in the thick air.

"The eyes?" Harvey's voice carried a casual, unsettling disinterest. "Creepy, right."

"Above them... in the shadows... the mark."

"No..." Harvey's denial was a void, dismissing the very thing that clawed at Jack's sanity. "Just the eyes."

The last photo turned over, revealing nothing but an overexposed blur—a maelstrom of what could have been fur. The ambiguity of the image, a mere suggestion of form, left Jack gasping, teetering on the edge of an unspoken horror. Harvey's unease grew to seemingly mirror Jack's.

Jack exhaled slowly, attempting to dispel the tension, and ordered a porto. Their conversation drifted through trivialities—a feeble attempt to escape the ominous undercurrent of Paul's absence. Yet, as Harvey spoke of his own hardships, Jack's thoughts remained ensnared by the implications of the photographs, his own role in the night's mysteries a question mark looming large in his mind.

Offering aid, Jack sought to escape the conversation's invisible bindings, the promise of a meal a temporary reprieve from the haunting uncertainty of Paul's fate and his own tangled involvement.

"Did you go to the races?"

"No. Not since Sunday."

"Heard anything from the States?"

"Nothing. Absolutely nothing."

"What happened?"

"I don't know. I'm done with them. Totally done." He leaned in, his gaze piercing into Jack's eyes.

"Want to hear something, Jack?"

"Sure."

"I haven't eaten for five days."

Jack quickly did the math. Harvey had won two hundred francs three days ago from him shaking poker dice in the New York Bar.

"What happened?"

"Out of cash. The money hasn't come," he paused. "It's odd, Jack. When I'm like this, I want solitude. I just want to stay in my room. I'm like a cat."

Jack reached into his pocket. "Would a hundred help, Harvey?"

"It would."

"Come on. Let's grab some food."

"No rush. Have a drink first."

"We should eat."

"No, when I'm in this state, food doesn't matter to me."

They shared a drink. Harvey discreetly added Jack's saucer to his teetering stack.

"Do you know Mencken, Harvey?"

"Yes. Why?"

"What's he like?"

"He's all right. He says some pretty funny things. Last time I had dinner with him, we talked about Hoffenheimer. 'The trouble is,' he said, 'he's a garter snapper.' That's not bad."

"That's not bad."

"He's through now," Harvey went on. "He's written about all the things he knows, and now he's on all the things he doesn't know."

"I guess he's all right," Jack said. "I just can't read him."

"Oh, nobody reads him now," Harvey said, "except the people that used to read the Alexander Hamilton Institute."

"Well," Jack said. "That was a good thing, too."

"Sure," said Harvey, and the pair sat and thought deeply for a while.

"Have another port?"

"All right," said Harvey.

"There comes Ctholh'en," Jack said. Ro'brt Ctholh'en was crossing the street.

"That moron," said Harvey. Ctholh'en came up to their table.

"Hello, you bums," he said.

"Hello, Ro'brt," Harvey said. "I was just telling Jack here that you're a moron."

"What do you mean?" Ctholh'en's eyes grew larger, and he looked even more stygian than usual.

"Tell us right off. Don't think. What would you rather do if you could do anything you wanted?"

Ctholh'en started to consider.

"Don't think. Bring it right out."

"I don't know," Ctholh'en said. "What's it all about, anyway?"

"I mean, what would you rather do. What comes into your head first. No matter how silly it is."

"I don't know," Ctholh'en said. "I think I'd rather play football again with what I know about handling myself now."

"I misjudged you," Harvey said. "You're not a moron. You're only a case of arrested development."

"You're awfully funny, Harvey," Ctholh'en said, shooting daggers into Harvey, but in his state, Harvey was as dagger-proof as mist. "Some day somebody will push your face in."

Harvey Stone let out a hollow laugh. "You think so. They won't, though. Because it wouldn't make any difference to me. I'm not a fighter."

"It would make a difference to you if anybody did it."

"No, it wouldn't. That's where you make your big mistake. Because you're not intelligent."

"Cut it out about me."

"Sure," said Harvey. "It doesn't make any difference to me. You don't mean anything to me."

"Come on, Harvey," Jack said. "Have another porto."

"No," he said. "I'm going up the street to eat. See you later, Jack."

He walked out and up the street. Jack watched him crossing through the taxis, small, heavy, slowly sure of himself in the traffic.

"He always gets me sore," Ctholh'en said. "I can't stand him."

"I like him," Jack said. "I'm fond of him. You don't want to get sore at him."

"I know it," Ctholh'en said. "He just gets on my nerves."

"Write this afternoon?"

"No. I couldn't get it going. It's harder to do than my first book. I'm having a hard time handling it."

When he returned from America early in the spring, the sort of healthy conceit he had was gone. Then, he had been sure of his work, only with these personal longings for adventure. Now the sureness was gone.

Jack considered Ro'brt Ctholh'en carefully before deciding the reason was that until he fell in love with Brett, Jack had never heard him make one remark that would, in any way, detach him from other people. He was nice to watch on the tennis court; he had a good body, kept it in shape, handled his cards well at bridge, and had a funny sort of undergraduate quality about him. In a crowd, nothing he said stood out. He wore polo shirts like the ones they'd worn at school and probably still called them that. But he wasn't trying to look young or fashionable. Jack didn't think he thought about clothes much.

Externally, he had been formed at Princeton. Internally, he had been molded first by dark family secrets wound too tight and second by the two women who had trained him. He had a nice, boyish sort of cheerfulness that hadn't been trained out of him, though Jack doubted he'd brought it out himself. He loved to win at tennis. He probably loved to win as much as Lenglen, for instance. But he wasn't angry about losing. His game fell apart when he fell in love with Brett. People who had never had a chance against him started beating him, and he was very nice about it.

They were sitting on the terrace of the Café Select, and Harvey Stone had just crossed the street.

"Come on up to the Lilas," Jack said.

"I have a date."

"What time?"

"Frances is coming here at seven-fifteen."

"There she is."

Frances Clyne was coming toward them from across the street. She was a very tall girl who walked with a great deal of movement. She waved and smiled. They watched her cross the street.

"Hello," she said, "I'm so glad you're here, Jack. I've been wanting to talk to you."

"Hello, Frances," said Ctholh'en. He smiled, but his eyes were dull, lifeless.

"Why, hello, Ro'brt. Are you here?" She continued, words tumbling out in a rapid torrent. "I've had the most difficult time. This one"—shaking her head at Ctholh'en—"didn't come home for lunch."

"I wasn't supposed to."

"Oh, I know. But you didn't say anything about it to the cook. Then I had a date myself, and Paula wasn't at her office. I went to the Ritz and waited for her, and she never came, and of course, I didn't have enough money for lunch at the Ritz—"

"What did you do?"

"Oh, went out, of course." She spoke in a sort of imitation joyful manner. "I always keep my appointments. No one keeps theirs nowadays. I ought to know better. How are you, Jack, anyway?"

"Fine."

"That was a fine girl you had at the dance and then went off with that Brett one."

"Don't you like her?" Ctholh'en asked.

"I think she's perfectly charming. Don't you?"

Ctholh'en said nothing.

"Look, Jack. I want to talk with you. Would you come over with me to the Dome? You'll stay here, won't you, Ro'brt? Come on, Jack."

They crossed the Boulevard Montparnasse and sat down at a table.

A boy came up with the *Paris Times*, and Jack bought one and opened it.

"What's the matter, Frances?"

"Oh, nothing," she said, "except that he wants to leave me."

"How do you mean?"

"Oh, he told everyone that we were going to be married, and I told my mother and everyone, and now he doesn't want to do it."

"What's the matter?"

"He's decided he hasn't lived enough. I knew it would happen when he went to New York."

She looked up, eyes unnaturally bright as she feigned nonchalance.

"I wouldn't marry him if he doesn't want to. Of course, I wouldn't. I wouldn't marry him now for anything. But it does seem to me to be a little late now after we've waited three years, and I've just gotten my divorce."

Jack said nothing.

"We were going to celebrate so, and instead, we've just had scenes. It's so childish. We have dreadful scenes, and he cries and begs me to be reasonable, but he says he just can't do it."

"It's rotten luck."

"I should say it is rotten luck. I've wasted two and a half years on him now. And I don't know now if any man will ever want to marry me. Two years ago, I could have married anybody I wanted down at Cannes. All the older ones who wanted to marry someone chic and settle down were crazy about me. Now, I don't think I could get anybody."

"Sure, you could marry anybody."

"No, I don't believe it. And I'm fond of him, too. I don't mind his look so much; I've even gotten used to it. And I'd like to have children. I always thought we'd have children."

She looked at Jack with a forced brightness. "I never liked children much, but I don't want to think I'll never have them. I always thought I'd have them and then like them."

"He's got children."

"Oh, yes. He's got children, and he's got money, and he's got a rich mother, and he's written a book, and nobody will publish his stuff; nobody at all. It isn't bad, either. And I haven't got any money at all. I could have had alimony, but I got the divorce the quickest way."

She looked at Jack again, her eyes glistening. "It isn't right. It's my own fault, and it's not, too. I ought to have known better. And when I tell him, he just cries and says he can't marry. Why can't he marry? I'd be a good wife. I'm easy to get along with. I leave him alone. It doesn't do any good."

"It's a rotten shame."

"Yes, it is a rotten shame. But there's no use talking about it, is there? Come on, let's go back to the café."

"And, of course, there isn't anything I can do."

"No. Just don't let him know I talked to you. I know what he wants." Now, for the first time, she dropped her bright, terribly cheerful manner. "He wants to go back to New York alone and be there when his book comes out when a lot of little admirers like it. That's what he wants."

"Maybe they won't like it. I don't think he's that way. Really."

"You don't know him like I do, Jack. That's what he wants to do. I know it. I know it. That's why he doesn't want to marry. He wants to have a big triumph this fall all by himself."

"Want to go back to the café?"

"Yes. Come on."

They got up from the table—they had never brought them a drink—and started across the street toward the Select, where Ctholh'en sat smiling at them from behind the marble-topped table.

"Well, what are you smiling at?" Frances asked him. "Feel pretty happy?"

"I was smiling at you and Jack with your secrets."

"Oh, what I've told Jack isn't any secret. Everybody will know it soon enough. I only wanted to give Jack a decent version."

"What was it? About your going to England?"

"Yes, about my going to England. Oh, Jack! I forgot to tell you. I'm going to England."

"Isn't that fine!"

"Yes, that's the way it's done in the very best families. Ro'brt's sending me. He's going to give me two hundred pounds, and then I'm going to visit friends. Won't it be lovely? The friends don't know about it yet."

She turned to Ctholh'en and smiled at him. He was not smiling now.

"You were only going to give me a hundred pounds, weren't you, Ro'brt? But I made him give me two hundred. He's really very generous. Aren't you, Ro'brt?"

Jack could not understand how people could say such terrible things to Ro'brt Ctholh'en and how there were people to whom you could not say insulting things. They gave you a feeling that the world would be destroyed—would actually be destroyed before your very eyes—if you said certain things. But here was Ctholh'en taking it all. It was all happening right in front of Jack, and he didn't even feel the impulse to try and stop it. And this was friendly joking compared to what went on later.

"How can you say such things, Frances?" Ctholh'en interrupted.

"Listen to him. I'm going to England. I'm going to visit friends. Ever visited friends who didn't want you? Oh, they'll have to take me, all right. 'How do you do, my dear? Such a long time since we've seen you. And how is your dear mother?' Yes, how is my dear mother? She put all her money into French war bonds. Yes, she did. Probably the only person in the world who did. 'And what about Ro'brt?' Or else be very careful talking around Ro'brt. 'You must be most careful not to mention him, my dear. Poor Frances has had a most unfortunate experience.' Won't it be fun, Ro'brt? Don't you think it will be fun, Jack?"

She turned to Jack with that terribly bright smile. It was very satisfying for her to have an audience for this.

"And where are you going to be, Ro'brt? It's my own fault, all right. Perfectly my own fault. When I made you get rid of your little secretary in the magazine, I should have known you'd get rid of me the same way. Jack doesn't know about that. Should I tell him?"

"Shut up, Frances, for God's sake."

"Yes, I'll tell him. Ro'brt had a little secretary in the magazine. Just the sweetest little thing in the world, and he thought she was wonderful, and then I came along, and he thought I was pretty wonderful, too. So I made him get rid of her, and he had brought her to Arkham from Carmel when he moved the magazine, and he didn't even pay her fare back to the coast. All to please me. He thought I was pretty fine then. Didn't you, Ro'brt?

"You mustn't misunderstand, Jack; it was absolutely platonic with the secretary. Not even platonic. Nothing at all, really. It was just that she was so nice. And he did that just to please me. Well, I suppose that they that live by the sword shall perish by the sword. Isn't that literary, though? You'll want to remember that for your next book, Ro'brt.

"You know, Ro'brt is going to get material for a new book. Aren't you, Ro'brt? That's why he's leaving me. He's decided I don't film well. You see, he was so busy all the time that we were living together, writing this book, that he doesn't remember anything about us. So now he's going out and getting some new material. Well, I hope he gets something frightfully interesting. Really frightful, Jack." Frances' eyes were wild behind her mask of civility. "Maybe I'm prone to do something really wild, too; maybe that would wake him up, make him remember."

"Don't be a fool, Frances," Jack said.

"Listen, Ro'brt, dear. Let me tell you something. You won't mind, will you? Don't have scenes with your young ladies. Try not to. Because you can't have scenes without crying, and then you pity yourself so much you can't remember what the other person said. You'll never be able to remember any conversations that way. Just try and be calm. I know it's awfully hard. But remember, it's for literature. We all ought to make sacrifices for literature. Look at me. I'm going to England without a protest. All for literature. We must all help young writers. Don't you think so, Jack? Writers need all the help they can get."

Frances paused—a deceptive calm before the tempest roiling beneath her poised exterior.

"But you're not a young writer. Are you, Ro'brt?" Her words, seemingly casual, carried the weight of a seasoned boxer's feint, probing for weaknesses. "You're thirty-four," she continued, her tone weaving between admiration and accusation. "Still, I suppose that is young for a great writer. Look at Hardy. Look at

Anatole France. He just died a little while ago. Ro'brt doesn't think he's any good, though. Some of his French friends told him. He doesn't read French very well himself. He wasn't a good writer like you are, was he, Ro'brt? Do you think he ever had to go and look for material? What do you suppose he said to his mistresses when he wouldn't marry them? I wonder if he cried, too? Oh, I've just thought of something." She put her gloved hand up to her lips. "I know the real reason why Ro'brt won't marry me, Jack. It's just come to me. I've seen it in a vision at the Café Select. Isn't it mystic? Someday, they'll put a tablet up. Like at Lourdes. Do you want to hear, Ro'brt?"

Ro'brt stood stoically, absorbing each verbal blow. His eyes were distant, as if he stood alone in a boxing ring, ropes pressing against his back, nowhere to go but forward into the onslaught. Frances kept at him, relentless, laying out her case like she was lining up jabs. Ro'brt didn't dodge or weave, just took them, standing there, enduring.

Frances pressed on, her words relentless like the churning of a locomotive. "I'll tell you. It's so simple. I wonder why I never thought about it. Why, you see, Ro'brt's always wanted to have a mistress, and if he doesn't marry me, why, then he's had one. I was his mistress for over two years. See how it is? And if he marries me, like he's always promised he would, that would be the end of all the romance. Don't you think that's bright of me to figure that out? It's true, too. Look at him and see if it's not. Where are you going, Jack?"

"I've got to go in and see Harvey Stone a minute."

Cthulh'en's wide eyes locked onto Jack's, silently pleading for rescue as Jack retreated inside. His face had taken on a grey, lifeless hue. Why did he sit there? Why did he keep on taking it like that?

As Jack stood against the bar, eyes fixed on their reflection in the window, he could see them through the glass. Frances was still talking to him, smiling brightly, looking into his face each time she asked: "Isn't it so, Ro'brt?" Or maybe she didn't ask that now. Perhaps she said something else. Jack told the bartender he didn't want anything to drink and went out through the side door. As he went out the door, Jack looked back through the two thicknesses of glass and saw them sitting there. She was still talking to him.

Walking away, Jack pondered the weight of silent endurance. Ro'brt was doing that, hanging on, just trying to make it to the bell.

The night took Jack in, the city fading behind him. He thought about Ro'brt, about endurance, about the quiet kind of strength it takes to stand there and take the hits. That was something. Maybe that was everything.

Jack slipped into the shadowed embrace of Boulevard Raspail. A lone taxi emerged from the night's shroud, the gibbous moon transforming it into a phantom barque, delivering Jack to the shrouded penumbra of his deepest fears and unspoken desires. Settling into the backseat, fleeting visions of a distant señorita's warmth flickered through his mind. Yet, it was the silent echo of something far more sinister that drew him—a nameless hunger awaiting him in his flat. Like a dark mirror, it reflected the chasm within him, its pulse a quiet yet insistent summons. As the city's lights blurred past, he returned to his flat, where whispers from the depths awaited—the unseen abyss that had quietly claimed him long ago.

CHAPTER 7

HOWL

AS JACK STARTED UP THE stairs, the concierge knocked on the lodge door. When Jack paused, she emerged with some letters and a telegram.

"Here is the post. A lady was here to see you."

"Did she leave a card?"

"No. She was with a gentleman—the one who was here last night. She's very nice."

"Was he a friend of mine?"

"I don't know. He was never here before. Very large. She was very nice, though. Last night, perhaps a little—" She rested her head on one hand, rocking it gently. "I'll speak frankly,

96

Monsieur Schitt. Last night, I saw her differently. But she is très, très gentille. You can see it."

"They didn't leave any word?"

"They said they'd be back in an hour."

"Send them up when they arrive."

"Oui, Monsieur Schitt. And that lady there is someone... an eccentric, perhaps, but quelqu'une!"

Before becoming a concierge, Madame Duzinell ran a beverage stand at the Paris racetracks. Her realm was the *pelouse*, yet her gaze often drifted to the *pesage* elite. She enjoyed advising Jack on his guests' breeding and sportsmanship. Those who didn't meet her standards were turned away from *chez* Schitt. One such outsider was the gaunt painter, Pablo Picasso. Despite his recent acclaim, he failed to impress Madame Duzinell. He once wrote Jack seeking a pass to bypass the gatekeeping concierge for evening visits, recently with a Chinese guest, Chen Zizhuang—an impressionist painter. Regardless, Pablo was the best master forger Jack had ever seen.

Jack went up to the flat, wondering what Brett had done to the concierge. He received a message from Bill Gorton, saying he was arriving in France. Jack placed the mail on the table, returned to the bedroom, undressed, and showered. While rubbing down, he heard the doorbell pull. Jack donned a bathrobe and slippers and answered the door. It was Brett, accompanied by the Count, holding a large bouquet of roses.

"Hello, darling," Brett greeted. "Aren't you going to invite us in?"

"Come in. I was just bathing."

"Aren't you the fortunate man. Bathing."

"Only a shower. Sit down, Count Mippipopolous. What will you drink?"

"I don't know if you like flowers, sir," the Count said, "but I brought these roses."

"Here, take them." Brett accepted the roses, their red contrasting her delicate hands. "Water, Jack," she murmured, her voice distant. Jack watched the roses bend in the earthen jug, their brightness fading in the dim light. Brett placed them on the dining table.

"I say, we've had a day."

"You don't remember a date with me at the Crillon?"

"No. Did we have one? I must have been blind."

"You were quite drunk, my dear," the Count observed.

"Wasn't I? And the Count's been incredible, truly."

"You've made quite an impression on the concierge now."

"I ought to have. Gave her two hundred francs."

"Don't be foolish."

"His," she nodded at the Count.

"I thought we should give her something for last night. It was very late."

"He's wonderful," Brett said. "He remembers everything."

"So do you, my dear."

"Imagine, who'd want to? Jack, do we get a drink?"

"You get it while I dress. You know where it is."

"Of course."

As Jack dressed, he heard Brett put down glasses and a siphon, their conversation muffled. His movements were lethargic, each action dragging more than the last. He sat heavily on the bed, a deep exhaustion seeping into the room's air. Brett entered with a glass in hand and sat beside him.

"What's the matter, darling? Do you feel unwell?"

She kissed Jack gently on the forehead.

"Oh, Brett, I love you so much."

"Darling," she said. "Do you want me to send him away?"

"No. He's nice."

"I'll send him away."

"No, don't."

"Yes, I'll send him away."

"You can't just like that."

"Can't I? You stay here. He's infatuated with me, I tell you."

She left the room. Jack lay face down on the bed, struggling. He heard them talking but didn't listen. Brett returned and sat on the bed.

"Poor dear." She stroked his head.

"What did you say to him?" Jack lay with his face away, not wanting to see her.

"Sent him for champagne. He loves champagne."

"Do you feel better, darling? Is your head any better?"

"It's better."

"Rest. He's gone to the other side of town."

"Couldn't we live together, Brett? Just live together?"

"I don't think so. I'd deceive you with everybody. You couldn't stand the cheating."

"I stand it now."

"That would be different. It's my fault, Jack. It's the way I'm made."

"Couldn't we go off to the country for a while?"

"It wouldn't be any good. I'll go if you like. But I couldn't live quietly in the country. Not with my true love."

"I know."

"Isn't it terrible? There's no use in my telling you—I love you."

"You know I love you."

"Let's not talk. Talking's nonsense. I'm going away, and then Michael's coming back."

"Why are you going away?"

"Better for you. Better for me."

"When are you going?"

"As soon as I can."

"Where?"

"San Sebastián."

"Can't we go together?"

"No. That would be a terrible idea after we'd just talked it out."

"We never agreed."

"Oh, you know as well as I do. Don't be stubborn, darling."

"Oh, sure," Jack said. "I know you're right. I'm just down, and when I'm down, I talk foolishly."

Jack sat up, found his shoes beside the bed, and put them on. He rose with effort.

"Don't look like that, darling."

"How do you want me to look?"

Brett glanced out the window, her voice barely a whisper. "Oh, don't be foolish. I'm going away tomorrow."

"Tomorrow?"

"Yes. Didn't I say so? I am."

"Let's have a drink, then. The Count will be back."

"Yes. He should be back. You know he's particular about buying champagne. It means a great deal to him."

They moved to the dining room. Jack poured Brett a drink and one for himself. The doorbell rang. The Count arrived, followed by the chauffeur carrying a basket of champagne.

"Where should I put it, sir?" asked the Count.

"In the kitchen," Brett replied.

"Put it in there, Henry," the Count instructed. "Now go get the ice." He watched the basket enter the kitchen. "I think you'll find this is very good wine. I got it from a friend in the business."

"Oh, you always have someone in the trade," Brett said.

"This fellow grows the grapes. He's got thousands of acres."

"What's his name? Veuve Clicquot?"

"No," said the Count. "Mumm. He's a baron."

"Isn't it amazing? They all have titles. Why don't you have a title, Jack?"

"I assure you, sir," the Count placed his hand on his arm, "it never does a man any good. Most of the time, it costs you money."

"Oh, I don't know. It's quite useful sometimes," Brett responded.

"I've never known it to do me any good."

"You haven't used it properly. I've had considerable credit on mine."

"Do sit down, Count," Jack said. "Let me take that stick."

The Count looked at Brett under the gaslight. She was smoking a cigarette, flicking ashes on the rug. "I say, Jack, I don't want to ruin your rugs. Can't you give someone an ashtray?"

Jack found some ashtrays and spread them around. The chauffeur returned with a bucket of salted ice. "Put two bottles in it, Henry," the Count instructed.

"Anything else, sir?"

"No. Wait down in the car." He turned to Brett and Jack. "We'll ride out to the Bois for dinner?"

"If you like," Brett said. "I couldn't eat a thing."

"I always enjoy a good meal," the Count replied.

"Should I bring the wine in, sir?" asked the chauffeur.

"Yes. Bring it in, Henry," the Count said, taking out a heavy cigar case. "Like to try a real American cigar?"

"Thanks," Jack said. "I'll finish the cigarette."

The Count cut the cigar with a gold cutter on his watch chain.

"I like a cigar to really draw," said the Count. "Half the cigars you smoke don't draw."

He lit the cigar, puffed, and looked at Brett. "And when you're divorced, Lady Ashley, you won't have a title."

"No. What a pity."

"No," said the Count. "You don't need a title. You have class all over you."

"Thanks. Very kind of you."

"I'm not pulling your leg," the Count blew a smoke cloud. "You have the most class of anybody I've ever seen. That's all."

"Nice of you," said Brett. "Mom would be pleased. Couldn't you write it out, and I'll send it in a letter to her?"

"I'd tell her, too," said the Count. "I'm not pulling your leg. I never pull people's legs. Pull enough legs, and you make enemies. That's what I always say."

Jack stared through the Count.

"You're right," Brett said. "You're absolutely right. I always pull legs, and I don't have many friends. Except Jack here."

"You don't pull my leg."

"That's it."

"Do you, now?" asked the Count. "Do you pull his leg?"

Brett looked at Jack and squinted slightly.

"No," she said. "I wouldn't pull his leg."

"See," said the Count. "You don't pull his leg."

"This is a dull conversation," Brett said. "How about some of that champagne?"

The Count spun the bottles in the shiny bucket. "It isn't cold yet. You're always drinking, my dear. Why don't you just talk?"

"I've talked too much. I've talked Jack's ears clean off. It was a mess."

"I'd like to hear you really talk, my dear. When you talk to me, you never finish your sentences."

"Leave 'em for you to finish. Let anyone finish them as they like."

"It's an interesting system," the Count spun the bottles again. "Still, I'd like to hear you talk sometime."

"Isn't he a fool?" Brett asked.

"Now," the Count brought up a bottle. "I think this is cool."

Jack took a towel, and the Count wiped the bottle dry, holding it up. "I like to drink champagne from magnums. The wine is better, but it would have been too hard to cool." He held the bottle, looking at it. Jack put out the glasses.

"I say, you might open it," Brett suggested.

"Yes, my dear. Now I'll open it."

The Count's gaze settled on Jack's desk as he impulsively pulled open a drawer. Jack's heart skipped, lips parted but voice trapped. The Count's fingers closed around a velvet-lined sack; eyes widened. Jack felt the Count's pulse, racing in his temples.

"An opener, Jack?"

Swallowing hard, Jack provided it, locking the drawer. The cork popped.

Jack smiled earnestly because it was amazing champagne.

"I say, that is wine," Brett held up her glass. "They ought to toast something. 'Here's to royalty.'"

"This wine is too good for toasting, my dear. You don't want to mix emotions with a wine like that. You lose the taste."

Brett's glass was empty.

"You ought to write a book on wines, Count," Jack said.

"Mr. Schitt," answered the Count, "all I want from wines is to enjoy them." His gaze lingered longer, boring into Jack and then back to Jack's desk drawer.

"Let's enjoy a little more of this," Brett pushed her glass forward. Jack shut the drawer as he moved to refill their glasses.

The Count poured carefully. "There, my dear. Enjoy that slowly, and then you can get tipsy."

"Tipsy? Tipsy?"

"My dear, you are charming when you are tipsy."

"Listen to the man."

"Mr. Schitt," the Count poured his glass full, "she is the only lady I have ever known who was as charming when she was tipsy as when she was sober."

"You haven't been around much, have you?"

"Yes, my dear. I have been around a great deal," the Count said dustily.

"Drink your wine," said Brett. "We've all been around. I dare say Jack here has seen as much as you have."

"My dear, I'm sure Mr. Schitt has seen a lot. Don't think I don't think so, sir. I have seen a lot, too."

"Of course you have, my dear," Brett said. "I was only teasing."

"I have been in seven wars and four revolutions," the Count said.

"Soldiering?" Brett asked.

"Sometimes, my dear. And I've got arrow wounds. Have you ever seen arrow wounds?"

"Let's have a look at them."

The Count stood, unbuttoned his vest, and opened his shirt. He pulled up his undershirt, revealing his chest and large stomach muscles bulging under the light.

"Do you see them?"

Below his ribs were two raised white welts. Just above the small of his back were the same two scars, raised as thick as a finger.

"I say, those are something."

"Clean through."

The Count tucked in his shirt.

"Where did you get those?" Jack asked.

"In Abyssinia."

"What were you doing? Were you in the army?"

"I was on a business trip, my dear."

"I told you he was one of us. Didn't I?" Brett turned to him. "I love you, Count. You're a darling."

"You make me very happy, my dear. But it isn't true."

"Don't be foolish."

"You see, Mr. Schitt," the Count observed, "true enjoyment comes with... perspective. One learns to appreciate the details. In living, one gathers layers of appreciation. It's the accumulation of experiences that refines our tastes."

"Yes. Absolutely," Jack said, sounding dull.

"I know. That is the secret. You must get to know the values."

"Doesn't anything ever happen to your values?" Brett asked.

"No. Not anymore."

"Never fall in love?"

"Always," said the Count. "I am always in love."

"What does that do to your values?"

"That, too, has its place in my values."

"You don't have any values. You're dead, that's all."

"No, my dear. You're not right. I'm not dead at all."

They drank three bottles of champagne, and the Count left the basket in Jack's kitchen. They dined at a restaurant in the Bois. It was a good dinner. Food held an excellent place in the Count's values, as did wine. The Count was in fine form during the meal, as was Brett. It was a good party.

"Where would you like to go?" asked the Count after dinner. They were the only people left in the restaurant. The two waiters stood by the door, eager to leave.

"Let's go up on the hill," Brett said. "Haven't we had a splendid party?"

The Count was beaming. He was very happy.

"You are very nice people," he said. He was smoking a cigar again. "Why don't you two get married?"

"We want to lead our own lives," Jack said.

"We have our careers," Brett said. "Come on. Let's get out of this."

"Have another brandy," the Count said.

"Get it on the hill."

"No. Have it here where it's quiet."

"You and your quiet," said Brett. "What is it men feel about quiet?"

"They like it," said the Count. "Like you like noise, my dear."

"All right," said Brett. "Let's have one."

"Sommelier!" the Count called.

"Yes, sir."

"What's the oldest brandy you have?"

"Eighteen eleven, sir."

"A fine year. Bring us a bottle."

"I say, don't be ostentatious. Call him off, Jack."

"Listen, my dear. I get more value for my money in old brandy than in any other antiquities."

"Got many antiquities?"

"I've got a houseful."

Finally, they went up to Montmartre. Inside Zelli's, it was crowded, smoky, and noisy. The music hit them as they entered. Brett and Jack danced. It was so crowded they could barely move. The drummer waved at Brett. They were caught in the jam, dancing in one place in front of him.

"How are you?"

"Great."

"That's good."

"He's a great friend of mine," Brett said. "A darn good drummer."

The music stopped, and they started toward the table where the Count sat. Then the music started again, and they danced. Jack looked at the Count. He was sitting at the table, smoking a cigar. The music stopped again.

"Let's go over."

Brett started toward the table. The music started, and again they danced, tight in the crowd.

"You're not a great dancer, Jack. Michael's the best dancer I know."

"He's splendid."

"He's got his points."

"I like him," Jack said. "I'm quite fond of him."

"I'm going to marry him," Brett said. "Funny. I haven't thought about him for a week."

"Don't you write to him?"

"No, I never write letters."

"I bet he writes to you."

"Indeed. Excellent letters, too."

"When are you going to get married?"

"How do I know? As soon as we can get the divorce. Michael's trying to get his mother to pay for it."

"Could I help you?"

"Don't be silly. Michael's family has plenty of money."

The music stopped. They walked over to the table. The Count stood up.

"Very nice," he said. "You looked very, very nice."

"Don't you dance, Count?" Jack asked.

"No. I'm too old."

"Oh, come off it," Brett said.

"My dear, I would do it if I would enjoy it. I enjoy watching you dance."

"Splendid," Brett said. "I'll dance again for you sometime. What about your friend, Zizi?"

"Let me tell you. I support that boy, but I don't want to have him around."

"He is rather hard."

"You know, I think that boy has a future. But personally, I don't want him around."

"I feel the same way."

"He gives me the creeps."

"Well," the Count shrugged his shoulders. "About his future, you can't ever tell. Anyway, I was a great friend of his father, in his younger days."

"Come on. Let's dance," Brett said.

Jack and Brett danced. It was crowded and close.

"Oh, darling," Brett said, "I'm so miserable."

Jack had that feeling of going through something that had all happened before. "You were happy a minute ago."

The drummer shouted: "You can't two-time—"

"It's all gone."

"What's the matter?"

"I don't know. I just feel terrible."

The drummer chanted and then turned to his sticks.

"Want to go?"

Jack had the feeling as in a nightmare of it all being something repeated, something he had been through and that now he must go through again.

His heart quickened. Somewhere, he—a part of him, if not the conscious him, then the deep, restless part of him he had lost at sea, long ago—pounded, futilely, against a black mirror's cool glass.

"Let's go," said Brett. "You don't mind."

The drummer shouted and grinned at Brett.

"All right," Jack said. They extricated themselves from the crowd, and Brett went to the dressing room.

"Brett wants to go," Jack said to the Count.

He nodded. "Does she? That's fine. You take the car. I'm going to stay here for a while, Mr. Schitt."

They shook hands.

"It was a wonderful time," Jack said, although he was fighting the out-of-body experience—to remain—corporeal. "I wish you would let me pay for this." Jack took a note out of his pocket.

"Mr. Schitt, don't be absurd," the Count said.

Brett came over with her wrap on. She kissed the Count and put her hand on his shoulder to prevent him from standing up. As they went out the door, Jack looked back and saw three girls at his table. They got into the large car. Brett gave the chauffeur the address of her hotel.

"No, don't come up," she said at the hotel. She had rung, and the door was unlatched.

"Really?"

"No. Please."

"Good night, Brett," Jack said. "I'm sorry you feel unwell."

"Good night, Jack. Good night, darling. I won't see you again."

They kissed, standing at the door. She pushed Jack away. They kissed again. "Oh, don't!" Brett said.

She turned and entered the hotel. The chauffeur drove Jack to his apartment. After handing him twenty francs, Jack's solitary return was a journey into a thick silence charged with unspoken dread. Familiar corners now harbored unnaturally stretching shadows, hinting at a presence lurking just beyond sight—a silent observer from a dimension where human fears were mere playthings.

As Jack crossed the threshold, a magnetic pull seized him, an irresistible call deeper than any forbidden tryst. Each step toward the desk was laden with a yearning that transcended the physical, as if his very fibers were entwined with the destiny awaiting him in the shadows of his sanctum.

The air was heavy with anticipation and the fragrant perfume of ancient mysteries, as Jack navigated the dimly lit path to his desk. This was a pilgrimage to an altar of otherworldly power, blurring the line between seducer and seduced. The drawer, keeper of secrets, beckoned with a siren's call, promising both revelation and damnation.

His fingers trembled with dread and desire, tracing the contours of the lock—a prelude to unveiling. Unlocking the drawer was akin to the delicate undressing of a lover, each movement fraught with the electricity of discovery and the shadow of guilt. The velvet sack within symbolized his pact with the arcane, its cool, smooth fabric a contrast to the fever pitch of his pulse.

Drawing the sack out, Jack's breath caught. The mirror, framed in cracked ivory, emerged slowly from the velvet folds. It wasn't just a reflective surface—it was a portal, dark and heavy with secrets. Each step of the unveiling pulled him closer to the edge. When the mirror lay bare, it whispered of power and danger, tempting him with the promise of forbidden knowledge and the risk of losing everything.

As he gazed into the glass, Jack's reflection was swallowed by the abyss, replaced by a vision dancing on the edge of comprehension. The room spun, a vortex of whispers and shadows, as if the mirror itself breathed, its murmurs weaving through Jack's mind like a lover's caress—seductive and terrifying. The abyss pulled him, a physical caress promising ecstasy and oblivion in equal measure.

Jack stood transfixed, his body a battleground of fear and fascination. The whispers grew louder, a chorus of the ancient and the damned, their voices a tapestry of seduction weaving through his consciousness, promising truths too terrible for mortal understanding. The mirror, in silent communion, offered a glimpse of eternity—a place where time and sanity unraveled, leaving Jack naked before the vast, indifferent cosmos.

Jack's gaze penetrated inscrutable depths across dimensions until he found his Spanish *señorita*. Heart racing, he was captivated by her figure clad in a red lace corset, barely containing hidden depths of passion, while the fringes of her skirt danced with a life of their own—a silent music only she could hear. The room filled with the intoxicating fragrance of her perfume, pulling Jack closer with a magnetic allure. It was as if her soul infused the space, wrapping him in a cloak of desire and yearning.

He gazed into her eyes as the lustful vision soured. In an instant, her beauty splintered, revealing the nightmare beneath. Her allure was a thin veil—behind it lurked something dark, predatory. Her eyes, once sparkling with laughter, now opened into an abyss—ancient and unyielding. A cold radiated from her, not of winter, but of the grave. Her smile twisted, lips peeling back to reveal a jagged maw, sharp as hunger itself. Her whisper, once sweet and low, coiled around him like a noose. "Ven a mí, Jack," she hissed, her voice dragging him not to her villa but to something far deeper—Hell itself.

The whispers around Jack swelled into a deafening roar, a cacophony of ancient voices speaking not of love, but of eternal hunger and darkness. Caught in her gaze, Jack stood at the precipice, facing a truth far more terrifying than any known horror—a cosmic abyss where humanity's light was but a fleeting spark against the endless night.

Jack's return to the world of the living came with a jolt, like a diver surfacing too fast from the deep. His first conscious breath filled his nostrils with the sharp tang of fear, a scent tangible in the opulent yet shadowed confines of the Count's bedroom. In the gloom, the Count's eyes bore into him—wide, horrified, raw expressions of fear. The room, with its rich tapestry and heavy, suffocating drapes, suddenly became a crypt, the air thick with anticipation of something unspeakable.

As the initial tremor of fear subsided, the Count's visage contorted into an abomination of the night. The noble lines of his face distorted into a grotesque mask, mouth gaping into an abyss lined with savage fangs sharp as daggers. His eyes, once bright, were now fathomless pits. The air grew thick with the scent of death.

Between them, a spear hung loosely in the Count's grasp—impaled in Jack's side. He looked down in confusion to see blood pooling around matted fur amid the curling smoke.

In the dim flickers, lit only by the capricious dance of candle flames and the hungry crackle of fire consuming velvet draperies, Jack's form became an ever-shifting horror. Shadows clung to his skin like living tar, hinting at a beastly form too ghastly for the human mind to comprehend. His breaths were ragged and wet, the sound of a creature lurking at the edge of madness, while the scant light revealed glimpses of what seemed like fur—matted and dark, bristling with an animal's ferocious intent. As the flames flickered, he held the Count ever tighter.

The air itself seemed to shudder with the weight of unspoken terrors, the shadows at the room's edge undulating as if alive with malevolent intent.

The Count's form began to dissolve into mist, dreamlike, but Jack's fury surged beyond the natural world, a force no shadow could outrun. His hands, twisted and strange, plunged into the swirling vapor, his fingers—elongated, jointed in ways that defied human anatomy—slithered through the Count's dissolving form. They found purchase, sinking deep into the impossible solidity of flesh and bone hidden within the spectral haze, as if Jack himself had become a vessel for something far more ancient and dangerous.

Old flesh split, filling the room with the sharp tang of blood and the stench of raw fear. Jack's grip tightened, his fingers sinking into the Count's skull and shoulder in a wet, unrelenting hold. Flesh tore with a sickening rip, the crackle of the fire punctuating the horror. The Count's scream died in his throat, drowned in blood, as Jack, cold and merciless, wrenched his head from his body.

Silence descended, broken only by the fire's roar and the drip of blood from Jack's hands onto the marble floor. Jack's howl, a sound bearing the weight of grief and fury, echoed into the night, momentarily overpowering the storm outside with a lone, terrifying note of madness in the night's symphony—a meaningless nightmare in the vast, unknowable, apathetic darkness.

LIBRO DOS

II

PARIS, FRANCE TO PAMPLONA, SPAIN
SUMMER, 1924

Nyarlathotep

By H. P. Lovecraft

Nyarlathotep . . . the crawling chaos . . . I am the last . . . . I will tell the audient void. . . .
I do not recall distinctly when it began, but it was months ago. The general tension was horrible. To a season of political and social upheaval was added a strange and brooding apprehension of hideous physical danger; a danger widespread and all-embracing, such a danger as may be imagined only in the most terrible phantasms of the night. I recall that the people went about with pale and worried faces, and whispered

warnings and prophecies which no one dared consciously repeat or acknowledge to himself that he had heard. A sense of monstrous guilt was upon the land, and out of the abysses between the stars swept chill currents that made men shiver in dark and lonely places. There was a daemoniac alteration in the sequence of the seasons— the autumn heat lingered fearsomely, and everyone felt that the world and perhaps the universe had passed from the control of known gods or forces to that of gods or forces which were unknown.

And it was then that Nyarlathotep came out of Egypt. Who he was, none could tell, but he was of the old native blood and looked like a Pharaoh. The fellahin knelt when they saw him, yet could not say why. He said he had risen up out of the blackness of twenty-seven centuries, and that he had heard messages from places not on this planet. Into the lands of civilisation came Nyarlathotep, swarthy, slender, and sinister, always buying strange instruments of glass and metal and combining them into instruments yet stranger. He spoke much of the sciences—of electricity and psychology— and gave exhibitions of power which sent his spectators away speechless, yet which swelled his fame to exceeding magnitude. Men advised one another to see Nyarlathotep, and shuddered. And where Nyarlathotep went, rest vanished; for the small hours were rent with the screams of nightmare. Never before had the screams of nightmare been such a public problem; now the wise men almost wished they could forbid sleep in the small hours, that the shrieks of cities might less horribly disturb the pale, pitying moon as it glimmered on green waters gliding under bridges, and old steeples crumbling against a sickly sky.

I remember when Nyarlathotep came to my city—the great, the old, the terrible city of unnumbered crimes. My friend had told me of him, and of the impelling fascination and allurement of his revelations, and I burned with eagerness to explore his uttermost mysteries. My friend said they were horrible and impressive beyond my most fevered imaginings; that what was thrown on a screen in the darkened room prophesied things none but Nyarlathotep dared prophesy, and that in the sputter of his sparks there was taken from men that which had never been taken before yet which shewed only in the eyes. And I heard it hinted abroad that those who knew Nyarlathotep looked on sights which others saw not.

It was in the hot autumn that I went through the night with the restless crowds to see Nyarlathotep; through the stifling night and up the endless stairs into the choking room. And shadowed on a screen, I saw hooded forms amidst ruins, and yellow evil faces peering from behind fallen monuments. And I saw the world battling against blackness; against the waves of destruction from ultimate space; whirling, churning; struggling around

*the dimming, cooling sun. Then the sparks played
amazingly around the heads of the spectators, and hair
stood up on end whilst shadows more grotesque than I
can tell came out and squatted on the heads. And when I,
who was colder and more scientific than the rest,
mumbled a trembling protest about "imposture" and
"static electricity", Nyarlathotep drave us all out, down
the dizzy stairs into the damp, hot, deserted midnight
streets. I screamed aloud that I was not afraid; that I
never could be afraid; and others screamed with me for
solace. We sware to one another that the city was exactly
the same, and still alive; and when the electric lights
began to fade we cursed the company over and over
again, and laughed at the queer faces we made.
I believe we felt something coming down from the
greenish moon, for when we began to depend on its light
we drifted into curious involuntary formations and
seemed to know our destinations though we dared not
think of them. Once we looked at the pavement and
found the blocks loose and displaced by grass, with scarce
a line of rusted metal to shew where the tramways had
run. And again we saw a tram-car, lone, windowless,
dilapidated, and almost on its side. When we gazed
around the horizon, we could not find the third tower by
the river, and noticed that the silhouette of the second
tower was ragged at the top. Then we split up into
narrow columns, each of which seemed drawn in a*

different direction. One disappeared in a narrow alley to
the left, leaving only the echo of a shocking moan.
Another filed down a weed-choked subway entrance,
howling with a laughter that was mad. My own column
was sucked toward the open country, and presently felt a
chill which was not of the hot autumn; for as we stalked
out on the dark moor, we beheld around us the hellish
moon-glitter of evil snows. Trackless, inexplicable snows,
swept asunder in one direction only, where lay a gulf all
the blacker for its glittering walls. The column seemed
very thin indeed as it plodded dreamily into the gulf. I
lingered behind, for the black rift in the green-litten
snow was frightful, and I thought I had heard the
reverberations of a disquieting wail as my companions
vanished; but my power to linger was slight. As if
beckoned by those who had gone before, I half floated
between the titanic snowdrifts, quivering and afraid,
into the sightless vortex of the unimaginable.
Screamingly sentient, dumbly delirious, only the gods
that were can tell. A sickened, sensitive shadow writhing
in hands that are not hands, and whirled blindly past
ghastly midnights of rotting creation, corpses of dead
worlds with sores that were cities, charnel winds that
brush the pallid stars and make them flicker low.
Beyond the worlds vague ghosts of monstrous things;
half-seen columns of unsanctified temples that rest on
nameless rocks beneath space and reach up to dizzy

vacua above the spheres of light and darkness. And through this revolting graveyard of the universe the muffled, maddening beating of drums, and thin, monotonous whine of blasphemous flutes from inconceivable, unlighted chambers beyond Time; the detestable pounding and piping whereunto dance slowly, awkwardly, and absurdly the gigantic, tenebrous ultimate gods—the blind, voiceless, mindless gargoyles whose soul is Nyarlathotep.

CHAPTER 8

DANUBE SHADOW PLAY

JACK SCHITT DID NOT SEE Brett again until she returned from San Sebastián. He received a single card bearing a picture of the Concha and the message:

"Darling. Very quiet and healthy.

Love to all the chaps. BRETT."

Nor did Jack see Ro'brt Ctholh'en again. He heard Frances had left for England and received a note from Ctholh'en stating he was going out in the country for a couple of weeks. Jack did not know where, but Ctholh'en insisted on a fishing trip in Spain they had discussed last winter. He wrote that Jack could always reach him through his bankers.

Brett was gone. Jack wasn't troubled by Ctholh'en's affairs, burdened as he was with his own. He somewhat enjoyed not playing tennis, despite waking up with a bizarre gash on his belly that healed swiftly without scarring. The town buzzed with scandalous rumors: a wild celebration at Count Mippipopolous's manor had erupted into a devastating blaze, claiming the lives of the Count and several others. Amidst this, Jack's routine was filled with work, social engagements, and horse racing. When bored, he dedicated extra hours at the office, getting things ahead to leave in charge of his secretary before his upcoming trip to Spain with Bill Gorton.

Bill Gorton arrived, visibly worn. His face was thinner, his steps faltering. "Publishing's a beast," he said with a tired grin. They slipped into their old rhythm of conversation. Bill's eyes lingered on Jack. "Aren't you the picture of Dorian Gray?" he teased. "While I look like his cursed canvas." Jack's laughter was too forced.

"I'd complain to the almighty, but he's too busy mixing our aging potions," Bill continued before falling silent. After Vienna, Bill returned looking defeated. Jack chose silence over questions.

Bill was happy to share that he'd made a lot of money on his last book and planned to make more. He was coming back in three weeks, and they would leave for Spain to fish and attend the fiesta at Pamplona. He wrote that Vienna was wonderful. Then a card from Budapest: "Jack, Budapest is wonderful." Followed by a wire: "Back on Monday."

On Monday evening, Bill's arrival, heralded by the soft purr of a taxi, broke the evening's silence. Jack called to him, his voice cutting through the chill air. Bill's response—a wave and a smile that didn't quite reach his eyes—struck Jack as offputting. The man ascending the stairs bore little resemblance to the friend Jack remembered. This Bill moved with vigor that belied his pallor, his eyes alight with an inner fire. It was as if Bill had returned from Budapest not just rejuvenated but reborn.

"Well," Jack began, "Budapest was quite the experience, I hear."

Bill's gaze was distant. "Budapest is a labyrinth, Jack. Not just of streets, but of... revelations." His voice trailed off, leaving the words hanging heavy between them.

"What happened there, Bill?"

A flicker of hesitation crossed Bill's features before he continued. "I met someone—a guide of sorts. Viktor... back from Cefalù in Sicily. He opened doors I never knew existed. Showed me paths... paths that lead to understanding."

Jack noted the peculiar emphasis on the name *Cefalù*.

"Cefalù... are you talking about Crowley?"

The corners of Bill's mouth twitched into a knowing smile. "Bingo, Jacky boy."

Jack chuckled, mentioning Yeats in an attempt to lighten the mood. "Just steer clear of magical duels, yeah? Wouldn't want you tumbling down stairs like some occult showdown."

But Bill's countenance remained earnest, devoid of amusement. "It's no time for jest, Jack," he asserted, a trace of warning in his tone. "Crowley's realm is darker and more potent than ever."

"You're alright, though?" Jack asked, his voice threading a needle in the heavy air. "Ro'brt told me his Thelma folk were poor dinner guests in the Hamptons. Thugs, he called them."

"Thelema," Bill corrected. "Well, he's your friend, not mine. Budapest was... enlightening. Let's just leave it at that."

Jack nodded, unsatisfied. "And Vienna?" he pressed, unwilling to let the thread drop just yet.

"Vienna..." Bill's voice trailed off, lost. "Got a bit lost there, too. I can resist everything except temptation."

Jack grinned, "Ok, Lady Windermere."

"Let's eat," Bill suggested, a shade of his old self returning.

They descended into Boulevard St. Michel, enveloped by the warmth of a June evening.

"Where shall we head?" Jack inquired.

"How about the island?"

"Sounds good."

Strolling down the Boulevard towards Rue Denfert-Rochereau, Bill's gaze landed on a statue adorned in flowing robes. "Pharmacists," he quipped.

Jack's eyes flickered to the statue, catching an unsettling shift in the shadows, reminiscent of tentacles weaving through darkness. A second glance dispelled the illusion, leaving only the play of light and shadow.

They moved on.

"Here's a taxidermist's," Bill said. "Want to buy anything? Nice stuffed dog?"

"Come on," Jack said. "You're pie-eyed."

"Pretty nice stuffed dogs," Bill replied. "Certainly brighten up your flat."

"Come on."

"Just one stuffed dog. I can take 'em or leave 'em alone. But listen, Jack. Just one stuffed dog."

"Kind of morbid."

Bill's smile widened, his gaze drifting to a point beyond Jack. "In Budapest, they'll stuff anything. And I mean anything. It becomes a part of you, that simple exchange. You give them money, they give one silent companion."

"We'll get one on the way back."

"All right. Have it your own way. Road to hell paved with unbought stuffed dogs. Not my fault."

They continued walking.

"How'd you feel that way about dogs so suddenly?"

"Always felt that way about dogs. Always been a great lover of stuffed animals."

They stopped and had a drink.

"Certainly like to drink," Bill said. "You ought to try it sometimes, Jack."

"You're about a hundred and forty-four ahead of me."

"Ought not to daunt you. Never be daunted. Secret of my success. Never been daunted. Never been daunted in public."

"You'll be daunted after about three more pernods."

"Not in public. If I begin to feel daunted, I'll go off by myself. I'm like a cat that way."

"When did you see Harvey Stone?"

"At the Crillon. Harvey was just a little daunted. Hadn't eaten for three days. Doesn't eat anymore. Haunted eyes. Just goes off like a cat. Pretty sad."

"He's all right."

"Splendid. Wish he wouldn't keep going off like a cat, though. Makes me nervous."

"Would you prefer he stuff himself like a dog?" Jack laughed, but Bill didn't find him funny.

"What'll we do tonight?"

"Doesn't make any difference. Only let's not get daunted. Suppose they got any hard-boiled eggs here? If they had hard-boiled eggs here, we wouldn't have to go all the way down to the island to eat."

"Nix," Jack said. "We're going to have a regular meal."

"Just a suggestion," said Bill. "Want to start now?"

"Come on."

They started down the Boulevard again. A horse-cab passed by them. Bill looked at it.

"See that horse-cab? Going to have that horse-cab stuffed for you for Christmas. Going to give all my friends stuffed animals. I'm a gen-u-ine nature writer."

A taxi passed; someone in it waved, then banged for the driver to stop. The taxi backed up to the curb. In it was Brett.

"Beautiful lady," said Bill, staring intently. "Going to kidnap us."

"Hullo!" Brett said. "Hullo!"

"This is Bill Gorton. Lady Ashley."

Brett smiled at Bill. "I say I'm just back. Haven't bathed even. Michael comes in tonight."

"I've heard so much about you, Lady Ashley," Bill said.

"Good," Jack said. "Come on and eat with us, and we'll all go to meet him."

"Must clean myself."

"Oh, rot! Come on."

"Must bathe. He doesn't get in till nine."

"Come and have a drink, then, before you bathe."

"Might do that. Now you're not talking rot."

They got in the taxi. The driver looked around.

"Stop at the nearest bistro," Jack said.

"We might as well go to the Closerie," Brett said. "I can't drink these rotten brandies."

"Closerie des Lilas."

Brett turned to Bill.

"Have you been in this pestilential city long?"

"Just got in today from Budapest."

"How was Budapest?"

"Wonderful. Budapest was wonderful."

"It did something wonderful to him. Ask him about Vienna."

"Vienna," said Bill, "is a strange city."

"Very much like Paris," Brett smiled at him, wrinkling the corners of her eyes.

"Exactly," Bill said, his attention on Brett sharpening. "In places like Budapest, you discover desires you didn't know you had. The city promises encounters that could change everything."

Brett laughed, a spark of challenge in her eyes. "Is that so? Paris has its own depths, I assure you. One just needs to know where to look."

Sitting out on the terraces of the Lilas, Brett ordered a whiskey and soda, Jack took one too, and Bill took another pernod.

"How are you, Jack?"

"Great," Jack said. "I've had a good time."

Brett looked at him. "I was a fool to go away," she said. "One's an ass to leave Paris."

"Did you have a good time?"

"Oh, all right. Interesting. Not frightfully amusing."

"See anybody?"

"No, hardly anybody. I never went out."

"Didn't you swim?"

"No. Didn't do a thing."

"Sounds like Vienna," Bill said.

Brett wrinkled the corners of her eyes at him.

"So that's the way it was in Vienna."

"It was like everything in Vienna."

Brett smiled at him again.

"You've a nice friend, Jack."

"He's all right," Jack said. "He's a taxidermist."

"That was in another country," Bill said. "And besides, all the animals were dead."

"One more," Brett said, "and I must run. Do send the waiter for a taxi."

"There's a line of them. Right out in front."

"Good."

They had the drink and put Brett into her taxi. "Mind you're at the Select around ten. Make him come. Michael will be there."

"We'll be there," Bill said. The taxi started, and Brett waved.

"Quite a girl," Bill said. "She's damned nice. Who's Michael?"

"The man she's going to marry."

"Well, well," Bill said. "That's always just the stage I meet anybody. What'll I send them? Think they'd like a couple of stuffed racehorses?"

"We'd better eat."

"Is she really Lady something or other?" Bill asked in the taxi on their way down to the Île Saint-Louis.

"She is. You said that you'd heard all about her," Jack furrowed his brow.

"I'm sure it was from you."

"I'm certain it was not."

They ate dinner at Madame Lecomte's restaurant on the far side of the island. It was crowded with Americans, and they had to stand and wait forty-five minutes for a table. Bill had eaten there in 1918, right after the armistice, and Madame Lecomte made a great fuss over seeing him.

"Doesn't get us a table, though," Bill said. "Grand woman, though."

The meal was satisfactory: roast chicken, fresh beans, mashed potatoes, a simple salad, and apple pie with cheese to follow. Jack tore at the meat, the chicken crossing his mind—a kinship with this bird, once caged and ignorant of its end. Its life, a span of dull routine cut by fleeting unease, culminating in final terror. Not unlike our own lives, Jack reflected, marked by the long drag of days and sporadic discomforts, all marching us toward an end shrouded more in dread than in peace.

His mind wandered to life's smaller denizens—mosquitos, ants—free until they inadvertently stir human annoyance and are crushed or swatted out of existence—insignificant ends for insignificant beings. A parallel struck him then; perhaps to the eldritch deities he'd glimpsed, humans were but specks, their notice a thing to be eluded, for attention from such beings spelled inexplicable furies, with lives no more significant than insects are to us.

This contemplation stayed with Jack, a thread weaving together the destinies of all creatures beneath the indifferent gaze of mightier forces. With the final bite of pie, the sweetness on his palate did nothing to thaw the cold creeping through him—a cold from the awareness of a cosmos vast, indifferent, and unfathomably random.

"You've got the world here all right," Bill said to Madame Lecomte.

She raised her hand. "Oh, my God!"

"You'll be rich."

"I hope so."

After the coffee and a clope, they got the bill, chalked it up the same as ever on a slate—one of the "quaint" features—paid it, shook hands, and left.

"You never come here anymore, Monsieur Schitt," Madame Lecomte said.

"Too many compatriots."

"Come at lunchtime. It's not crowded then."

"Good. I'll be down soon."

They walked along under the trees that grew out over the river on the Quai d'Orléans side of the island. Across the river were the broken walls of old houses being torn down.

"They're going to cut a street through."

"They would," Bill said.

They walked on and circled the island. The river was dark, and a bateau-mouche passed by, bright with lights, moving fast and quiet out of sight under the bridge. Down the river, Notre Dame stood against the night sky. They crossed to the left bank of the Seine via the wooden footbridge from Quai de Bethune, stopped on the bridge, and looked down the river at Notre Dame. Some lights flashed on the bank, a bustle of nocturnal activity that made Jack shudder. He breathed slowly, steadily.

Standing on the bridge, the island looked dark; the houses were high against the sky, and the trees were shadows.

"It's pretty grand," Bill said. "God, I love to get back."

They leaned on the wooden rail of the bridge and looked up the river to the lights of the big bridges. Below, the water was smooth and black. It made no sound against the piles of the bridge. A man and a girl passed them, walking with their arms around each other.

They crossed the bridge and walked up Rue du Cardinal Lemoine. It was steep walking, and they went all the way up to Place Contrescarpe. The arc light shone through the leaves of the trees in the square, and underneath the trees was an S bus ready to start. Music poured from the door of Nègre Joyeux. Through the window of Café Aux Amateurs, Jack saw the long zinc bar. Outside on the terrace, working people were drinking. In the open kitchen of the Amateurs, a girl cooked potato chips in oil. An iron pot of stew simmered. The girl ladled some onto a plate for an old man who stood holding a bottle of red wine in one hand.

"Want to have a drink?"

"No," said Bill. "I don't need it."

They turned right off Place Contrescarpe, walking along smooth, narrow streets lined with high old houses on both sides. Some of the houses jutted out toward the street, while others were set further in. They continued onto Rue du Pot de Fer and followed it to the straight, rigid lines of Rue Saint-Jacques. From there, they walked south, past Val de Grâce, tucked behind the courtyard and the iron fence, to Boulevard du Port Royal.

"What do you want to do?" Jack asked. "Go up to the café and see Brett and Mike?"

"Why not?"

They walked along Port Royal until it became Montparnasse, and then past the Lilas, Lavigne's, and all the little cafés—Damoy's—crossed the street to Rotonde, past its lights and tables to the Select.

Michael Hawk approached them from the tables, looking tanned and healthy.

"Hello, Jack," he said. "Hello! Hello! Jack Schitt! How are you, old lad?"

"Mike Hawk," Jack crowed. "You look fit. Positively glowing."

"Oh, I am. I'm incredibly fit. I've done nothing but walk. Walk all day long. One drink a day with mother at tea."

Bill had gone into the bar. He was standing, talking with Brett, who was sitting on a high stool, her legs crossed. She wore no stockings.

"It's good to see you, Jack," Michael said. "I'm a little tipsy, you know. Amazing, isn't it? Did you see my nose?"

There was a patch of dried blood on the bridge of his nose.

"An old lady's bags did that," Mike said. "I reached up to help her with them, and they fell on me."

Brett gestured at him from the bar with her cigarette holder and wrinkled the corners of her eyes.

"An old lady," said Mike. "Her bags fell on me. Let's go in and see Brett. I say she's something. You are a lovely lady, Brett. Where did you get that hat?"

"A guy bought it for me. Don't you like it?"

"It's a dreadful hat. Do get a good hat."

"Oh, we have so much money now," Brett said. "I say, haven't you met Bill yet? You're a lovely host, Jack."

She turned to Mike. "This is Bill Gorton. This tipsy fellow is Mike Hawk. Mr. Hawk is an undischarged bankrupt."

"Am I not, though? You know I met my ex-partner yesterday in London. The guy who did me in."

"What did he say?"

"Bought me a drink. I thought I might as well take it. I say, Brett, you're a lovely sight. Don't you think she's beautiful?"

"Beautiful. With this nose?"

"It's a lovely nose. Go on, point it at me. Isn't she a lovely sight?"

"Couldn't they have kept the man in Scotland?"

"I say, Brett, let's turn in early."

"Don't be indecent, Michael. Remember, there are ladies at this bar."

"Isn't she a lovely sight? Don't you think so, Jack?"

"There's a fight tonight," Bill said. "Want to go?"

"Fight," said Mike. "Who's fighting?"

"Ledoux and somebody."

"He's very good, Ledoux," Mike said. "I'd like to see it, rather"—he was making an effort to pull himself together. "But

I can't go. I have a date with this lovely lady here. I say, Brett, do get a new hat."

Brett pulled the felt hat down far over one eye and smiled out from under it. "You two go on to the fight. I'll have to take Mike Hawk home shortly."

"I'm not tipsy," Mike said. "Perhaps just a little. I say, Brett, you're a lovely sight."

"Go on to the fight," Brett said. "Mr. Hawk's getting difficult. What are these outbursts of affection, Michael?"

"I say, you're a lovely sight."

They said good night. "I'm sorry I can't go," Mike said. Brett laughed. Jack looked back from the door. Mike had one hand on the bar coolly, but the corners of her eyes were smiling.

Outside on the pavement, Jack said, "Do you want to go to the fight?"

"Sure," said Bill. "If we don't have to walk."

In the back of the taxi, the lights of Paris danced across their faces, casting fleeting shadows. "Mike's got it bad for her," Jack mused, a casual observer to the unfolding drama.

Bill's laughter was nonchalant. "Ensnared, you could say," he replied, "ensorcelled. Positively enchanted." His tone was laced with an untraceable depth. "Fate has a peculiar way of weaving its threads, doesn't it?"

Jack blushed in silence. In the mercurial glow of Paris, their faces caught in a dance of light and shadow. Jack, entangled in Bill's veiled words, drifted through the shadows of regret and the silent echoes of the past, a ghost among lost chances, worlds apart.

CHAPTER 9

CRYPTIC CROSSROADS

THE LEDOUX-KID FRANCIS FIGHT was a tightrope of tension and technique, each boxer's style starkly contrasting the other. In a surprising twist, the underdog Eugene Ledoux claimed victory, despite being lighter and less aggressive. His strategic prowess outmaneuvered the favored Francis. The match's aftermath buzzed through Paris—a blend of shock and admiration that clung to the city like sweat on a boxer's brow.

The morning after the fight, Jack received a letter from Ro'brt Ctholh'en, written from Hendaye. He was having a quiet time—bathing, playing golf, and bridge. Hendaye had a splendid beach, but he was restless to start the fishing trip. When would Jack arrive? If Jack could buy him a double-tapered line, he'd repay him upon arrival.

Later that morning, Jack wrote to Ctholh'en from the office that he and Bill would leave Paris on the 25th unless Jack wired otherwise, and they'd meet him at Bayonne. From there, they could take a bus over the mountains to Pamplona. That same evening, around seven o'clock, Jack stopped in at the Select to see Michael and Brett. They weren't there, so Jack went over to the Dingo and found them sitting at the bar.

"Hello, darling," Brett said, extending her hand.

"Hello, Jack," Mike said. "I understand I was tight last night."

"Weren't you, though," Brett replied. "Disgraceful business."

"Look," Mike said, "when do you go down to Spain? Would you mind if we came with you?"

"It would be grand."

"You wouldn't mind, really? I've been to Pamplona, you know. Brett's mad to go. You're sure we wouldn't just be a bloody nuisance?"

"Don't be a fool."

"I'm a little tight, you know. I wouldn't ask you like this if I weren't. You're sure you don't mind?"

"Oh, shut up, Michael," Brett said. "How can the man say he'd mind now? I'll ask him later."

"But you don't mind, do you?"

"Don't ask that again unless you want to make me sore. Bill and I go down on the morning of the 25th."

Brett leaned forward, her eyes sparkling like twin galaxies. "By the way, where is Bill?"

"He's out at Chantilly dining with some people."

"He's a good chap. Intense."

"He's a bit...," Mike muttered, a hint of wariness in his voice. "Not quite right," he added.

"You don't remember him," Brett said.

"I do. Remember him perfectly. He was just a bit... creepy."

Jack smiled.

"Look, Jack, we'll come down the night of the 25th. Brett can't get up in the morning. Can't stand the sun in her eyes."

"Indeed not!"

"If our money comes and you're sure you don't mind."

"It will come, all right. I'll see to that."

"Tell Jack what tackle to send for."

"Get two or three rods with reels and lines, and some flies."

"I won't fish," Brett added.

"Get two rods, then, and Bill won't have to buy one."

"Right," said Mike. "I'll send a wire to the keeper."

"Won't it be splendid," Brett said. "Spain! We will have fun."

"The 25th. When is that?"

"Saturday."

"We will have to get ready."

"I say," said Mike, "I'm going to the barber's."

"I must bathe," said Brett. "Walk up to the hotel with me, Jack. Be a good chap."

"We've got the loveliest hotel," Mike said. "I think it's a brothel!"

"We left our bags here at the Dingo when we got in, and they asked us at this hotel if we wanted a room for the afternoon only. They seemed frightfully pleased we were going to stay all night."

"I believe it's a brothel," Mike said with certainty. "And I should know."

"Oh, shut it and go get your hair cut."

Mike went out. Brett and Jack remained at the bar, the tension between them palpable. Jack enjoyed the pressure playfully until it soured.

"Have another?" Brett finally asked.

"Might."

"I needed that," Brett admitted, her husky voice a mix of relief and vulnerability.

They walked up Rue Delambre, the heavy silence between them finally breaking.

"I haven't seen you since I've been back," Brett said.

"No."

"How are you, Jack?"

"Fine."

Brett looked at Jack, her eyes searching his face. "I say, is Ro'brt Ctholh'en going on this trip?"

"Yes. Why?"

"Don't you think it will be a bit rough on him?"

"Why should it?"

"Who did you think I went down to San Sebastián with?"

"Congratulations," Jack said bitterly.

They walked along, the tension building with each step.

"What did you say that for?"

"I don't know. What would you like me to say?"

They turned a corner, the weight of their conversation growing heavier.

"He behaved rather well, too. He gets a little dull."

"Does he?"

"I rather thought it would be good for him."

"You might take up social service."

"Don't be nasty."

"I won't."

"Didn't you really know?"

"No," Jack said, his voice strained. "I guess I didn't think about it."

"Do you think it will be too rough on him?"

"That's up to him," Jack said. "Tell him you're coming. He can always not come."

"I'll write him and give him a chance to pull out of it."

Jack didn't see Brett again until the night of June 24th, the tension between them still lingering.

"Did you hear from Ctholh'en?"

"Rather. He's keen about it."

"My God!"

"I thought it was rather odd myself."

"Says he can't wait to see me."

"Does he think you're coming alone?"

"No. I told him we were all coming down together. Michael and all."

"He's wonderful."

"Isn't he?"

They expected their money the next day and arranged to meet at Pamplona. They would go directly to San Sebastián and take the train from there. They would all meet at the Montoya in Pamplona. If they didn't turn up on Monday at the latest, they would go on ahead up to Burguete in the mountains to start fishing. There was a bus to Burguete. Jack wrote out an itinerary so they could follow.

Bill and Jack took the morning train from the Gare d'Orsay. It was a lovely day, not too hot, and the countryside was beautiful from the start. They went back into the diner and had breakfast. Jack left the dining car and asked the conductor for tickets for the first service.

"Nothing until the fifth."

"What's this?"

There were never more than two servings of lunch on that train, and always plenty of places for both of them.

"They're all reserved," the dining-car conductor said. "There will be a fifth service at three-thirty."

"This is serious," Jack said to Bill.

"Give him ten francs."

"Here," Jack said. "We want to eat in the first service."

The conductor pocketed the ten francs.

"Thank you," he said. "I would advise you gentlemen to get some sandwiches. All the places for the first four services were reserved at the office of the company."

"You'll go a long way, brother," Bill said to him in English. "I suppose if I'd given you five francs, you would have advised us to jump off the train."

"Comment?"

"Go to hell!" said Bill. "Get the sandwiches made and a bottle of wine. You tell him, Jack."

"And send it up to the next car," Jack added, describing their location.

In their compartment were a man, his wife, and their young son.

"I suppose you're Americans, aren't you?" the man asked. "Having a good trip?"

"Wonderful," said Bill.

"That's what you want to do. Travel while you're young. Mother and I always wanted to get over, but we had to wait a while."

"You could have come over ten years ago if you'd wanted to," the wife said. "What you always said was: 'See America first!' I will say we've seen a good deal, take it one way and another."

"Say, there's plenty of Americans on this train," the husband said. "They've got seven cars of them from Dayton, Ohio. They've been on a pilgrimage to Rome, and now they're going down to Biarritz and Lourdes."

154

"So that's what they are. Pilgrims. Goddamn Puritans," Bill said.

"What part of the States you boys from?"

"Kansas City," Jack said. "He's from Chicago."

"You both going to Biarritz?"

"No. We're going fishing in Spain."

"Well, I never cared for it myself. There's plenty that do out where I come from, though. We've got some of the best fishing in the state of Montana. I've been out with the boys, but I never cared for it any."

"Mighty little fishing you did on those trips," his wife said.

He winked at us.

"You know how the ladies are. If there's a jug that goes along, or a case of beer, they think it's hell and damnation."

"That's the way men are," his wife said. She smoothed her comfortable lap. "I voted against Prohibition to please him and because I like a little beer in the house, and then he talks that way. It's a wonder they ever find anyone to marry them."

"Say," said Bill, "do you know that gang of Pilgrim Fathers has cornered the dining car until half past three this afternoon?"

"How do you mean? They can't do a thing like that."

"You try and get seats."

"Well, Mother, it looks as though we'd better go back and get another breakfast."

She stood up and straightened her dress.

"Will you boys keep an eye on our things? Come on, Hubert."

155

All three went up to the wagon-restaurant. A little while after they were gone, a steward announced the first service, and pilgrims with their priests began filing down the corridor. Our friend and his family did not return. A waiter passed in the corridor with our sandwiches and the bottle of Chablis, and they called him in.

They ate the sandwiches and drank the Chablis, gazing at the countryside through the window. The grain was ripening, and the fields were awash with poppies. The pastureland was verdant, and majestic trees dotted the landscape, occasionally accompanied by grand rivers and hidden châteaux.

At Tours, they disembarked to buy another bottle of wine. When they returned to their compartment, the gentleman from Montana, his wife, and his son Hubert were seated comfortably.

"Is the swimming good in Biarritz?" Hubert inquired.

"That boy's just itching to get in the water," his mother said.

"Traveling can be tough on kids," Jack remarked. "The swimming's good, but it can be dangerous when the water's rough."

"Did you manage to eat?" Bill asked.

The man from Montana recounted how they had joined the pilgrims' dining party, which ultimately led to them being served.

"It really shows the influence of the Catholic Church," the man said. "Too bad you boys aren't Catholics. You could have gotten a meal, too."

"I am," Jack retorted. "That's why I'm so irritated."

Finally seated for lunch at a quarter past four, a noticeable tension emanated from Bill. His usual frustration had deepened into something more complex. Inside the dining car, they were served the fifth consecutive table d'hôte meal. The exhausted waiter's white jacket was stained purple under his arms.

"He must drink a lot of wine."

"Or wear purple undershirts."

"Let's ask him."

"No. He's too tired."

After their meal, they stumbled into a priest. Bill's response was startling—a low, guttural sound, the words foreign and archaic. Jack couldn't place the language, yet it stirred uneasy memories of war and his sickness. Jack hastily excused himself. He sought refuge in the passing scenery outside the train window. The fleeting landscapes offered a momentary escape, a brief respite from the shadows that hung over them.

The train paused for half an hour at Bordeaux, allowing them to take a brief walk through the station. They didn't have time to venture into the town. Afterward, they journeyed through the Landes, watching the sunset. Wide fire gaps cut through the pines, revealing avenues with wooded hills in the distance. Around seven-thirty, they had dinner, observing the countryside through the open window in the dining car. The landscape was sandy and filled with pine trees and heather. Occasionally, they passed little clearings with houses or a sawmill. As darkness fell, they sensed the heat and shadows of the country outside the window.

At around nine o'clock, they arrived in Bayonne. The man, his wife, and Hubert bid them farewell, continuing to La Negresse to transfer to Biarritz.

"Take care at those bullfights," the man advised Jack.

Exiting the dark station, they saw Ro'brt Ctholh'en among the hotel runners. After exchanging greetings, Ro'brt led them to his hotel in a cab he had arranged. The cabman loaded their bags onto the seat beside him, and they drove into the town.

Ro'brt eagerly anticipated meeting Bill, intrigued by his writings. Upon reaching the hotel, they were greeted by a warm ambiance and amiable staff, with snug rooms awaiting them.

Jack spotted Bill in the common room, about to greet him, but stopped. Bill was engaged in something unusual, intently marking an old parchment with precise details before discreetly sliding it into the sofa. His actions were quiet but intentional.

This secret act left Jack uneasy, torn between inquiry and restraint. He chose to withdraw, retreating to his room as the mystery of Bill's actions lingered silently into the quiet hours of the night.

CHAPTER 10

MONTOYA'S MIASMAL MYSTERIES

IN THE BRIGHT MORNING, THEY strolled through the town streets and had breakfast at a café. Bayonne was a pleasant town, mirroring its pristine Spanish counterpart by a vast river. The morning heat pressed against them as they crossed the river bridge and wandered through the languid town.

Uncertain about Mike's rods arriving from Scotland, they found a tackle store. While waiting for the seller, Bill's mood darkened, but Jack pretended not to notice. When the seller arrived, they bought a decent rod at a low price and two landing nets.

They emerged into the street, the cathedral casting a long, oppressive shadow. Jack pointed it out, but Bill lingered at the threshold, his red, swollen eyes fixed on the shadows clinging to the ancient stones.

"It's oppressive... stuffy air," Bill murmured, his voice tight.

"Did you get any sleep last night? Maybe we can stop for a bite to eat," Jack asked.

Bill's response was low, barely audible. "These stones, Jack... do you hear them? Echoing secrets... unsettling whispers. Time, sanity—it's all different here." Then, without another word, Bill drifted away, his mutterings lost as he disappeared from sight.

Jack noticed Ctholh'en eyeing Bill with an odd, inexplicable gaze before the two exchanged a look. "Perhaps genius takes a toll," Ro'brt commented with a tight smile, their laughter ringing hollow as they stepped into the cathedral's somber sanctuary.

Under the cathedral's towering arches, Jack's thoughts began to unravel. As he bowed his head in prayer, candlelight twisted into ghostly forms, casting shadows that stretched into grasping hands. An eerie vision unfolded—a village in eternal dusk, where human cries merged into despair. Bill, shrouded like the Grim Reaper, gestured toward the dark heart of the sea, summoning a leviathan so immense its emergence threatened to capsize Jack's sanity.

The vision intensified—shards, bloodstains, and flames. Amid this terror, Jack's plea for guidance through shadowed streets drew him closer to doom. As an ancient deity rose, a symbol of primal fear, Jack's resolve faced its ultimate test. The upcoming bullfights morphed from mere contests into a crucible for his soul.

Startled awake, Jack blinked quickly, disoriented as candles flickered, casting ominous shapes around the sigil. The eye and spirals etched a tale of dread onto the ancient walls. Ro'brt's hand on his shoulder grounded him, pulling him back to reality as the symbols vanished as quickly as they had appeared.

Afterward, they proceeded past the old fort to the local *Syndicat d'Initiative* office, where the bus was supposed to depart. Jack learned that the bus service wouldn't begin until July 1st. At the tourist office, he discovered the fee for a motor car to Pamplona and rented one from a large garage near the Municipal Theatre for four hundred francs. The car would pick them up at the hotel in forty minutes.

In the café, Bill sat, his hypnotic words weaving an erratic tapestry. One moment, his laughter bubbled over a trivial joke; the next, his eyes clouded, his voice dipping into solemn. Jack, nursing his drink, watched Bill's mood swings with concern, wondering what deeper currents stirred beneath his surface. The heat persisted, but a cool, fresh morning scent permeated the town, making the café a comfortable spot. A sea breeze blew, pigeons gathered in the square, and the sunbaked houses glowed with a warm, yellow hue. Reluctantly, they left the café to pack their bags and settle the hotel bill.

Ro'brt trailed behind as they left the café, sharing a look with Bill. There was something unspoken between them. He looked toward Jack and then quickly away.

They returned to the hotel, the heavy door closing behind them with a resonant thud. The innkeeper approached, her steps uneven, a slight limp betraying her youthful vigor. Bill couldn't resist. "Madame Foothurtz, huh? How did you earn that?" he teased, a playful smirk curling his lips.

She delivered the bill with a weary roll of her eyes. Sixteen francs each, plus a ten percent service fee. Jack waited, the air thick with unspoken tension, and after a tense moment, the innkeeper chuckled lightly—a sound that seemed to momentarily ease the evening's unease.

Jack watched as Bill's smile remained steady, but a shadow flickered across his features. "Well, it suits you. You run this place with such flair."

She blushed, adjusting her apron. "Thank you, gentlemen. If you need anything for your fishing trip, don't hesitate to ask."

As she limped away, Bill leaned back, his eyes slightly glassy, a hint of darkness lurking beneath his mirth.

"That was mean of you," Jack remarked.

Bill only shrugged.

A paranoid chill crept up Jack's spine. He wondered if Bill's teasing banter was just a little too-Bill-like, as he'd been acting so bizarre since his return to Paris. Perhaps Jack was just drunk, haunted by ghosts.

They sent their bags down and waited for Ro'brt Ctholh'en. Jack shivered as the hotel's atmosphere grew tense, a subtle undercurrent of unease prickling his skin. A large cockroach scuttled across the floor, driven by unseen fear. Jack's reaction was swift, decisive: he stomped it with a heavy bootheel.

Bill's laughter, tinged with a chilling edge, echoed hollowly. "Cold-blooded killer," he whispered icily.

"Why don't you stuff it like one of your dogs?" Jack shot back flippantly, but Bill just shrugged and pointed to the tiny pool of goo. There was nothing left to stuff. They speculated that it came from the garden. Despite this, the hotel remained immaculate.

Ctholh'en finally arrived, and they all headed to the car. It was a large, closed vehicle with a driver in a white duster, blue collar, and cuffs. They had him lower the back of the car before piling in the bags and setting off. They drove past beautiful gardens and enjoyed a final glimpse of the town before venturing into the verdant, rolling countryside. Along the way, they encountered many Basques with oxen or cattle hauling carts along the road and admired the low-roofed, white-plastered farmhouses. The Basque country's land appeared fertile and green, with prosperous, tidy houses and villages. Every village had a *pelota* court where children played under the scorching sun. Church walls displayed signs prohibiting *pelota*, and village houses boasted red-tiled roofs. The road veered off, ascending along a hillside with a valley below and hills stretching back toward the sea. The sea was invisible, too distant to see. Only hills upon hills were visible, indicating the sea's location.

Approaching the Spanish frontier's bridge, Bill murmured, his voice blending with a whisper from the stream. The carabineers eyed Bill uneasily, their glances tinged with wary anticipation of some unspoken threat. Bill's voice faded, and the whisper with it, as if quelled by an unseen force. The frontier, a silent witness to this fleeting moment, returned to its mundane vigil, watched over by Spanish carabineers and French guards, each immersed in their duties, oblivious to the subtle undercurrents at play.

An old man with long, sunburned hair and beard approached the bridge, his clothing like rough, weathered sackcloth. He carried a long staff, and something limp was slung across his back. A howl tore through the air—sharp, desperate, almost human. Jack felt a cold unease rise in him. The creature's head lolled, eyes vacant. Its legs were bound tight—it was a kid, a goat. The carabineer raised his sword, motioning the man away. Without a word, the old man turned and vanished back up the white road into Spain.

"What's the matter with the old one?" Jack asked.

"He hasn't got any passport," the carabineer replied.

Jack offered him a cigarette, which he accepted with gratitude. Jack continued, "What will he do?"

The guard spat in the dust. "Oh, he'll just wade across the stream."

"Do you have much smuggling?" Jack inquired.

"Oh," the carabineer said, "they go through."

The chauffeur emerged with the paperwork, folding it and storing it in his coat pocket. They all reentered the car and continued up the white, dusty road into Spain. The landscape remained familiar for a while before they climbed to the top of a *col*, the road winding back and forth. Then, they truly entered Spain—long brown mountains, scattered pines, and distant beech-tree forests graced the mountainsides. The road followed the summit of the *col*, then descended, requiring the driver to honk and slow down to avoid hitting two sleeping donkeys in the road. They left the mountains behind, passing through an oak forest where white cattle grazed. Below, grassy plains and clear streams beckoned, and they crossed a stream and drove through a gloomy village before climbing once more.

Jack caught Ro'brt casting sidelong glances at Bill, his face conflicted. The countryside rolled past in shades of green and brown, the train rocking them gently. Bill's light banter seemed to cover something deeper, something Ro'brt sensed but didn't name. Jack could feel it too—the unspoken tension, hovering between knowledge and loyalty.

As they crawled through the Basque heartland, Ro'brt wiped his spectacles and spoke with sudden intensity. "These woods," he said, "harbor more than beasts. They hold legends. The Basajaun, they call them. Lords of the forest. Protectors and enigmas, bridging the known with the unfathomable wild." His gaze, wide and searching, seemed to pierce the dense wall of pine outside the window.

Jack leaned forward, curious. "Still the Princeton boy, eh? Do tell. Like shepherds of the wild?"

"Far more," Ro'brt said, his voice low and steady, almost a chant. It carried an echo, like the forest itself had spoken through him. "Guardians of a primordial order, revered and dreaded. They live in the dark spaces, where the known world frays. Much like the Carlist Wars. Beliefs clashing, weaving a tapestry of fear and reverence."

Jack frowned, thinking of the war. Across from him, Bill, usually dismissive, was silent. His sneer was gone, replaced by something darker, his mouth set in a line of thought.

Ro'brt's words lingered, winding through the small car like smoke, a reminder of the ancient powers that outlast men and their wars. The forest seemed to press against the windows, heavy and watchful.

Bill leaned forward, breaking the silence. His voice was low, gravelly, laced with something unspoken. "You like ghost stories?" he asked. "I've got one." He didn't wait for an answer. "In the heart of Sardinia," he began, "they speak of the *Accabadòra*. The last visitor to the dying. A figure cloaked in shadow. She's no ghost, though. She's the final mother, the one who comes to end it."

His eyes flickered, catching the dim light, his words wrapping around them like a fog. The rest he left unsaid, but the car felt smaller, colder. The car seemed to tighten around them, the weight of the tale pressing in, cold and inescapable.

"She comes in silence, clad in black, wielding a hammer of olive wood, shrouded in wool. A gentle caress, a whispered prayer, then a swift, merciful blow to the suffering soul," Bill continued, his words painting a macabre picture.

Jack shuddered.

"She's a murderer," Bill said, his gaze briefly catching Ro'brt's, "but to others, she's an angel of mercy, liberating souls from their mortal coil."

The air in the car grew colder, the story's gravity settling like a shroud. Bill's voice, now a whisper, resonated with the grim acceptance of life's finality. "In our journey, might we not be like her? Choosing when to end the suffering, when the weight of living becomes too heavy to bear."

Ro'brt shifted uncomfortably, his feigned sleep faltering under the weight of Bill's words. Bill's story, cloaked in the guise of folklore, carried an ominous undercurrent, a veiled warning or perhaps a promise.

After a while, they came out of the mountains, and the road was lined with trees on both sides, with a stream and ripe fields of grain nearby. The road went straight ahead, then lifted to a slight rise, and to the left was a hill with an ancient castle surrounded by buildings. The grain field reached right up to the walls, undulating in the wind. Jack was in the front with the driver and turned around. Ro'brt Ctholh'en was asleep, but Bill looked and nodded his head, seeming a shade of his old self.

They crossed a vast plain and saw a big river to the right, shimmering in the sun between the lines of trees. In the distance, they could see the plateau of Pamplona rising out of the plain, the city walls, the great brown cathedral, and the broken skyline of other churches. Behind the plateau were mountains, and everywhere they looked, there were more mountains. The white road stretched out across the plain, leading toward Pamplona.

They entered the town on the other side of the plateau, the road sloping up steeply, shaded by trees on both sides, before leveling out through the new part of town built outside the old walls. They passed the bull-ring, a high, white, concrete structure in the sun, and arrived at the big square by a side street, stopping in front of the Hotel Montoya.

The driver helped them unload their bags. A crowd of children watched the car, the square hot and the trees green. Escaping the sun and finding shade under the arcade that ran around the square was a relief. Montoya greeted them warmly, shaking hands and providing them with nice rooms overlooking the square. They washed up and went downstairs to the dining room for lunch. The driver also stayed for lunch, and they paid him afterward before he left for Bayonne.

The Hotel Montoya had two dining rooms. One was upstairs on the second floor, overlooking the square. The other was one floor below the square's level, with a door that opened onto the back street where the bulls would pass during their early morning run to the ring. The downstairs dining room was always cool, and they enjoyed a delicious lunch. The first meal in Spain was always a shock with its multiple courses, requiring copious amounts of wine to wash it all down. Ro'brt Ctholh'en tried to refuse the second meat course, but they wouldn't interpret for him, and he ended up with a plate of cold meats instead. Ctholh'en had been nervous since they met at Bayonne, uncertain whether they knew Brett had been with him at San Sebastián, which made him feel awkward.

"Well," Jack said, "Brett and Mike should arrive tonight."

Bill, gazing out into the encroaching dusk, murmured, "Night ushers in more than travelers in the darkness, Jack. Shadows hide unfathomable inky tendrils deeper than the eye sees."

"I'm not sure they'll come," Ctholh'en said, his intense gaze searing through Bill's enigmatic rambling.

"Why not?" Bill said. "Of course they'll come." He grinned crookedly.

"I thought they might," Jack replied.

"I rather think they're not coming," Ro'brt Ctholh'en said.

He spoke with an air of superior knowledge that irritated both Jack and Bill. Bill, angered, foolishly bet fifty *pesetas* that they would arrive that night. Ctholh'en took the bet, raising it to one hundred *pesetas*. Jack tried to smooth things over, but the tension remained.

Later, they walked under the arcade to the Café Iruña for coffee. Ctholh'en said he was going to get a shave. Bill asked Jack about his chances with the bet.

"You've got a rotten chance. They've never been on time anywhere. If their money doesn't come, it's a cinch they won't get in tonight," Jack replied.

Jack saw Ctholh'en approach from across the square.

"Here he comes."

"Let's hope he doesn't act superior and ... Arkhame."

"The barber shop is closed," Ctholh'en informed them. "It won't open until four."

They enjoyed coffee at the Iruña, seated in cozy wicker chairs, gazing out from the coolness of the arcade onto the vast square. Eventually, Bill left to write some letters, and Ctholh'en headed to the barbershop. Discovering it was still closed, he opted to return to the hotel for a bath. Jack remained in front of the café for a while, then strolled around the town. The heat was oppressive, but he stayed in the shade of the streets, meandered through the market, and delighted in exploring the town once more. Jack visited the city hall and found the old man who reserved bullfight tickets for him every year. The man had received the money Jack had sent from Paris and renewed his subscriptions, so everything was in order. He was the archivist, and the town's archives filled his office. Jack exited the building, leaving the archivist surrounded by archives, and the porter stopped Jack to brush off his coat.

"You must have been in a motor car," he remarked.

The back of Jack's collar and the upper part of his shoulders were coated in gray dust.

"From Bayonne."

"Well, well," he said. "I could tell you were in a motor car by the way the dust settled." Jack then handed him two copper coins.

At the end of the street, the cathedral beckoned Jack with its stoic presence, its façade growing more profound with each visit. Inside, past towering pillars, the quiet hum of prayers resonated amidst the lingering incense and the dance of colors from grand stained-glass windows.

Kneeling, Jack's thoughts flickered between Brett, Mike, Bill, Ro'brt Ctholh'en, and himself. Half-drifting in a trance, grotesque images pierced his prayer: a shadowy cult, Brett's bare form laid on an altar, her body trembling under a blinding flash of light, and the hulking silhouette of a dormant god rising from a churning sea. Spain burned in his mind, flames licking the edges of his vision until the terror dulled, swallowed by the pull of a dark mirror—memories of witchcraft and war merging into one. His body jerked, dragging him awake. He muttered prayers for bullfights, fiestas, anything to push the horror away. Wealth drifted into his thoughts, the count's face forming in his mind, but the solid pew beneath him anchored him back.

When he stepped outside into the burning sun, the remnants of his devotion clung to his fingers, now dry and sticky. He moved toward the hotel, drawn into the cloying shadows, seeking refuge from the light.

At dinner that night, they discovered that Ro'brt Ctholh'en had bathed and shaved his head. He was anxious, and Jack didn't attempt to help him. The train from San Sebastián was scheduled to arrive at nine o'clock, and if Brett and Mike were coming, they'd be on it. With twenty minutes to spare, they were only halfway through dinner. Ro'brt Ctholh'en stood up from the table and declared he'd go to the station. Jack announced that he'd accompany him just to tease him. Bill declared that he'd be damned if he'd leave his dinner. Jack assured him they'd be right back.

They strolled to the station, Jack relishing Ctholh'en's wide-eyed stygian unease. Jack hoped Brett would be on the train. At the station, the train was tardy, and they perched on a baggage cart, waiting in the darkness. Jack had never witnessed a civilian as agitated and eager as Ro'brt Ctholh'en. Jack enjoyed it, albeit guiltily. Ctholh'en had a remarkable knack for bringing out the worst in others.

Eventually, they heard the train whistle from afar, on the other side of the plateau, and spotted the headlight approaching up the hill. They went inside the station and stood among a crowd of people just behind the gates. The train arrived and halted, and everyone began exiting through the gates.

They weren't in the throng. They lingered until everyone had departed the station and boarded buses or cabs or strolled with friends or relatives into the town through the darkness.

"I knew they wouldn't come," Ro'brt said as they headed back to the hotel.

"I thought they might," Jack replied.

Upon their return, Bill was eating fruit and finishing a bottle of wine.

"Didn't come, huh?"

"No."

"Do you mind if I give you that hundred *pesetas* in the morning, Ctholh'en?" Bill inquired. "I haven't exchanged any money here yet."

"Oh, forget about it," Ro'brt Ctholh'en replied. "Let's wager on something else. Can you bet on bullfights?"

"You could," Bill answered, "but you don't need to."

"It'd be like betting on the war," Jack chimed in. "You don't require an economic interest."

"I'm quite curious to see them," Ro'brt admitted.

Montoya approached their table with a telegram in hand. "It's for you." He handed it to Jack.

It read: "Stopped night San Sebastian."

"It's from them," Jack declared. "They've stopped over in San Sebastian. They send their regards to you."

Jack couldn't understand why he had to hack on Ro'brt. He also recognized that as a lie. Deep down, he understood. It was a blind, unforgiving envy of what had transpired between Ro'brt and Brett. His acceptance of their relationship as normal changed nothing; deep inside, Jack harbored a profound resentment.

Jack didn't think he ever truly hated him until his moment of superiority at lunch and the extensive grooming. So Jack pocketed the telegram. The telegram was addressed to him, after all.

"Well," Jack said, "they should catch the noon bus to Burguete. They can follow us if they arrive tomorrow night."

There were only two trains from San Sebastián: an early morning train and the one they had just met.

"That sounds like a good idea," Ctholh'en agreed.

"The sooner we get on the stream, the better."

"It's all the same to me when we start," Bill said. "The sooner the better."

They sat in the Iruña for a while, enjoying their coffee, then strolled to the bull-ring, wandering across the field, under the trees at the cliff's edge, to gaze down at the river shrouded in darkness. Bill paused, his gaze fixed on the field. "More than wind stirs these fields," he murmured. A sudden chill swept over Jack, unexplained, prompting him to excuse himself. Bill and Ro'brt lingered at the café well into the night, as Jack was already asleep by the time they returned.

In the morning, Jack purchased three tickets for the bus to Burguete. It was scheduled to leave at two o'clock. There was nothing earlier.

Bill stood apart, his gaze fixed on the bustling square. "See the dance, Jack?" he mused softly. "Every step, every turn, like they're avoiding something unseen. It's all a delicate balance, on the edge of a knife." Jack scanned the square, seeing nothing but the ordinary hustle of morning.

Jack wandered away, biting his tongue once again, and sat for a while at the Iruña reading the papers when he saw Ro'brt coming across the square. He approached the table and sat down in one of the wicker chairs.

"This is a comfortable café," he said. "Did you have a good night, Jack?"

"I slept like a log."

"I didn't sleep very well. Bill and I were out late, too."

"Where were you?"

"Here. And after it closed, we went to that other café. The old man there speaks German and English."

"The Café Suizo."

"That's it. He seems like a nice old fellow. I think it's a better café than this one."

"It's not so good in the daytime," Jack said. "Too hot. By the way, I got the bus tickets."

Ro'brt hesitated, his gaze fixed somewhere in the distance. "I think I'll stay back," he said quietly, the words hanging in the air as he turned away.

"I've got your ticket."

"Give it to me. I'll get the money back."

"It's five *pesetas*."

Ro'brt took out a silver five-*peseta* piece and handed it to Jack.

"I ought to stay," he said. "You see, I'm afraid there's some sort of misunderstanding."

"Why," Jack said. "They may not come here for three or four days now if they start on parties at San Sebastian."

"That's just it," said Ro'brt. "I'm afraid they expected to meet me at San Sebastian, and that's why they stopped over."

"What makes you think that?"

"Well, I wrote suggesting it to Brett."

"Why in hell didn't you stay there and meet them then?" Jack started to say but stopped. He thought that idea would come to him by itself, but he didn't believe it ever did.

Ro'brt was being confidential now, and it was giving him pleasure to be able to talk with the understanding that Jack knew there was something between him and Brett.

"Well, Bill and I will go up right after lunch," Jack said.

"I wish I could go. We've been looking forward to this fishing all winter." He was being sentimental about it. "But I ought to stay. I really should. As soon as they come, I'll bring them right up."

"Let's find Bill."

"I want to go over to the barbershop," Ro'brt said, rubbing a layer of stubble on his head.

"See you at lunch."

As Jack prepared to leave, Ro'brt's voice lowered. "It's always wise to stay alert, Jack. Especially now." His glance subtly swept toward where Bill had been.

Jack found Bill in his room. He was shaving.

Jack knocked on the slightly ajar door and entered, catching a glimpse of a tattered notebook in Bill's hands, his movements quick, almost secretive. Bill glanced up, the notebook vanishing into his jacket.

"Everything alright?" Jack asked, eyeing Bill's pocket.

"Just jotting something down," Bill answered, his voice light but his hand not quite steady.

Jack nodded, but the moment hung in the air, another silent question unanswered.

"Have you seen Ro'brt?" Bill asked, eager to lead Jack's penetrating gaze away. "He's a great little confider. He bragged about a date with Brett at San Sebastian."

"The lying scoundrel!"

"Oh, no," said Bill. "Don't get upset. Don't get upset at this stage of the trip. How did you ever happen to know this fellow, anyway?"

"Don't rub it in."

Bill looked around, half-shaved, and then continued talking into the foggy mirror while he lathered his face.

"Didn't you send him with a letter to me in New York last winter? Thank God, I'm a traveling man. Haven't you got some more friends you could bring along?" He rubbed his chin with his thumb, looked at it, and started scraping again.

"You've got some fine ones yourself."

"Oh, yes. I've got some great ones. But not alongside this Ro'brt. The funny thing is he's nice, too. I like him. But he's just so awful."

"He can be really nice."

"I know it. That's the terrible part."

Jack laughed.

"Yes. Go on and laugh," said Bill. "You weren't out with him last night until two o'clock."

"Was he very bad?"

"Awful. What's all this about him and Brett, anyway? Did she ever have anything to do with him?"

He raised his chin up and pulled it from side to side. "Sure. She went down to San Sebastian with him."

"What a foolish thing to do. Why did she do that?"

"She wanted to get out of town and can't go anywhere alone. She said she thought it would be good for him."

"What ridiculous things people do. Why didn't she go off with some of her own people? Or you?"—he slurred that over—"or me? Why not me?" He looked at his face carefully in the glass and put a big dab of lather on each cheekbone. "It's an honest face. It's a face any woman would be safe with."

"She'd never seen it."

"She should have. All women should see it. It's a face that ought to be displayed on every screen in the country. Every woman ought to be given a copy of this face as she leaves the altar. Mothers should tell their daughters about this face. My son"—he pointed the razor at Jack—"go west with this face and grow up with the country."

He ducked down to the bowl, rinsed his face with cold water, put on some alcohol, and then looked at himself carefully in the glass, pulling down his long upper lip. "My God!" he said, "isn't it an awful face?" He looked in the glass. "And as for this Ro'brt," Bill said, "he makes me sick, and he can go to hell, and I'm damn glad he's staying there so we won't have him fishing with us."

"You're damn right."

"We're going trout fishing. We're going trout fishing in the Irati River, and we're going to enjoy ourselves now at lunch on the wine of the country, and then take a fantastic bus ride."

"Come on. Let's go over to the Iruña and start," Jack said.

CHAPTER 11

WHISPERING WINESKINS

AS THEY STEPPED INTO THE square, the day's heat enveloped them like a suffocating cloak, and the sweltering sun bore down mercilessly. The bus, packed with people jostling for space, pulsed with chaotic energy—a cacophony of voices and frenzied movement. Jack watched as Ro'brt's silhouette dissolved into the arcade's cool shade, his departure marked by a silent, enigmatic nod from the shadows. Feeling the oppressive weight of the journey ahead, Jack hoisted himself and slid into the vacant wooden seat, warm and scarred under his touch. As the Basque man casually passed the wineskin, his and Bill's eyes locked in a silent exchange thick with understanding.

A flicker of something dark and unspoken crossed Bill's features, cracking his affable facade. It passed swiftly. Accepting the wine, Jack was startled by the Basque's perfect imitation of a klaxon horn, causing the wine to spill. Laughter erupted around them.

He apologized, prompting the Basque to make Jack take another drink. The Basque sounded the klaxon again a little later, fooling Jack a second time. Adept at the trick, the Basques enjoyed the joke. The man beside Bill spoke to him in Spanish, but Bill wasn't following, so he offered him one of their wine bottles. The man waved it off, saying it was too hot and he'd had too much at lunch. When Bill offered the bottle again, the man took a long pull, then the bottle wandered across the bus. Everyone took a sip politely before insisting their friends cork it and put it away. The group urged each other to drink from their leather wine bottles instead.After a few more false klaxons, the bus finally started. Ro'brt Ctholh'en waved goodbye, and all the Basques waved back. As they left the town, a sudden coolness crept over them, sharp and unsettling. The trees lining the road seemed to bend inward, their branches brushing the bus, casting long, twisted shadows. Initially, the breeze felt like a welcome relief, but beneath it lurked something else—a faint, unspoken warning.

The Basque gestured toward the view with his wine bottle. "That's something, isn't it?" he murmured.

"These Basques are swell people," Bill said.

The Basque lying against his legs was tanned like worn saddle leather, wearing a black smock and creased with wrinkles on his neck. He turned around and offered his wine bag to Bill, who handed him a bottle. The Basque wagged a forefinger, slapped the cork with his palm, and shoved the wine bag up. "Arriba! Arriba! Lift it up," he said.

Bill raised the wineskin and let the stream of wine spurt into his mouth, his head tipped back. When he stopped drinking and tipped the leather bottle down, a few drops ran down his chin.

"No! No!" several Basques exclaimed. "Not like that." One snatched the bottle away from the owner, who was about to demonstrate. He was a young man holding the wine bottle at full arm's length, raising it high, squeezing the leather bag so the stream of wine hissed into his mouth. He held the bag out, the wine tracing a flat, complex trajectory into his mouth, swallowing smoothly and regularly.

"Hey!" the bottle's owner shouted. "Whose wine is that?"

The drinker wagged his little finger and smiled at his friends with his eyes. Then he abruptly stopped the stream, lifted the wine bag quickly, and lowered it to the owner. He winked at them. The owner shook the wineskin sadly.

They traveled through a farming country with rocky hills sloping into fields. The grain climbed the hillsides as they ascended higher, a wind blowing the grain fiercely. The road, a stark ribbon through the landscape, stirred a dense dust that lingered behind them like a ghostly veil.

They turned sharply off the road to give room to a long string of six mules hauling a high-hooded wagon loaded with freight, covered in dust. Close behind was another string of mules and another wagon loaded with lumber. The arriero driving the mules leaned back and put on the thick wooden brakes as they passed. The country was barren up here, with rocky, hard-baked clay hills furrowed by rain.

As the bus rounded the curve, the green valley of the town unfolded. The stream running through it moved with unsettling vigor, its currents eddying in a desperate dance. Nearby, grapevines twisted away from the soil, their shapes contorted as though in quiet defiance of the earth that nurtured them.

The bus stopped in front of a posada, and many passengers disembarked. Baggage was unstrapped from the roof under big tarpaulins and lifted down. Bill and Jack got off and entered the posada. The low, dark room held saddles, harnesses, hay forks, clusters of canvas rope-soled shoes, hams, slabs of bacon, white garlic, and long sausages hanging from the roof. It was cool and dusky as they approached a long wooden counter with two women serving drinks. Behind them were shelves stacked with supplies and goods.

They each had an *aguardiente* and paid forty centimes for the drinks. Jack gave the woman fifty centimes as a tip, but she returned the copper piece, thinking he had misunderstood the price.

Two of their Basque friends came in and insisted on buying a round. They bought a drink, then their friends did the same, and soon they were slapping each other on the backs and buying another round. Venturing out into the sunlight and heat, they climbed onto the bus's top again. There was plenty of room now for everyone to sit on the seat, and the Basque who had been lying on the tin roof now sat between them. The woman who had been serving drinks came out, wiping her hands on her apron, and spoke to someone inside the bus. Then the driver appeared, swinging two flat leather mail pouches, and climbed up. With everyone waving, they set off.

The road left the green valley at once, and they were up in the hills again. Bill and the wine-bottle Basque conversed. A man leaned over from the other side of the seat and asked in English,

"You're Americans?"

"Sure."

The old man leaned in, his weathered face a roadmap of untold stories, his voice a low echo of days long gone. "Once, I called America home," he murmured, more to himself than his listeners. "A long time ago. Now it feels like... a dream." His gaze drifted to a horizon seen only by him.

"How was it?"

"What you say?"

"How was America?"

"Oh, I was in California. It was fine."

"Why did you leave?"

"What you say?"

"Why did you come back here?"

"I returned for... the heart," he said, the words trailing into silence. "But sometimes, in the still of night, I find myself... wandering ..." His words lingered, and then he asked, "Where are you from?"

"Kansas City."

"I been there," he said. "I been in Chicago, St. Louis, Kansas City, Denver, Los Angeles, and Salt Lake City." He named them carefully.

"How long were you over?"

"Fifteen years. Then I came back and got married."

"Have a drink?"

"All right," he said. "You can't get this in America, eh?"

"There's plenty if you can pay for it."

"What did you come over here for?"

"We're going to the fiesta at Pamplona."

"You like the bull-fights?"

"Sure. Don't you?"

"Yes," he said. "I guess I like them." Then, after a little:

"Where are you going now?"

"Up to Burguete to fish."

"Well," he said, "I hope you catch something." He shook hands and turned to the rear seat again. The other Basques were impressed. He settled in comfortably and smiled at Jack when he turned to look at the country. But the effort of speaking English seemed to have tired him. He didn't say anything after that.

The bus climbed steadily up the road. The country was barren, and rocks stuck up through the clay. No grass beside the road. Looking behind, they saw the country spread out below. Far in the distance, fields were squares of green and brown on the hillsides. The horizon was the brown mountains, strangely shaped. As they climbed higher, the horizon kept changing. As the bus slowly descended, they could see other mountains in the south. Then the road came over the crest, flattened out, and went into a forest of cork oaks. The sun filtered through the trees in patches, and cattle grazed among them. They traveled through the forest, and the road turned along a rise of land, revealing a rolling green plain with dark mountains beyond it— wooded, with clouds descending from them. The green plain stretched off, cut by fences, and the white road showed through the trunks of a double line of trees that crossed the plain toward the north. At the edge of the rise, they saw the red roofs and white houses of Burguete ahead, strung out on the plain, and off on the shoulder of the first dark mountain was the gray metal-sheathed roof of the monastery of Roncesvalles.

"There's Roncesvalles," Jack said.

"Where?"

"Way off there where the mountain starts."

"It's cold up here," Bill said.

"It's high," Jack said. "It must be twelve hundred meters."

"It's awfully cold," Bill said.

The bus leveled down onto the straight road that ran to Burguete. They passed a crossroads and crossed a bridge over a stream. The houses of Burguete lined both sides of the road with no side streets. They passed the church and the schoolyard, and the bus stopped. They got off, and the driver handed down their bags and the rod case. A carabineer in his cocked hat and yellow leather cross-straps approached.

"What's in there?" he pointed to the rod case.

Jack opened it and showed him. He asked to see their fishing permits, and Jack got them out. He looked at the date and then waved them on.

"Is that all right?" Jack asked.

"Yes. Of course."

They went up the street, past whitewashed stone houses with families sitting in doorways watching them, to the inn. The plump woman running the inn came out from the kitchen and shook hands with them. She took off her spectacles, wiped them, and put them on again. Inside, a chill lingered, unnatural in its depth, seeping into the marrow. The wind outside began its ascent, its mournful song weaving through the eaves as if lamenting forgotten tales. The girl guiding them upstairs quickened her pace, her glances toward the trembling windows betraying a shared unease. Each gust carried a ghostly whisper, a dread felt but unseen.

The room had two beds, a washstand, a clothes chest, and a framed steel engraving of *Nuestra Señora de Roncesvalles*. The wind blew against the shutters. The room was on the north side of the inn. They washed, put on sweaters, and came downstairs into the dining room. It had a stone floor and low ceiling, oak-paneled. The shutters were up, and it was so cold you could see your breath.

"My God!" said Bill. "It can't be this cold tomorrow. I'm not going to wade a stream in this weather."

An upright piano stood in the far corner, and Bill went over and started to play.

"I got to keep warm," he said.

Jack went out to find the woman and ask her how much the room and board was. She put her hands under her apron and looked away.

"Twelve pesetas."

"Why, we only paid that in Pamplona."

She didn't say anything, just took off her glasses and wiped them on her apron.

"That's too much," Jack said. "We didn't pay more than that at a big hotel."

"We've put in a bathroom."

"Haven't you got anything cheaper?"

"Not in the summer. Now is the big season."

They were the only people in the inn. "Is the wine included?"

"Oh, yes."

"Well," Jack said. "It's all right."

He went back to Bill. He blew his breath at Jack to show how cold it was and went on playing. Jack sat at one of the tables and looked at the pictures on the wall. There was one panel of dead rabbits, one of dead pheasants, and one of dead ducks. The panels were dark and smoky-looking. There was a cupboard full of liqueur bottles. He looked at them all. Bill was still playing.

"How about a hot rum punch?" he said. "This isn't going to keep me warm permanently."

Jack went out and told the woman what a rum punch was and how to make it. In a few minutes, a girl brought a steaming stone pitcher into the room. Bill came over from the piano, and they drank the hot punch and listened to the wind.

"There isn't too much rum in that."

Jack went over to the cupboard, brought the rum bottle, and poured a half-tumblerful into the pitcher.

"Direct action," said Bill. "It beats legislation."

The girl came in and laid the table for supper.

Bill paused, his words trailing off as he listened to the howl of the wind, its roar almost drowning out his thoughts.

The girl brought in a big bowl of hot vegetable soup and the wine. They had fried trout afterward and some sort of stew and a big bowl of wild strawberries. They didn't skimp on the wine; the girl was shy but nice about bringing it. The old woman looked in once and counted the empty bottles.

After supper, they went upstairs, smoked, and read in bed for warmth.

"Have you ever delved into... the hidden realms woven into the fabric of reality?" Bill asked slyly, comfortably snuggled in his bed. Jack stared wistfully at the night sky out the window, not turning around.

"There are catacombs beneath St. Stephen's Cathedral in Vienna, you see," Bill said, a little gleefully. "It was once a shrine devoted to a long-forgotten deity." Jack turned at the mention of Vienna and watched Bill, who now continued down his track with the lumbering power of locomotion. His eyes were glazed, and he spoke with the feverish conviction of a cultist.

"Have you heard of the Blackstone?" Bill asked, waiting for a signal from Jack, who shook his head. "It's a curious and sinister monolith, brooding amongst the mountains of Hungary. Viktor told me numerous dark legends about it... Oh, you know, he mentioned the hidden chambers beneath the Great Pyramids..."

"Egypt?" Jack said, raising a brow. Ro'brt had been on about Egypt lately, too.

"Yes, and in the desolate expanse of the Syrian desert, deep inside the *French Mandate for Syria and Lebanon*—there are mysteries amidst the crumbling ruins of Babylon, too. The remnants of forgotten civilizations, esoteric lore beyond our comprehension, and power, Jack, real power. You couldn't imagine the taste of it."

"I could, though," Jack said with a wince, "and I don't like it."

"Oh Jack, we're not far now. Close to... specific places, concealed realms, where one could sense the eerie presence of these... entities. In the stygian recesses of these very lightless forests, peculiar glades where trees contort at unnatural angles, bowing to eldritch forces."

Jack yawned and checked his wrist, but he wore no watch.

"Most steer clear of their lurking malevolence, while some oddballs are drawn right to it. If you discovered the arcane knowledge in the mountains of British Raj, of Tibet, you could listen to the whispering winds and hear the tales of ages past, their gods are still here, sleeping."

"That sounds like a good idea," Jack said, excusing himself to rest.

In the nebulous realm of sleep, Jack drifted into a dream where Brett's image emerged, both beguiling and subtly distorted as if seen through a warped lens. Her voice echoed, a haunting melody with words that tantalized and eluded comprehension. Around them, shadowy figures in hoods loomed, their presence more sensed than seen, their chants a soft, unsettling thrum that resonated through time itself. Abruptly, the dream shattered, leaving Jack to awaken with a disquieted start. Outside, the wind's cadence echoed his racing heart.

CHAPTER 12

CHTHONIAN SUSURRUS

WHEN JACK WOKE, HE WENT to the window and looked out. The sky was clear, the mountains bare of clouds. Below, old carts and a weathered diligence sat abandoned, the wood splitting like old bones under the sun. Among them, a goat balanced on a cart, its eyes fixed on something beyond Jack's understanding. It didn't move, but its gaze penetrated deep within him. Jack felt a brief pull, as if the air itself had shifted. He waved, and the goat tilted its head, unhurried, before bounding down into the stillness below.

Bill was still sleeping, so Jack dressed, put on his shoes outside in the hall, and went downstairs. No one was stirring, so he unbolted the door and stepped out. It was cool in the early morning, and the sun had not yet dried the dew that had settled when the wind died down. Jack searched the shed behind the inn, found a mattock, and headed toward the stream to dig some worms for bait.

The stream was clear and shallow but did not look trouty. On the damp grassy bank, Jack drove the mattock into the earth, loosening a chunk of sod. Worms wriggled out of sight as he lifted the sod and dug carefully, gathering many. The mirror nestled in his satchel hummed with a subtle vibration, reflecting shadows that didn't align with their surroundings.

Digging at the edge of the damp ground, Jack filled two empty tobacco tins with worms and sifted dirt onto them. The goats watched him dig.

When Jack went back into the inn, the woman was in the kitchen. He asked her to get coffee and prepare lunch. Bill was not in his usual languid state. Instead, he sat on the edge of the bed, his gaze locked on the closet with an intensity that bordered on unnerving.

"I saw you out the window," Bill remarked, eyes glued to the closet. "What were you digging up out there?"

"Just worms," Jack replied, studying Bill. "What's so fascinating about that closet?"

Bill sat, frozen. "Come on," Jack said, uneasy with Bill's uncharacteristic behavior. "Get up."

"What? Get up?" Bill jolted awake with feigned surprise. "I never get up. I'm waiting for an audience with the unseen." He climbed into bed, pulling the sheet up to his chin, his eyes never leaving the closet. "This room, Jack, it's... a portal of sorts. Vanishes with its occupant, only to return years later. I'm waiting for it to reveal its secrets."

Jack paused, the tackle bag in his hand, feeling a cold draft of absurdity. "Aren't you interested?" Bill prodded, his voice a mix of earnestness and mockery.

"I'm going down to eat," Jack dismissed, unwilling to entertain what seemed like a fanciful delusion.

"Eat? Why didn't you say so?" Bill's demeanor shifted, the bizarre fascination with the closet momentarily forgotten. "Eat? Fine. Now you're talking sense. You go out and dig some more worms, and I'll be right down."

"Oh, go to hell!" Jack retorted, the odd exchange leaving an unsettling aftertaste.

"Work for the good of all," Bill chimed in, a trace of his usual humor returning. "Show irony and pity."

Jack started out of the room with the tackle bag, the nets, and the rod case. "Hey! Come back!"

Jack put his head in the door. "Aren't you going to show a little irony and pity?"

Jack thumbed his nose. "That's not irony."

As Jack went downstairs, he heard Bill singing, "Irony and pity. When you're feeling... Oh, give them irony and give them pity. Oh, give them irony. When they're feeling... Just a little irony. Just a little pity..." He kept on singing until he came downstairs. The tune was: "The bells are ringing for me and my gal."

As Jack settled in the dining area, he picked up a week-old Spanish paper. "What's all this irony and pity?"

"What? Don't you know about irony and pity?"

"No. Who got it up?"

"Everybody. They're mad about it in New York. It's just like the Fratellinis used to be."

The girl came in with the coffee and buttered toast. Or rather, it was bread toasted and buttered.

"Ask her if she's got any jam," Bill said. "Be ironical with her."

"Have you got any jam?"

"That's not ironical. I wish I could talk Spanish."

The coffee was good, and they drank it out of big bowls. The girl brought in a glass dish of raspberry jam.

"Thank you."

"Hey! That's not the way," Bill said. "Say something ironical. Make some crack about Primo de Rivera."

"I could ask her what kind of a jam they think they've gotten into in the Riff."

"Poor," said Bill. "Very poor. You can't do it. That's all. You don't understand irony. You have no pity. Say something pitiful."

"Ro'brt Ctholh'en."

"Not so bad. That's better. Now, why is Ctholh'en pitiful? Be ironic." He took a big gulp of coffee.

"Aw, hell!" Jack said. "It's too early in the morning."

"There you go. And you claim you want to be a writer, too. You're only a newspaperman. An expatriated newspaperman. You ought to be ironical the minute you get out of bed. You ought to wake up with your mouth full of pity."

"Go on," Jack said. "Who did you get this stuff from?"

"Everybody. Don't you read? Don't you ever see anybody? You know what you are? You're an expatriate. Why don't you live in New York? Then you'd know these things. What do you want me to do? Come over here and tell you every year?"

"Take some more coffee," Jack said.

"Good. Coffee is good for you. It's the caffeine in it. Caffeine puts a man on his horse and a woman in his grave. You know what's the trouble with you? You're an expatriate. One of the worst types. Haven't you heard that? Nobody that ever left their own country ever wrote anything worth printing. Not even in the newspapers."

He drank the coffee. "You're an expatriate. You've lost touch with the soil. You get precious. Fake European standards have ruined you. You drink yourself to death. You become obsessed with sex. You spend all your time talking, not working. You are an expatriate, see? You hang around cafés."

"I never thought of it that way," Jack said. "It sounds like a swell life. When do I work?"

"You don't work. One group claims women support you. Another group claims you're impotent."

"No," Jack said. "I just had an accident."

"Never mention that," Bill said. "That's the sort of thing that can't be spoken of. That's what you ought to work up into a mystery. Like Henry's bicycle."

He had been going splendidly, but he stopped, worried he had hurt Jack with the remark about impotence. Jack wanted to start him again.

"It wasn't a bicycle," Jack said. "He was riding horseback."

"I heard it was a tricycle."

"Well," Jack said. "A plane is sort of like a tricycle. The joystick works the same way."

"But you don't pedal it."

"No," Jack said. "I guess you don't pedal it."

"Let's lay off that," Bill said.

"All right. I was just standing up for the tricycle."

"I think he's a good writer, too," Bill said. "And you're a hell of a good guy. Anybody ever tell you you were a good guy?"

"I'm not a good guy."

"Listen. You're a hell of a good guy, and I'm fonder of you than anybody on earth. I couldn't tell you that in New York. It'd mean I was Uranian, you know, bent. That was what the Civil War was about. Abraham Lincoln was bent. He was in love with General Grant. So was Jefferson Davis. Lincoln just freed the slaves on a bet. The Dred Scott case was framed by the Anti-Saloon League. Sex explains it all. The colonel's lady and Judy O'Grady are Lebanese under their skin. No, from Lesbos, that."

He stopped and considered his next words. "Want to hear some more?"

"Shoot," Jack said.

"I don't know anymore. Tell you some more at lunch."

"Old Bill," Jack said.

"You bum!"

They packed the lunch and two bottles of wine in the rucksack, and Bill put it on. Jack carried the rod case, and the landing nets were slung over his back. They started up the road, crossed a meadow, and found a path leading toward the woods on the first hill's slope. The rolling fields, cropped by grazing sheep, stretched before them. Cattle bells echoed from the hills as they walked the sandy path.

The path crossed a stream on a foot-log. The log was surfaced off, and a sapling bent across for a rail. In the flat pool beside the stream, tadpoles spotted the sand. They went up a steep bank and across the fields. Looking back, they saw Burguete—white houses and red roofs, the white road with a truck along it, and dust rising.

Beyond the fields, they crossed another faster-flowing stream. A sandy road led down to the ford and beyond into the woods. The path crossed the stream on another foot-log below the ford and joined the road, and they ventured into the woods.

It was a beech wood, and the trees were very old. Their roots bulged above the ground, and the branches were twisted. They walked on the road between the thick trunks of the old beeches, sunlight filtering through the leaves in dappled patterns on the grass. The trees were big, and the foliage was thick, but it was not gloomy. There was no undergrowth, only smooth, very green grass and big gray trees well spaced as though it were a park.

"This is country," Bill said.

The road climbed a hill into thick woods, sometimes dipping down but rising again steeply. All the time, they heard the cattle in the woods. Finally, they reached the summit, the highest point of the wooded hills visible from Burguete. Wild strawberries were growing on the sunny side of the ridge in a clearing.

Ahead, the road came out of the forest and ran along the shoulder of the ridge of hills. The hills ahead were not wooded, and there were great fields of yellow gorse. Way off, they saw the steep bluffs, dark with trees and jutting with gray stone, that marked the course of the Irati River.

"We have to follow this road along the ridge, cross these hills, go through the woods on the far hills, and come down to the Irati Valley," Jack pointed out to Bill.

"That's a hell of a hike."

"It's too far to go and fish and come back the same day, comfortably."

"Comfortably. That's a nice word. We'll have to go like hell to get there and back and have any fishing at all."

It was a long walk through beautiful country, but they were tired when they finally descended the steep road into the valley of the Rio de la Fábrica. The road came out from the shadow of the woods into the hot sun. Ahead was a river valley. Beyond the river was a steep hill. There was a field of buckwheat on the hill.

They saw a white house under some trees on the hillside. It was very hot, and they stopped under some trees beside a dam that crossed the river.

Bill put the pack against one of the trees, and they jointed up the rods, put on the reels, tied on leaders, and got ready to fish.

"You're sure this thing has trout in it?" Bill asked.

"It's full of them."

"I'm going to fish a fly. You got any McGintys?"

"There are some in there."

"You going to fish bait?"

"Yeah. I'm going to fish the dam here."

"Well, I'll take the fly-book, then." He tied on a fly. "Where'd I better go? Up or down?"

"Down is the best. There are plenty up above, too."

Bill went down the bank. "Take a worm can."

"No, I don't want one. If they won't take a fly, I'll just flick it around."

Bill was down below watching the stream. "Say," he called against the noise of the dam, "how about putting the wine in that spring up the road?"

"All right," Jack shouted. Bill waved his hand and started down the stream. Jack found the two wine bottles in the pack and carried them up the road to where water flowed out of an iron pipe. There was a board over the spring, and Jack lifted it, knocking the corks firmly into the bottles, and lowered them into the water. It was so cold, Jack's hand went numb. He put back the wood slab and hoped nobody would find the wine.

Jack got his rod leaning against the tree, took the bait can and landing net, and walked out onto the dam. It was built to provide a head of water for driving logs. The gate was up, and Jack sat on one of the squared timbers and watched the smooth apron of water before the river tumbled into the falls. The white water at the foot of the dam was deep.

As he baited up, a trout leaped from the churning water, arcing gracefully before vanishing back into the depths. Before Jack could finish baiting, another trout jumped at the falls, making the same arc and disappearing into the thundering water. Jack put on a good-sized sinker and dropped into the white water close to the edge of the timbers of the dam.

Jack did not notice the first trout strike. When he started to pull up, a sudden resistance announced he had one. He brought it, fighting and bending the rod almost double, out of the boiling water and swung it onto the dam. It was a good trout; Jack slammed its head against the timber. The fish shuddered, then went still before he slipped it into his bag.

While Jack had him on, several trout had jumped at the falls. As soon as he baited up and dropped in again, Jack hooked another and brought him in the same way. In a little while, Jack had six. They were all about the same size. Jack laid them out, side by side, all their heads pointing the same way, and looked at them. They were beautifully colored and firm from the cold water. It was a hot day, so Jack slit them open, removing the insides, gills and all, and tossed the entrails into the river. He took the trout ashore, washed them in the cold water above the dam, and then picked some ferns and packed them in the bag—three trout on a layer of ferns, then another layer of ferns, then three more trout, and covered them with ferns. The bag was now bulky, and Jack put it in the shade of the tree.

It was very hot on the dam, so Jack put his worm can in the shade with the bag, got a book out of the pack, and settled down under the tree to read until Bill should come up for lunch.

It was a little past noon, and there was not much shade, but Jack sat against the trunk of two trees that grew together and read. The book was something by A. E. W. Mason, about a man frozen in the Alps who vanished into a glacier. His bride vowed to wait twenty-four years for his body to emerge, while her true love waited too, and they were still waiting when Bill came up.

"Get any?" Bill asked. He had his rod, bag, and net all in one hand and was sweating. Jack hadn't heard him come up because of the noise from the dam.

"Six. What did you get?"

Bill sat down, opened his bag, and laid a big trout on the grass. He took out three more, each a little bigger than the last, and laid them side by side in the shade of the tree. His face was sweaty and happy.

"How are yours?"

"Smaller."

"Let's see them."

"They're packed."

"How big are they really?"

"They're all about the size of your smallest."

"You're not holding out on me?"

"I wish I were."

"Get them all on worms?"

"Yes."

"You lazy bum!"

"You've certainly set the standard high, the very model of a master baiter extraordinaire, Bill!"

Bill glowered at Jack for a moment. "Indeed," was all he said, and suddenly Jack blushed, his jest skewered back upon himself.

Bill gave up the pretense and grinned. "Now that was irony and pity in spades, Jack. You may be a writer yet."

As Bill stowed the trout, his movements were deliberate, as if sending a secret message to unseen watchers. Jack shook his head, laughing at his own paranoia, and walked up the road to get the two bottles of wine. They were cold. Moisture beaded on the bottles as Jack walked back to the trees. Jack spread the lunch on a newspaper, uncorked one of the bottles, and leaned the other against a tree. Bill came up, drying his hands, his bag plump with ferns.

"Let's see that bottle," he said. He pulled the cork, tipped up the bottle, and drank. "Whew! That makes my eyes ache."

"Let's try it."

The wine was icy cold and tasted faintly rusty.

"That's not such filthy wine," Bill said.

"The cold helps it," Jack said.

They unwrapped the little parcels of lunch.

"Chicken."

"There are hard-boiled eggs."

"Find any salt?"

"First, the egg," said Bill. "Then the chicken. Even Bryan could see that."

Jack smiled and nodded. "He's dead. I read it in the paper yesterday."

"No," Jack stopped. "Not really?"

"Yes. Bryan's dead. Murdered." Bill laid down the egg he was peeling.

Jack's heart raced. "Found torn apart, drained of blood. Animal attack, they said. Strange, in this modern age, in the heart of the city," Bill murmured, his expression grim.

The news settled like a drop in still water, rippling outward, leaving something cold in its wake. Jack felt it in his spine—a slow tightening—as a bead of sweat traced a line down his neck. The mirror in his satchel hummed softly, reflecting shadows that seemed to listen.

Around them, the natural sounds of the wilderness quieted. It was as if the world had held its breath in anticipation of something deeper, a more ancient rhythm, a sense of something just beyond the veil of the known, waiting, watching.

"I reverse the order," Bill said stiffly. "For Bryan's sake. As a tribute to the Great Commoner. First the chicken, then the egg."

"Wonder what day God created the chicken?"

"Oh," said Bill, sucking the drumstick, "how should we know? We should not question. Our stay on earth is not for long. Let us rejoice and believe and give thanks."

"Eat an egg."

Bill gestured with the drumstick in one hand and the bottle of wine in the other. "Let us rejoice in our blessings. Let us utilize the fowls of the air. Let us utilize the product of the vine. Will you utilize a little, brother?"

"After you, brother."

Bill took a long drink. "Utilize a little, brother," he handed Jack the bottle. "Let us not doubt, brother. Let us not pry into the holy mysteries of the hen-coop with simian fingers. Let us accept on faith and simply say—I want you to join me in saying—what shall they say, brother?" He pointed the drumstick at Jack and continued. "Let me tell you. They will say, and I, for one, am proud to say—and I want you to say with me, on your knees, brother. Let no man be ashamed to kneel here in the great out-of-doors. Remember, the woods were God's first temples. Let us kneel and say: 'Don't eat that, lady—that's Mencken.'"

"Here," Jack said. "Utilize a little of this."

They uncorked the other bottle. "What's the matter?" Jack said. "Didn't you like Bryan?"

"I loved Bryan," said Bill. "We were like brothers."

"Where did you know him?"

"He and Mencken and I all went to Holy Cross together."

"And Frankie Frisch."

"It's a lie. Frankie Frisch went to Fordham."

"Well," Jack said, "I went to Loyola with Bishop Manning."

"It's a lie," Bill said. "I went to Loyola with Bishop Manning myself."

"You're cockeyed," Jack said.

"On wine?"

"Why not?"

"It's the humidity," Bill said. "They ought to take this damn humidity away."

"Have another shot."

"Is this all we've got?"

"Only the two bottles."

"Do you know what you are?" Bill looked at the bottle affectionately.

"No," Jack said.

"You're in the pay of the Anti-Saloon League."

"I went to Notre Dame with Wayne B. Wheeler."

"It's a lie," said Bill. "I went to Austin Business College with Wayne B. Wheeler. He was class president."

"Well," Jack said, "the saloon must go."

"You're right there, old classmate," Bill said. "The saloon must go, and I will take it with me."

"You're cockeyed."

"On wine?"

"On wine."

"Well, maybe I am."

"Want to take a nap?"

"All right."

They lay with their heads in the shade, Jack's hand unconsciously resting near the mirror in his satchel, as they looked up into the trees.

"You asleep?"

"No," Bill said. "I was thinking."

Jack shut his eyes, his fingers brushing the edge of the mirror in his satchel. It was good lying on the ground, yet the world buzzed and hummed around him. He tried to steer his thoughts away from the mirror's dark history—a silent sentinel of his eternal youth and unfulfilled desires—but Bill's presence pulled him back.

"Say," Bill said, "what about this Brett business?"

"What about it?"

"Were you ever in love with her?"

"Sure."

"For how long?"

"Off and on for a hell of a long time."

"Oh, hell!" Bill's eyes held a distant, feverish glint as he spoke. "I'm sorry, fella," he murmured, his voice carrying an undercurrent that reminded Jack of Budapest.

"It's all right," Jack said. "I don't give a damn anymore."

"Really?"

"Really. Only I'd a hell of a lot rather not talk about it."

"You aren't sore I asked you?"

"Why should I be?"

"I'm going to sleep," Bill said, covering his face with a newspaper. "Technically."

"What does that mean?"

"I don't know."

"All right, I'll try," Bill said, his voice strangely heavy.

Jack drifted into fitful sleep, but something unseen pressed down on him. When he awoke, the world had shifted. Shadows stretched as though alive, whispering secrets in the fading light. Bill was packing the rucksack with precise, ritualistic movements. The low sun cast long, dark shadows from the trees, turning the world into a web of unease.

"You're up?" Bill sounded disappointed, as though Jack had interrupted something. "You could've stayed with Morpheus a little longer." His eyes gleamed with something unreadable.

"I dreamt," Bill said, his voice distant, echoing with the weight of unseen worlds. "A dream of significance, now just a fading shadow. It was... necessary, though its purpose eludes me."

"I didn't dream," Jack whispered, a fleeting sense of relief crossing his face.

Bill's gaze sharpened. "Dreams are more than you think, Jack. They're where destinies meet. Ford, Coolidge, Rockefeller— they weren't just men. They saw the bigger picture, part of a hidden narrative." His words hinted at a world beyond their own, some secret order guiding unseen threads.

Jack packed the fishing rods, aware of Bill's gaze. The rucksack, meticulously packed, felt like part of something larger, some unknown design.

"Well," Bill finally said, "do we have everything?"

"The worms," Jack said, shivering despite the warm breeze.

Bill's hands hovered as he dropped the worm cans into the rucksack. "Ah, yes, the worms." They squirmed inside, too much like rats. Jack heard it again—the gnawing, relentless scraping through walls—the sound of endless feeding—the taste of fear tracing a line down his neck. His mother's voice flickered in his memory, but he forced it down, jaw tight with revulsion.

"Everything now?" Jack's voice was strained, heavy with unspoken fears.

Bill met Jack's gaze. "Yes, we have everything. Let's go."

As they ventured into the woods, the air shifted, growing thicker. Tension seemed to rise from the ground itself. The darkness, once familiar, closed in, alive and watching. The lights of Burguete faded to distant specks, swallowed by the encroaching night.

With each step, the woods transformed, the familiar path becoming a corridor to an older, wilder world. Jack's senses, attuned to a primal urgency, detected an eerie watchfulness. The rustle of leaves and crack of twigs weren't just night sounds anymore—they were the breaths of unseen watchers, hidden in the gloom, observing with ancient eyes.

The embrace of the forest tightened. Jack's heart pounded out a relentless rhythm, a primal drumbeat warning of unseen horrors lurking just beyond the veil of shadows. The comforting glow of Burguete, now lost to the abyss, was replaced by the suffocating presence of the night, alive and watchful, waiting to reveal its hidden truths.

Beside Jack, Bill's form wavered, his murmurs weaving a disturbing melody into the fabric of the night. Jack's gaze, drawn irresistibly to Bill, captured a terrifying transformation: his eyes, once familiar, now abyssal voids reflecting an alien reality.

"Shub-Niggurath, I invoke thee! Ygnaiih, ygnaiih, thflthkh'ngha! The Black Goat with a Thousand Young, your servant calls! Y'hah, y'hah, Shub-Niggurath! Iä! Iä! Y'ai 'ng'ngah, Yog-Sothoth h'ee—L'geb f'ai throdog! Uaah!"

Bill's voice cut through the darkness, a discordant mix of tones that sliced the stillness like a knife. His arms rose toward the black sky, and the sound that followed wasn't a scream but something worse—a call, raw and primal, reaching for gods older than memory. Jack stood frozen, the bitter taste of fear thick on his tongue. Cold sweat traced his spine, a silent warning—they had crossed into a place where human understanding held no power.

Out of the suffocating dark, grotesque shapes emerged, writhing beneath the distant stars. Their towering forms, tangled with undulating tendrils, moved with a fluid grace that mocked their size. They circled Jack and Bill, silent sentinels of madness older than the sky itself.

"Bill, run!" Jack's voice broke the stillness, a plea swallowed by the night. Bill didn't move, his chant deepening, pulling the forest's ancient rhythm into his chest.

Jack stumbled, his breath catching as something cold and slick coiled around his ankle. A thick tentacle snaked through the grass, tightening its grip. Without thinking, Jack pulled the pocket knife from his belt, slashing at the appendage. The blade cut deep, splitting the thing open. Black fluid oozed from the wound, and for a heartbeat, Jack thought he had won.

But the severed limb twitched, pulsed, and grew. It doubled, then tripled, thickening as it climbed up his leg. Jack's pulse hammered in his ears as he hacked again, only to watch in horror as the pieces multiplied, growing stronger with each desperate cut. The grass writhed beneath him, alive with the ever-spawning mass of limbs.

A cold, creeping dread spread through him. He wasn't cutting them down—they were feeding, growing with every slice. The more he struggled, the more they multiplied, a sea of flesh and shadow consuming him inch by inch.

Jack's hand shook as he slashed again, but it was useless. The knife might as well have been cutting air. He could feel them now, whispers crawling through his mind, speaking a language no human should hear. His heart raced, every beat pushing him closer to the edge of something vast and unknowable, something that laughed at his efforts.

The tentacles tightened, wrapping him in their cold, pulsing grip. The weight of their ancient purpose pressed down on him, too immense to comprehend. The last thing he heard before the dark swallowed him was Bill's voice, rising in an eerie chant, calling out to gods that had long forgotten the world.

From the heart of this nightmare, Bill emerged—yet not Bill. A being, transmuted, half-lost to the darkness he invoked. With an authority that stilled the air, he commanded the retreat of the grotesque entities. In his hand, a chalice glowed with eldritch light, its contents deeper than night.

"Drink," the entity urged, its voice a dissonant harmony of Bill and otherness, an avatar of an immortal god now in control. With resigned dread, Jack obeyed. The darkness welcomed him like an old friend, swallowing his consciousness whole. The last thing he heard was a whisper, barely audible above the wind, slithering into his ear—a voice not heard but felt, emanating from the dark mirror in his satchel. It spoke a single word: "Deeper."

Jack's scream tore through the quiet inn. Bill, calm and serene, assured him it was just a fevered dream. But as Jack lay there, the weight of an unseen truth pressed down—a certainty that the woods, the mirror, and the night had witnessed something far more terrifying than any dream.

Jack spent the day resting, the weight of the previous night pressing like a burden. His mind refused solace in the daylight's clarity. Instead, paranoia gnawed at him—the haunting suspicion that what happened in the woods had been real.

Seeking distraction, Jack descended to the inn's dining hall for a meal and drinks. Bill, unaffected by the night's ordeal, was his old jovial self. Yet Jack couldn't shake the shadow at the edge of his perception—the darkness still clinging, waiting.

The days at Burguete unfolded in a surreal haze. Crisp nights contrasted with sweltering days, but even the refreshing breeze couldn't disperse Jack's unease. The sun's warmth, once comforting, now felt distant, a mere illusion of comfort.

Evenings brought Howard, the affable American from Providence, whose presence brought some normalcy. Together, they fished the Irati River—a routine that would have been peaceful if not for Jack's lingering tension, the silent anticipation of unseen forces lurking beyond the veil of reality.

Days passed with no word from Ro'brt Ctholh'en, Brett, or Mike. Their silence deepened the mystery. Jack found himself returning to the cursed mirror in his satchel. It hummed with a vibration, pulsing with the heartbeat of some otherworldly entity. A faint whisper, like distant locomotion, grew nearer with each passing day.

219

CHAPTER 13

DEBTS OF THE DAMNED

ONE MORNING, JACK WENT DOWN to breakfast. The American, Howard, was already at the table, spectacles perched on his nose as he scanned the newspaper. He looked up with bleary, bloodshot eyes and smiled.

"Salutations," he slurred. "A most curious missive for your attention. It arrived with mine at the postal establishment—clearly misdirected, yet... fateful, perhaps." When they only glared at him, he shrugged and said, "I got this letter by mistake."

A letter rested at Howard's place on the table, leaning against a coffee cup. Howard returned to his paper, ignoring the letter's presence. Jack opened it. It had been forwarded from Pamplona and was postmarked San Sebastián on a Sunday:

DEAR JACK,

We got here Friday. Brett passed out on the train, so brought her here for three days' rest with old friends of ours. We go to Montoya Hotel Pamplona Tuesday, arriving at I don't know what hour. Will you send a note by the bus to tell you what to do to rejoin you all on Wednesday. All our love and sorry to be late, but Brett was really done in and will be quite all right by Tues. and is practically so now. I know her so well and try to look after her, but it's not so easy. Love to all the chaps,

MICHAEL.

"What day of the week is it?" Jack asked Howard.

"It seems to be Wednesday. There's a peculiar charm in how the days become so elusive, almost ethereal, in the high mountain air."

"Yes. We've been here nearly a week."

"I sincerely hope you're not thinking of leaving?"

"Yes. We'll go on the afternoon bus, I'm afraid."

"What a deplorable turn of events. I had envisioned us traversing the mysterious waters of the *Irati* together. I don't imagine I could handle going there alone."

"We have to go into Pamplona. We're meeting people there."

"What abysmal luck. Our time here at *Burguete* has been like a fleeting dream."

"Come on into Pamplona. We can play bridge there, and there's a fine fiesta."

"The invitation tempts my spirit greatly. It is kind of you to offer. I'd best stay here, though. I haven't much more time to fish."

"You want those big ones in the *Irati*."

"I do, you know. The trout there are prodigious and unfathomable."

"I'd like to try them once more."

"Extend your stay one day more. Do this kindness, good fellow."

"Do you always speak with such pompous self-importance?" Bill asked with a chuckle, and Howard blushed.

"We really have to get into town," Jack said.

"What a pity," Howard replied.

After breakfast, Bill and Jack sat in the sun on a bench in front of the inn, discussing their plans. A girl approached from the center of town, pulling a telegram from her leather wallet.

"Por ustedes?"

Jack looked at it. The address was: "Schitt, Burguete."

"Yes. It's for us."

She brought out a book for Jack to sign, and he handed her a couple of coppers. The telegram was in Spanish: "Vengo *Jueves* Ctholh'en."

Jack handed it to Bill.

"What does the word *Ctholh'en* mean?" he asked.

"What a lousy telegram!" Jack exclaimed. "He could send ten words for the same price. 'I come Thursday.' That gives you a lot of dope, doesn't it?"

"It gives you all the dope that's of interest to *Ctholh'en*."

"We're going in, anyway," Jack said. "There's no use trying to move Brett and Mike out here before the fiesta. Should we answer it?"

Jack's words seemed to drift past Bill, who tilted his head, listening intently to the silent room. "Not now," he whispered, a cryptic smile directed at an empty space beside him.

"Bill?" Jack waited for a sign he was pulling their leg. "Bill?" he repeated stubbornly. "For God's sake, Bill!"

"We might as well," Bill finally said, looking sore. "There's no need for us to be snooty."

Jack whistled a mournful tune as they walked up to the post office and asked for a telegraph blank.

"What will we say?" Bill asked.

"Arriving tonight. That's enough."

They paid for the message and walked back to the inn. Howard was there, and the three of them walked up to *Roncesvalles*. They went through the monastery.

"It's a remarkable place," Howard said when they came out. "But you know I'm not much into those sorts of places."

"Me either," Bill replied.

"It's a remarkable place, though," Howard repeated. "I wouldn't have seen it. I'd been intending to come up each day."

"It isn't the same as fishing, though, is it?" Bill asked, pausing as if he heard a reply from the shadows. He stared intently into the darkness for a long moment.

"I say not."

They stood in front of the old chapel of the monastery. Bill kept his gaze trained on the horizon.

"Isn't that a pub across the way?" Howard asked. "Or do my eyes deceive me?"

"It has the look of a pub," Bill replied.

"It looks like a pub to me," Jack agreed.

"I say," said Howard, "let's utilize it." He had adopted 'utilize' from Bill.

They each had a bottle of wine. Howard wouldn't let them pay. He spoke Spanish well, and the innkeeper accepted his gestures instead.

"Really, it means a lot, having you all here. It's been a great comfort to me, more than you might realize."

"We've had a grand time, Howard."

Howard was a little tight, and it mixed with his sedatives to make him fluttery.

"I say... Really, you've no idea the difference it makes. Since arriving, fun's been scarce. I've been chasing inspiration, but in its absence, your company... it's a welcome diversion."

"We'll fish together again sometime. Don't you forget it, Howard."

"We must. We have had such a jolly good time."

"How about another bottle around?"

"Good idea," said Howard.

"This is mine," Bill declared. "Or we don't drink it."

"I wish you'd let me pay for it. It does give me pleasure, you know."

"This is going to give me pleasure," Bill insisted.

The innkeeper brought in the fourth bottle. They kept their glasses the same. Howard lifted his glass.

"I say. You know this does utilize well."

Bill slapped him on the back. "Good old Howard."

"I say. You know my name isn't really Howard. It's Howard Philips Lovecraft. All one name."

"Good old H.P. Lovecraft," Bill said. "We call you Howard because we're so fond of you."

"I say, Schitt. You don't know what this all means to me."

"Come on and utilize another glass," Jack urged.

"Schitt. Really, Schitt. Schitt, man, you can't know. That's all."

"Drink up, Howard."

Jack and Bill walked back down the road from *Roncesvalles* with Howard between them.

They had lunch at the inn, and Howard walked them to the bus. He gave them his card, with his address in America and his club and his business address, and as they got on the bus, he handed them each an envelope. Jack opened his, finding a dozen flies inside. Howard had tied them himself. He tied all his own flies.

"I say, Howard —" Jack began.

"No, no!" Howard interrupted, climbing down from the bus. "They're not first-rate flies at all. I only thought if you fished them some time, it might remind you of what a good time we had."

As the bus rumbled to life, Howard stood, a solitary figure against the backdrop of the old post office, his silhouette tinged with a cyclopean sense of desolation as he waved them towards their inevitable fate. As they started along the road, he turned and walked back toward the inn.

"Say, wasn't that Howard nice?" Bill commented.

"I think he really did have a good time. Not a bad chap."

"I wish he'd come into Pamplona."

"He wanted to fish. No luck with his writing, he claimed."

"Perhaps a lack of inspiration—he didn't seem well traveled."

"I suppose not."

They arrived in Pamplona late in the afternoon, and the bus stopped in front of the *Hotel Montoya*. In the plaza, they stringed electric light wires to illuminate the area for the fiesta. A few kids approached as the bus stopped, and a customs officer made all passengers open their bundles on the sidewalk. They entered the hotel, and on the stairs, Jack met Montoya. He shook hands with them, smiling in his embarrassed way.

"Your friends are here," he said.

"Mr. Mike Hawk?"

"Yes. Mr. Ctholh'en and Mr. Hawk and Lady Ashley."

He smiled as though there were something Jack would hear about.

"When did they get in?"

"Yesterday. I've saved you the rooms you had."

"That's fine. Did you give Mr. Hawk the room on the plaza?"

"Yes. All the rooms we looked at."

"Where are our friends now?"

"I think they went to the pelota," Bill whispered to Montoya.

Montoya smiled. "Tonight," he said. "Tonight at seven o'clock, they bring in the Villar bulls, and tomorrow come the Miuras. Do you all go down?"

"Oh, yes. They've never seen a *desencajonada*."

Montoya placed his hand on Jack's shoulder. "I'll see you there."

He smiled again, as though bullfighting was a very special secret between them—a shocking but deeply understood bond. It would not do to expose it to those who wouldn't comprehend.

"Your friend, is he aficionado, too?" Montoya smiled at Bill.

"Yes. He came all the way from New York to see the *San Fermines*."

"Yes?" Montoya politely disbelieved. "But he's not aficionado like you."

He placed his hand on Jack's shoulder again, embarrassedly.

"Yes," Jack said. "He's a real aficionado."

"But he's not aficionado like you are."

"*Afcion* means passion. An aficionado is one who is passionate about the bullfights. All the good bullfighters stayed at Montoya's hotel; those with *aficion* stayed there. The commercial bullfighters perhaps stayed once and then did not return. The good ones came each year."

In Montoya's room were their photographs. The photographs were dedicated to Juanito Montoya or his sister. The photographs of bullfighters Montoya had truly believed in were framed. Photographs of bullfighters without *aficion* Montoya kept in a drawer of his desk. They often had the most flattering inscriptions but did not mean anything. One day, Montoya took them all out and dropped them in the waste basket. He did not want them around.

They often discussed bulls and bullfighters. Jack had frequented Montoya's for several years, enjoying brief exchanges that revealed their shared passion for the sport. Men would come in from distant towns and, before they left Pamplona, stop and talk for a few minutes with Montoya about bulls. These men were aficionados. Those who were aficionados could always get rooms even when the hotel was full. Montoya introduced Jack to some of them. They were always very polite at first, and it amused them that Jack was an American. Somehow, it was taken for granted that an American could not have *aficion*. He might simulate it or confuse it with excitement, but he could not really have it. When they saw that Jack had *aficion*, and there was no password, no set questions that could bring it out—rather it was a sort of oral spiritual examination with questions always a little defensive and never apparent—there was this same embarrassed putting the hand on the shoulder, or a *"Buen hombre."* But nearly always, there was the actual touching. It seemed as though they wanted to touch you to make it certain.

Montoya could forgive anything of a bullfighter who had *aficion*. He could forgive attacks of nerves, panic, bad, unexplainable actions, all sorts of lapses. For one who had *aficion*, he could forgive anything. At once, he forgave Jack and all his friends. Without his ever saying anything, they were simply a little something shameful between us, like the spilling open of the horses in bullfighting.

Bill had gone upstairs as they came in, and Jack found him washing and changing in his room.

"Well," he said, "talk a lot of Spanish?"

"He was telling me about the bulls coming in tonight."

"Let's find the gang and go down."

"All right. They'll probably be at the café."

"Have you got tickets?"

"Yes. I got them for all the unloadings."

"What's it like?" Bill pulled his cheek before the glass, checking for unshaved patches under his jawline.

"It's pretty good," Jack said. "They let the bulls out of the cages one at a time, and they have steers in the corral to receive them and keep them from fighting, and the bulls tear in at the steers, and the steers run around like old maids trying to quiet them down."

"Do they ever gore the steers?"

"Sure. Sometimes, they go right after them and kill them."

"Can't the steers do anything?"

"No. They're trying to make friends."

"What do they have them in for?"

"To quiet down the bulls and keep them from breaking horns against the stone walls or goring each other."

"Must be swell being a steer."

They went down the stairs and out the door, walking across the square toward *Café Iruña*. Two lonely-looking ticket houses stood in the square. Their windows, marked *SOL, SOL Y SOMBRA*, and *SOMBRA*, were shut. They would not open until the day before the fiesta.

Across the square, white wicker tables and chairs from *Iruña* spread out, creeping toward the street's edge. Jack's gaze wandered over them, eventually resting on Brett, Mike, and Ro'brt Ctholh'en. Vibrant yet oddly pale beneath her Basque beret, Brett had Mike in a matching one beside her. Ro'brt Ctholh'en, bare-headed, his black dome gleaming faintly, was harder to read behind those spectacles, which reflected more than they revealed. Brett's eyes lit up as they approached.

"Hello, you chaps!" she greeted, joy evident.

Her spirit seemed lifted. Mike greeted with his usual intense handshake, while Ro'brt Ctholh'en's was more reserved. Under the table, there was a subtle shift. But the moment passed, buried under pleasantries and the afternoon sun.

"Where the hell have you been?" Jack asked.

"I brought them up here," Ctholh'en replied.

"What rot," Brett retorted. "We'd have gotten here earlier if you hadn't come."

"You'd never have gotten here."

"What rot! Your chaps are brown. Look at Bill. Look at Jack, I swear, darling, you look younger. You look as young as the day I met you, while the rest of us..."

Jack smiled tightly, reaching one comforting hand into his satchel, while the mirror hummed faintly with a promise unrequited.

"Did you get good fishing?" Mike asked. "We wanted to join you."

"It wasn't bad. We missed you."

"I wanted to come," Ctholh'en said, "but I thought I ought to bring them."

"You bring us," Brett snorted. "What rot."

"Was it really good?" Mike asked. "Did you take many?"

"Some days, we took a dozen apiece. There was an American up there."

"Named Howard," Bill said. "Ever know him, Mike? He said he was in the war, too."

"You don't listen well for a writer, Bill," Jack said with a grin. "He enlisted but his mother prevented him from serving. Over protective."

"Fortunate fellow," Mike said. "What times we had. How I wish those dear days were back."

"Don't be an ass."

"Were you in the war, Mike?" Ctholh'en asked.

"Was I not."

"He was a very distinguished soldier," Brett said. "Tell them about the time your horse bolted down Piccadilly."

"I'll not. I've told that four times."

"You never told me," Ro'brt Ctholh'en said.

"I'll not tell that story. It reflects discredit on me."

"Tell them about your medals."

"I'll not. That story reflects great discredit on me."

"What story's that?"

"Brett will tell you. She tells all the stories that reflect discredit on me."

"Go on. Tell it, Brett."

"Should I?"

"I'll tell it myself."

"What medals have you got, Mike?"

"I haven't got any medals."

"You must have some."

"I suppose I've the usual medals. But I never sent in for them. Once, there was this big dinner, and the Prince of Wales was to be there, and the cards said medals would be worn. So naturally, I had no medals, and I stopped at his tailor's, and he was impressed by the invitation. I said to him: 'You've got to fix me up with some medals.' He said: 'What medals, sir?' And I said: 'Oh, any medals. Just give me a few medals.' So he said: 'What medals have you, sir?' And I said: 'How should I know?' Did he think I spent all my time reading the gazette? 'Just give me a good lot. Pick them out yourself.' So he got me some medals, miniature medals, and handed me the box, and I put it in my pocket and forgot it. Well, I went to the dinner, and it was the night they'd shot Henry Wilson, so the Prince didn't come and the King didn't come, and no one wore any medals, and all these guys were busy taking off their medals, and I had mine in my pocket."

He paused for them to laugh.

"Is that all?"

"That's all. Perhaps I didn't tell it right."

"You didn't," Brett said. "But no matter."

They were all laughing.

"Ah, yes," said Mike. "I know now. It was a dull dinner, and I couldn't stick it, so I left. Later on in the evening, I found the box in my pocket. What's this? I said. Medals? Bloody military medals? So I cut them off their backing—and gave them all around. Gave one to each girl. Form of souvenir. They thought I was hell's own shakes of a soldier. Give away medals in a nightclub. Dashing fellow."

"Tell the rest," Brett said.

"Don't you think that was funny?" Mike asked. They were all laughing. "It was. I swear it was. At any rate, my tailor wrote me and wanted the medals back. Sent a man around. Kept on writing for months. Seems some chap had left them to be cleaned. Frightfully military guy. Set hell's own store by them." Mike paused. "Rotten luck for the tailor," he said.

"You don't mean it," Bill said. "I should think it would have been grand for the tailor."

"Frightfully good tailor. Never believe it to see me now," Mike said. "I used to pay him a hundred pounds a year just to keep him quiet. So he wouldn't send me any bills. Frightful blow to him when I went bankrupt. It was right after the medals. Gave his letters rather a bitter tone."

"How did you go bankrupt?" Bill asked.

"Two ways," Mike said. "Gradually and then suddenly."

"What brought it on?"

"Friends," said Mike. "I had a lot of friends. False friends. Then I had creditors, too. Probably had more creditors than anybody in England."

"Tell them about in the court," Brett said.

"I don't remember," Mike said. "I was just a little tight."

"Tight!" Brett exclaimed. "You were blind!"

"Extraordinary thing," Mike said. "Met my former partner the other day. Offered to buy me a drink."

"Tell them about your learned counsel," Brett said.

"I will not," Mike said. "My learned counsel was blind, too. I say this is a gloomy subject. Are they going down and see these bulls unloaded or not?"

"Let's go down."

They called the waiter, paid, and started to walk through the town. Jack walked with Brett, but Ro'brt Ctholh'en joined her on the other side. The three of them walked along, past the *Ayuntamiento* with banners hung from the balcony, down past the market, and down the steep street that led to the bridge across the *Arga*. Many people walked to see the bulls, and carriages drove down the hill and across the bridge, drivers, horses, and whips rising above the walking crowd. Across the bridge, they turned up a road to the corrals. They passed a wine shop with a sign in the window: *Good Wine 30 Centimes A Liter.*

"That's where we'll go when funds get low," Brett said.

The woman by the wine shop's entrance gave them a long, measured look as they strolled by. A hushed exchange occurred, and three girls rushed to the window, their eyes immediately finding Brett. Something in their stares—a shadow of unease or perhaps foreboding—unsettled Jack, though he couldn't say why.

At the gate of the corrals, two men took tickets from those entering. They walked through the gate. Trees lined the area and a low, stone house stood nearby. At the far end was the stone wall of the corrals, with apertures like loopholes running along each side. A ladder led up to the top of the wall, and people climbed up, spreading down to stand on the walls separating the two corrals. As they ascended, walking across the grass under the trees, they passed the big, gray-painted cages with the bulls inside. Each cage bore the name and brand of the bull-breeder.

They climbed up and found a place on the wall overlooking the corral. The stone walls were whitewashed, with straw on the ground and wooden feed-boxes and water troughs against them.

"Look up there," Jack said.

Beyond the river rose the plateau of the town. Along the old walls and ramparts, people stood in three black lines. Above the walls, heads peeked from windows of houses. At the plateau's far end, boys had climbed into the trees.

"They must think something is going to happen," Brett said.

"They want to see the bulls."

Mike and Bill were on the other wall across the corral pit. They waved. People who arrived late pressed against them as others crowded around.

"Why don't they start?" Ro'brt Ctholh'en asked.

A single mule hitched to one of the cages was dragged up against the corral wall with crowbars. Men pushed and lifted it into position against the gate. At the other end of the corral, a gate opened, and two steers came in, swaying their heads and trotting, their lean flanks swinging. They stood together at the far end, heads toward the gate where the bull would enter.

"They don't look happy," Brett observed.

Men on the wall pulled up the corral gate, then the cage gate. Jack leaned over the wall, trying to see into the cage. It was dark. Someone rapped on the cage with an iron bar. Inside, something seemed to explode. The bull struck the wood side to side with his horns, making a great noise. For a moment, smoke or fire might've erupted from the dog-faced monstrosity's nostrils—a fleeting vision of tentacles, scales, and unyielding eyes from his dream clouded Jack's mind. Brett's pale, naked flesh on a stone altar under him flashed back, and he jerked his head violently. With a clattering on the wood in the hollow box, the bull charged and emerged into the corral, skidding with his forefeet in the straw as he stopped. His head up, the great hump of muscle on his neck swollen tight, his body quivering as he looked up at the crowd on the stone walls. The two steers backed away against the wall, heads sunken, eyes watching the bull.

The bull saw them and charged. A man shouted from behind one of the boxes and slapped his hat against the planks, and the bull, before reaching the steer, turned, gathered himself, and charged where the man had been, trying to reach him behind the planks with a half-dozen quick, searching drives with the right horn.

"My God, isn't he beautiful?" Brett's voice sounded underwater, distant and dreamy. Jack stuck his thumb in his ear and shook his head. They were looking right down on him.

"Look how he knows how to use his horns," Jack said, attempting to find his *aficion*. "He's got a left and a right, just like a boxer."

"Not really?"

"You watch."

"It goes too fast."

"Wait. There'll be another one in a minute."

They had backed up another cage into the entrance. In the far corner, a man, from behind one of the plank shelters, attracted the bull's attention, and while the bull faced away, the gate was pulled up, and a second bull came out into the corral.

He charged straight for the steers, and two men ran out from behind the planks, shouting to divert him. The bull remained unwavering in his course, and the shouts grew more desperate: "Hah! Hah! Toro!" The two steers braced, turning sideways, but the bull crashed into one with force.

"Don't look," Jack murmured to Brett, who gazed on in wonder.

"Fine," Jack said, the scene unfolding dangerously fresh. "If it doesn't buck you."

"I saw it," she whispered. "I saw him shift from his left to his right horn."

"Damn good," Jack replied, though a shadow loomed over them.

The steer's neck was bloodied and stretched, his head twisted grotesquely as he lay where he had fallen. Suddenly, the bull left off and made for the other steer, who stood at the far end, head swinging, watching it all. The steer ran awkwardly, and the bull caught him, hooking him lightly in the flank, then turned away and looked up at the crowd on the walls, his crest of muscle rising. The steer approached him, made as though to nose at him, and the bull hooked perfunctorily. The next time, he nosed at the steer, and then the two trotted over to the other bull.

When the next bull came out, all three—the two bulls and the steer—stood together, heads side by side, horns against the newcomer. In a few minutes, the steer picked the new bull up, quieted him down, and made him one of the herd. When the last two bulls had been unloaded, the herd was all together.

The gored steer leaned against the wall, bleeding. Bulls kept their distance. Jack's memory cast out to the suit in the Seine. *Plum* and a muddy bloody mess. What had been in his wine?

They climbed down from the wall with the crowd and had a last look at the bulls through the loopholes in the corral wall. They were all quiet now, heads down. They got a carriage outside and rode up to the café. Mike and Bill came in half an hour later. They had stopped on the way for several drinks.

"That's an extraordinary business," Brett said, sitting in the café.

"Will those last ones fight as well as the first?" Ro'brt Ctholh'en asked. "They seemed to quiet down awfully fast."

"They all know each other," Jack said. "They're only dangerous when they're alone, or only two or three of them together."

"What do you mean, dangerous?" Bill said. "They all looked dangerous to me."

"They only want to kill when they're alone. Of course, if you went in there, you'd probably detach one of them from the herd, and he'd be dangerous."

"That's too complicated," Bill said. "Don't you ever detach me from the herd, Mike."

"I say," Mike Hawk said, "they were fine bulls, weren't they? Did you see their horns?"

"Did I not," Brett said. "I had no idea what they were like."

"Did you see the one hit that steer?" Mike asked. "That was extraordinary."

"It's no life being a steer," Ro'brt Ctholh'en said.

"Don't you think so?" Mike said. "I would have thought you'd loved being a steer, Ro'brt."

"What do you mean, Mike?"

"They lead such a quiet life. They never say anything, and they're always hanging about so."

They were embarrassed. Bill laughed. Ro'brt Ctholh'en was angry. Mike continued talking.

"I should think you'd love it. You'd never have to say a word. Come on, Ro'brt. Do say something. Don't just sit there."

"I said something, Mike. Don't you remember? About the steers." Ro'brt's wide eyes glanced at Jack and back to Mike Hawk as if he were a shark circling a terrified marlin.

"Oh, say something more. Say something funny. Can't you see we're all having a good time here?"

"Come off it, Michael. You're drunk," Brett said.

"I'm not drunk. I'm quite serious. Is Ro'brt Ctholh'en going to follow Brett around like a steer all the time?"

"Shut up, Michael. Try and show a little breeding."

"Breeding be damned. Who has any breeding, anyway, except the bulls? Aren't the bulls lovely? Don't you like them, Bill? Why don't you say something, Ro'brt? Don't sit there looking like a bloody funeral. What if Brett did sleep with you? She's slept with lots of better people than you."

"Shut up," Ctholh'en said. He stood up. "Shut up, Mike."

"Oh, don't stand up and act as though you were going to hit me. That won't make any difference to me. Tell me, Ro'brt.

Why do you follow Brett around like a poor bloody steer? Don't you know you're not wanted? I know when I'm not wanted. Why don't you know when you're not wanted? You came down to San Sebastián, where you weren't wanted, and followed Brett around like a bloody steer. Do you think that's right?"

"Shut up. You're drunk."

"Perhaps I am drunk. Why aren't you drunk? Why don't you ever get drunk, Ro'brt? You know you didn't have a good time at San Sebastián because none of our friends would invite you to any of the parties. You can't blame them hardly. Can you? I asked them to. They wouldn't do it. You can't blame them now. Can you? Now, answer me. Can you blame them?"

"Go to hell, Mike."

"I can't blame them. Can you blame them? Why do you follow Brett around? Haven't you any manners? How do you think it makes me feel?"

"You're a splendid one to talk about manners," Brett said. "You've such lovely manners."

"Come on, Ro'brt," Bill said.

"What do you follow her around for?"

Bill stood up and took hold of Ctholh'en.

"Don't go," Mike said. "Ro'brt Ctholh'en's going to buy a drink."

Bill went off with Ctholh'en. Ctholh'en's face was sallow. Mike continued talking. Jack sat and listened for a while. Brett looked disgusted.

"I say, Michael, you might not be such a bloody ass," she interrupted.

"I'm not saying he's not right, you know."

She turned to Jack.

The emotion left Mike's voice. They were all friends together.

"I'm not so damn drunk as I sounded," he said.

"I know you're not," Brett said.

"We're none of us sober," Jack said.

"I didn't say anything I didn't mean."

"But you put it so badly," Brett laughed.

"He was an ass, though. He came down to San Sebastián, where he damn well wasn't wanted. He hung around Brett and just looked at her the way he does. It made me damned well sick."

"He did behave very badly," Brett said.

"Mark you. Brett's had affairs with men before. She tells me all about everything. She gave me this chap Ctholh'en's letters to read. I wouldn't read them."

"Damned noble of you."

"No, listen, Jack. Brett's gone off with men. But they weren't ever so... *Arkhamian*, and they didn't come and hang about afterward."

"Damned good chaps," Brett said. "It's all rot to talk about it. Michael and I understand each other."

"She gave me Ro'brt Ctholh'en's letters. I wouldn't read them."

"You wouldn't read any letters, darling. You wouldn't read mine."

"I can't read letters," Mike said. "Funny, isn't it?"

"You can't read anything."

"No. You're wrong there. I read quite a bit. I read when I'm at home."

"You'll be writing next," Brett said. "Come on, Michael. Do buck up. You've got to go through with this thing now. He's here. Don't spoil the fiesta."

"Well, let him behave, then."

"He'll behave. I'll tell him."

"You tell him, Jack. Tell him either he must behave or get out."

"Yes," Jack said, "it would be nice for me to tell him."

"Look, Brett. Tell Jack what Ro'brt calls you. That is perfect, you know."

"Oh, no. I can't."

"Go on. We're all friends. Aren't we all friends, Jack?"

"I can't tell him. It's too ridiculous."

"I'll tell him."

"You won't, Michael. Don't be an ass."

"He calls her *Circe*," Mike said. "He claims she turns men into swine. Damn good. I wish I were one of these literary chaps."

"He'd be good, you know," Brett said. "He writes a good letter."

"I know," Jack said. "He wrote me from San Sebastián."

"That was nothing," Brett said. "He can write a damned amusing letter."

"Come on," Jack said, "We must go in and eat."

"How should I meet Ctholh'en?" Mike said.

"Just act as though nothing had happened."

"It's quite all right with me," Mike said. "I'm not embarrassed."

"If he says anything, just say you were tight."

"Quite. And the funny thing is I think I was tight."

"Come on," Brett said. "Are these poisonous things paid for? I must bathe before dinner."

They walked across the square. It was dark, and all around the square were the lights from the cafés under the arcades. They walked across the gravel under the trees to the hotel.

They went upstairs, and Jack stopped to speak with Montoya.

"Well, how did you like the bulls?" he asked.

"Good. They were nice bulls."

"They're all right"—Montoya shook his head—"but they're not too good."

"What didn't you like about them?"

"I don't know. They just didn't give me the feeling that they were so good."

"I know what you mean."

"They're all right."

"Yes. They're all right."

"How did your friends like them?"

"Fine."

"Good," Montoya said.

Jack went upstairs. Bill was in his room, standing on the balcony, looking out at the square. Jack stood beside him.

"Where's Ctholh'en?"

"Upstairs in his room."

"How does he feel?"

"Like hell, naturally. Mike was awful. He's terrible when he's tight."

"He wasn't so tight."

"The hell he wasn't. I know what they had before they came to the café."

"He sobered up afterward."

"Good. He was terrible. I don't like Ctholh'en, God knows, and I think it was a silly trick for him to go down to San Sebastián, but nobody has any business to talk like Mike."

"How'd you like the bulls?"

"Grand. It's grand the way they bring them out."

"Tomorrow come the Miuras."

"When does the fiesta start?"

"Day after tomorrow."

"We've got to keep Mike from getting so tight. That kind of stuff is terrible."

"We'd better get cleaned up for supper."

"Yes. That will be a pleasant meal."

"Won't it?"

Supper unfolded, a pleasant meal amid an eerie calm. Brett, pale in a black, sleeveless evening dress, radiated haunting beauty. Jack had to go up and bring Ro'brt Ctholh'en down. He was reserved and formal, his face still taut and sallow, but he cheered up finally. He couldn't stop looking at Brett. It seemed to make him happy. It must have been pleasant for him to see her looking so lovely and know he had been away with her and that everyone knew it. They could not take that away from him. Mike Hawk acted as though nothing had happened. Bill's laughter, dark-edged, and Michael's banter wove tension.

Jack's fingers brushed the cold surface of the mirror, a shiver crawling up his spine. It whispered of borrowed time, of debts not easily paid. Their laughter felt thin, barely hiding the yawning abyss beneath. Each sip of wine blurred reality a little more, replacing unease with fleeting warmth. But the chill of the mirror stayed with him, a cold weight pressing in—a reminder that they were all just dancing on the edge of the inevitable.

CHAPTER 14

THE CALM BEFORE

JACK COULDN'T RECALL THE EXACT moment he settled into bed. The routine was automatic—undressing, slipping on a bathrobe, stepping into the balcony's cool air. Inside, Turgenieff's *A Sportsman's Sketches* beckoned, soothing yet unfamiliar, a balm for the weight in his head. But with closed eyes, a subtle vertigo whispered, shadows stretching and twisting in his fragile mind. He turned to reading. In the haunting quiet, the mirror in his satchel hummed beside the bed, emitting an unsettling tune from unknown depths.

After a fleeting moment, Jack heard Brett and Ro'brt Ctholh'en on the stairs. Ctholh'en's peculiar goodnight lingered, charged with unspoken warnings, before he ascended into the darkness. Jack swore he heard a faint whine, a whisper from the abyss, then silence. Through paper-thin walls, Brett entered the adjoining room. Mike was already there, their shared laughter a bright contrast to the growing darkness in Jack's thoughts.

Exhaustion draped over Jack. He extinguished the light, seeking slumber's embrace. But closed eyes didn't bring peace, only a magnetic tug towards the satchel. The urge to peer into the mirror's depths was irresistible, a silent call from the void. In his mind's depths, fragments of dark horrors stirred, subtly unsettling. He pushed them away, focusing on the enveloping darkness of the room. The night altered perceptions, didn't it? The absence of light made everything different. It had to.

Jack had once resolved never to sleep without electric light. It was a bright idea then. Women, especially Brett, were like another kind of light—just as blinding. To hell with women, he mused. To hell with Brett Ashley.

Women were great friends, in theory. To be friends with a woman, you first had to love her, or so Jack believed. He had been Brett's friend without considering her perspective. A delayed invoice for affection—the bill always came, a constant in the chaos of relationships.

Jack thought he had paid for everything in life. Unlike women, who paid endlessly, his exchanges were straightforward. You gave something, you got something. Life was about knowing the value of your experiences. But at night, old philosophies haunted him, echoing in the silence, never knowing if the horrors of the night were the soldier's price of admission. That was true too, wasn't it?

In the stillness of night, when inhibitions lowered and the world took on a surreal sheen, Jack's thoughts echoed British sensibilities, musing on language, limitations, and nuances. His nocturnal reflections, while profound, drifted into the whimsical, offering respite from the lurking shadows. Jack shifted again. He wished Mike would not behave so terribly towards Ctholh'en. Mike was a lousy drunk. Brett was a good drunk. Bill was a good drunk. Ctholh'en was never drunk. Mike was unpleasant after a certain point. Jack liked to see him hurt Ctholh'en. He wished he would not do it because afterward, it made him disgusted with himself. That was morality, things that made you disgusted afterward. No, that must be immorality. That was a vast statement.

At night, Jack's mind spun tales of shadowed bilge, each more unsettling than the last. "What rot?" Jack could hear Brett say. "What rot!" When you were with English, you got into the habit of using English expressions in your thinking. The English spoken language—the upper classes, anyway—must have fewer words than Inuit languages. Of course, Jack didn't know anything about the Inuit. Maybe their languages were fine. Say the Cherokee. Jack didn't know anything about the Cherokee, either. The English talked with inflected phrases— one phrase to mean everything. Jack liked them, though. He liked the way they spoke. He liked Canadians, too.

Jack turned on the light once more and immersed himself in Turgenieff's prose. The book, read in his brandy-heightened sensitivity, imprinted on him as if the experiences were his own. These memories, paid for in moments of solitude and reflection, would always be part of him. Some time toward daylight, he went to sleep.

In the following days, Pamplona lay in a quiet lull, its streets brimming with silent anticipation for the Fiesta. Workmen, like specters of the coming revelry, erected gateposts to guide the charging bulls. On the outskirts, vague figures flickered at the edge of Jack's vision, ethereal and elusive, vanishing when directly observed. The bull-ring stood as a dormant colossus on the plateau, its picador horses galloping, their movements strangely rigid against the sun-baked earth. Inside the ring, an open gate led to an amphitheater in preparation. Carpenters mended the battered barrera while old women, bent and wraithlike, swept the stands, their brooms whispering against the ground.

Outside, the fence leading from the last street of the town to the bull-ring was already in place, forming a long pen; the crowd would come running down with the bulls on the morning of the first bullfight. Across the plain, where the horse and cattle fair would be, some gypsies had camped under the trees. Wine and aguardiente sellers were putting up their booths. One booth advertised *ANIS DEL TORO*. The cloth sign hung against the planks in the hot sun. In the big square at the town center, there was no change yet. They sat in white wicker chairs on the café's terrasse, watching motor buses come in and unload peasants from the country entering the market. They watched the buses fill up and start out with peasants carrying saddlebags full of their purchases. The tall gray motor buses were the only life of the square except for pigeons and the man with a hose who sprinkled the graveled square and watered the streets.

In the evening was the paseo. For an hour after dinner, everyone—the good-looking girls, the officers from the garrison, and all the fashionable people of the town—walked along one side of the square while café tables filled with the regular after-dinner crowd.

Jack's days followed a predictable pattern: perusing newspapers, walks with or without Bill, who often wandered off at all hours on his own, and writing sessions. Ro'brt Ctholh'en, ever aloof, immersed himself in Spanish studies or frequented the barber. Brett and Mike, emerging like phantoms past noon, carried the remnants of tumultuous dreams in their eyes. Jack went to church a couple of times, once with Brett. Her smile was tight, her eyes ringed with sleepless nights, but she exuded her usual charm and said she wanted Jack to go to confession. He told her it was impossible and not as interesting as it sounded, and besides, it would be in a language she did not know. They met Ctholh'en as they came out of the church, and although it was obvious he had followed them, he was very pleasant and nice, and all three went for a walk to the gypsy camp.

Their walk culminated in an unsettling encounter with a fortune-teller. As Brett entered the tent, Jack paused outside, muttering that he needed some air. He peeked in but held back, watching the old gypsy woman draw cards for Brett. Her gnarled hands moved with a practiced yet unsteady rhythm, her weathered face deeply lined, like a map of curses and ancient sorrow. Yet, as her piercing gaze darted across the cards, something about her struck Jack deeply—hauntingly familiar. It wasn't her appearance exactly, but a shadow of what might have been. For a moment, Jack imagined her as she once was, long before time and tragedy had taken their toll. She reminded him of the Spanish señorita lost in the village fire during the Civil War, as though this woman might have been her, had she lived to see her beauty consumed by the years.

Suddenly, the gypsy woman shrieked madly, clutching her face in a desperate cry that echoed Jack's darkest visions of hell and the slumbering gods below. She tossed Brett's money back and demanded she leave at once. Ro'brt swiftly escorted her out, and the group left the camp, their discomfort palpable as they sheepishly wandered off to get a drink.

The day before the Fiesta, dawn was pristine, with white clouds drifting over the mountains and the air refreshed by nocturnal rain. Yet beneath the tranquility, Jack sensed a subtle disquiet, a pulse of unease throbbing beneath the surface. The presence of Ctholh'en, a silent anchor in their shifting group dynamics, brought a fleeting sense of equilibrium. On such a day, with the sky a canvas of serenity and the air crisp with the promise of festivities, it seemed impossible to be upset about anything.

That was the last day before the Fiesta.

CHAPTER 15

ALL THE COLORS OF SAN FERMIN

AT NOON ON SUNDAY, JULY 6th, the fiesta burst into life like a vibrant tapestry unfurling. The streets of Pamplona transformed into a kaleidoscope of colors. Vivid banners and streamers adorned balconies, fluttering in the summer breeze. The air was filled with the scents of sizzling *chorizo*, sweet *churros*, and freshly brewed coffee from the food stalls. Laughter, chatter, and the rhythmic beats of traditional music created a lively soundscape, setting the town's heartbeat. Amidst the fiesta's awakening, a familiar stir awakened within Jack. The vibrant colors, sounds, and scents evoked nostalgia and a whisper of hope.

Throughout the morning, people from the countryside flowed into town, blending seamlessly with the locals. Jack watched, fascinated, as the square filled with a vibrant crowd. Farmers in worn hats mingled with city dwellers in bright attire. Children ran through the throngs, their laughter rising above the excited conversations. The town pulsed with shared anticipation, a communal heartbeat waiting to erupt into celebration. The square was as quiet in the hot sun as any other day, with peasants in outlying wine shops preparing for the fiesta. Having recently arrived from the plains and hills, they were careful with their spending, seeking value where their money still held old-world worth.

That morning, the streets echoed with anticipation. Jack could hear jovial songs blending with distant, haunting chants that prickled his skin. San Fermín's day wasn't just for celebration; it had religious roots too. Many attended the eleven o'clock mass in the cathedral, marking the fiesta's religious facet.

Later, descending from the cathedral hill, Jack made his way to the café in the square. Ro'brt Ctholh'en and Bill were already seated. The café's familiar furnishings had been replaced, suggesting wartime austerity. A waiter approached as Jack sat.

"What are you drinking?" Jack asked.

"Sherry," Ctholh'en replied, his gaze distant.

"*Jerez*," Jack confirmed to the waiter.

As they awaited their drinks, a rocket burst into the sky, its smoky trail casting a foreboding shadow over the plaza, now a hive of frenetic energy. The air, once serene, thrummed with an ancient melody carried by a *gaita* and a steady drum, as the square came alive with an age-old dance. Ro'brt's gaze drifted over the revelers—an outsider to the spectacle. Bill's delight was unmistakable. "This is life!" he proclaimed.

As dusk descended, the streets began their nightly transformation. Lamps flickered to life with a hesitant glow, their light faltering as if sharing Jack's growing dread. Amidst this eerie dance of light and shadow, a solitary figure emerged, his silhouette stark against the dimming glow. The reed pipe at his lips sang a melody, drawing children into a dance as ancient as fear itself. Their laughter wove through the air like mist—shifting and unsettling.

Jack shivered as the piper's tune twisted through the night, whispering secrets from a dark, forgotten realm. The piper's pocked face held a knowing smirk, each note dragging Jack closer to the edge of reason.

"He must be the village idiot," Bill muttered, eyes fixed on the piper. "Every town's got one, but there's something wrong about that tune. Look."

Children danced around them, their laughter stretching into hollow moans. Their steps broke free from any earthly rhythm, a warped ritual echoing from the depths of night. The melody thickened, pulling Jack deeper into something ancient and wrong. Around him, the sigil—a spiraled eye—began to spread across walls, tables, faces, its mark staining the night. Jack felt its weight pressing into him, gnawing at his sanity. Faces around him twisted into masks caught between life and death, grinning and grimacing in the dance.

The air thickened with rot, as if the ground exhaled death. Shadows pulsed and closed in, pressing on him with the weight of something unseen, alive. His heartbeat pounded as he squeezed his eyes shut, desperate to escape, but the darkness around him tightened, twisting nightmare and reality into one.

When he opened his eyes, his gaze caught a figure at the edge of the square, half-veiled in shadow. Dressed in tattered yellow robes and crowned with tarnished metal, the figure's hollow eyes glowed faintly, filled with spectral malice. Jack felt his skin crawl as he stared back, feeling something unravel inside him. The figure remained still, watching from beyond.

Everything else faded—the warped laughter, the twisted faces, the sound of the festival's music. The King in Yellow lifted a gloved hand, beckoning slowly. Silence fell, the sounds of the festival dulling to a hum. A single scrap of paper drifted from the King's fingers, catching candlelight as it floated toward Jack. The words seemed etched into his mind: *"The mask slips only for the worthy. Dare you seek what lies beneath?"*

A deep wave of nausea hit him, the stench of decay choking him as shadows swallowed him whole. The laughter and moans distorted into a cacophony, pressing on him, suffocating him. Darkness pulsed, feeding on his terror.

Then—Ro'brt's hand on his shoulder. A solid touch. Jack blinked, the sigils and shadows dissolving, the sickening smell fading into the night air. He was back, standing in the square.

The crowd bustled around them, oblivious, and the King in Yellow had vanished as if he'd never been.

Outside, rockets split the sky as café tables filled and the square emptied.

"Where's Brett and Mike?" Bill repeated.

"I'll fetch them," Ctholh'en offered, sullenly. "Bring them here."

The fiesta had truly begun. Seven days of day and night, the revelry unwound in a dreamlike sequence where every action merged into the festival's tapestry, devoid of real consequence. Outcomes seemed out of place amid such celebration.

Outside the chapel, the crowd gathered. The aroma of incense filled the air. They attempted to enter, but Brett was stopped at the door for not wearing a hat. They walked along a street back to town. With wreaths of white garlic around their necks, dancers encircled Brett and began to dance. Some howled with faces painted like the dead, others hid in shadows or offered grotesque rictus grins. Unsettlingly, they pulled Bill and Jack into the circle, whisking the group into a nearby wine shop.

Inside the dusky wine shop, men sang with powerful voices. A haunting chant echoed faintly. Brett sat on a wine cask while Jack attempted to pay. One man refused the money, placing it back in Jack's pocket.

"I want a leather wine bottle," Bill said.

"There's a place down the street," Jack replied. "I'll get a couple."

ERNEST HEMINGWAY AND JORAH KAI

The dancers seemed reluctant as Jack left. Three were close to Brett, their eyes distant and hypnotic. They taught her to drink from the wineskins and hung a garlic wreath around her neck. Across the room, someone whispered a song to Bill, tapping him rhythmically.

Reassuring them, Jack made his way outside, feeling as if unseen eyes traced his every step. Entering the shop, the air smelled of tanned leather and hot tar. All wineskins were marked for the fiesta with unusual symbols.

Returning to the wine shop, the atmosphere grew denser, joviality veiled by muted anticipation and whispered secrets. Brett and Bill, seated on barrels, were encircled by ritualistic dancers, while Mike delved into conversation and food.

From afar, the procession's music seeped in, occasionally discordant, sending ripples of unease through the attendees.

"Isn't that the procession?" Mike queried.

"Nada," a voice answered, eyes briefly avoiding Mike's. "Just the wind. Drink up. Lift the bottle."

Catching Jack's eye, Mike inquired, "Where did they find you?"

"Someone ushered me here," Jack answered. "They said you were around."

"And Ctholh'en?"

"Resting," Brett interjected, her tone suggesting more. "Somewhere in the back."

Bill chuckled. "I reckon he's beyond just sleep."

Mike waved it off. "He's just had too much *Anis del Mono*." Jack caught a figure at the table subtly roll up his sleeve, revealing a tattoo of a familiar glyph.

In a dimly lit back chamber, Ro'brt Ctholh'en rested among wine casks. The stillness was palpable, unsettling amidst the fiesta. A garlic wreath lay around his neck.

Time slipped, and Ctholh'en emerged, his gaze adrift as if journeying through realms beyond dreams. As the crowd greeted him, he blinked away his daze.

"I took a brief respite," he mused.

"A momentary escape," Brett teased.

"Seemed more like an eternity," Bill remarked.

A pang of hunger struck Ctholh'en. "Anyone fancy a meal?"

Mike gestured to the garlic wreath. "How about starting with that?"

Ctholh'en stood uneasily, the day's weight pressing upon him. "Let's go and eat," Brett said, her voice trembling slightly. "I must get a bath."

"Come on," Bill urged. "Let's get Brett to the hotel."

They said farewell to familiar and unfamiliar faces, expressions inscrutable in the dimming twilight. The world blurred into darkness faster than usual.

"What time do you suppose it is?" Ctholh'en asked, looking at a starless sky.

"It's tomorrow," Mike replied. "Feels like we've crossed into a different reality."

As they walked to the hotel, echoes of laughter carried an unsettling undercurrent for Jack. Shadows darted between buildings, and the celebratory atmosphere felt eerie.

"Bit creepy, isn't it?" Bill broke the silence.

"Takes one to know one," Ro'brt replied, and Jack laughed.

The hotel meal was abundant, but every dish seemed too rich, infused with the festival's essence, making it both enticing and overwhelming. Despite the festivities outside, Jack's fatigue pulled him to bed. His dreams were restless, punctuated by eerie cries and distant drumbeats. The outside world was a cacophony, interspersed with growing whispers of something primal awakening.

Jolted from sleep, Jack's room was bathed in the eerie light of a gibbous moon, declaring the night's deep silence. The sigil—an eye within spirals—imprinted upon his vision, open or closed, was a relentless echo of ancient whispers. He tried to dismiss it, yet the sigil stirred, its gaze slicing through him in communion with an ancient presence. A shock of fear sent him crashing to the floor, a howl of terror escaping as he fell.

Desperate, he rubbed his eyes, flashes of red momentarily obscuring the cursed symbol. As the kaleidoscope behind his lids faded, so did the sigil. Still on the floor, he stared at the indifferent ceiling, fearful of inviting the vision's return with a blink.

Only with the day's first light creeping in did he find the courage to return to bed and close his eyes. The dawn, a tenuous shield against the shadow invading his thoughts, left a residue of dread as the new day unfolded.

Ro'brt woke Jack later in the afternoon. As Jack began to change and approached to close the window, he hesitated. The silhouettes of people on the balcony across the street seemed wrong—limbs too long, heads tilted unnaturally. They froze, meeting Ro'brt's odd gaze. Shuddering, he quickly closed the curtains.

"Did you see the show?" Jack asked.

"Yes. They were all there," Ctholh'en replied.

"Anybody get hurt?"

"One of the bulls got into the crowd and tossed six or eight people."

"How did Brett like it?"

"It was sudden; there wasn't time to bother anyone."

"I wish I'd been up."

"They didn't know where you were. They went to your room, but it was locked. I heard... whispers beneath the door," Ctholh'en added with a grin.

"Where did you stay up?" Jack asked evasively. Whispers? Had he been alone?

"We danced at some club. An old one, deep underground."

"I got sleepy," Jack said, avoiding Ctholh'en's unsettling gaze.

"My gosh! I'm sleepy now," Ctholh'en laughed softly. "Doesn't this thing ever stop?"

"Not for a week."

Bill opened the door, putting his head in with wider, manic eyes. "You felt it too?" he whispered, looking suspiciously at Ctholh'en.

Ro'brt froze, eyes unblinking.

"Where you going?"

"To sleep."

No one was up before noon. The town was full of people with smiles too wide, laughter a shade too sharp. Eyes sparkled, but with what? Joy or something else? The fiesta's spirit, joyous on the surface, masked a restless energy. They waited for a table and finally ate under the arcade. After lunch, the gang went to the Iruña. It filled up as the bullfight time approached, the tables crowded closer. A close, crowded hum filled the café, unlike any other time, making them part of it.

Jack had six seats for all the fights—three barreras (first row ringside) and three sobrepuertos (wooden-backed seats halfway up the amphitheater). Mike thought Brett should sit high for her first time, and Ctholh'en wanted to join them. Bill and Jack sat in the barreras, and Jack gave an extra ticket to a waiter to sell. Bill advised Ctholh'en on how to look so he wouldn't mind the horses. Bill had seen one season of bullfights.

"I'm not worried about how I'll stand it. I'm only afraid I may be bored," Ctholh'en said.

"You think so?"

"Don't look at the horses after the bull hits them," Jack advised Brett. "Watch the charge and see the picador try to keep the bull off, but don't look again until the horse is dead if it's been hit."

"I'm a little nervy about it," Brett admitted. "I'm worried whether I'll be able to go through with it all right."

"You'll be all right. There's nothing but that horse part that will bother you, and they're only in for a few minutes with each bull. Just don't watch when it's bad."

"She'll be all right," Mike said. "I'll look after her."

"I don't think you'll be bored," Bill added.

"I'm going to the hotel to get the glasses and the wineskin," Jack said. "See you back here. Don't get cock-eyed."

"I'll come along," Bill said. Brett smiled at them.

They walked through the arcade to avoid the square's heat.

"That Ctholh'en gets me," Bill said. "He's got this blue-blooded superiority, thinking the only emotion he'll get from the fight will be boredom."

"We'll watch him with the glasses," Jack replied.

"Oh, to hell with him! Bloody coward is more like it!"

"He spends a lot of time there."

"I want him to stay there."

In the hotel stairs, they met Montoya.

"Come on," Montoya said. "Do you want to meet Pedro Romero?"

"Fine," Bill agreed. "Let's go see him."

They followed Montoya up a flight and down the corridor.

"He's in room eight," Montoya explained. "He's getting dressed for the bullfight."

Montoya knocked and opened the door. It was a gloomy room with little light from the window. Two beds were separated by a monastic partition. The electric light was on. A boy stood straight and unsmiling in bullfighting clothes. His jacket hung over a chair. They were finishing his sash. His black hair shone under the light. He wore a white linen shirt, and the sword-handler finished his sash, stood, and stepped back. Pedro Romero nodded, appearing far away and dignified as they shook hands. Montoya praised their enthusiasm and wished him luck. Romero listened seriously before turning to Jack. Jack thought he was the best-looking boy he had ever seen.

"You go to the bullfight," Romero said in English.

"You know English," Jack remarked, feeling foolish.

"No," Romero replied, smiling.

One of the three men on the beds approached. "Would you like me to interpret? Anything you'd like to ask Pedro Romero?"

They thanked him. What was there to ask? Romero was nineteen, alone except for his sword-handler and three hangers-on. The bullfight was to start in twenty minutes. Jack wished him "*Mucha suerte,*" shook hands, and left. Romero stood alone with his hangers-on as Montoya shut the door.

"He's a fine boy, don't you think?" Montoya asked.

"He's a good-looking kid," Jack agreed.

"He looks like a *torero,*" Montoya said. "He has the type."

"He's a fine boy."

"We'll see how he is in the ring," Montoya added.

They found the big leather wine bottle in Jack's room, took it and the field glasses, locked the door, and went downstairs.

It was a good bullfight. Bill and Jack were excited about Pedro Romero. Montoya sat about ten places away. After Romero killed his first bull, Montoya caught Jack's eye and nodded. This was a real one. There hadn't been a real one for a long time. Of the other two matadors, one was fair, the other passable. But neither compared to Romero, although his bulls weren't much either.

Several times during the bullfight, Jack looked up at Mike, Brett, and Ctholh'en with his glasses. They seemed fine. Brett did not look upset. All three leaned forward on the concrete railing.

"Let me take the glasses," Bill said.

"Does Ctholh'en look bored?" Jack asked.

"That son of a bitch!"

Outside the ring, after the bullfight, movement through the crowd became impossible. They couldn't forge their own path but were swept along like a glacier back toward town. Emotions churned within them, disturbed by the bullfight's violence and elation from its artistry. The fiesta's pulse beat on. Drums throbbed a primal rhythm, resonating deep in the bones, while pipes' melodies wove through the air, eerie and enthralling—a siren's call to something long buried. The crowd moved fragmented by islands of dancers, bobbing heads and shoulders obscured intricate footwork. Eventually, they emerged from the throng, seeking refuge in the café. The waiter held chairs for the latecomers, and with absinthes ordered, they settled to observe the square's vibrant life and the crowd's fluid dance.

"What do you suppose that dance is?" Bill asked.

"It's a sort of *jota*."

"They're not all the same," Bill replied. "They dance differently to all the different tunes."

"It's swell dancing."

A company of boys danced in front of them on a clear street section. Their intricate steps showed intent and concentration. They danced with downcast eyes, their rope-soled shoes tapping the pavement. The toes, heels, and balls of their feet touched in rhythm. Then the music broke wildly, the step finished, and they danced up the street.

"Here come the gentry," Bill noted as they crossed the street.

"Hello, men," Jack greeted.

"Hello, gents!" Brett responded. "You saved us seats? How nice."

"I say," Mike added, "that Romero, what's his name, is somebody. Am I wrong?"

"Oh, isn't he lovely," Brett said. "And those green trousers."

"Brett never took her eyes off them."

"I must borrow your glasses tomorrow," Brett remarked.

"How did it go?"

"Wonderfully! Simply perfect. It is a spectacle!"

"How about the horses?"

"I couldn't help looking at them."

"She couldn't take her eyes off them," Mike said. "She's an extraordinary wench."

"They do have some rather awful things happen to them," Brett said. "I couldn't look away, though."

"Did you feel all right?"

"I didn't feel badly at all."

"Ro'brt Ctholh'en did," Mike interjected. "You were quite green, Ro'brt."

"The first horse did bother me," Ctholh'en replied.

"You weren't bored, were you?" Bill asked.

Ctholh'en laughed. "No. I wasn't bored. I wish you'd forgive me that."

"It's all right," Bill said, "so long as you weren't bored."

"He didn't look bored," Mike observed. "I thought he was going to be sick."

"It wasn't that bad. It was just for a minute."

"I thought he was going to be sick. You weren't bored, were you, Ro'brt?"

"Let up on that, Mike. I said I was sorry I said it."

"He was, you know. He was positively green."

"Oh, shove it along, Michael."

"You mustn't ever get bored at your first bullfight, Ro'brt," Mike said. "It might make such a mess."

"Oh, shove it along, Michael," Brett added.

"He said Brett was a sadist," Mike said. "Brett's not a sadist. She's just a lovely, healthy wench."

"Are you a sadist, Brett?" Jack asked.

"Hope not."

"He said Brett was a sadist just because she has a good, healthy stomach."

"Won't be healthy long," Bill said, and they fell silent.

Bill diverted Mike's attention from Ctholh'en. The waiter brought the absinthe glasses.

"Did you really like it?" Bill asked Ctholh'en.

"No, I can't say I liked it. I think it's a wonderful show."

"Gad, yes! What a spectacle!" Brett exclaimed.

"I wish they didn't have the horse part," Ctholh'en said.

"They're not important," Bill replied. "After a while, you never notice anything disgusting."

"It is a bit strong just at the start," Brett added. "There's a dreadful moment for me just when the bull starts for the horse."

"The bulls were fine," Ctholh'en responded.

"They were very good," Mike agreed.

"I want to sit down below next time." Brett drank from her absinthe glass.

"She wants to see the bullfighters close by," Mike said.

"They are something," Brett remarked. "That Romero lad is just a child."

"He's a damned good-looking boy," Jack said. "When we were up in his room, I never saw a better-looking kid."

"How old do you suppose he is?"

"Nineteen or twenty."

"Just imagine it."

The bullfight on the second day was much better than the first. Brett sat between Mike and Jack in the barrera, while Bill and Ctholh'en sat above. Romero was the main attraction. Brett didn't see any other bullfighters, nor did anyone else except the technicians. It was all Romero. Two other matadors didn't compare. Jack sat beside Brett, explaining the fight. He told her to watch the bull, not the horse, and observe the picador's attempts to keep the bull off. This approach gave the fight a definite end and made it less of a spectacle with unexplained horrors. Jack showed her how Romero took the bull away from a fallen horse with his cape, holding and turning him smoothly without wasting the bull. She saw Romero avoid brusque movements, saving his bulls for the kill—calmly wearing them down. Brett watched, her face a mask of fascination and horror, eyes fixed on the bull's relentless charge. Each moment Romero faced the bull, she seemed to catch her breath, living every dodge and turn. She saw how Romero worked closely with the bull, and Jack whispered the tricks other bullfighters used to appear closely involved. She appreciated Romero's cape work and disliked the others'.

Romero never contorted. His movements were straight, pure, and natural. The others twisted like corkscrews, their elbows raised, leaning against the bull's flanks after the horns passed, creating a fake look of danger. Afterward, their fakery turned unpleasant. Romero's bullfighting showed real emotion, maintaining pure line and calm dominance, making the bull realize he was unattainable and preparing him for the kill.

272

Ro'brt's usually calm eyes widened at each pass of the bull. The fight's raw, primal nature unsettled him deeply. Jack would have imagined he loved the sport, but Ro'brt's composure was replaced by visible unease.

"I've never seen him do an awkward thing," Brett said.

"You won't until he gets frightened," Jack replied.

"He'll never be frightened," Mike said. "He knows too damned much."

"He knew everything when he started. The others can't ever learn what he was born with."

"And God, what looks," Brett trailed off.

"I believe she's falling in love with this bullfighter chap," Mike said.

"I wouldn't be surprised."

"Be a good chap, Jack. Don't tell her anything more about him. Tell her how he beats his old mother. Tell her what a drunk he is. Drunk all day and spends all their time beating his poor old mother."

"He looks that way," Brett said.

"Doesn't he?" Jack replied.

They hitched the mules to the dead bull, whips cracked, men ran, and the mules broke into a gallop. The bull, one horn up, his head on its side, swept smoothly across the sand and out the red gate.

"This next is the last one."

"Not really," Brett said, leaning forward in the barrera. Romero waved his picadors to their places, then stood with his cape against his chest, looking across the ring where the bull would emerge.

Afterward, they were pressed tightly into the crowd.

"These bullfights are hell on one," Brett said. "I'm limp as a rag."

"Oh, you'll get a drink," Mike offered.

The next day, Pedro Romero did not fight. It was Miura bulls and a very bad bullfight. The day continued with no scheduled bullfight, but the fiesta persisted day and night.

CHAPTER 16

DAWN OF THE DEEP ONE

THE MORNING GREETED PAMPLONA WITH relentless rain. Thick fog crept over the mountains, obscuring their peaks and cloaking the plateau in a ghostly veil. Cracking thunder echoed through the mist as Jack gazed toward the horizon. An unease settled over him, something he couldn't quite place. He walked past the town limits, feeling the weather's heaviness pressing down, as if the deep sea whispered of an old, unsettled debt.

Flags in the square hung limp and drenched, their vibrant colors muted. Rain forced everyone beneath the arcades, turning streets into muddy rivers that mirrored the fiesta's decorations. Yet, undeterred, the fiesta roared on. Music, laughter, and conversations seeped through the rain, infusing the damp air with an unyielding spirit of celebration.

The bullring was packed, its covered seats offering scant refuge. Basque dancers and Navarrese singers continued their performances, moving fluidly despite the soggy conditions. The Val Carlos dancers emerged onto the streets, their drums beating a hollow rhythm resonating with the melancholic rain. Band leaders rode ahead, their elaborate costumes and horses soaked like the flags around them. Inside the cafés, patrons huddled together, dancers wringing out their costumes, seeking warmth until the rain subsided.

Jack left the bustling café and returned to his hotel, needing a clean shave before dinner. In his modest room, razor in hand, he heard a soft knock.

"Come in," Jack called.

Montoya entered, awkward hesitation marking his presence.

"How are you?" he asked nervously.

"Fine," Jack replied curtly.

"No bulls today," Montoya noted, eyes darting away.

"No. Nothing but rain."

"Where are your friends?"

"Over at the Iruña."

Montoya forced a smile that didn't reach his eyes. "Do you know the American ambassador?"

"Yes. Everybody knows him."

"He's here in town now."

"Yes. Everybody's seen him."

"I've seen him too," Montoya added, searching Jack's face.

Jack continued shaving.

"No, I have to go," Montoya insisted, shaking his head.

Jack finished, splashed cold water on his face, and saw Montoya standing awkwardly.

"Look," Montoya said again, "I've received a message from the Grand Hotel. They want Pedro Romero and Marcial Lalanda to join us for coffee tonight."

"Well, it can't hurt Marcial."

"Marcial has been in San Sebastián all day. I don't think they'll be back tonight," Montoya replied, frustration evident.

"Don't give Romero the message," Jack stated firmly.

"You think so?"

"Absolutely."

Montoya's face brightened with relief. "I wanted to ask you because you're an American."

"That's what I'd do."

"People take a boy like Romero for granted. They don't know his true worth. Any foreigner can flatter him, start this Grand Hotel business, and within a year, they're through."

"Like Algabeno."

"Yes, like Algabeno."

"They're a fine lot," Jack remarked with irony. "There's one American woman here who collects bullfighters."

"I know. They only want the young ones."

"Yes. The old ones get fat."

"Or crazy like Gallo."

"It's easy. Just don't give him the message."

"He's such a fine boy," Montoya sighed. "He ought to stay with his own people."

"Won't you have a drink?" Jack offered.

"No, I have to go." Montoya exited, leaving Jack alone.

Jack descended the stairs into the rain-soaked streets. The arcades were deserted, stone columns casting elongated shadows. He wandered aimlessly, the steady patter of rain doing nothing to ease his tension. Passing the Iruña, he found it empty. Shrugging, he circled the square before returning to his hotel.

Inside, the hotel's warmth didn't soothe his nerves. He took a seat at the bar, ordering whiskey, hoping the sharp burn might ground him. Unease clung to him like a second skin. The bar lights flickered, casting shifting shadows across the walls. His grip on the glass tightened as his heart raced, the air humming with a sinister charge. When the lights steadied, the shadows pulsed at the edges of his vision.

Out of the dimness, a sigil seared into reality, alive and ravenous. Its twisted lines glowed with malevolent intent, etching into Jack's world like a dark curse. Tendrils slithered forward, wrapping around Bill and dragging him into suffocating darkness. Jack stood paralyzed, watching in horror as Bill's body contorted, bones cracking like dry twigs. Tentacles sprouted from his back, each reflecting the nightmare creatures haunting Jack's sleep.

The horror didn't stop at Bill. The sigil pulsed with ancient hunger, gnawing at reality itself. Jack felt its gaze—cold, calculating—probing his mind, twisting the world around him. A deep memory surfaced: dark figures in a black forest, eyes gleaming with ancient knowledge, offering him a cup of something thick and pulsing with life. The same dread was spilling into his waking world.

His heart pounded as he staggered back, breath sharp and shallow. He bit down on his tongue, tasting blood, anchoring himself to the whiskey's weight and burn as he swallowed. The bar came back into focus—the buzz of conversation, faint laughter from the dining room.

The sigil flickered, testing him. But Jack, will hardened, resisted its pull. The vision wavered; the tendrils retreated, leaving a cold residue on his skin. Shadows danced one last time before disappearing, leaving him with gnawing silence and unspoken questions.

Ahead, the gang remained oblivious. Bill, back to his usual self, laughed while buying shoe shines for Mike. Each time the bootblacks opened the street door, Bill teased Mike as if nothing had happened. Jack steadied his breath, eyes lingering on Bill, waiting for something to break the fragile veil of normalcy.

"This is the eleventh time my boots have been polished," Mike said. "I say, Bill is an ass."

Another bootblack entered.

"¿*Limpia* botas?" he asked Bill.

"No. For this señor."

The bootblack knelt beside Mike's shoe, which already shone under electric light.

"Bill's a yell of laughter," Mike muttered.

Jack drank red wine, feeling increasingly uncomfortable. He glanced around. At the next table sat Pedro Romero. When Jack nodded, Romero stood and approached with a friend—a Madrid bullfight critic. Jack introduced himself, expressing admiration for Romero's work, which pleased him. They conversed in Spanish, the critic adding bits of French. As Jack reached for his wine, the critic took his arm, and Romero laughed.

"Drink here," Romero said in English.

He was bashful about his English but pleased. They continued talking, Romero stumbling over words, asking for translations. "Do you know the English for *corrida de toros*? The exact translation? Bullfight?" he questioned.

Jack explained that "*corrida*" translates to "running of bulls." The critic noted, "There is no Spanish word for bullfight."

"I learned a little English in Gibraltar," Romero shared. "I was born in Ronda. I started bullfighting in Málaga. I've only been at it three years." The critic joked about his Malagueño expressions. "I'm nineteen," Romero added. "My older brother is with me as a *banderillero*."

He asked Jack how many times he'd seen him in the ring. Jack lied, saying three times.

"Where did you see me the other time? In Madrid?"

"Yes," Jack lied smoothly.

"The first or the second time?"

"The first."

"I was very bad," Romero confessed. "The second time, I was better. You remember?" He turned to the critic.

"I like it very much that you like my work," Romero said. "But you haven't seen it yet. Tomorrow, if I get a good bull, I'll show you."

He smiled, anxious not to seem boastful.

"I am anxious to see it," the critic responded. "I would like to be convinced."

"He doesn't like my work much," Romero said seriously to Jack.

The critic explained he liked Romero's work but found it incomplete.

"Wait till tomorrow if a good one comes out."

"Have you seen the bulls for tomorrow?" the critic asked.

"Yes. I saw them unloaded."

"What did you think of them?" Romero leaned forward.

"Very nice. About twenty-six *arrobas*. Very short horns. Haven't you seen them?"

"Oh, yes."

"They won't weigh twenty-six *arrobas*," the critic interjected.

"No," Romero confirmed.

"They've got bananas for horns," the critic remarked.

"You call them bananas?" Romero asked, smiling. "You wouldn't call them bananas?"

"No. They're horns, all right."

"They're very short. Very, very short. Still, they aren't bananas."

"I say, Jack," Brett called from the next table, "you have deserted us."

"Just temporarily. We're talking bulls."

"You are superior."

"Tell him that bulls have no balls," Mike shouted, clearly drunk.

Romero looked at Jack inquisitively.

"Drunk. ¡Borracho! ¡Muy borracho!'"

"You might introduce your friends," Brett suggested, watching Romero intently. Jack invited Romero to join them for coffee. Romero's face was very brown, and he had nice manners.

They moved to a larger table. Mike ordered a bottle of Fundador, leading to drunken conversation.

"Tell him I think writing is lousy," Bill said. "Tell him I'm ashamed of being a writer."

Romero sat beside Brett, listening.

"Go on. Tell him!" Bill insisted.

Romero looked up, smiling.

"This gentleman is a writer," Jack said.

Romero was impressed. "This other one, too," Jack added, pointing at Ctholh'en.

"He looks like Villalta," Romero observed about Bill. "Doesn't he look like Villalta?"

"I can't see it," the critic responded.

"Really, he looks a lot like Villalta. What does the drunken one do?"

"Nothing."

"Is that why he drinks?"

"No. He's waiting to marry this lady."

"Tell him bulls have no balls!" Mike shouted.

"What does he say?"

"He's drunk."

"Jack," Mike called out again. "Tell him bulls have no balls!"

"You understand?" Jack said.

"Yes."

Mike proceeded, "Tell him Brett wants to see him put on those green pants."

"Pipe down, Mike."

"Tell him Brett is dying to know how he can get into those pants."

"Pipe down."

Romero fidgeted with his glass, conversing with Brett, who spoke French while he toggled between Spanish and English, laughing.

Bill refilled the glasses. "Tell him Brett wants to come into—"

"Oh, pipe down, Mike, for Christ's sake!" Romero interjected, still smiling.

Just then, Montoya entered. He smiled at Jack, then noticed Romero with cognac, laughing between Jack and a woman with bare shoulders at a table full of drunks. He didn't nod in greeting.

Montoya exited, and Mike stood to propose a toast. "Let's all drink to—"

"Pedro Romero," Jack finished. Everyone stood. Romero took the toast seriously; they touched glasses and drank. Romero shook hands before leaving with the critic.

"My God! He's a lovely boy," Brett exclaimed. "And how I would love to see him get into those clothes. He must use a shoehorn."

"I started to tell him," Mike began, "and Jack kept interrupting me. Do you think you talk Spanish better than I do?"

"Oh, shut up, Mike! Nobody interrupted you."

"No, I'd like to get this settled." He turned to Ctholh'en. "Do you think you amount to something? Do you think you belong here among us? Don't be so noisy, Ctholh'en!"

"Oh, cut it out, Mike," Ctholh'en retorted.

"Do you think Brett wants you here? Do you think you add to the party? Why don't you say something?"

"I said all I had to say the other night, Mike."

"I'm not one of you literary chaps." Mike stood shakily. "I'm not clever. But I do know when I'm not wanted. Why don't you see when you're not wanted, Ctholh'en? Go away. Go away, for God's sake. Take that wretched Arkham-face away. Don't you think I'm right?"

He looked at Jack.

"Sure. Let's all go over to the Iruña."

"No. Don't you think I'm right? I love that woman."

"Oh, don't start that again. Do shove it along, Michael," Brett interjected.

"Don't you think I'm right, Jack?"

Ctholh'en remained seated, his face adopting a sallow hue yet seeming to enjoy the drunken antics.

"Jack," Mike said, almost crying. "You know I'm right. Listen, you!" He turned to Ctholh'en, voice cracking, "Go away! Go away now!"

"But I won't go, Mike," Ctholh'en responded defiantly.

"Then I'll make you!" Mike started to stand, swaying as he moved toward Ctholh'en.

Ctholh'en stood, removed his glasses, and faced Mike, hands held low—ready to defend himself.

Jack grabbed Mike's arm. "Come on to the café. You can't hit him here."

"Good! Good idea!"

They started off. Jack glanced back and saw Ctholh'en putting his glasses back on. Bill was pouring another glass of Fundador; Brett sat quietly, staring at nothing.

Outside, the rain had ceased. A gust of wind carried the military band's music as the crowd gathered. Don Manuel Orquito and his son were attempting to send up fire balloons. Balloons started up jerkily, torn apart by the wind or blown against houses. Some fell into the crowd, magnesium flaring as fireworks exploded. No one danced in the square; the gravel was too wet.

Brett emerged with Bill and joined Jack and Mike, watching Don Manuel meticulously ignite the balloons. The wind would soon bring them all down, and Don Manuel's face was slick with sweat as fireworks descended into the crowd. The crowd shouted as each luminous bubble careened, caught fire, and fell.

"They're razzing Don Manuel," Bill commented.

"How do you know he's Don Manuel?" Brett inquired.

"His name's on the program. Don Manuel Orquito, *el pirotécnico de esta ciudad,*" Bill replied.

"*Globos iluminados,*" Mike added. "A collection of *globos iluminados.*"

"I wish one would go up," Brett said. "That Don Manuel chap is furious."

"He's probably worked for weeks fixing them to go off, spelling out 'Hail to San Fermín,'" Bill explained.

"*Globos iluminados,*" Mike repeated. "A bunch of bloody *globos iluminados.*"

"Come on," Brett urged. "We can't stand here."

"Her ladyship wants a drink," Mike interjected.

"How you know things," Brett remarked, a hint of frustration.

Inside, the café was crowded and noisy. They struggled to find a table amid the chaos.

"Come on, let's get out of here," Bill suggested.

Outside, the paseo hummed with life under the arcade. English and American tourists from Biarritz lounged in sports attire. Some women scrutinized passersby through lorgnons. Among them was a friend of Bill's from Biarritz.

"Here's the pub," Mike announced as they approached Bar Milano. They settled at a table and ordered a bottle of Fundador. The bar was subdued.

"This is a hell of a place," Bill commented.

"It's too early," Mike replied.

"Let's take the bottle and come back later," Bill suggested. "I don't want to waste a night like this sitting around."

"Let's go and look at the English," Mike proposed. "I love to watch the English."

"They're awful," Bill grumbled. "Where did they all come from?"

"They come from Biarritz," Mike answered. "They flock here to witness the last day of our quaint little Spanish fiesta."

"I'll *festa* them," Bill muttered.

Jack's gaze shifted to the street, drawn to a movement in the shadows of the arcade. Unease crept over him as he noticed a figure lurking just beyond the light. He took a deep breath through his nose—the scent of tobacco mingled with hints of impatience, anger, and violence. Instinctively, he wanted to steer Brett away, protectively shielding her from whatever presence watched them.

"You're an extraordinarily beautiful girl," Mike turned to Bill's friend. "When did you come here?"

"Come off it, Michael."

"I say, she is a lovely girl. Where have I been? Come along with me and Bill. We're going to *festa* the English."

"I'll *festa* them," Bill responded. "What the hell are they doing at this fiesta?"

"Come on," Mike insisted. "Just us three. We're going to *festa* the bloody English. I hope you're not English? I'm Scotch. I hate the English."

Through the window, they saw three Englishmen heading toward the café as rockets exploded in the square.

"I'm going to sit here," Brett declared.

"I'll stay with you," Ctholh'en offered.

"Oh, don't!" Brett protested. "For God's sake, go off somewhere. Can't you see Jack and I want to talk?"

"I didn't," Ctholh'en replied. "I thought I'd sit here because I felt a little tight."

"What a hell of a reason for sitting with anyone. If you're tight, go to bed. Go on to bed."

"Was I rude enough to him?" Brett asked, noticing Ctholh'en was gone. "My God! I'm so sick of him!"

"He doesn't add much to the gaiety."

"He depresses me so."

"He's behaved very badly."

"Damned badly. He had a chance to behave so well."

"He's probably waiting just outside the door now."

"Yes. He would. You know I do know how he feels. He can't believe it didn't mean anything."

"I know."

"Nobody else would behave as badly. Oh, I'm so sick of the whole thing. And Michael. Michael's been lovely, too."

"It's been damned hard on Mike."

"Yes. But he didn't need to be a swine."

"Everybody behaves badly," Jack remarked. "Give them the proper chance."

"You wouldn't behave badly," Brett countered, looking at Jack.

"I'd be as big an ass as Ctholh'en."

"Darling, don't let's talk a lot of rot."

"All right. Talk about anything you like."

"Don't be difficult. You're the only person I've got, and I feel rather awful tonight."

"You've got Mike."

"Yes, Mike. Hasn't he been pretty?"

"Well, it's been damned hard on Mike, having Ctholh'en around and seeing him with you."

"Don't I know it, darling? Please don't make me feel any worse than I do."

Brett was more nervous than Jack had ever seen her. She kept looking away, staring ahead at the wall.

"Want to go for a walk?"

"Yes. Come on."

Jack corked up the Fundador bottle and handed it to the bartender.

"Let's have one more drink of that," Brett suggested. "My nerves are rotten."

They each drank a glass of the smooth brandy.

"Come on," Brett urged.

As they exited, Jack noticed Ctholh'en emerging from under the arcade. He seemed to be washing blood off his hand. Jack blinked several times. Maybe not.

"He was there," Brett noted.

"He can't be away from you."

"Poor devil!"

"I'm not sorry for him. I hate him."

"I hate him, too," she shivered, her voice barely above a whisper. "I hate his damned suffering."

Arm in arm, they veered off the main thoroughfare, the clamor of the crowd dissolving as they entered a shadowy side street. The pavement glistened underfoot, reflecting flickers of light from occasional wine shops where laughter spilled out before being snatched away by the wind.

"Want to go in?" Jack's voice cut through the distant music.

"No." Her reply was terse.

They continued, footsteps muffled on wet grass leading to ancient stone fortifications. Jack spread a newspaper atop the cold stone, and Brett sat silently, her silhouette merging with the darkness. The plains stretched vast into the night, mountains looming as silent sentinels. High winds herded clouds across the moon, casting fleeting shadows.

Behind them, the cathedral's shadow loomed ominously. "Don't feel bad," Jack murmured.

"I feel like hell," Brett's tone was hollow. "Don't let's talk."

Silence fell between them, broken only by rustling trees and the distant hum of a car ascending the mountain. The fort's lights flickered like far-off stars, the river whispering secrets in the darkness. Brett shivered, her body tensing. "It's cold."

"Want to walk back?" Jack suggested, eyes darting nervously toward the park, its gates framing the darkness.

"Through the park."

As they climbed down, clouds gathered, plunging the park into deeper shadow. Under ancient trees, the darkness felt tangible. Jack's senses sharpened; each snap of a twig echoed loudly. He could smell the lingering scent of tobacco and a hint of violence in the air. Every rustle seemed laden with threat. He reached for Brett's arm, wanting to steer her away protectively.

She was a few steps ahead, a ghostly figure drifting through the darkness. He caught up; the exit of the park promised escape from the oppressive gloom. But as they neared the gate, the night felt watchful. Jack could feel it—the weight of unseen eyes. He wanted to run, to break the spell, but the darkness held him.

"Do you still love me, Jack?"

"Yes," he replied softly.

"Because I'm a goner," Brett confessed.

"How?"

"I'm mad about the Romero boy. I'm in love with him, I think."

"I wouldn't be if I were you."

"I can't help it. It's tearing me up inside."

"Don't do it."

"I've never been able to help anything."

"You ought to stop it."

"How can I stop? Feel that?" Her hand trembled. "I'm like that all through."

"You oughtn't to do it."

"I can't help it. I'm a goner now. Don't you see the difference?"

"No."

"I've got to do something I really want to do. I've lost my self-respect."

"You don't have to do that."

"Oh, darling, don't be difficult. What do you think it's meant to have that damned fish face about, and Mike the way he's acted?"

"Sure."

"I can't just stay tight all the time."

"No."

"Oh, darling, please stay by me. Please see me through this."

"Sure."

"I don't say it's right. It is right for me. God knows I've never felt such a bitch."

"What do you want me to do?"

"Come on," Brett said. "Let's go and find him."

They walked down the gravel path, under the trees, then out past the gate into the street leading back into town.

Pedro Romero was in the café, sitting with other bullfighters and critics, smoking cigars. When they entered, Romero smiled and bowed. They sat at a table halfway down the room.

"Ask him to come over and have a drink."

"Not yet. He'll come over."

"I can't look at him."

"He's nice to look at," Jack said.

"I've always done just what I wanted."

"I know."

"I do feel such a bitch."

"Well."

"My God! The things a woman goes through."

"Yes?"

"Oh, I do feel such a bitch."

Jack looked across. Romero smiled, said something to his table, and stood up. He came over. Jack stood, and they shook hands.

"Won't you have a drink?"

"You must have a drink with me," Romero said. He seated himself, asking Brett's permission without words. He kept smoking his cigar; it suited him.

"You like cigars?" Jack asked.

"Oh, yes. I always smoke cigars."

It was part of his authority, making him seem older. Jack noticed his clear, smooth, very brown skin. A triangular scar on his cheekbone. He was watching Brett. An undeniable spark passed between them when Brett gave him her hand. He was careful, not wanting to make a mistake.

"You fight tomorrow?" Jack said.

"Yes. Algabeno was hurt today in Madrid. Did you hear?"

"No. Badly?"

He shook his head. "Nothing. Here," he showed his hand. Brett reached out and spread the fingers apart.

"Oh!" he said in English. "You tell fortunes?"

"Sometimes. Do you mind?"

"No. I like it." He spread his hand flat. "Tell me I live forever and be a millionaire."

He was polite but surer of himself. "Look," he said, "do you see any bulls in my hand?"

He laughed. His hand was fine, the wrist small.

"There are thousands of bulls," Brett said, not nervous now. She looked lovely.

"Good," Romero laughed. "At a thousand *duros* apiece," he said to Jack in Spanish. "Tell me some more."

"It's a good hand," Brett said. "I think he'll live a long time."

"Say it to me. Not to your friend."

"I said you'd live a long time."

"I know it," Romero said. "I'm never going to die."

Jack tapped his fingertips on the table. Romero saw it and shook his head.

"No. Don't do that. The bulls are my best friends."

Jack translated to Brett.

"You kill your friends?" she asked.

"Always," he said in English and laughed. "So they don't kill me." He looked at her across the table.

"You know English well."

"Yes. Pretty well, sometimes. But I must not let anybody know. It would be very bad, a *torero* who speaks English."

"Why?" asked Brett.

"It would be bad. The people would not like it. Not yet."

"Why not?"

"They would not like it. Bullfighters are not like that."

"What are bullfighters like?"

He laughed, tipped his hat over his eyes, changed the angle of his cigar, and altered his expression.

"Like at the table," he said. Jack glanced over. He had mimicked Nacional's expression exactly. He smiled naturally again. "No. I must forget English."

"Don't forget it yet," Brett said.

"No?"

"No."

"All right." He laughed again.

"I would like a hat like that," Brett said.

"Good. I'll get you one."

"Right. See that you do."

"I will. I'll get you one tonight."

Jack stood, and Romero followed.

"Sit down," Jack said. "I need to go find our friends and bring them here."

Romero gave Jack a penetrating look, a silent request for confirmation.

"Sit down," Brett urged him. "You have to teach me Spanish."

Romero reseated himself, gaze locked with hers. Jack left, his departure drawing intense scrutiny from the bullfighters' table. Their stares were unsettling. Twenty minutes later, when Jack returned and peered into the café, Brett and Pedro Romero were gone. Only the remnants remained—a trio of empty cognac glasses and coffee cups. A waiter collected the glasses and wiped the table clean.

CHAPTER 17

CTHULHU'S ECLIPSE

JACK SAT AT THE CAFÉ, staring into the night. The mirror in his satchel thrummed faintly against his side. Across the street, the shop where Brett and Romero had vanished loomed in shadow, its crooked sign swaying in the breeze. Jack's chest tightened. He could still see the barman earlier, furtively tampering with their drinks. Brett had laughed, her head tilted back, while Romero leaned close, his hand grazing hers.

He'd seen it. Known something was wrong. He should have spoken up, should have stopped them. But the words stuck in his throat. Fear held him—sharp and familiar, the same fear he tried to drink away every night. Was it the barman he feared? Or Brett? The way she might look at him if he interfered?

Maybe it was easier to stay silent, to watch and pretend it wasn't his problem. He'd told himself it was their choice, their risk. But the hollow ache in his chest told him the truth: he'd failed her.

The street was silent, except for the faint hum of a car in the distance. Jack gripped the edge of the table, his knuckles white, as shadows flickered across the shop's windows. Ro'brt and Mike appeared, their faces grim.

"Where's Brett?" Ro'brt's voice broke the silence.

"Inside—they've been drugged," Jack said, his throat dry. Bill. He realized Bill was missing.

As they approached the shop, a chill slid through them. The building loomed like a black silhouette against the dying light. From the shadows, two matadors stepped forward, their eyes gleaming cold and sharp, like knives catching the last light of the day.

"*Váyanse,*" one growled, his voice heavy with threat. The other waved them off. "*Este no es lugar para ustedes.*"

Jack opened his mouth, but Ro'brt didn't hesitate. In a blur of fury, he lunged. His fist connected with the guard's jaw, sending him sprawling like a broken doll. The second swung a bat; Ro'brt dodged, delivering a lightning-fast combination: jab, cross, hook, hook. A final uppercut lifted the man off his feet, crashing him through the door in a shower of splintered wood.

Crossing the threshold, the walls seemed to pulse with an unseen heartbeat, the air heavy with dread. The shop was abandoned, but Jack felt a chant echoing through the floorboards, calling them deeper into the abyss. They found a door to the basement and descended into darkness, following the faint candlelight flickering below. The musky chill wrapped around Jack, and the mirror in his satchel reverberated with hungry anticipation.

In the shadow-draped cellar, hooded figures chanted in eerie cadence, their voices weaving a malevolent symphony that reverberated through the stone chamber. The words were ancient, forgotten by time, carrying a darkness that pulsed with the candles' flames. Bill stood at the center, next to a hooded face Jack recognized as the visiting American ambassador, but Jack was transfixed by Bill's grotesque visage—a waxy nightmare given flesh.

His chant was both summoning and declaration, swirling around him like a dark cloak:

"Ph'nglui mglw'nafh Cthulhu R'lyeh wgah'nagl fhtagn! Ia! Ia! Yog-Sothoth! Throdog r'luhhor l'goth Y'ai'ng'gah! Rise and leave R'lyeh—our call summons you!"

The voices rose, shadows twisting into grotesque hands that clawed at reality's fabric. Bill's face, now a mask of otherworldly terror, pulsed with the rhythm of the chant. His mouth and nose were gone, replaced by writhing tentacles tasting the fear in the air, each slimy appendage squirming independently, dripping with a viscous fluid that hissed upon contact with the air.

Jack tore his gaze from his transformed friend and recognized the tome in Bill's hands—the *Necronomicon*, bound in human skin, seeping madness from its pages. The cellar buzzed as hooded figures chanted with fervor, their voices vibrating through the stone, rousing ancient horrors. Jack stood defiant as reality frayed at the edges, torn between fleeing and trying to save Brett. The acolytes, twisted by dark forces, moved in grotesque synchronization, their bodies warping as their chants became otherworldly howls. The cellar had become a tomb of horrors, the air a suffocating miasma. Jack could feel the despair of *Shub-Niggurath* rising.

The grotesque herald of darkness wearing Bill's skin stood before the assembly, his humanity consumed. His voice echoed the rise of Cthulhu, the god-priest who sleeps.

In the vortex of madness, Brett lay vulnerable, her torn attire marked with sinister sigils pulsing with unearthly energies. Jack's heart thundered in protest, defying the encroaching abyss. The chant swelled to a deafening crescendo, weaving a suffocating tapestry of terror. Violations inside the cultists quivered and burst from their stomachs and chests. Abominations surged forward, dripping with ichor—unfathomable beings desecrating the earth with each step, their non-Euclidean contortions a blasphemy to the three-dimensional world.

In the corner, Pedro Romero, once a proud matador, lay broken and discarded, overtaken by a swarm of ghastly spawn enveloping his still body.

Bill held a cursed dagger aloft, its blade etched with symbols shimmering with dark energy. The chanting swelled around him, a feverish cacophony that reverberated through the chamber. Bill brought the blade down slowly, the tip hovering above Brett's pale, exposed breast. With deliberate care, he drew a single drop of blood—crimson against alabaster skin. The dagger pulsed hungrily, drinking it in—and in that instant, the chanting ceased. The room plunged into a suffocating, unnatural silence.

Jack gasped, the sound echoing in the oppressive stillness. Bill's head snapped up, his abyssal eyes locking onto them.

"Ah, Jack, my dear friend," Bill's voice resonated, a chilling blend of the known and the unfathomable. "You've brought companions. How touching. I wasn't certain you'd make it to witness my triumph." He stood over Brett, the dagger tracing patterns across her skin, forming an evil sigil in crimson. The tentacles around his mouth quivered with perverse excitement. "Tell me, Jack," he taunted, "do you know the worst part of being mortal? It's the dying." He smiled—or rather, the tentacles curled upward in a mockery of a grin—creating a sight both terrifying and surreal. "Yes, the dying. Your kind perishes from trivial afflictions—a mere scratch, a simple infection, and you crumble. So fragile, so pathetically weak."

Bill's voice rose, echoing off the stone walls as the tentacles flailed, emphasizing each word. "You are but mayflies, dancing briefly before night descends. But me?" He spread his arms, shadows swirling around him. "I shall become eternal—a storm to sweep away humanity's detritus."

He stopped before Brett, his abyssal gaze never leaving Jack. "Yet, your fragility has its uses. You make excellent cattle and, even better, a fine sacrifice." He dragged the blade softly, drawing another thin line of blood, the tentacles reaching out as if tasting the air heavy with fear. Jack's fists clenched, jaw set in defiance. The air thickened with malevolent energy. "You're here to bear witness," Bill continued, mocking. The tentacles writhed more intensely, their movements hypnotic and repulsive. "To watch me transcend this pitiful shell and embrace something greater. I am the chrysalis from which a god shall emerge."

Jack strained against the shadowy tendrils that ensnared him, each grip tightening like spectral vines, but to no avail.

Bill tilted his head, the tentacles twisting and curling in a grotesque dance. His abyssal eyes narrowed, brow furrowed just so—a poker tell Jack recognized from countless games. Bill raised the dagger just so, the blade gleaming with unholy light, poised to strike Brett's heart.

Ro'brt unleashed an otherworldly wail, a sound that sliced through the fetid air, reverberating with primal fury, causing the candles to flare with a searing brilliance that pushed back the darkness and scattered the lurking abominations. The *Necronomicon's* pages quivered violently, as if an unseen force ripped at them. Jack lunged forward—part man and part beast—as Bill plunged the dagger toward Brett's heart. A furious leap propelled him across the distance, and the dagger pierced his own abdomen—a sacrifice born of desperation.

At that instant, Jack caught a glimpse of a dangerous-looking Turk—Viktor, it must be—standing beside Bill. Viktor regarded Jack with steely eyes and produced a Luger, aiming it directly at him.

With a wild haymaker, Ro'brt struck the American ambassador, sending the man staggering forward, and he collided violently with Viktor, causing the gun to discharge and ricochet through the cellar. He crawled away, turned, and fled into the darkness.

Bill gazed down at the wounded Jack as grotesque appendages swarmed his face, ready to devour him. With a surge of adrenaline-fueled fury, Jack tore the dagger from his belly and plunged it into Bill's eye. A sickly gurgle escaped Bill as his writhing protuberances went limp. Jack knelt over Brett, Bill's blood mingling with his own on the stone altar.

From the shadows, Viktor muttered an ancient incantation, and something alien coiled within Jack. *Shub-Niggurath's* essence pulsed in his veins, twisting his will, forcing his hand to betray his heart.

Jack's mind screamed, trapped within his body as he was compelled to reach into Bill's skull, retrieve the ceremonial blade, and raise the bloody dagger over Brett once more. His movements were not his own.

Ro'brt charged at Viktor, his punch a blur—like the toll of a bell. Viktor went limp, the Luger clattering from his hand and skidding across the floor, coming to rest at Mike's feet.

The dark enchantment over Jack shattered. Collapsing from the ordeal, his hand reached for the satchel, fingers closing around the mirror—its hunger palpable even in chaos.

Ro'brt cradled Brett with one arm and propped up Jack with the other. "Help me!"

Spurred into action, Mike rushed to Jack, hauling him up.

"I'm fine," Jack lied, grip tightening on the mirror, drawn to its dark allure. Pain-wracked but resolute, they helped carry Pedro, the gang limping after Ro'brt through the fiery chaos, emerging into Pamplona's streets—now unrecognizable, forever altered.

Above them, space-time rippled, struggling to contain the non-Euclidean horror. Jack's mind buckled as he gazed upon the leviathan rising from the sea.

Cthulhu, a towering abomination, rose impossibly vast—a nightmarish fusion of octopus, dragon, and humanoid. His head writhed with slimy tentacles, pulsing with malevolent life, each one oozing primordial filth that hissed on shattered stone.

His leathery wings stretched wide, blotting out the sun and casting the world in shadow. As they unfurled, the sky warped, bending to his will, unable to contain the magnitude of his presence. His eyes glowed with twin suns, ancient and unfathomable, seething with the madness of eons.

As his body emerged, the ground trembled, waves crashing with the force of a thousand storms. The air hummed, low and otherworldly, vibrating through bone and mind. Cobblestones rippled absurdly, illusions battered by an unseen wind.

Reality itself twisted, contorting to accommodate the eldritch presence. Pamplona's streets warped; buildings leaned at impossible angles, their structures unraveling like threads pulled from a tapestry. Jack's own tongue and teeth felt strange in his mouth—contorting, foreign, as though his body was no longer his.

Cthulhu gazed down, indifferent, ancient. His eyes, vast and unfathomable, locked onto the minuscule figures below. The weight of eons crushed Jack's spirit—staring into that starless abyss, hopelessness consumed him. Around the god, the *Byakhee* circled, their bat-like wings beating against the tortured air, a sound that reverberated deep into Jack's bones. These abominations—twisted amalgamations of bird and insect—moved with unnatural grace, their soulless eyes scanning the chaos below.

The ground shook, buildings collapsed, and villagers screamed. *Byakhee* swooped, claws sinking into flesh, lifting their prey skyward with predatory elegance. The harrowing screams faded into silence. Above, Cthulhu blotted out the dawn, his monstrous silhouette devouring the sun's light. Shadow enveloped the world, the air thick with unspeakable dread.

Jack stood paralyzed, each breath a struggle. Madness gnawed at his mind, whispering promises of release. Beneath him, the earth trembled. Fissures opened, swallowing humanity's remains. Despair settled in his bones.

Then came the pain. A pulse, rhythmic and sharp, beat through Jack's core. His hand found the mirror's handle buried in his side, trembling with a life of its own. The surface burned against his skin, its heat searing through his palm. Smoke curled faintly where his fingers clutched the glass, but he didn't let go. A whisper slid through his mind: *Deeper.*

Memories flared—fires raging, the señorita's voice low and sure: *"Tómalo. Es un regalo."* Her smile, faint and sad, stayed with him. The way she pressed it into his hands, her eyes dark and glinting like the mirror itself. He had believed it was a gift. Or had it been a curse? The screams came back to him, louder now. The screams of the innocent.

His righteous mask cracked, each memory splitting it wider. He'd thought he was the hero. He'd been wrong. The mirror hadn't been vengeance. It had been protection.

Deeper. The whisper grew louder. The mirror shuddered in his grip, the heat blistering his palm. He felt his flesh crack, but still he held on. His mind splintered, the cracks glowing with a searing, alien light. Through them, the light erupted. It rushed through him, expanding, illuminating. His vision sharpened. He saw everything. Every sin, every choice, every thread of existence stretched unbroken before him, infinite and unbearable.

The light wasn't warmth. It wasn't peace. It was raw. Blinding. It peeled him open, layer by layer, until there was nothing left but truth. Jack didn't resist. He let it in. He let it burn.

The light rose higher, but beneath it, the darkness stirred. It threaded through the cracks, low and hungry. Jack felt it pulling at him. It whispered without words. A weight, heavy and inevitable, dragged at the edges of his mind.

Deeper.

His hands trembled, his body straining. The mirror grew heavier, the light inside it roaring against the darkness. Jack raised it, arms shaking, and turned it toward the god. He met Cthulhu's unblinking gaze.

The mirror rippled like water. Time froze. The universe exhaled.

Cthulhu's eyes widened. A flicker of something—confusion, perhaps—passed through his vast gaze. His tentacles froze mid-writhe, suspended in stillness. He stared into his own reflection, vast and incomprehensible.

Reality buckled. Buildings twisted. Streets melted into liquid. The sky fractured into colors that burned the eyes. Existence, torn apart by the god's being, seemed to hesitate. The light pouring from Jack, reflected in the mirror, consumed the shadow of the god.

Jack's mind burned, brighter than ever. He saw it all—the terror wasn't power. It was absence. An endless void devouring itself.

Cthulhu stared into the mirror, the abyss meeting its own gaze. A crease formed on his brow. For a fleeting instant, the ancient god hesitated. The light surged again. The void screamed.

Then it happened. A suddenness beyond comprehension—a *VWOOP*. Cthulhu spiraled inward, drawn into the abyss within the glass. His immense form collapsed, sucked into the mirror.

Reality snapped back with a violent shudder. The heavens groaned. Streets convulsed. A collective scream rose from the world as the void devoured the god.

The roar tore through the air, wrenching Jack's face as though hurled into a tornado. Then the city plunged into silence.

Cthulhu was gone, pulled into the black depths of the mirror. Pamplona stood in silence, its streets a charred ruin—a ghost of what had been. Jack collapsed, the mirror slipping from his blistered hand. Its surface, dark and inscrutable as the cosmos, no longer hummed. Somehow, they were still sane—still themselves. The mirror's terrible light must have cast more than destruction. Perhaps, in its burning truth, it sheltered them too. The storm had passed, leaving only the quiet of something too vast to name.

Jack lay there, his breaths shallow. His arm burned, the skin raw and seared where the mirror's light had torn through him. For the first time, he understood *deeper*. It wasn't the depths of the world. It was the abyss of his own soul, where the darkness waited, eternal and unforgiving.

Pain flared in his abdomen where the eldritch blade had struck. He tore a strip from his shirt and pressed it against the wound, gritting his teeth as he bound it tight. His burned hand trembled as he worked, the pain sharp and relentless. He glanced at Brett, unconscious in Ro'brt's arms, and felt the hollow weight of her absence. But there was no time for rest.

The survivors—Jack, Ro'brt, Brett, Mike, and Pedro Romero—stood amidst the ruins. Ash and despair hung thick in the air. The city lay in smoldering silence, a scar on the earth, a witness to the horror that had almost devoured the world.

Mike surveyed the devastation. "Well," he muttered. "That was a bloody nightmare."

Pedro wiped his bloodied nose and glanced at Jack, his eyes ringed with exhaustion. *Nunca tuve tanto miedo,* he said softly.

Jack nodded, his voice low. *Yo también.*

Ro'brt shifted Brett in his arms. "We need to move."

Mike squinted at them. "What's he saying?"

"He said he's never been so afraid," Jack replied, tightening the knot on his bandage with his trembling, burned hand.

Mike gave a hollow laugh. "Join the club."

Ro'brt started off. "Can't stand here all day."

Jack winced as he fell in step, the ache in his body sharp with each movement. His burned arm throbbed with each swing, and he held it close to his chest. Mike sighed, scanning the ruins. "Don't suppose there's a bar still standing."

Dawn broke over Pamplona with deceptive grace. The sun's light touched the smoldering ruins, casting the streets in shades of lavender and bronze—a fragile beauty against the charred remains. Thin columns of smoke twisted upward as the sun climbed higher, its warmth an illusion of comfort. Jack stared at it, unmoved.

The rising sun offered no solace. It only reminded him of how small they were, how fleeting their struggles seemed beneath its indifferent glow.

LIBRO TRES

III

PAMPLONA TO PARIS, AND MADRID
SUMMER TO FALL, 1924

The Dark Beyond

By Jorah Kai

*There's a species of silence that clings to the edge of
things,
thicker than ink, darker than death—a silence beyond
sound,
as if the cosmos itself has turned away,
and left us to stare, trembling, into the dark beyond.*

*They promised stars, a silver sea, galaxies spinning in
endless dance,
but out there, there's no warmth, no gleam, just a void,
cold as a widow's hands, black as a godless night.*

A darkness that feeds on light, eats stars whole,
leaving only echoes of screams that never reach our ears.

I looked back once—just once—toward Earth,
that fragile, blue breath afloat in the cradle of light.
Gaia, with her clouds and her seas,
the last gasp of life in an endless night.
But out here, she's nothing, a speck in the maw of
eternity,
a candle struggling against the winds of the void.

It was supposed to be glory, this flight,
a soaring communion with the stars,
a plunge into the mysteries where gods keep their secrets.
But the secrets are empty; the gods are dead or never
were.
And I am left spinning, caught in the jaws of the dark
beyond,
swallowed by an ancient silence that knows only hunger.

So here I am, an orphan of stardust,
adrift in the cold veins of the universe,
where light is swallowed and stars are bones.
There's no song, no solace, only the yawning maw,
the dark beyond, waiting, watching,
a promise that all we know, all we are,
will vanish into its endless, pitiless mouth.

CHAPTER 18

TWILIGHT OF FORGOTTEN GODS

JACK STAGGERED INTO THE MIDDAY streets of Pamplona, his body aching, a scarred shell. His abdomen throbbed faintly beneath the tight bandages he'd wound there. His hand, also wrapped, hung stiff at his side, the burned skin hidden but not forgotten. Somehow, though, the pain had dulled overnight. Sleep had done more than it should have.

The city buzzed with rumors of last night's "gas leak," whispers brushing over the unspeakable truth. At Bar Milano, he found Howard, Mike, and Sonia already there, wrapped in their own silence.

Sonia glanced up, her dark hair falling loose over her shoulders. She was Howard's girlfriend from New York, a writer like him, though far gentler in her ambition.

"An explosion, they say?" Sonia broke through the quiet, her voice laced with disbelief. "They're saying Bill died in it. How is that even possible?" Her words hovered, unanswered.

Jack shifted in his seat, pressing a hand to his side. The motion wasn't necessary—it hardly hurt now—but it grounded him. Howard glanced over.

"They say you took some metal last night," Howard said, his tone casual, almost amused.

Jack nodded. "Through and through," he murmured. "They patched it up at the hotel."

Howard raised an eyebrow. "Lucky," he said, then paused. "Really metal?"

Jack hesitated, then shook his head. "A knife."

Howard took that in, saying nothing. Just a slight nod, as if that explained everything.

Mike shifted, uneasy. "Strange types asking questions," he muttered. "Not just any police. Too sharp. Too tailored." His eyes shifted away, scanning the room as though those men might walk in at any moment.

Howard leaned forward, his voice smooth with sedatives. "The official story is a gas leak... mass hallucination." His gaze held on Jack. "But what really happened?"

Jack's silence was weighted, his gaze fixed on the table as the truth settled, shared yet unsaid.

When their *huevos rotos con jamón* arrived, they ate in quiet, savoring the warmth of the crispy potatoes and rich jamón. The *pacharán* came next, each bottle promising a gentler release from their thoughts.

Sonia's voice softened, breaking the silence again. "Did you see him? Bill... before..." Her words trailed off, laced with grief.

Howard's curiosity sparked. "What did you see?" His voice was gentle, coaxing. He shared his sedatives like they were breath mints, and with the *pacharán* warming their veins, Jack and Mike began to speak.

They skirted the edges of the truth, leaving details raw, sharing only as much as they dared. They touched on Bill's change, on rituals stained with blood, on Cthulhu's shadow over Pamplona. Howard listened, enraptured, laughing and crying with them, his mind threading together fragments of a nightmare he couldn't fathom.

In the dim comfort of Bar Milano, with the *pacharán* stacked between them, they balanced on the edge of madness, telling a story the city would never believe.

Jack glanced around, seeing his own emptiness reflected in their eyes—all but Howard, who seemed alive with the need to understand.

"You can't write about this," Jack said abruptly, his tone sharp.

Howard's smile was enigmatic. "Of course, Jack," he murmured, though his eyes hinted at a different story.

Amid the tense backdrop, two inebriated locals erupted in shouts near their table. One stumbled across their space, sending bottles of *pacharán* flying. The whirlwind of fists and fury spilled out the doorway, leaving disheveled calm in its wake.

"Make that four brawls sidestepped," Sonia declared, her tone sharp with resolve. A cluster of irate townsfolk brushed against their proximity but retreated under her formidable glare. "Seems we're needing reinforcements."

"Dance with Mike, Sonia," Howard urged, his voice tinged with a medicated haze. "It's all foolishness."

"Let's reclaim the pub," Mike said, rallying his spirits. "They can't commandeer it all."

"True, Mike," Howard said, a bitter edge in his voice. "Insults during fiesta are intolerable. Don't they know you saved Spain?"

Howard, buoyed by drink and the sweet *pacharán*, slipped into Bill's guise of the merry prankster.

Jack's eyes caught a wiry man in expensive clothes and tinted lenses—Edward Bausch, whom Bill always called "Ray" to avoid remembering his real name.

Jack tightened his grip on his glass as Ray muttered something about bankruptcy, his tone dripping with condescension. Bill's voice echoed in Jack's head: "Never written a damn thing worth reading."

Jack stood abruptly. "Hey, Ray," he called. The room fell silent. "Why don't you take your fancy eyewear outside so I can remove it from your weaselly little face?"

Edward adjusted his glasses, his grin faltering.

Jack stepped closer, fists clenched. "You've been living off your father's dime for years. Bill saw right through you."

Edward's companions shifted uneasily, their eyes darting between Jack and the exit.

"What's it going to be, *Ray Ban?*" Jack's voice was cold and steady. "Walk out, or do I walk you out like Bill used to? *Vámonos, hombre.*"

Edward blinked, his shoulders sagging. He muttered something to his group, and they hurriedly settled their tab before slinking out.

Jack turned back to the table and drained his glass. "*Suizo,*" he said, the word clipped. "Let's not waste any more time."

In front of the ticket booths in the square, two lines of people waited. Some sat on chairs, others crouched on the ground with blankets and newspapers wrapped around them. The morning's wicket openings promised tickets for the bullfight. The night was clearing, and the moon hung low. A few people in line were already asleep.

At the Café Suizo, hands curled around glasses of Fundador as murmurs filled the room. The door slammed open, and Ro'brt Ctholh'en's entry cut through the noise. His gaze, wild and haunted, swept the café.

"Where's Brett?" His demand sliced the air, sharp and raw.

"She's safe. She's fine," Jack said calmly, not looking up.

"She was with you," Ro'brt accused, stepping closer.

"She must still be resting."

"She's not."

"I don't know where she is."

Ro'brt's face was sallow under the dim light. He leaned over the table, his voice low but tense. "Tell me where she is."

"Sit down," Jack said. "I'm sure she's fine now."

"The hell she is!" Ro'brt's voice cracked, anger rising.

"You can shut your face."

"Tell me where Brett is."

"I won't tell you a damn thing."

"You know where she is."

"If I did, I wouldn't tell you."

"Oh, go to hell, Ctholh'en," Mike called from the corner, his tone languid. "Brett's gone off with the bullfighter chap. They're on their honeymoon."

"You shut up."

"Oh, go to hell!" Mike said again, stretching his legs out under the table.

"Is that where she is?" Ro'brt turned back to Jack, his voice dangerous.

"Go to hell!"

"She was with you. Is that where she is?"

"Go to hell!"

Ro'brt lunged at Jack, his aggression palpable. "I'll make you tell me, you damned pimp!"

Jack's reaction was instinctive. He swung at Ro'brt, but Ro'brt was faster, ducking the blow and catching Jack in the gut.

The café blurred. Jack went down hard, and the cold splash of water from a carafe jolted him back to awareness.

Leaning on Mike, Jack managed to find a chair. Mike tugged on Jack's ear, his grin lazy. "I say, you were out cold."

"Where the hell were you?" Jack asked, wiping his face.

"Oh, I was around."

"You didn't want to mix in it?"

"He knocked Mike down, too," Sonia said.

"He didn't knock me out," Mike said. "I just lay there."

Sonia brushed her hair back and glanced at the waiters moving around. "Does this happen every night at your fiestas? Wasn't that Mr. Ctholh'en?"

"I'm all right," Jack said, though his head throbbed. "My head's a little wobbly."

There were several waiters and a crowd of people standing around, their whispers buzzing like flies.

"¡Vaya!" said Mike. "Get away. Go on." He waved his hand irritably, and the waiters herded the gawkers away.

"It was quite a thing to watch," Sonia said. "He must be a boxer."

"He is," Jack muttered, running a hand through his damp hair.

"I wish Bill had been here," Sonia said, her voice softening. "I'd like to have seen Bill knocked down, too. I've always wanted to see Bill knocked down..." She stopped, her gaze distant. "He was so big."

Jack grimaced, the mention of Bill cutting deeper than the fight.

"I was hoping Ro'brt would knock down a waiter," Mike said, pouring himself another drink. "Get arrested. I'd like to see Mr. Ctholh'en in jail."

"No," Jack said firmly.

"Oh, no," Sonia added. "You don't mean that."

"I do, though," Mike said. "I'm not one of these chaps who likes being knocked about. I never play games, even."

Mike took a slow drink, his grin returning. "I never liked to hunt, you know. There was always the danger of having a horse fall on you. How do you feel, Jack?"

"All right."

"You're nice," Sonia said to Mike. "Are you really a bankrupt?"

"I'm a tremendous bankrupt," Mike said with a flourish. "I owe money to everybody. Don't you owe any money?"

"Tons," Sonia replied, sipping her drink.

"I owe everybody money," Mike said. "I borrowed a hundred pesetas from Montoya tonight."

"The hell you did," Jack said, his voice sharper now.

"I'll pay it back," Mike said, waving him off. "I always pay everything back."

"That's why you're a bankrupt, isn't it?" Sonia teased.

Jack stood, the ache in his ribs making the movement slow. Their voices seemed far away, like an overheard conversation in a bad play.

"I'm going over to the hotel," Jack said, his voice flat. Then he heard them talking about him as though he weren't there.

"Is he all right?" Sonia asked.

"We'd better walk with him," Mike said, leaning back lazily.

"I'm all right," Jack said again, his tone sharper now. "Don't come. I'll see you all later."

Jack left the café behind, the murmur of voices fading into the cool night. He glanced back once—Howard and the others still seated, a waiter slumped at an empty table, head in his hands.

The square unfolded before him, strangely vivid in the moonlight. Trees whispered in the breeze, flagpoles cast strange shadows, and the theater loomed with unfamiliar menace. It felt like walking through a dream of his hometown, where every detail—each leaf, each wisp of smoke—seemed charged with hidden meaning, as if the world itself had been rewritten.

The cobblestones beneath his feet didn't seem real. Each step echoed faintly, like a memory from another life. He thought of a football game long ago, the dazed clarity after a kick to the head. The world had been oddly beautiful then, too—familiar, yet made alien by pain.

Ascending the stairs of the hotel felt like climbing into a cloud. The steps stretched endlessly, and Jack moved as though both participant and observer in his own life. At the top, light spilled down the corridor like a beacon, and Howard stood silhouetted against it.

"Say," Howard said, his voice casual but edged. "Go up and see Ctholh'en. He's been in a jam, and he's asking for you."

"The hell with him."

"Go on. Go on up and see him."

Jack hesitated. The thought of climbing another flight made his legs feel leaden. "What are you looking at me that way for?"

"I'm not looking at you," Howard replied, his tone tinged with drunken detachment. "Just go. He's in bad shape."

"You were drunk a little while ago."

"I'm drunk now," Howard said, a faint grin flickering across his face. "But you should see him. He wants to meet you."

Jack pushed past him, his steps heavy on the wooden stairs.

In the dim room, Ro'brt's silhouette trembled, his frame wracked by sobs that pierced the silence. Jack stood in the doorway, his calm unsettling against Ro'brt's raw grief.

"I'm sorry, Jack," Ro'brt gasped, each word jagged and soaked in sorrow. "I'm leaving tonight. For everything I've put you through... I'm sorry."

Jack's voice was low, almost a whisper. "No apologies needed."

"The book..." Ro'brt's voice cracked. "It's unleashed pure torment."

Jack's spine prickled as memories surged back—Bill's grotesque transformation, the chanting, the *Necronomicon's* malevolent pages. He latched onto something solid. "How the hell did Bill even have it?"

Ro'brt wiped his face with trembling hands. "He wasn't meant to. I was tracking it—trying to stop this before it began. From the theft at my parents' Hampton manor, to the Thelma Thieves in Paris, to Viktor at Cefalù or Constantinople...a damned Ottoman Turk playing with forces he shouldn't have. Bill was a step ahead every time, tipping them off. Bloody Bill, leaving notes in San Sebastián, warning them I was coming."

"Why?" Jack's voice was tight.

Ro'brt shook his head, eyes hollow. "He thought he was clever. Playing a game he didn't understand. He thought the book was power. A way out. He was dying, you know..."

Jack said nothing. The words sat heavy in the air.

Ro'brt continued, his voice dropping to a whisper. "The *Necronomicon...* the mirror ...it was never about power. It's about the unraveling. That book, in the wrong hands, would bring the absolute disintegration of our reality. Cthulhu would have torn through space-time itself, awakening the sleeping elder gods. Time, matter, meaning—gone. Only chaos."

Jack stared, unblinking.

"I knew," Ro'brt admitted, his words trembling. "I kept silent. You've shouldered this alone, and now it's yours to bear. Forever."

Jack's chest tightened. The air in the room seemed to thicken, pressing against him.

Ro'brt's tear-soaked eyes met Jack's, the weight of his confession unbearable. "That *señorita...* she wasn't what you think. The mirror... it's unearthly. My father, Jack. My true father. I found him. In Egypt. *Nyarlathotep.*"

The name hit Jack like a physical blow. It echoed from the forbidden chapters of the *Necronomicon,* a name synonymous with chaos and humanity's darkest nightmares.

"Egypt," Jack managed to choke out, his voice thin. "Why? Your dreams...?"

Ro'brt's body trembled as if clutched by unseen hands. "Nyarlathotep's whims are not for us to understand," he said, his voice frail but laden with dread. "Last night wasn't just about halting Cthulhu's rise—it was about using you, Jack."

Tears streamed down Ro'brt's face. "You're now the keeper," he said, the words heavy with finality.

"Keeper?" Jack repeated, the term foreign and ominous.

"The mirror," Ro'brt murmured. "It restrains the absolute disintegration of our reality. But the burden remains yours. Forever."

Jack stood frozen, hollowed by the revelation.

"You knew about Bill... about everything," Jack said flatly. "Why Brett?"

Ro'brt's shadowed figure seemed to shrink in the sparse light. "Because she loves you, Jack," he said softly. "True love was the key. It had the power to transform Bill. He was dying, you know."

Jack's breath caught. "But the... rising?"

"Maybe Bill loved you as well," Ro'brt murmured.

Jack recoiled slightly. "I can't hate you, Ro'brt. There's nothing left to feel."

Ro'brt's face twisted in sorrow, his silhouette dimming against the room's faint glow.

"Maybe one day you'll understand why I did it," Ro'brt said. He reached out, gripping Jack's hand. Their handshake was brief, awkward, and unbearably heavy.

"Goodbye, Ro'brt," Jack said, turning away. His steps were slow and deliberate, each one carrying the weight of an epoch. He left Ro'brt behind in the dark, silent room.

Jack woke with a throbbing headache, street bands weaving through his foggy mind. A vague promise to escort Sonia to the bull procession lingered. He changed the bandage on his hand and abdomen, marveling at how well he had healed overnight—it was almost like a dream. Dressing slowly and painfully, he stepped into the cool morning air, the bloodied bandage around his abdomen a silent reminder of past horrors. Navigating the crowded square, an unsettling vision seized him—two cities overlaid like cyclopean remnants from forgotten dimensions. This Pamplona thrived with morning bustle; the other, a desolate specter where fire devoured twisted, non-Euclidean structures and lifeless bodies lay scattered like broken offerings. He shook his head, trying to dismiss the vision. His hand instinctively clutched the satchel at his side, feeling the mirror's pulse beneath his fingers—a silent heartbeat echoing with malevolent intent. What had he unleashed? What was he trapping? And for how long?

As the two worlds teetered on the edge of reality, the full weight of his choices pressed upon him—the mirror's dark power, an unspoken pact of dire consequences and lurking fears. Reaching the square, he observed two lines of men before the ticket booths, their calm patience stark against the ticking clock nearing seven. He quickened his pace toward the café, the echoes of cyclopean whispers fading as he arrived. The waiter greeted him with news that his companions had already gone.

"How many were they?"

"Two gentlemen and a lady."

That was all right. Howard and Mike were with Sonia. She had been afraid last night they would pass out. That was why Jack was to be sure to escort her. Jack drank the coffee and hurried with the other people toward the bull ring. Jack was not groggy now. There was only a bad headache. Everything looked sharp and clear, and the town smelled of the early morning.

The stretch of ground from the edge of town to the bull ring was muddy. A crowd filled the fence that led to the ring, and the outside balconies and the top of the bull ring were packed with people. Jack heard the rocket and knew he could not get into the ring in time to see the bulls come in, so he shoved through the crowd to the fence, being pushed close against the planks. Between the two fences of the runway, the police were clearing the crowd. They walked or trotted into the bull ring. Then people began to run. A drunk slipped and fell. Two policemen grabbed him and rushed him over to the fence. The crowd was running fast now. A great shout echoed as Jack, putting his head between the boards, saw the bulls just coming out of the street into the long-running pen. They were gaining on the crowd. Just then, another drunk staggered from the fence, waving a blouse. He wanted to do capework with the bulls. Two policemen grabbed him, one hit him with a club, and they dragged him to the fence, pressing themselves flat as the bulls and the crowd rushed past. There were so many people running ahead of the bulls that the mass thickened and slowed as they went through the gate into the ring.

As the bulls galloped past—heavy, muddy-sided, horns swinging—one surged ahead, caught a man in the back, and lifted him into the air. The man's arms were by his sides; his head snapped upward as the horn pierced him. The bull lifted and then dropped him. The bull lunged at another runner, but he vanished into the crowd. The mass of people pushed through the gate into the ring, the bulls close behind. The red door of the ring shut, and the crowd on the outside balconies pressed to the inside; there was a shout, then another.

The man who had been gored lay face down in the trampled mud. People climbed over the fence, and Jack could not see him because the crowd was so thick around. From inside the ring came shouts; each one signaled a bull charging into the crowd. The intensity of the cries revealed how bad things were. Then the rocket went up, meaning the steers had gotten the bulls out of the ring and into the corrals. Jack left the fence and headed back to town.

Back in town, Jack returned to the café for a second coffee and some buttered toast. The waiters were sweeping out the café and mopping the tables. One came over and took his order.

"Anything happen at the *encierro*?"

"I didn't see it all. One man was badly *cogido*."

"Where?"

"Here." Jack put one hand on the small of his back and the other on his chest, where it looked as though the horn must have come through. The waiter nodded and swept the crumbs from the table with his cloth.

"Badly *cogido*," he said. "All for sport. All for pleasure."

He went away and returned with the long-handled coffee and milk pots. He poured the milk and coffee. It came out of the long spouts in two streams into the big cup. The waiter nodded.

"Badly *cogido* through the back," he said. He put the pots down on the table and sat down. "A big horn wound. All for fun. Just for fun. What do you think of that?"

"I don't know."

"That's it. All for fun. Fun, you understand."

"You're not an *aficionado*?"

"Me? What are bulls? Animals. Brute animals." He stood up and put his hand on the small of his back. "Right through the back. A *cornada* right through the back. For fun—you understand."

He shook his head and walked away, carrying the coffee pots. Two men were going by in the street. The waiter shouted to them. They were grave-looking. One shook his head. "¡Muerto!" he called.

The waiter nodded. The two men went on. They were on some errand. The waiter came over to Jack's table.

"Did you hear? *Muerto*. Dead. He's dead. With a horn through him. All for morning fun. *Es muy flamenco*."

"It's bad."

"Not for me," the waiter said. "No fun in that for me."

Later in the day, they learned that the man who was killed was named Vicente Girones and came from near Tafalla. The next day, in the paper, they read that he was twenty-eight years old and had a farm, a wife, and two children. He had continued to come to the fiesta each year after he was married. The next day, his wife came in from Tafalla to be with the body, and the day after, there was a service in the chapel of San Fermín, and the coffin was carried to the railway station by members of the dancing and drinking society of Tafalla. The drums marched ahead, and there was music on the fifes, and behind the men who carried the coffin walked the wife and two children. Behind them marched all the members of the dancing and drinking societies of Pamplona, Estella, Tafalla, and Sanguesa who could stay over for the funeral. The coffin was loaded into the baggage car of the train, and the widow and the two children rode, sitting together, in an open third-class railway carriage. The train started with a jerk and then ran smoothly, going downhill around the edge of the plateau and out into the fields of grain that blew in the wind on the plain on the way to Tafalla.

The bull who killed Vicente Girones was named Bocanegra, Number 118 of the bull-breeding establishment of Sánchez Tabemo, and was killed by Pedro Romero as the third bull of that same afternoon. His ear was cut by popular acclamation and given to Pedro Romero, who, in turn, gave it to Brett, who wrapped it in a handkerchief belonging to Jack and left both the ear and the handkerchief, along with a number of Muratti cigarette stubs, shoved far back in the drawer of the bed-table that stood beside her bed in the Hotel Montoya in Pamplona.

Back in the hotel, the night watchman was sitting on a bench inside the door. He had been there all night and was very sleepy. He stood up as Jack came in. Three of the waitresses entered at the same time. They had been to the morning show at the bull ring. They went upstairs laughing. Jack followed them upstairs and went into his room. He took off his shoes and lay down on the bed. The window was open onto the balcony, and the sunlight was bright in the room. Jack did not feel sleepy. It must have been half past three when he had gone to bed, and the bands had woken him at six. His jaw was sore on both sides. Jack rubbed it with his thumb and fingers. That damn Ctholh'en. He should have hit somebody the first time he was insulted and then gone away. He was so sure that Brett loved him. He was going to stay, and true love would conquer all. Someone knocked on the door.

"Come in."

It was Howard and Mike. They sat down on the bed.

"Some *encierro*," Howard said.

"I say, weren't you there?" Mike asked. "Ring for some beer, Howard."

"What a morning!" Howard said. He mopped his face. "My God! What a morning! And here's old Jack. Old Jack, the human punching bag."

"What happened inside?"

"Good God!" Howard exclaimed. "What happened, Mike?"

"There were these bulls coming in," Mike said. "Just ahead of them was the crowd, and some chap tripped and brought the whole lot of them down."

"And the bulls all came in right over them," Howard said.

"I heard them yell."

"That was Sonia," Howard said.

"Chaps kept coming out and waving their shirts."

"One bull went along the *barrera* and hooked everybody over."

"They took about twenty chaps to the infirmary," Mike said.

"What a morning!" Howard said. "The damn police kept arresting chaps that wanted to go and commit suicide with the bulls. It makes for great inspiration, though."

"The steers took them in, in the end," Mike said.

"It took about an hour."

"It was really about a quarter of an hour," Mike objected.

"Oh, go to hell," Howard said. "You've been in the war. It was two hours and a half for me."

"Where's that beer?" Mike asked.

"What did you do with the lovely Sonia?"

"We took her home just now. She's gone to bed."

"How did she like it?"

"Fine. We told her it was just like that every morning."

"She was impressed," Mike said.

"She wanted us to go down in the ring, too," Howard said. "She likes action."

"I said it wouldn't be fair to my creditors," Mike said.

"What a morning," Howard said. "And what a night!" His eyes shone.

"How's your jaw, Jack?" Mike asked, looking a little sheepish.

"Sore," Jack said.

Howard laughed.

"Why didn't you hit him with a chair?"

"You can talk," Mike said. "He'd have knocked you out, too. I barely saw him before suddenly I was sitting in the street, and you were lying under a table."

"Where did he go afterward?" Jack asked.

"Here she is," Mike said. "Here's the beautiful lady with the beer."

The chambermaid put the tray with the beer bottles and glasses down on the table.

"Now, bring up three more bottles," Mike said.

"Where did Ctholh'en go after he hit me?" Jack asked Howard.

"Don't you know about that?" Mike was opening a beer bottle. He poured the beer into one of the glasses.

"Really?" Howard asked.

"Why, he went in and found Brett and the bullfighter chap in the bullfighter's room, and then he massacred the poor, bloody bullfighter."

Jack closed his eyes and saw a vision of the bloody dagger piercing the Spaniard's chest and the blood pooling on the stone below. "No."

"Yes."

"What a night!" Howard said.

"He nearly killed the poor, bloody bullfighter. Then Ctholh'en wanted to take Brett away. Wanted to make an honest woman of her, I imagine. Damned touching scene."

He took a long drink of the beer.

"He is an ass."

"What happened?"

"Brett gave him what for. She told him off. I think she was rather good."

"I'll bet she was," Howard said.

"Then Ctholh'en broke down and cried and wanted to shake hands with the bullfighter fellow. He wanted to shake hands with Brett, too."

"I know. He shook hands with me."

"Did he? Well, they weren't having any of it. The bullfighter fellow was rather good. He didn't say much, but he kept getting up and getting knocked down again. Ctholh'en couldn't knock him out. It must have been damned funny."

"Where did you hear all this?"

"Brett. I saw her this morning."

"What happened finally?"

"It seems the bullfighter fellow was sitting on the bed. He'd been knocked down about fifteen times, and he wanted to fight some more. Brett held him and wouldn't let him get up. He was weak, but Brett couldn't hold him, and he got up. Then Ctholh'en said he wouldn't hit him again. Said he couldn't do it. Said it would be wicked. So the bullfighter chap sort of staggered over to him. Ctholh'en went back against the wall."

"So you won't hit me?"

"No," said Ctholh'en. "I'd be ashamed to."

"So the bullfighter fellow hit him just as hard as he could in the face and then sat down on the floor. He couldn't get up, Brett said. Ctholh'en wanted to pick him up and carry him to the bed. He said if Ctholh'en helped him, he'd kill him, and he'd kill him anyway this morning if Ctholh'en wasn't out of town. Ctholh'en was crying, and Brett had told him off, and he wanted to shake hands. I've told you that before."

"Tell the rest," Howard said.

"It seems the bullfighter chap was sitting on the floor. He was waiting to get strength enough to get up and hit Ctholh'en again. Brett wasn't having any shaking hands, and Ctholh'en was crying and telling her how much he loved her, and she was telling him not to be a ruddy ass. Then Ctholh'en leaned down to shake hands with the bullfighter fellow. No hard feelings, you know. All for forgiveness. And the bullfighter chap hit him in the face again."

"That's quite a kid," Howard said.

"He ruined Ctholh'en," Mike said. "You know, I don't think Ctholh'en will ever want to knock people about again."

"When did you see Brett?"

"This morning. She came in to get some things. She's looking after this Romero lad."

He poured another beer.

"Brett's rather cut up. But she loves looking after people. That's how we came to go off together. She was looking after me."

"I know," Jack said.

"I'm rather drunk," Mike said. "I think I'll stay rather drunk. This is all awfully amusing, but it's not too pleasant."

He drank the beer.

"I gave Brett what for, you know. I said if she would go about with Arkhamites and bullfighters and such people, she must expect trouble." He leaned forward.

"I say, Jack, do you mind if I drink that bottle of yours? She'll bring you another one."

"Please," Jack said. "I wasn't drinking it, anyway."

Mike started to open the bottle. "Would you mind opening it?" Jack pressed up the wire fastener and poured it for him.

"You know," Mike went on, "Brett was rather good. She's always rather good. I gave her a fearful hiding about Arkhamites and bullfighters and all those sorts of people, and do you know what she said: 'Yes. I've had such a hell of a happy life with the British aristocracy!'"

He took a drink.

"That was rather good. Ashley, the chap she got the title from, was a sailor, you know. Ninth baronet. When he came home, he wouldn't sleep in a bed. Always made Brett sleep on the floor. Finally, when he got really bad, he used to tell her he'd kill her. Always slept with a loaded service revolver. Brett used to take the shells out when he'd gone to sleep. She hasn't had an absolutely happy life. Brett. Damned shame, too. She enjoys things so."

He stood up. His hand was shaky.

"I'm going in the room. Try and get a little sleep."

He smiled.

"They go too long without sleep in these fiestas. I'm going to start now and get plenty of sleep. Damn bad thing not to get sleep. Makes you frightfully nervy."

"We'll see you at noon at the Iruña," Howard said.

Mike went out the door. They heard him in the next room.

He rang the bell, and the chambermaid came and knocked at the door.

"Bring up half a dozen bottles of beer and a bottle of Fundador," Mike told her.

"*Sí, señorito.*"

"I'm going to bed," Howard said. "Poor old Mike. I had a hell of a row about him last night."

"Where? At that Milano place?"

"Yes. There was a fellow there who had helped pay Brett and Mike out of Cannes once. He was damned nasty."

"I know the story."

"I didn't. Nobody ought to have a right to say things about Mike."

"That's what makes it bad."

"They oughtn't to have any right. I wish to hell they didn't have any right. I'm going to bed."

"Was anybody killed in the ring?"

"I don't think so. Just badly hurt."

"A man was killed outside in the runway."

"Was there?" said Howard.

CHAPTER 19

SHRIMPS, BEER, AND COSMIC FEAR

AT NOON, THE CAFÉ BUZZED, its atmosphere thick with echoes of last night's turmoil and today's forced merriment. They sat among the press of bodies, peeling shrimp whose beady eyes and twisted forms offered an eerie counterpoint to the boisterous crowd. Beer flowed freely, its frothy head a flimsy disguise for the dread beneath the revelry.

Jack picked up a shrimp and tore off its head. The creature's remaining body, with dangling legs and curled tail, resembled a miniature sea monster, tentacles splayed in a mock threat. For a moment, the sight unsettled him—a flash of cosmic horror stirring in his mind. The shrimp's twisted form mirrored nightmarish shapes of eldritch terrors.

He stared at it, the world around him dimming. Then he laughed, breaking the spell.

"Fuck you, Cthulhu," he said, popping the shrimp into his mouth.

Howard and Mike looked at him, startled. Catching the mischievous glint in his eye, they each grabbed a shrimp.

"Fuck you, Cthulhu," Howard echoed, grinning as he bit into it.

"Here's to you, old god," Mike added, chuckling as he took a bite.

Jack glanced at him as if Mike had sprouted a dozen eyes, then sighed.

"Fuck you, Cthulhu."

They cheered, drained their beers, and signaled for another round. The tension eased, the shared rebellion lifting their spirits. Jack felt a vibration from his shoulder bag—the mirror a simmering sea of defiance. He ignored it, savoring the brief respite from his ennui.

Overhead, the sky loomed heavy and gray, clouds gathering like omens of a storm, mirroring the unease beneath the surface. The mayor had made his rounds earlier, a brief beacon of reassurance that the fiesta would go on despite the shadow over Pamplona. A memorial had sprung up spontaneously for the workers caught in the previous night's chaos, uniting the town in a somber parade of solidarity. A collection was taken for the wounded and unhoused before the fiesta drew everyone back into its frenetic embrace. Pamplona, nursing a hangover of shock and grief, decided to dress its wounds with more revelry.

Motor cars from Biarritz and San Sebastián cut through the town, spilling out tourists with detached gazes. Sightseeing cars paraded through, including one filled with Englishwomen who surveyed the fiesta through binoculars, an alien spectacle within the spectacle. The dancers, lost in inebriation, seemed oblivious to these foreign onlookers, their revelry undimmed.

The fiesta surged around these interruptions, its vitality undeterred. The tourists, distinct in sports clothes against locals in mourning, were reclaimed by the fiesta's energy, their individuality fading into the crowd like specters. Music melded with discordant laughter, creating a tapestry of sound that smothered reflection. Drums pounded with a heartbeat's insistence, driving the day forward, while pipes sang a mournful dirge for what was lost.

Inside the café, men clung to each other and the moment, their singing a raw expression of life's persistence amidst unseen horrors beyond the fiesta's facade.

As Brett approached, threading through the bustling square with untroubled grace, her arrival seemed theatrical, as if she were the protagonist of the fiesta, delighting in the spectacle crafted for her amusement. Her stride, confident and light, betrayed none of the night's shadows.

"Hello, you chaps!" Brett greeted them, her voice a cheerful melody amidst the cacophony. "I say, I have a thirst."

"Get another big beer," Howard told the waiter, his gaze lingering on Brett with concern.

Jack smiled ruefully, acknowledging Brett's indomitable spirit—or perhaps her blissful ignorance. It was as if the horrors were nothing more than vivid nightmares, now dispelled by morning light.

"Shrimps?"

"Is Ctholh'en gone?" Brett asked.

"Yes," Howard said. "He hired a car."

The beer arrived. Brett lifted the glass mug, her hand shaking. She noticed and smiled, leaned forward, and took a long sip.

"Good beer."

"Very good," Jack said.

Jack was nervous about Mike. He didn't think Mike had slept. He must have been drinking the whole time, but he seemed under control.

"I heard Ctholh'en hurt you, Jack," Brett said.

"No. Knocked me out. That's all."

"He did hurt Pedro Romero," Brett said. "He hurt him badly."

"How is he?"

"He'll be all right. He won't leave the room."

"Does he look bad?"

"Very. He was really hurt. I wanted to pop out and see you chaps for a minute."

"Is he going to fight?"

"Rather. I'm going with you if you don't mind."

"How's your beau?" Mike's question hung in the air. His eyes glossed over—a mirror to the chaos beneath.

"Brett's off with some bullfighter now," he mumbled, his façade of indifference clashing with the jittery tilt of his head. "Before, it was a Dunwich dullard, some Miskatonic miser named Ro'brt Ctholh'en." The corners of his mouth twitched into a semblance of a smile, a dark parody devoid of joy. "Turned out rotten."

Brett stood up. "I'm not going to listen to that sort of rot from you, Michael."

"How's your boyfriend?"

"Damned well," Brett said. "Watch him this afternoon."

"Brett's got a bullfighter," Mike said. "A beautiful, bloody bullfighter."

"Would you mind walking over with me? I want to talk to you, Jack."

Mike's eyes flickered, dimmed by drink and something darker. He had played a losing hand and knew it.

Jack looked at Brett, and the anger softened. Her face held something worth forgetting.

"Your matador," Mike sneered. "Oh, to hell with your *torero!*"

His arm swung in a wild arc, sending the table's contents crashing to the floor. Beer flew, glass broke, and shrimp skidded across the tiles like fleeing insects.

"Come on," Brett said. "Let's get out of this."

In the crowd crossing the square, Jack said, "How is it?"

"I'm not seeing him after lunch until the fight. His people come in and dress him. They're very angry about me, he says."

Brett was radiant. The sun was out, and the day was bright.

"I feel altogether changed," Brett said. "You've no idea, Jack."

"You look well, Brett. Anything you want me to do?"

"No, just go to the fight with me."

"We'll see you at lunch?"

"No. I'm eating with him."

Under the hotel's arcade, as workers arranged tables for the festivities, Jack and Brett found a moment of calm.

"Did you see Ro'brt earlier?" Jack ventured.

Brett shook her head, regret flickering in her eyes. "No, I was out when he came in. I feel awful about Romero; he was beaten, and I didn't even stir. Must've been the drink," she mused.

"And how are you feeling now?" Jack asked, watching her closely.

She responded quickly, vitality in her voice. "Strangely, I've never felt better. Had bizarre dreams, but now I'm just... buzzing with life."

They walked past the theater and out of the square, moving with the crowd between lines of booths. They reached a cross street leading to the Paseo de Sarasate, seeing the crowd of fashionably dressed people.

"Let's not go there," Brett said. "I don't want to be stared at right now."

They stood in the sunlight. It was hot after the rain and clouds from the sea.

"I hope the wind goes down," Brett said. "It's bad for him."

"So do I."

"He says the bulls are all right."

"They're good."

"Is that San Fermín's?" Brett looked at the yellow chapel wall.

"Yes. Where the show started Sunday."

"Let's go in. Do you mind? I'd like to pray for him or something."

They went in through the heavy leather door that moved lightly. It was dark inside. Many people were praying. They knelt at a long wooden bench. After a moment, Brett stiffened and gazed ahead.

"Come on," she whispered. "Let's get out of here. Makes me damned nervous."

Outside in the bright street, Brett looked up at the treetops in the wind. The praying had not been a success.

"Don't know why I get so nervy in church," Brett said. "Never does me any good."

They walked along.

"I'm bad for a religious atmosphere," Brett said. "I've the wrong type of face. You know, I'm not worried about him at all. I just feel happy about him."

"Good."

"I wish the wind would drop, though."

"It's likely to go down by five o'clock."

"Let's hope."

"You might pray," Jack laughed.

"Never does me any good. I've never gotten anything I prayed for. Have you?"

"Oh, yes."

"Oh, rot," Brett said. "Maybe it works for some people, though. You don't look very religious, Jack."

"I'm pretty religious."

"Oh, rot," Brett said. "Don't start proselytizing today. Today's going to be bad enough as it is."

It was the first time Jack had seen her happy and carefree since before she went off with Ctholh'en. They were back in front of the hotel. All the tables were set, and several were filled with people eating.

"Do look after Mike," Brett said. "Don't let him get too bad."

"Your friends have gone upstairs," the German maître d'hôtel said in English. He was a continual eavesdropper.

Brett turned to him. "Thank you so much. Have you anything else to say?"

"No, ma'am."

"Good," said Brett.

"Save us a table for three," Jack said to the German. He smiled his dirty pink-and-white smile.

"Is madam eating here?"

"No," Brett said.

"Then I think a table for two will be enough."

"Don't talk to him," Brett said. "Mike must have been in bad shape," she said on the stairs.

They passed Montoya on the stairs. He bowed but did not smile.

"I'll see you at the café," Brett said. "Thank you so much, Jack."

They stopped at their floor. She went straight down the hall into Romero's room without knocking.

Jack stood in front of Mike's room and knocked. No answer. He tried the knob, and it opened.

Inside, the room was in disorder. Bags were opened, clothing strewn around. Empty bottles lay beside the bed. Mike lay on the bed, looking like a death mask of himself.

He opened his eyes and looked at Jack.

"Hello, Jack," he said slowly. "I'm getting a little sleep. I've wanted a little sleep for a long time."

"You've been a very bad boy, Mike."

"You don't know, Schitt."

Jack turned to leave before things got ugly.

"Don't go. I haven't gotten to sleep yet."

"You'll sleep, Mike. Don't worry."

"Brett's got a bullfighter," Mike said. "But her Arkham idiot has gone away."

He turned and looked at Jack. "Damned good thing, what?"

"Yes. Now go to sleep, Mike. You ought to sleep."

Mike's silence filled the room, heavy and ominous. Jack stared at the closed eyes, sensing a stillness beyond sleep. A glance revealed the culprits: empty bottles, quiet heralds of a bitter retreat. No chuckle escaped Jack; the room was grim.

Brett's image flickered through his mind—sharp, insistent. It spurred him into action, saving Mike from his own bleak bargain. The job done, Mike was left to the night.

The door clicked shut, sealing the chapter. In the next room, Howard sat, turning pages, unknowing.

"See Mike?"

"Yes."

"Let's go and eat."

"I won't eat downstairs with that German head waiter. He was snotty when I was getting Mike upstairs."

"He was snotty to us, too."

"Let's go out and eat in the town."

They went down the stairs. On the way, they passed a girl coming up with a tray.

"There goes Brett's lunch," Howard said.

"And the kid's," Jack said.

Outside on the terrace under the arcade, the German head waiter approached. His red cheeks were shiny. He was being polite.

"I have a table for two for you gentlemen," he said.

"Go sit at it," Jack said. They went across the street.

They ate at a restaurant off the square. It was full of smoke, drinking, and singing. The food was good, and so was the wine. They did not talk much.

When the fiesta surged toward the bullring, they moved with the crowd. Brett sat at ringside between Howard and Jack. Directly below them was the callejón, the passageway between the stands and the red fence of the barrera. Behind them, the concrete stands stood solidly. Out in front, beyond the red fence, the sand of the ring was smooth-rolled and yellow. It looked a little heavy from the rain but was dry, firm, and smooth in the sun.

The sword handlers and bullring servants descended the callejón, carrying wicker baskets of fighting capes and muletas on their shoulders. The capes were bloodstained, compactly folded, and neatly packed in the baskets. The sword handlers opened heavy leather sword cases, revealing the red-wrapped hilts of the sheaf of swords as the cases leaned against the fence. They unfolded the dark-stained red flannel of the muletas and fixed batons in them to spread the fabric, giving the matador something to hold. Brett watched it all, absorbed in the professional details.

"His name is stenciled on all the capes and muletas," she said.

"Why do they call them muletas?"

"I don't know."

"I wonder if they ever launder them."

"I don't think so. It might spoil the color."

"The sanguine essence must congeal them," Howard intoned whimsically.

"Funny," Brett replied. "How one doesn't mind the blood."

Below, in the narrow passage of the callejón, the sword handlers arranged everything. All the seats were occupied. Above, all the boxes were full. There was not an empty seat except in the President's box. When he arrived, the fight would start. Across the smooth sand, in the high doorway leading into the corrals, the bullfighters stood with their arms furled in their capes, talking and waiting for the signal to march into the arena. Brett watched them through her glasses.

"Here, would you like to look?"

Jack looked through the glasses and saw the three matadors. Romero was in the center, Belmonte on his left, and Marcial on his right. Behind them were their people, followed by the banderilleros in the passageway and the open space of the corral. Jack also saw the picadors, their picas rising like lances into the morning fog that seemed to writhe unnaturally. Romero wore a black suit, his tricorne hat low over his eyes and looking badly marked. He stared straight ahead, his gaze piercing. Marcial smoked a cigarette guardedly, holding it in his hand. Belmonte looked ahead, his face wan and yellow, his long wolf jaw jutting out. He was looking at nothing, or perhaps something unseen to others. Neither he nor Romero seemed to have anything in common with the others—they were all alone, or so it seemed under the surface of the fiesta's vibrant chaos.

The President entered; there was handclapping above them in the grandstand, and Jack handed the glasses to Brett. Applause filled the air as the music started, a discordant symphony that seemed to resonate with the eldritch whispers Jack could barely hear through the cursed mirror. Brett looked through the glasses.

"Here, take them," she said.

Through the glasses, Jack saw Belmonte speak to Romero. Marcial straightened and dropped his cigarette, then, looking straight ahead with their heads back and free arms swinging, the three matadors walked out. Behind them came the entire procession, opening out, striding in step, capes furled, everybody with free arms swinging. Behind rode the picadors, their picas rising like lances into the morning fog that seemed to writhe unnaturally. Following them were two trains of mules and the bullring servants. The matadors bowed, holding their hats on, before the President's box, and then approached the barrera below. Pedro Romero took off his heavy gold-brocaded cape and handed it over the fence to his sword handler. He said something to the handler. Close below them, Romero's lips were puffed, and both eyes were discolored. His face was a deep purple and swollen. The sword handler took the cape, looked up at Brett, and handed the cape to her.

"Spread it out in front of you," Jack said.

Brett leaned forward. The cape was heavy and smoothly stiff with gold. The sword handler looked back, shook his head, and said something. A man beside Jack leaned toward Brett.

"He doesn't want you to spread it," he said. "You should fold it and keep it in your lap."

Brett folded the heavy cape.

Romero did not look up at them. He was speaking to Belmonte, whose formal cape had been sent over to some friends. Belmonte looked across at them and smiled, his wolf smile limited to his mouth. Romero leaned over the barrera and asked for the water jug. The sword handler brought it, and Romero poured water over the percale of his fighting attire, then scuffed the lower folds in the sand with his slippered foot.

"What's that for?" Brett asked.

"To give it weight in the wind," Romero replied.

"His face looks bad," Howard remarked.

Jack's thoughts mulled over the possibilities: Did Ro'brt really assault him, or was it the work of the cultists? Hadn't Pedro been beaten unconscious in the cellar? The ambiguity of the night's chaos, intertwined with shadows and whispers, left a residue of doubt. In the aftermath, the lines between friend, foe, and frenzied actions under a moonlit terror blurred, leaving Jack to grapple with the unsettling notion of uncertainty.

"He feels very badly," Brett said. "He should be in bed."

The first bull was Belmonte's. Belmonte was very good. But because he received thirty thousand pesetas and people had stayed in line all night to buy tickets to see him, the crowd demanded that he should be more than very good. Belmonte's great attraction was working close to the bull. In bullfighting, they speak of the terrain of the bull and the terrain of the bullfighter. As long as a bullfighter stays in his own terrain, he is comparatively safe. Each time he enters into the bull's terrain, he is in great danger. Belmonte, in his best days, always worked in the bull's terrain. This way, he gave the sensation of impending tragedy. People went to the corrida to see Belmonte, to experience tragic sensations, and perhaps to witness Belmonte's death. Fifteen years ago, they said if you wanted to see Belmonte, you should go quickly while he was still alive. Since then, he has killed more than a thousand bulls. When he retired, the legend grew about how his bullfighting had been, and when he came out of retirement, the public was disappointed because no real man could work as close to the bulls as Belmonte was supposed to have done—not even Belmonte himself.

Belmonte also imposed conditions and insisted that his bulls should not be too large nor too dangerously armed with horns, so the element necessary to give the sensation of tragedy was missing. The public, who wanted three times as much from Belmonte—who was sick with a fistula—as Belmonte had ever been able to give, felt defrauded and cheated. Belmonte's jaw jutted further out in contempt, and his face turned yellower as he moved with greater difficulty, his pain increasing. Finally, the crowd was actively against him, and he became utterly contemptuous and indifferent. He had meant to have a great afternoon, but instead, it became an afternoon of sneers, shouted insults, and finally, a volley of cushions and pieces of bread and vegetables thrown at him in the plaza where he had had his greatest triumphs. His jaw only jutted further out. Sometimes he turned to smile that toothed, long-jawed, lipless smile when he was called something particularly insulting, and the pain from any movement grew stronger until finally, his yellow face was parchment-colored. After his second bull was dead and the throwing of bread and cushions was over, after he had saluted the President with the same wolf-jawed smile and contemptuous eyes, and handed his sword over the barrera to be wiped and put back in its case, he passed into the callejón and leaned on the barrera below them, his head on his arms—not seeing, not hearing anything, only enduring his pain. When he looked up finally, he asked for a drink of water. He swallowed a little, rinsed his mouth, spat the water, took his cape, and returned to the ring.

Because they were against Belmonte, the public was for Romero. From the moment he left the barrera and went toward the bull, they applauded him. Belmonte watched Romero, too, always watching without seeming to. He paid no attention to Marcial, who was the sort of thing Belmonte knew all about. Marcial had come out of retirement to compete with him, knowing it was a competition arranged in advance. He had expected to compete with Marcial and the other stars of the decadent period of bullfighting, and he knew that the sincerity of his own bullfighting would be so set off by the false aesthetics of the bullfighters of the decadent period that he would only have to be in the ring. His return from retirement had been spoiled by Romero. Romero always did, smoothly, calmly, and beautifully, what Belmonte could only bring himself to do now, sometimes. The crowd felt it; even the people from Biarritz and the American ambassador, sporting a fresh purple shiner, saw it, finally. It was a competition that Belmonte would not enter because it would lead only to a bad horn wound or death. Belmonte was no longer well enough. He no longer had his greatest moments in the bullring. He was not sure that there were any great moments. Things were not the same, and now life only came in flashes. He had flashes of the old greatness with his bulls, but they were not of value because he had discounted them in advance when he had picked the bulls out for their safety, getting out of a motor and leaning on a fence, looking over at the herd on the ranch of his friend, the bull breeder. So he had two small, manageable bulls without many horns, and when he felt the greatness again coming, just a little of it through the pain that was always with him, it had been discounted and sold in advance, and it did not give him a good feeling. It was greatness, but it did not make bullfighting wonderful to him anymore.

Pedro Romero embodied greatness. He loved bullfighting, and Jack believed he loved the bulls and, probably, Brett as well. Everything he could control in the locality, he did in front of her all afternoon. Never once did he look up. He made it stronger that way, doing it for himself as well as for her. Because he did not look up to ask if it pleased, he did it all for himself inside, strengthening him, yet he did it for her too. But he did not do it at any loss to himself. He gained from it all throughout the afternoon.

His first "cuarto" was directly below them. The three matadors took the bull in turn after each charge it made at a picador. Belmonte was first, Marcial second, and then Romero. The three stood to the left of the horse. The picador, his hat down over his eyes, the shaft of his pic angling sharply toward the bull, kicked in the spurs and held them. With the reins in his left hand, he walked the horse forward toward the bull. The bull was watching. Seemingly, he watched the white horse, but really, he watched the triangular steel point of the pic. Romero, watching, saw the bull start to turn his head. He did not want to charge. Romero flicked his cape so the color caught the bull's eye. The bull charged reflexively, finding not the flash of color but the white horse. A man leaned far over the horse, shooting the steel point of the long hickory shaft into the hump of muscle on the bull's shoulder, and pulled his horse sideways as he pivoted on the pic—making a wound, enforcing the iron into the bull's shoulder, making him bleed for Belmonte.

The bull did not insist under the iron. He did not really want to get at the horse. He turned, and the group broke apart, and Romero was taking him out with his cape. He took him out softly and smoothly, then stopped and, standing squarely in front of the bull, offered him the cape. The bull's tail went up, and he charged. Romero moved his arms ahead of the bull, wheeling, his feet firm. The dampened, mud-weighted cape swung open and full as a sail fills, and Romero pivoted with it just ahead of the bull. At the end of the pass, they were facing each other again. Romero smiled. The bull wanted it again, and Romero's cape filled again, this time on the other side. Each time, he let the bull pass so close that the man, the bull, and the cape that filled and pivoted ahead of the bull were all one sharply etched mass. It was all so slow and so controlled. It was as though he were rocking the bull to sleep. He made four veronicas like that and finished with a half-veronica that turned his back on the bull and came away toward the applause, his hand on his hip, his cape on his arm, and the bull watching his back as he went away.

In his own bulls, he was perfect. His first bull did not see well. After the first two passes with the cape, Romero knew exactly how badly the vision was impaired. He worked accordingly. It was not brilliant bullfighting. It was only perfect bullfighting. The crowd wanted the bull changed. They made a great row. Nothing very fine could happen with a bull that could not see the lures, but the President would not order him replaced.

"Why don't they change him?" Brett asked.

"They've paid for him. They don't want to lose their money."

"It's hardly fair to Romero."

"Watch how he handles a bull that can't see the color."

"It's the sort of thing I don't like to see."

It was not nice to watch if you cared anything about the person who was doing it. With the bull who could not see the colors of the capes or the scarlet flannel of the muleta, Romero had to make the bull consent with his body. He had to get so close that the bull saw his body and would start for it, and then shift the bull's charge to the flannel and finish out the pass in the classic manner. The Biarritz crowd did not like it. They thought Romero was afraid, and that was why he gave that little sidestep each time as he transferred the bull's charge from his own body to the flannel. They preferred Belmonte's imitation of himself or Marcial's imitation of Belmonte. There were three of them in the row behind them.

"What's he afraid of the bull for? The bull's so dumb he only goes after the cloth."

"He's just a young bullfighter. He hasn't learned it yet."

"But I thought he was fine with the cape before."

"Probably he's nervous now."

Out in the center of the ring, all alone, Romero was going on with the same thing, getting so close that the bull could see him plainly, offering the body, offering it again a little closer, the bull watching dully, then so close that the bull thought he had him, offering again and finally drawing the charge and then, just before the horns came, giving the bull the red cloth to follow with a little, almost imperceptible jerk that so offended the critical judgment of the Biarritz bullfight experts.

"He's going to kill now," Jack said to Brett. "The bull's still strong. He wouldn't wear himself out."

Out in the center of the ring, Romero profiled in front of the bull, drew the sword out from the folds of the muleta, rose on his toes, and sighted along the blade. The bull charged as Romero charged. Romero's left hand dropped the muleta over the bull's muzzle to blind him, his left shoulder went forward between the horns as the sword went in, and for just an instant, he and the bull were one. Romero was way out over the bull, his right arm extended high up to where the hilt of the sword had gone in between the bull's shoulders. Then, the figure was broken. There was a little jolt as Romero came clear, and then he was standing, one hand up, facing the bull, his shirt ripped out from under his sleeve, the white blowing in the wind, and the bull, the red sword hilt tight between his shoulders, his head going down and his legs settling.

"There he goes," Howard said.

Romero was close enough that the bull could see him. His hand still up, he spoke to the bull. The bull gathered himself, then his head went forward, and he went over slowly, then all over suddenly, four feet in the air.

With each bull's demise, as its dark crimson essence seeped into the parched earth, an unsettling vibration began to resonate from within the leather satchel at Jack's side. It was a macabre chorus thirsting for the bloodshed unfolding in the arena. It was a hunger for the spectacle of death.

"Eat your god and shut up," Jack muttered. With Brett by his side, he pushed aside the unsettling vibrations, immersing himself in the fiesta's vibrant distraction—an echo of the ancient chaos that so recently threatened to tear Europe asunder.

They handed the sword to Romero, and carrying it blade-down, the muleta in his other hand, he walked over in front of the President's box, bowed, straightened, and handed over the sword and muleta.

"Bad one," said the sword handler.

"He made me sweat," Romero replied. He wiped off his face. The sword handler handed him the water jug. Romero wiped his lips. It hurt him to drink out of the jug. He did not look up at Brett.

Marcial had a big day. They were still applauding him when Romero's last bull came in. It was the bull that had sprinted out and killed the man running in the morning—a mad bull who had tasted blood.

During Romero's first bull, his hurt face had been very noticeable. Everything he did showed it. All the concentration of the awkwardly delicate work with the bull that could not see well brought it out. The beating had not touched his spirit, but his face had been smashed, and his body hurt. He was wiping all that out now. Each thing he did with this bull wiped that out a little cleaner. It was a good bull, a big bull with horns, and it turned and recharged easily and surely. He was what Romero wanted in bulls.

When he had finished his work with the muleta and was ready to kill, the crowd made him go on. They did not want the bull killed yet; they did not want it to be over. Romero went on. It was like a course in bullfighting. All the passes he linked up, all completed, all slow, templed, and smooth. There were no tricks and no mystifications. There was no brusqueness. And each pass as it reached the summit gave you a sudden ache inside. The crowd did not want it ever to be finished.

The bull was squared on all four feet to be killed, and Romero killed directly below Brett. He killed not as he had been forced to by the last bull but as he wanted to. He profiled directly in front of the bull, drew the sword out of the folds of the muleta, and sighted along the blade. The bull watched him. Romero spoke to the bull and tapped one of his feet. The bull charged, and Romero waited for the charge; the muleta held low, sighting along the blade, his feet firm. Then, without taking a step forward, he became one with the bull. The sword was high between the shoulders; the bull had followed the low-slung flannel that disappeared as Romero lurched clear to the left, and it was over. The bull tried to go forward, but his legs began to settle. He swung from side to side, hesitated, and then went down on his knees. Romero's older brother leaned forward behind him and drove a short knife into the bull's neck at the base of the horns. The first time, he missed. He drove the knife in again, and the bull went over, twitching and rigid.

Romero's brother, holding the bull's horn in one hand and the knife in the other, looked up at the President's box. Handkerchiefs waved all over the bullring. The President looked down from the box and waved his handkerchief. The brother cut the notched black ear from the dead bull and trotted over with it to Romero. The bull lay heavy and black on the sand, his tongue out. Boys ran toward him from all parts of the arena, making a little circle around him. They began to dance around the bull.

Jack reveled in the raw beauty of the corrida, his senses alight beside Brett.

Romero took the ear from his brother and held it up toward the President. The President bowed, and Romero, running to get ahead of the crowd, came toward them. He leaned against the barrera and gave the ear to Brett. He nodded his head and smiled. The crowd was all about him. Brett held down the cape.

"You liked it?" Romero called.

Brett did not say anything. They looked at each other and smiled. Brett had the ear in her hand.

"Don't get bloody," Romero said and grinned. The crowd wanted him. Several boys shouted at Brett. The crowd—comprising boys, dancers, and drunks—surrounded him, trying to lift him and put him on their shoulders. He fought and twisted away and started running toward the exit amidst them. He did not want to be carried on people's shoulders, but they held him and lifted him. It was uncomfortable; his legs were spraddled, and his body was very sore. They lifted him all the way toward the gate. He had his hand on somebody's shoulder. He looked around at them apologetically. The crowd, running, went out the gate with him.

Back at the hotel, Brett went upstairs. Howard and Jack sat in the downstairs dining room, eating hard-boiled eggs and drinking several bottles of beer. Belmonte came down in his street clothes with his manager and two other men. They sat at the next table and ate. Belmonte ate very little as they were leaving on the seven o'clock train for Barcelona. He wore a blue-striped shirt and a dark suit. The others ate a big meal, while Belmonte answered questions but did not talk much.

Howard was tired after the bullfight. So was Jack. They both took the bullfight very hard. They sat and ate the eggs, and Jack watched Belmonte and the people at his table. The men with him were tough-looking and businesslike.

"Come on over to the café," Howard said. "I want an absinthe."

It was the last day of the fiesta. Outside, the square was bustling with people and preparations for the evening. The music and the dancing continued unabated. The giants and the dwarfs were passing.

"Where's Sonia?" Jack asked Howard.

"I don't know."

They watched the beginning of the evening of the last night of the fiesta. The absinthe made everything seem better. Jack drank it without sugar in the dripping glass, and it was pleasantly bitter.

"I feel sorry about Ctholh'en," Howard said. "He had an awful time."

"Oh, to hell with Ctholh'en," Jack said.

"What do you suppose he'll do?" Howard asked.

"Pick up with his old girl, probably," Jack replied, thinking about somebody named Frances.

They had another absinthe. As Jack sipped his drink, the cursed mirror in his satchel pulsed with dormant power. He ignored it rather easily now, both feeling strangely satiated. Perhaps, he thought drunkenly, he could learn to sleep well again—in time.

"When do you go back?" Jack asked Howard.

"A few days."

"And then?"

"To New York. With Sonia, and then we're getting married."

"That's a shame. Still, you could do worse."

"Well, it was a swell fiesta," Howard said after a while.

"Yes," Jack agreed. "Something doing all the time."

"You wouldn't believe it. It's like a wonderful nightmare."

"Sure," Jack said. "I'd believe anything. Including nightmares."

"What's the matter? Feel low?"

"Low as hell."

"Have another absinthe. Here, waiter! Another absinthe for this señor."

As he drank, the world began to blur at the edges. He was more drunk than he'd ever been. He made his way to Brett's room, where Mike sat on the bed, waving a bottle. Jack sat down, the room spinning unless he focused on a fixed point.

"Brett's gone off with the bullfighter chap," Mike said.

Jack didn't reply, feeling an overwhelming sense of emptiness. Jack lay on the bed, eyes tracing the curling yellow wallpaper like the patterns of a fever dream. The fiesta outside meant nothing to him. Later, Howard and Mike came to get him for dinner, but Jack pretended to be asleep.

"He's blind as a tick," Mike said as they left.

Jack got up and went to the balcony, watching the dancing in the square. The world was clear and bright, but distant and surreal. After washing up, he joined Howard and Mike in the dining room.

"Hello, you old drunk," Mike greeted.

Jack's smile held a quiet knowing, shadowed by the night's deep secrets. The cursed mirror, a silent sentinel in his satchel, bore witness to their shared ordeal, its surface quiet for now. At the table, they sat—three marked by the unseen fourth, a sleeping god entwined with their fate. Their company felt larger, haunted by the absent six, their echoes lingering like the last notes of a forgotten song. Outside, the fiesta danced on, oblivious to the thin line they had walked between worlds.

CHAPTER 20

ELEGY OF THE ELDRITCH

THEY ROLLED POKER DICE FROM a deep leather cup. Howard was out on the first roll. Mike lost to Jack and handed the bartender a hundred-franc note. The whiskeys were twelve francs apiece. Another round began, and Mike lost again, tipping the bartender generously each time. In a room off the bar, a jazz band played. It was a pleasant bar.

They played another round. Jack went out first with four kings. Howard and Mike rolled. Mike won the first with four jacks. Howard took the second. On the final roll, Mike had three kings and let them stay. He handed the dice cup to Howard.

Howard rattled them and rolled: three kings, an ace, and a queen.

"It's yours, Mike," Howard said. "Old Mike, the gambler."

"I'm so sorry," Mike replied. "I can't get it."

"What's the matter?"

"I've no money. I'm stony. I've just twenty francs. Here, take twenty francs."

Howard's expression changed.

"I just had enough to pay Montoya. Damned lucky to have it, too."

"I'll cash you a check," Howard offered.

"That's damned nice of you, but I can't write checks."

"What are you going to do for money?"

"Oh, some will come through. I've two weeks' allowance should be here. I can live on tips at this pub in Saint Jean."

"What do you want to do about the car?" Howard asked Jack. "Do you want to keep it on?"

"It doesn't make any difference. Seems sort of idiotic."

"Come on, let's have another drink," Mike said.

"Fine. This one is on me," Howard replied. "Has Brett any money?" He turned to Mike.

"I shouldn't think so. She put up most of what Jack gave to old Montoya."

"She hasn't any money with her?" Jack asked.

"I hardly think so. She never has any money. She gets five hundred quid a year and pays three hundred and fifty of it in interest to bloody thieves. Blood-sucking vampires."

"I suppose they get it at the source," Howard mused.

"Hasn't she any at all with her?" Jack persisted.

"She gave it all to me when she left."

"Well," Howard said, "we might as well have another drink."

"Damned good idea," Mike agreed. "One never gets anywhere by discussing finances."

"No," Howard concurred.

Howard and Jack rolled for the next two rounds. Howard lost and paid. They went out to the car.

"Anywhere you'd like to go, Mike?" Howard asked.

"Let's take a drive. It might do my credit good. Let's drive around a little."

"Fine. I'd like to see the coast. Let's drive down toward Hendaye."

"I haven't any credit along the coast."

"You can't ever tell," Howard replied.

They drove along the coast road. The green headlands, white and red-roofed villas, patches of forest, and the deep blue ocean with the tide out and water curling along the beach created a picturesque scene. Passing through Saint Jean de Luz and villages further down the coast, they returned inland through rolling country, glimpsing the mountains they had crossed from Pamplona. The road stretched ahead. Howard checked his watch. It was time to head back. He knocked on the window and told the driver to turn around. The driver reversed the car into the grass to make the turn. Behind them lay the woods, a stretch of meadow, and then the sea.

They stopped at the hotel where Mike was to stay in Saint Jean, and he got out. The chauffeur carried in his bags. Mike stood by the car.

"Goodbye, you chaps," Mike said. "It was a damned fine fiesta."

"So long, Mike," Howard replied.

"I'll see you around," Jack added.

"Don't worry about money," Mike said. "You can pay for the car, Jack, and I'll send you my share."

"So long, Mike."

"So long, you chaps. You've been damned nice."

They shook hands and waved from the car to Mike. He stood in the road watching. They reached Bayonne just before the train left. A porter carried Howard's bags from the *consigne*. Jack went as far as the inner gate to the tracks.

"So long, fella," Howard said.

"So long, Lovecraft!"

"It was swell. I've had a swell time," said Howard simply.

"Will you be in Paris?"

"No, I have to sail on the 17th. So long!"

Howard entered through the gate to the train. The porter went ahead with the bags. Jack watched the train pull out. Howard was at one of the windows. The window passed, the rest of the train followed, and the tracks emptied. Jack went outside to the car.

"How much do we owe you?" Jack asked the driver. The price to Bayonne was fixed at one hundred and fifty *pesetas*.

"Two hundred *pesetas*," the driver replied.

"How much more if you drive me to San Sebastián on your way back?"

"Thirty-five *pesetas*."

"It's not worth it," Jack said. "Drive me to the Hotel Panier Fleuri."

At the hotel, Jack paid the driver and gave him a tip. The car was powdered with dust. Jack rubbed the rod case through the dust, feeling it was the last connection to Spain and the fiesta. The driver put the car in gear and left. Jack watched it turn off towards Spain. He entered the hotel and was given a room—the same one he had slept in when Bill, Ctholh'en, and he were in Bayonne. That felt like a lifetime ago. Jack washed, changed his shirt, and went out into town.

At a newspaper kiosk, Jack bought a copy of the *New York Herald* and sat in a café to read it. The mundane, comfortable routines of life in France felt safe, suburban, and strange. Jack wished he had gone up to Paris with Howard, but Paris would have meant more fiesta-ing. He was through with fiestas for a while. It would be quiet in San Sebastián. The season didn't open there until August. Jack could get a good hotel room, read, and swim. There was a fine beach, wonderful trees along the promenade, and many children sent down with their nurses before the season opened. In the evening, band concerts would play under the trees across from Café Marinas. Jack could sit in the Marinas and listen.

"How does one eat inside?" Jack asked the waiter. Inside the café was a restaurant.

"Well, very well. One eats very well."

"Good."

Jack entered and ate dinner. It was a big meal for France but seemed carefully portioned after Spain. He drank a bottle of wine for company—a Château Margaux. It was pleasant to drink slowly, tasting the wine alone. Afterward, Jack had coffee. The waiter recommended a Basque liqueur called *izarra*, made from the flowers of the Pyrenees. It looked like hair oil and smelled like Italian *strega*. Jack asked for a *vieux marc* instead. The *marc* was good. Jack had a second *marc* after the coffee.

The waiter's mood brightened after Jack's generous tip, showcasing the simplicity of pleasing people in France. Unlike Spain, where a waiter's gratitude can be uncertain, France operated on a clear financial basis. Simple expenses earned appreciation, making interactions straightforward and devoid of complex motivations. With a bit of money, Jack secured the waiter's favor, ensuring he would be warmly welcomed back, desired at his table for the genuine value he brought. In France, Jack found comfort in the ease of making connections through clear, simple acts of spending, affirming his place in a society that valued straightforward transactions.

The next morning, Jack tipped everyone a little too much at the hotel to make friends and left on the morning train for San Sebastián. He didn't tip the porter at the station more than necessary, as he didn't think he would see him again. Jack wanted a few good French friends in Bayonne to welcome him if he returned.

At Irun, changing trains and showing passports interrupted his journey. Jack felt foolish for returning to Spain, where certainty eluded him, yet he queued for passport inspection, submitted his bags to customs, secured a ticket, passed through the gate, boarded the train, and after forty minutes and eight tunnels, arrived in San Sebastián.

Even on a hot day, San Sebastián had an early-morning quality. The trees seemed as though their leaves were never quite dry. The streets felt as if they had just been sprinkled. It was always cool and shady on certain streets during the hottest days. Jack checked into a hotel where he had stayed before and was given a room with a balcony overlooking the town's roofs. Beyond them lay a green mountainside.

He unpacked his bags, set down his leather satchel, stacked his books beside the bed, put out his shaving kit, hung clothes in the armoire, and bundled laundry. Jack showered and went downstairs for lunch. Spain hadn't switched to summertime, so he was early. He reset his watch, recovering an hour by coming to San Sebastián.

In the dining room, the concierge brought him a police bulletin to fill out. Jack signed it, asked for two telegraph forms, and wrote a message to Hotel Montoya to forward all mail and telegrams to his new address. He sent a wire to the office to hold mail but forward all wires to San Sebastián. Then he had lunch.

After lunch, Jack read in his room and drifted off to sleep. For once, his dreams were peaceful. When he woke at half past four, he found his swimsuit, wrapped it with a comb in a towel, and headed downstairs to the *Concha*. The tide was halfway out. The beach stretched smooth and firm, the sand bright yellow under the soft light.

He changed in the bathing cabin, then walked barefoot across the warm sand, feeling it sink slightly beneath each step. The water stretched ahead, scattered with people bobbing in the surf or lounging on the beach. Far out, where the headlands of the *Concha* nearly met, a line of white breakers kissed the horizon. The tide was retreating, but a few slow waves still rolled in, gathering their weight before breaking softly on the shore.

Jack waded in. The water was cold, sharp against his skin. He dove into a wave, swam underwater, and surfaced as the chill faded. He struck out toward the raft, pulled himself onto the hot wooden planks, and stretched, feeling the sun bake the seawater from his skin.

He couldn't believe how cleanly it had healed. The skin smooth, untouched, as if nothing had pierced him at all. He ran his fingers over it, but there was nothing—just the memory, lingering like a distant, forgotten nightmare.

A boy and a girl were at the other end. The girl had undone her bathing suit strap, letting the sun bronze her skin. The boy lay beside her, murmuring softly, and she laughed, flipping to soak up more sun.

Jack lay there until he dried, then dove into the water again, this time going deep with eyes open. Beneath the surface, it was all green murk and shifting light. He swam up, hauled himself back onto the raft, dove again, and swam to shore.

Back on the beach, he lay in the sun until dry, then walked back to the cabin, rinsed off with fresh water, and rubbed himself dry, the warm day clinging to his skin.

Jack walked around the harbor under the trees to the casino and then up one of the cool streets to Café Marinas. An orchestra played inside. Jack sat on the terrace, enjoying the fresh coolness on the hot day with a glass of lemon juice and shaved ice, followed by a long whiskey and soda. He sat in front of the Marinas for a long time, read, watched people, and listened to music.

Later, as dusk fell, Jack walked around the harbor and along the promenade before returning to the hotel for supper. There was a bicycle race on the Tour du Pays Basque, with riders stopping that night in San Sebastián. In the dining room, a long table of bicycle riders ate with their trainers and managers. They were all French and Belgians, paying close attention to their meals but enjoying themselves. At the head of the table were two good-looking French girls with much Rue du Faubourg Montmartre chic. Jack couldn't discern if they were spoken for. They chatted in slang, sharing private jokes that some at the far end didn't repeat when the girls asked to hear them. The next morning at five o'clock, the race resumed with the last lap, San Sebastián–Bilbao. The riders drank a lot of wine and were burned and browned by the sun. They didn't take the race seriously except among themselves, racing so often it didn't matter who won, especially in a foreign country where money could be arranged.

A rider leading by two minutes had an attack of boils, which were very painful. He sat on the small of his back. His neck was very red, and his blond hair was sunburned. The other riders joked with him about his boils. He tapped his fork on the table.

"Listen," he said, "tomorrow, my nose is so tight on the handlebars that the only thing that touches those boils is a lovely breeze."

One of the girls looked at him down the table, and he grinned and turned red. "The Spaniards," they said, "do not know how to pedal."

Jack had coffee on the terrace with the team manager of a major bicycle manufacturer. He said it had been a pleasant race and would have been worth watching if Bottechia hadn't abandoned it at Pamplona. The dust had been bad, but in Spain, the roads were better than in France. Bicycle road racing was the only sport in the world, he said. Had Jack ever followed the Tour de France? Only in the papers. The Tour de France was the greatest sporting event in the world. Following and organizing road races had made him know France. Few people knew France. All spring, summer, and fall, he spent on the road with bicycle racers. Look at the number of motor cars now that followed the riders from town to town in a road race. It was a rich country and more *sportif* every year. It would be the most *sportif* country in the world. It was bicycle road racing and football that did it. He knew France. *La France sportive.* He knew road racing. They had a cognac. After all, it wasn't bad to get back to Paris. There is only one *Paname.* In all the world, that is. Paris is the town; the most *sportif* in the world. Did Jack know the Chope de Nègre? Jack did not. Jack would see him there sometime. He certainly would. They would drink another *fine* together. They certainly would. They started at six o'clock, less than a quarter in the morning. Would Jack be up for the departure? He would certainly try to. It was very interesting. Jack would leave a call at the desk. They said goodbye until the next morning.

In the morning, Jack awoke to find the bicycle riders and their following cars had been on the road for three hours. He had coffee and the papers in bed, then dressed and took his bathing suit to the beach. Everything was fresh, cool, and damp in the early morning. Nurses in uniform and peasant costumes walked under the trees with children. The Spanish children were beautiful. Some bootblacks sat together under a tree, talking to a soldier. The soldier had only one arm. The tide was in, and there was a good breeze and surf on the beach.

Jack undressed in one of the bath cabins, crossed the narrow line of beach, and entered the water. Swimming through the rollers, he sometimes dove to avoid them. In the calmer water beyond the break, he floated, seeing only the sky and feeling the swell's rhythmic drop and lift beneath him. Jack swam back toward the surf, riding face down on a big roller into the shore, then turned to swim parallel to the beach, striving to stay in the wave's trough to avoid being overtaken by a breaking wave. The effort of swimming in the trough exhausted him, prompting him to turn again and head out toward the raft. The buoyant, cold water seemed to defy the possibility of sinking. The swim to the raft, lengthened by the high tide, felt like a timeless, infinite struggle, but eventually, Jack pulled himself onto the raft and sat, water dripping from him, on the boards warming in the sun. He surveyed the bay: the ancient town, the casino, the treelined promenade, and the grand hotels with their white porches and gold-lettered names filled his view. To the right, a green hill crowned with a castle nearly enclosed the harbor. The raft swayed with the water's movements. Across the narrow passage to the open sea stood another towering headland. The idea of swimming across the bay intrigued Jack, yet the fear of cramps held him back.

On the shore, Jack found clarity in solitude. Hours blended into days, and days into weeks. He watched figures come and go while remaining resolute. Each distant bather echoed his thoughts, a note in life's symphony. The mirror, his silent companion, whispered muted, sputtering existential dread, yet Jack focused on his breath. With each passing moment, he contemplated wisdom hard-earned, justice served in shadowed corners, courage in quiet defiance, and temperance against unyielding tides. In that quiet moment, an inner strength to endure surged within him. "The path of the righteous is like the morning sun, shining ever brighter till the full light of day," Jack whispered, watching the horizon where sky met sea with profound calm. "Though the waters roar and foam and the mountains quake with their surging, there is a river whose streams make glad the city of God." He exhaled deeply, a breath laden with pain. His heart, once troubled, made space for forgiveness. Perhaps the real harm to Spain came from the boys of war, not Spain itself. Even Ro'brt, through each trial, marked a step toward serenity. Maybe, one day, home would beckon him back. Jack smiled under the cloudless sky.

One day—early fall by then, though still warm—as all the brilliant hues of twilight seemed to perform only for him, He rose, toes curled over the raft's edge as it tipped with his weight, and dove cleanly and deeply to come up through the lightening water, blew the salt water out of his head, and swam slowly and steadily into shore.

After he was dressed and had paid for the bath cabin, Jack walked back to the hotel. He glanced at the satchel. The mirror, dormant lately, hadn't caused much grief. He hoped to keep it under his thumb a while yet. The bicycle racers had left several copies of *L'Auto* around, and he gathered them up in the reading room, took them out, and sat in an easy chair in the sun to read about and catch up on French sporting life. While he was sitting there, the concierge came out with a blue envelope in his hand.

"A telegram for you, sir."

Jack poked his finger along under the fold that was fastened down, spread it open, and read it. It had been forwarded from Paris:

*COULD YOU COME HOTEL MONTANA MADRID
AM RATHER IN TROUBLE BRETT.*

He tipped the concierge and read the message again. A postman was coming along the sidewalk. He turned in the hotel. He had a big mustache and looked very military. He came out of the hotel again. The concierge was just behind him.

"Here's another telegram for you, sir."

"Thank you," Jack said.

He opened it. It was forwarded from Pamplona.

*COULD YOU COME HOTEL MONTANA MADRID
AM RATHER IN TROUBLE BRETT.*

The concierge stood there waiting for another tip, probably.

"What time is there a train for Madrid?"

"It left at nine this morning. There is a slow train at eleven and the Sud Express at ten tonight."

"Get me a berth on the Sud Express. Do you want the money now?"

"Just as you wish," he said. "I will have it put on the bill."

"Do that."

Well, that meant San Sebastián all shot to hell. Jack supposed, vaguely, he had expected something of the sort. He saw the concierge standing in the doorway.

"Bring me a telegram form, please."

He brought it, and Jack took out his fountain pen and printed:

*LADY ASHLEY HOTEL MONTANA MADRID
ARRIVING SUD EXPRESS TOMORROW LOVE JACK.*

That seemed to handle it. That was it. Send a girl off with one man. Introduce her to another to go off with him. Now go and bring her back. And sign the wire with love. That was it all right. Jack went in to lunch.

He did not sleep much that night on the Sud Express. In the morning, Jack had breakfast in the dining car and watched the rock and pine country between Ávila and El Escorial. He saw the Escorial out of the window, gray and long and cold in the sun, and did not give a damn about it. He saw Madrid come up over the plain, a compact white skyline on the top of a little cliff away off across the sun-hardened country.

The Norte station in Madrid is the end of the line. All trains finish there. They don't go on anywhere. Outside were cabs and taxis and a line of hotel runners. It was like a country town. Jack took a taxi, and they climbed up through the gardens, by the empty palace and the unfinished church on the edge of the cliff, and on up until they were in the high, hot, modern town. The taxi coasted down a smooth street to the Puerta del Sol, and then through the traffic and out into the Carrera San Jerónimo. All the shops had their awnings down against the heat. The windows on the sunny side of the street were shuttered. The taxi stopped at the curb. Jack saw the sign **HOTEL MONTANA** on the second floor. The taxi driver carried the bags in and left them by the elevator. Jack could not make the elevator work, so he walked up. On the second floor up was a cut brass sign:

HOTEL MONTANA. Jack rang, and no one came to the door. He rang again, and a maid with a sullen face opened the door.

"Is Lady Ashley here?" Jack asked.

She looked at Jack dully.

"Is an Englishwoman here?"

She turned and called someone inside. A very fat woman came to the door. Her hair was gray and stiffly oiled in scallops around her face. She was short and commanding.

"*Muy buenos,*" Jack said. "Is there an Englishwoman here? I would like to see this English lady."

"*Muy buenos.* Yes, there is a female English. Certainly, you can see her if she wishes to see you."

"She wishes to see me."

"The *chica* will ask her."

"It is very hot."

"It is very hot still this time of year in Madrid."

"And how cold in winter."

"Yes, it is very cold in winter."

Did Jack want to stay himself in person in the Hotel Montana?

Of that as yet, he was undecided, but it would give him pleasure if his bags were brought up from the ground floor in order that they might not be stolen. Nothing was ever stolen in the Hotel Montana. In other *fondas*, yes. Not here. No. The personages of this establishment were rigidly selected. Jack was happy to hear it. Nevertheless, he would welcome the upbringal of his bags.

The maid came in and said that the female English wanted to see the male English now, at once.

"Good," Jack said. "You see. It is as I said."

"Clearly."

He followed the maid's back down a long, dark corridor. At the end, she knocked on a door.

"Hello," said Brett. "Is it you, Jack?"

"It's me."

"Come in. Come in."

He opened the door. The maid closed it after him. Brett was in bed. She had just been brushing her hair and held the brush in her hand. The room was in that disorder produced only by those who have always had servants.

"Darling!" Brett said.

He went over to the bed and put his arms around her. She kissed him, and while she kissed Jack, he could feel she was thinking of something else. She was trembling in his arms, and she was very small.

"Darling! I've had such a hell of a time."

"Tell me about it."

"Nothing to tell. He only left yesterday. I made him go."

"Why didn't you keep him?"

"I don't know. It isn't the sort of thing one does. I don't think I hurt him any."

"You were probably damn good for him."

"It wasn't that. He shouldn't be living with anyone. I realized that right away."

"No."

"Oh, hell!" she said. "Let's not talk about it. Let's never talk about it."

"All right."

"It was rather a knock his being ashamed of me. He was ashamed of me for a while, you know."

"No."

"Oh, yes. They ragged him about me at the café, I guess. He wanted me to grow my hair out. Me, with long hair. I'd look so like hell."

"It's funny."

"He said it would make me more womanly. I'd look a fright."

"What happened?"

"Oh, he got over that. He wasn't ashamed of me long."

"What was it about being in trouble?"

"I didn't know whether I could make him go, and I didn't have a *sou* to go away and leave him. He tried to give me a lot of money, you know. I told him I had scads of it. He knew that was a lie. I couldn't take his money, you know."

"No."

"Oh, let's not talk about it. There were some funny things, though. Do give me a cigarette."

He lit the cigarette.

"He learned his English as a waiter in Gib."

"Yes."

"He wanted to marry me, finally."

"Really?"

"Of course. I can't even marry Mike."

"Maybe he thought that would make him Lord Ashley."

"No. It wasn't that. He really wanted to marry me. So I couldn't go away from him, he said. He wanted to make it sure I could never go away from him. After I'd gotten more womanly, of course."

"You ought to feel set up."

"I do. I'm all right again. He's wiped out that damned Ctholh'en."

"Good."

"You know I'd have lived with him if I hadn't seen it was bad for him. We got along damned well."

"Outside of your personal appearance."

"Oh, he'd have gotten used to that."

She put out the cigarette.

"I'm thirty-four, you know. I'm not going to be one of these bitches that ruins children."

"No."

"I'm not going to be that way. I feel rather good, you know. I feel rather set up."

"Good."

She looked away, her gaze distant, as if peering into some bleak horizon only she could see. "I've been having the most horrible nightmares, Jack," she whispered, her voice brittle with a barely concealed terror. "Dreams of Pamplona, of being trapped... by you, by Bill! Even poor, dead, Bill, all turning into... something else. Monstrous, end-of-the-world nightmares. Do you think it's fear of commitment?" Her laugh, meant to be light, carried a tremor of genuine fear.

Then he saw she was crying. The sobs came from a place deep within, wracking her frame. She wouldn't look up. Jack enveloped her in his arms.

"Don't let's ever talk about it. Please don't let's ever talk about it."

"Dear Brett."

"I'm going back to Mike." He could feel her crying as he held her close. "He's so damned nice and he's so awful. He's my sort of thing."

She would not look up. Jack stroked her hair. He could feel her shaking.

"I won't be one of those bitches," she said. "But, oh, Jack, please let's never talk about it."

They left the Hotel Montana. The woman who ran the hotel would not let him pay the bill. The bill had been paid.

"Oh, well. Let it go," Brett said. "It doesn't matter now."

They rode in a taxi down to the Palace Hotel, left the bags, arranged for berths on the Sud Express for the night, and went into the bar of the hotel for a cocktail. They sat on high stools at the bar while the barman shook the martinis in a large nickel shaker.

"It's funny what a wonderful gentility you get in the bar of a big hotel," Jack said.

"Barmen and jockeys are the only people who are polite anymore."

"No matter how vulgar a hotel is, the bar is always nice."

"It's odd."

"Bartenders have always been fine."

"You know," Brett said, "it's quite true. He is only nineteen. Isn't it amazing?"

They touched the two glasses as they stood side by side on the bar. They were coldly beaded. Outside the curtained window was the lingering summer heat of Madrid.

"I like an olive in a martini," Jack said to the barman.

"Right you are, sir. There you are."

"Thanks."

"I should have asked, you know."

The barman went far enough up the bar to avoid hearing their conversation. Brett had sipped from the martini as it stood on the wood. Then she picked it up. Her hand was steady enough to lift it after that first sip.

"It's good. Isn't it a nice bar?"

"They're all nice bars."

"You know, I didn't believe it at first. He was born in 1905. I was in school in Paris, then. Think of that."

"Anything you want me to think about it?"

"Don't be an ass. Would you buy a lady a drink?"

"We'll have two more martinis."

"As they were before, sir?"

"They were very good." Brett smiled at him.

"Thank you, ma'am."

"Well, bung-o," Brett said.

"Bung-o!"

"You know," Brett said, "he'd only been with two women before. He never cared about anything but bullfighting."

"He's got plenty of time."

"I don't know. He thinks it was me. Not the show in general."

"Well, it was you."

"Yes. It was me."

"I thought you weren't going to ever talk about it."

"How can I help it?"

"You'll lose it if you talk about it."

"I just talk around it. You know I feel rather damned good, Jack."

"You should."

"You know it makes one feel rather good deciding not to be a bitch."

"Yes."

"It's sort of what they have instead of God."

"Some people have God," Jack said. "Quite a lot."

"He never worked very well with me."

"Should we have another martini?"

The barman shook up two more martinis and poured them out into fresh glasses.

"Where will we have lunch?" Jack asked Brett. The bar was cool. You could feel the heat outside through the window.

"Here?" asked Brett.

"It's rotten here in the hotel. Do you know a place called Botín's?" he asked the barman.

"Yes, sir. Would you like to have me write out the address?"

"Thank you."

They lunched upstairs at Botín's. It is one of the best restaurants in the world. They had roast young suckling pig and drank *Rioja Alta*. Brett did not eat much. She never ate much. Jack ate a very big meal and drank three bottles of *Rioja Alta*.

"How do you feel, Jack?" Brett asked. "My God! What a meal you've eaten."

"I feel fine. Do you want a dessert?"

"Lord, no."

Brett was smoking.

"You like to eat, don't you?" she said.

"Yes," Jack said. "I like to do a lot of things."

"What do you like to do?"

"Oh," Jack said, "I like to do a lot of things. Don't you want a dessert?"

"You asked me that once," Brett said. She looked at him, her fingers running delicately through his hair. "Why don't you get old, Jack?"

Jack smiled faintly. "Maybe I am old. Just hiding it well."

She tilted her head, studying him. "No, you don't change. Not really."

"Yes," Jack said. "So I did ask you before. And getting old isn't all it's cracked up to be. Let's have another bottle of Rioja Alta."

"It's very good."

"You haven't drunk much of it," Jack said.

"I have. You haven't seen."

"Let's get two bottles," Jack said.

The bottles came. He poured a little in his glass, a glass for Brett, then filled his glass. They touched glasses.

"Bung-o!" Brett said.

Jack drank his glass and poured out another. Brett put her hand on his arm.

"Don't get drunk, Jack," she said. "You don't have to."

"How do you know?"

"Don't," she said. "You'll be all right."

"I'm not getting drunk," Jack said. "I'm just drinking a little wine. I like to drink wine."

"Don't get drunk," she said. "Jack, don't get drunk."

"Want to go for a ride?" Jack said. "Want to ride through the town?"

"Right," Brett said. "I haven't seen Madrid. I should see Madrid."

"I'll finish this," Jack said.

Downstairs, they came out through the first-floor dining room to the street. A waiter went for a taxi. It was hot and bright. Up the street was a little square with trees and grass where taxis were parked. A taxi came up the street, the waiter hanging out at the side. Jack tipped him, told the driver where to drive, and got in beside Brett. The driver started up the street. Jack settled back. Brett moved close to him. They sat close against each other. In his leather satchel, a little mirror swished with the hypnotic push and pull of the Mediterranean Spanish sea, and in it, the snoozing, light afternoon slumber of an elder god, Cthulhu. Perhaps, for a long time, if Jack was good, perhaps for long enough. Jack put his arm around Brett, and she rested against him comfortably. It was very hot and bright, and the houses looked sharply white. They turned out onto the Gran Vía.

"Oh, Jack," Brett said, shifting in her seat, and for a moment, he saw her eyes wide like saucers, and they both remembered the chaos of Pamplona. "Are we going to be okay?"

Ahead was a mounted policeman in khaki directing traffic. He raised his baton. The car slowed suddenly, pressing Brett against Jack.

"Yes," Jack said, a tight smile painted on his stoic visage. "We're all good, and all is well."

Her eyes, reflecting the endless cosmos, held a quiet certainty. "We could have had such a damned good time together."

"Isn't it pretty to think so?"

THE END

CHAPTER 21

EPILOGUE: REQUIEM OF NEON FURY
CHONGQING, 2025

THE TYPHOON BATTERED THE GLASS. Neon lights flickered against wet streets, their fractured reflections smeared by rain. Thunder cracked, rattling the pane like a gunshot.

Inside the apartment, Garrett H. Jones adjusted his spectacles, his hands unsteady. A manuscript lay closed on the desk, its weight felt in the silence.

"Intense," Garrett murmured, nearly swallowed by the roar outside. He leaned back, leather chair protesting, and stared at

Kai. "But timely," he said with a grin, lifting his steaming coffee cup as if it were champagne. "A literary renaissance after a century. Chin chin."

"Ninety-nine years, to be precise," Kai replied. His cup chimed softly as his gaze lingered on the city lights.

Garrett nudged the manuscript aside, studying Kai. "This idea of 'co-writing with Hemingway's ghost'... Another fantasy?"

Kai sat in shadow. The desk lamp cast enough light to hint at his figure—a leather satchel in his lap, a sleek guitar case at his side. His fingers tapped the satchel in a rhythm too measured to be casual. He watched the manuscript as if waiting for it to speak. "Reality bends, Garrett. Press hard enough, it breaks."

Garrett exhaled. "Boundaries exist, even in art."

Kai's smile sharpened. "Sand lines at low tide. One wave, and they're gone."

"You've been on a streak lately," Garrett said, forcing a smile. "Three albums and a novel in a year? Where's it coming from? Divine inspiration?"

Kai's smile thinned, his eyes drifting. "Not divine," he said softly. His fingers pressed flat on the satchel. "Something darker."

"The Dark Beyond." Garrett waited for a joke. None came. Kai nodded, his smile brittle. Silence stretched between them.

A faint vibration threaded the air. Garrett straightened. He first blamed the storm, but this was sharper, more insistent—a note plucked on unseen strings. He stared at the guitar case, then the satchel.

"New trinket in there?" he asked, noticing how the satchel had become a more constant presence lately. "Since this book's been on your plate, you carry that thing everywhere. What's in it?"

Kai lowered his eyes. His hand rested on the satchel. "Old. A very old trinket," he said lightly, though his tone lacked warmth. The satchel's weathered leather and layers of dusty cloth hinted at its origins, likely sourced from an antique shop downtown. The silence lengthened between them. Inside, the hum matched his heartbeat. "It's a mirror," he said finally, his voice low, as if naming it gave it power.

Garrett leaned forward, and Kai, startled, slipped his hand inside. The hum swelled, pulling at him, demanding, and his fingers found the handle. He froze, and the room seemed to ripple, the storm's howl stretching into a low, resonant drone.

"Kai?" Garrett's voice drifted, distant and distorted, as if coming through deep water.

Kai's vision blurred. Neon lights fell into amber and gold smears. The rain-slicked window faded, and the storm's roar gave way to low conversation and a jazz saxophone's soft lament. Smoke and wine thickened the air. Laughter, sharp and brittle, sliced through the haze. A saxophonist swayed in the corner, his tune languid yet mournful. The place felt both electric and intimate, a stage where dreams flared before dying to ash.

In the back, Ernest Hemingway leaned forward. Candlelight caught in his whiskey, turning the glass into a quiet beacon. His jaw cut through the smoke, his voice low and measured.

"Honesty, Zelda," he said. "If you're not honest on the page, you might as well write fairy tales."

Zelda Fitzgerald's laughter cracked like breaking glass. "Fairy tales? And what would you know about honesty, Ernest? Not as much as you know about fairies' tails, you hairy fairy, you." Her dress shimmered as she clutched her champagne. "All you write about are men drowning their sorrows in booze and war."

Scott winced, ash drooping from his cigarette. "Come on, darling," he said, reaching for her arm. "Let's not make a scene. He's only trying to help."

Zelda pulled free, her laughter gone bitter. "Help? From the man who treats heartbreak like a plot device?" She turned sharply, heels clicking as she left. Scott followed, throwing a helpless look over his shoulder.

Hemingway drained his whiskey, expression unchanged. As Scott hurried after Zelda, Hemingway's gaze shifted, pinning Kai with the precision of a rifle sight. "Back so soon? You're chasing it, aren't you?"

Kai frowned, a flicker of red eyes in the corner catching his attention—only the glow of a cigarette's trailing ember. Still, a faint sulfur scent prickled at his nose.

"The story," Hemingway said, lifting his empty glass so the candlelight danced. "The truth no one else dares touch because it burns."

Kai opened his mouth, but Hemingway leaned in, shadows scrawling hard lines across his face. "*The Sun Also Rises* wasn't about bullfights or booze. It's about wounds we carry, the ones we can't heal. Bring gods if you want. Just don't forget: the real horror's in us, not in some monster."

Kai's throat went dry. A whiff of brimstone tightened his chest. He grabbed Scott's abandoned drink and swallowed it in one go. "Thanks for everything, Ernest. You've lived up to your name. It matters to me that we've walked this road together."

Hemingway's eyes narrowed. "Do you even know what you're holding?"

Before Kai could reply, laughter erupted nearby. Hunter S. Thompson leaned into view, wild-eyed, sunglasses flashing. "You're ripping through the veil, kid!" he hissed. "Blending gods and madness, twisting nightmares with ours—it's genius or lunacy. Probably both!" He gripped Kai's shoulder, energy crackling in his fingertips. "Ernest frets about the cost. Me? I love it. Just promise me one thing."

"What is it?" Kai asked, catching another glimpse of red at the edge of his vision. Something felt off, as if this lucid dream were slipping its leash.

"Don't let the bastards tame it. You've birthed something raw and bloody. Let it breathe."

Hunter's laughter shattered the air. "And when it bites back?" he barked, standing. "Don't flinch!" He vanished into the haze, leaving Kai's mind spinning.

The café trembled. Shadows warped along the walls. Kai stumbled, but a firm hand steadied him.

"Waller?" he asked, blinking at the red-bearded figure who stood taller than memory. Rob's smile eased the tension a little.

"Does it make sense?" Rob asked, voice calm but curious. "Any of it?"

Kai tried to form words, but Rob continued. "Feels rushed. The mirror, the gods, all that cosmic madness—it's piling up fast. You sure the reader can keep up?"

Kai hesitated, ears still ringing with the mirror's hum. "Isn't that cosmic horror? Everything crumbling before you can hold it?"

Rob chuckled. "Maybe. Or maybe you like them fumbling in the dark."

Kai attempted a smile. "Ernest taught me to make them work for it." But when he glanced back, Hemingway's chair was empty. His stomach lurched, dizziness washing over him.

"Either way, you've got me thinking," Rob said. "Hope it's worth it, Kai."

Before Kai could answer, the café buckled. The jazz warped into a discordant wail. Rob faded, swallowed by shifting shadows. Kai reached out, grasping only emptiness. He lurched forward—and his hand struck wood.

Stillness. Air thick with old ink and aged timber. Kai blinked, head pounding. Beneath his fingers was a desk. On it lay a single envelope, the script on it elaborate, hauntingly familiar.

"To Jorah Kai," it read.

The mirror's hum lingered, faint yet insistent. Kai hovered over the envelope, parchment crackling under his fingers. Its weight pressed against him like a silent warning. The seal bore twisting tendrils that seemed to writhe in the flickering light, sending a pulse up his arm as he broke it. Outside his peripheral vision, shadows inched closer, as if tasting the air.

A whiff of brimstone drifted past. He stiffened. The room felt tighter now, as if the walls leaned in. Kai drew a breath and unfolded the letter, the ink shimmering like distant stars. Each stroke of the pen held a patience beyond mortal measure.

His pulse quickened as he read: "In this grand tapestry of tales, where ink and passion intertwine to capture the essence of the mortal coil, why dost thou summon me, Shakespeare, from the hallowed silence of eternity?"

The Bard's voice seemed to rise from the page, each phrase steeped in centuries. Kai leaned closer, forcing himself to ignore the creeping shadows along the floorboards. The brimstone smell lingered, faint but steady. He felt the mirror's hum deepen, a slow vibration threading through the words.

"Shall I weigh upon the merits of Ernest Hemingway and Jorah Kai, those two scribes of disparate eras, their quills weaving threads through the fabric of human frailty?"

The mirrorverse of Kai's lucid dreamspace answered with a low, pulsing note. He read on, eyes skimming lines of harmony and discord, truths that scratched at the veil. Outside the corner of his vision, the shadows stretched, and he sensed time thinning, as if he had to keep moving or be caught in their grasp.

Then the sonnet formed, perfect in measure, timeless in rhythm. Kai's heart thudded faster. He whispered the lines:

In shadows deep where truths and terrors meld,
A mirror turns, reflecting lives undone.
Its glass contains the stars' abyss, beheld
By those who'd challenge gods, yet fear the sun.
What light remains when courage meets despair?
What voice endures when silence claims its due?
Through wounds unseen, the heart must still declare
The echoes of a world both false and true.
Oh, fleeting muse, whose whispers haunt the page,
Thy ink runs black with stars that bled and died.
Yet love and loss are constants, age to age,
Their throbbing pulse the guide where gods abide.
So write, brave scribe, with fire against the cold,
And carve thy truths before the mirror folds.

The air thickened as he finished, charged and uneasy. A subtle tremor ran through the room. Only two words gleamed faintly at the end: "Big Willy."

Kai let out a sound—part laugh, part gasp. His heart drummed in his ears. The brimstone scent sharpened, the mirror's hum grew louder. He knew he could not linger. Shadows pooled beneath the desk and along the walls, pushing him forward without words. He leaned back, breath shallow, a chill settling in his chest. Time was short; he had to move.

The room shimmered into existence—a lavish fever dream of velvet and gold. Chandeliers dripped diamonds; bookshelves stretched impossibly high, their volumes stacked by whim, not reason. The air hung heavy with absinthe and old ink, spiced faintly with brimstone. Kai stood at the center, blinking against the dazzle.

Behind a mahogany desk polished to a mirror sheen lounged Oscar Wilde, his dark curls slightly tousled, catching the candlelight in subtle glints. Dressed in midnight blues and emeralds that shimmered like polished envy, he raised a glass of absinthe, his eyes gleaming with sharp amusement.

"Ah, another visitor," he drawled, voice rich as cream and sharp as glass.

"Interruptions are the luxury of the undisturbed. Sadly, I've known neither luxury nor peace since I met you."

Kai smirked, his eyes drifting to the quivering peacock feather quill, still and yet somehow alive in the candlelight. He tapped his fingers against his chin, watching its delicate tremor. "Better delinquents than dullards. A good mess always improves the décor." He leaned back slightly, letting his gaze roam over the room, lingering once more on the feather. "At least it keeps the furniture awake."

Wilde's brow arched. "A wit that dares to spark back. How novel," he said, stepping forward with deliberate grace. His hand swept through Kai's curls in a swift, theatrical flourish. "Ah, the messy-haired genius trope. How quaint. Shall I compose an ode to these disheveled locks?"

Kai inclined his head. "Not here to dethrone you, old chap. Just borrowing a spark or two to light my own pages." His gaze flicked to a backward-turning clock on the side table. "Time's running in reverse. Might as well collect a few souvenirs."

"Ah, existential terror," Wilde mused, sipping absinthe with deliberate grace. "You dabble in horrors beyond mortal ken, all for art. Admirable or absurd—who can say? Still, you've nerve, and that's more than most."

Kai dipped into a mock bow. "Nerve is cheap. I'm after something rarer. Maybe the meaning gods forgot to patent."

Wilde's laughter rang, musical and dangerous. "Meaning? We pilfer it. It's not gifted by gods; we snatch it from their feasts when they're too drunk to notice." He leaned closer, his voice dropping. "I've dined with Dionysus, you know. I've seen mortal minds snap like twigs. Yet here you are, haggling with me, unafraid."

Kai tasted brimstone on his tongue, the mirror stirring at the edges of his thoughts. Shadows flickered at the room's borders, but he met Wilde's gaze without flinching. "I've run with devils in jazz clubs and traded riddles with ghosts. Dancing with a dandy who outdresses the stars is just another page in my scrapbook."

Wilde studied him, surprise and delight mingling in his grin. "You have a gift, terrible and wonderful. I rather like that you don't beg for meaning. You'd rather pluck it from my cufflinks while I'm distracted."

Kai tapped his chin. "If you're offering, I'll take a cufflink or two. They might suit a nightmare I'm writing."

"Cheeky." Wilde's laughter warmed, genuine now.

He raised his glass. "You amuse me. Perhaps you deserve more than a lecture. I'm invited to Dionysus's estate tonight. Gods, monsters, and a fine vintage. Care to join?"

Kai felt the mirror's hum deepen, the air pressing tighter around him. The brimstone sharpness lingered. "A party with gods and poets? Cherry tomatoes and finer vices? Sounds like a Tuesday. Lead on."

Wilde winked. "Excellent. No need to linger here." He gestured to a tall mirror rippling like black water. "Shortcut. Step through, dear boy. The night is young."

Without waiting, Wilde crossed to the mirror and passed through. Kai grinned at the absurdity and followed. The opulent room dissolved behind him, leaving only the echo of Wilde's laughter.

Kai emerged into a marble hall, where a grand banquet table stretched beneath flickering candles. Vines heavy with overripe grapes curled around alabaster columns. The air smelled of wine, sweetness laced with faint brimstone. He stood steady, oddly at ease.

Oscar Wilde adjusted his emerald cravat, his dark curls slightly tousled from movement. "Welcome to the revels."

Jorah Kai surveyed the room, recognizing figures from old portraits and book covers. Their presence was both familiar and unsettling.

Mark Twain, in a rumpled white suit, leaned back, a cigar smoldering in his hand. "Mixing gods and ghosts like a mad bartender," he said, his voice warm with mischief. "Got the guts to swallow what you've brewed, kid?"

Kai grinned. "If ink, absinthe, and broken rules are on the menu, I'll have seconds. I've survived stranger hangovers." He tapped the table lightly. "Your words still echo down rivers I've never seen. That's gutsy enough for me."

Twain chuckled. "Fair answer. Just mind where those echoes lead."

Before Kai could respond, Edgar Allan Poe drifted closer, twisting a raven's feather quill. "Do you dread the heartbeat in your chest," he murmured, voice soft as midnight, "or the hush after it fails?"

Kai met Poe's hollow gaze, unblinking. "I dread the day I run out of stories worth telling. Hearts stop, but tales linger. I'll keep scratching ink on paper until silence forgets how to find me."

A ghost of a smile touched Poe's lips. "You speak like a man who knows midnight from within."

H.P. Lovecraft, arms folded, observed from a slight distance. His posture was taut, as though containing constellations within. "You've wandered into places no map records," he said, voice clipped. "Not all horrors require your belief. They simply exist."

Kai nodded. "I'm well aware, of that at least, Howard. I'm not here to tame horrors, just to acknowledge them. If I flinch, it's only to step aside and let them pass. Fear's a guide, not a cage."

Lovecraft studied him. "Then tread carefully."

The brimstone tang sharpened. Kai stood firm. After all, he'd come this far. Wilde sipped absinthe, content to watch. From somewhere distant came a low, feral howl. Kai's pulse quickened—not from dread, but the thrill of impossible odds.

A hush fell. The crowd parted. Dionysus entered, crowned with ivy, glowing as if lit from within. The god scanned the room, then addressed them all, his voice resonant and timeless.

"Wilde, Twain, Poe, Lovecraft—and you, Jorah Kai."

He paused, the name heavy with meaning.

"You, who plucked ghosts as though harvesting grapes, have shown both homage and recklessness. Your debts are paid. But beware the line you walk."

Kai squared his shoulders, calm but respectful. "I never meant offense, Lord Dionysus. If I danced too close to the fire, it's because I thought it offered light as well as heat. I'll mind my steps."

Dionysus nodded, stern yet fond. "See that you do." He raised his chalice. For a moment, the room settled, legends and a daring mortal caught in delicate balance.

Then Kai saw it: the authors' eyes flattened, their smiles fixed. Twain's cigar smoke curled and froze, suspended like a conjurer's trick. Poe's ink froze mid-drip, suspended like a cruel joke. Lovecraft's fingers clenched empty air. Wilde stood too still, his emerald pin flashing in the dim light, but no breath stirred his chest. Thin filaments of shadow descended from above, snaring each figure's limbs. Puppets. Every last one.

Kai's stomach turned, but he stayed steady. "So this is a play?" His voice was calm, almost quiet.

Dionysus flickered, his form thinning. "We... are stories," he said, the words unraveling. "Puppets... on a stage..."

From the shadows stepped Nyarlathotep, cloaked in writhing darkness that folded and unfurled like wings. As he emerged fully, the dark receded, revealing his human guise—an Egyptian pharaoh in gold and obsidian, robes edged with intricate hieroglyphs that seemed to shift and writhe. A tall crown rose from his head, glinting like ancient sunfire, and a broad, jeweled collar gleamed across his chest.

His face was too perfect, his smile too wide, the kohl-lined eyes burning with malice.

Black tendrils trailed from his fingers, snaking through the air to the authors. With a twitch, Twain's arm jerked, Poe's head tilted, Lovecraft's posture locked. Wilde bent in a stiff bow, as if hinged at the waist. The hieroglyphs on Nyarlathotep's robes flickered, as if laughing in a language too ancient to decipher.

Nyarlathotep's voice purred, low and mocking. "You thought they came of their own will? No, Kai. They dance at mine. You've chased truths, stolen sparks, toyed with cosmic ink. Did you think there'd be no one holding the strings?"

The howl outside grew louder, deeper, as if pressing against the walls. Kai felt something vast beyond the marble—Cthulhu's bulk warping the very geometry of reality. The grapes shriveled to black rot, the wine soured, but Kai refused to crumple. He lifted his chin.

"You've shown me your hand," he said, his voice steady. "A puppet show, cosmic scale. I won't pretend I can match you trick for trick, but I've written my share of endings. Maybe I'll find one you didn't expect."

Nyarlathotep's grin widened, darkly pleased. "By all means, try to flee. See how far your endings carry you. The abyss travels light, my friend, and it always follows."

The hall trembled. Shadows twisted into impossible angles, collapsing logic. The air thickened with brimstone. The howl rose, hungry and mournful. Kai knew better than to freeze now. If an escape existed, he would find it. He would not become another marionette, strung up for some cruel laughter.

He glanced one last time at the table. Twain, Poe, Lovecraft, Wilde—all hollow now, reduced to grotesque puppets. He would remember them as they had been, not this grim version. Then, without another moment's pause, he turned and ran. His boots rang against the marble as he searched for a door, a mirror—anything.

Behind him, Nyarlathotep chuckled, the sound fusing with the howl. Kai ran harder, the weight of his own story propelling him forward. He was determined to shape his own ending—or die trying.

A sharp rap cracked the humid silence like glass under pressure. The lights flickered ominously, their glow sputtering as shadows danced wildly on the walls. Kai blinked, his eyes unfocused, as though waking from a distant nightmare. He drew a ragged breath, shoulders slackening in a brief flash of relief—he was back in the apartment, no longer lost in that cosmic banquet of puppets and horrors.

But a crease formed between his brows. He pressed his lips together, wondering if he had brought something else back with him. The faint taste of brimstone lingered in the back of his throat, as if he hadn't fully closed the door on whatever lurked beyond.

Garrett frowned, unease sharpening into something colder. "Wasn't expecting anyone," he murmured, voice barely audible over the storm's relentless howl outside.

Kai tried to speak, but only managed a faint, mechanical smile. The tension in the room was thick, and he could feel the mirror's hum as a distant echo in his mind. "Perhaps those boundaries aren't as firm as most people believe," he said quietly, voice tinged with a distant weight. It was as if the words were not his own, or as if he feared an unseen audience might be listening.

A second knock, louder this time, reverberated through the room. Garrett's chest tightened. He glanced at the door, where the storm's roar mixed with something else—a silence too deep, too watchful.

Rising slowly, Garrett moved with caution, as though approaching a predator. His shadow stretched long and distorted. "Whoever it is," he said to no one in particular, "they've got rotten timing."

Kai remained seated, distant eyes fixed somewhere past the walls. His breathing came shallow and uneven, as though trying to tune in to a frequency beyond normal hearing. Garrett hesitated, looking back at him. "Kai, are you all right?"

Kai blinked, head tilting as if catching a distant signal only he could hear. "Time," he murmured, voice low. "Time bends. Time—breaks."

A third knock—sharp, insistent—shattered the fragile silence. Garrett's heart lurched, his pulse a relentless drumbeat in his ears. Cold sweat gathered on his brow, trailing down like icy fingertips. Every instinct screamed against opening the door, yet an unseen force—implacable, inexorable—compelled him forward. The knob turned with an unnatural smoothness, the motion too deliberate, too eager.

The door groaned open, revealing not the dim hallway he expected but a void—a churning abyss of shadows that seemed to writhe with malevolent purpose. The storm's roar died away, replaced by a resonant hum that burrowed deep into Garrett's bones, shaking the very foundation of his reason.

Behind him, Kai stirred. When he spoke, his voice was hollow, mechanical, like the toll of a distant bell. "Your last appointment," he intoned, his face twisted as though tasting something bitter.

Garrett's gaze fixed on the darkness. From its depths, a figure emerged, distorting the air around it, as if reality recoiled at its presence. Blue eyes burned with ancient fire, locking onto Garrett with a force that unraveled his thoughts.

"You're telling a dangerous story, Mr. Jones," the figure said softly, its voice a cruel harmony of frost and flame. "Consider the implications before you publish," it continued, its tone a twisted melody, mocking yet hypnotic. "Critics, after all, can be real killers."

The figure stepped forward, its flowing cape swallowing what little light remained. A tall top hat crowned a pale, angular face etched with menace. Its suit shimmered as though spun from nightmares, each fold catching the dim light like a trap. The air thickened, pressing Garrett's breath into his chest.

The lights flickered, dimming further as the figure's smirk cut through the room, sharp and mocking. Its searing gaze spiraled inward, unraveling the edges of Garrett's sanity. The walls themselves seemed to shudder, the room folding in upon itself, twisting into madness.

The figure moved with serpentine grace, closing the distance in a heartbeat. Jack—if that was its name—reached into the satchel and withdrew a mirror. Its surface rippled like liquid shadow, swallowing the faint light around it.

"You've toyed with dreams," Jack hissed, his voice slipping into Garrett's mind like a scalpel. "Written truths you don't understand. Now, see what lies beyond."

The mirror's surface revealed no familiar image, only a vast, ravenous void that beckoned with a silent hunger. Around them, sigils carved into the walls flared crimson, casting jagged, flickering shadows. Their malevolence painted the room in hellish strokes, each pulse biting at the edges of Garrett's mind.

Garrett stumbled back, the room trembling as the mirror's hum deepened. Jack loomed larger, his presence suffocating, as though the void itself had stepped through the door. Shadows coiled, the light retreating, until Garrett knew there was no escape. No door, no lock, no light could keep it out.

Jorah Kai struggled, but the mirror's hum wove tight around him, a spectral chain binding him to its will. The sigils spiraled inward, their fiery light clawing at his soul with ravenous intent. His reflection shimmered, warped, and finally dissolved into a yawning abyss. In its place, tendrils of darkness writhed, deliberate and hungry. Garrett staggered back, his breath hitching in broken gasps, clutching a silver cross as if it might guard him from the shadows that now twisted and coiled like serpents around the room. The sigils blazed one final, furious light, then dimmed, exhausted, their malevolent work complete. Kai's image stretched, fractured, and was consumed by the mirror's endless maw. No scream marked his passage— only a faint, hollow *vwoop* as he vanished into the void.

The universe shuddered. Threads of reality frayed, exposing the rotted heart of creation, where elder gods stirred in malignant slumber.

Their gaze pierced the tattered veil of time, their presence a putrid madness that seeped into every crack of existence. Space convulsed, folding and collapsing into an unfathomable chaos that warped reality's edges until nothing held firm—no light, no logic, no sanctuary. The sigils pulsed in rhythm with the mirror's song, tearing open a void that roared with a discordant chant, part prophecy, part curse, heralding the horrors that had waited, buried beneath the surface of all we dared to name real.

Then came the crunch—a hideous, maddening crunch—like unseen vermin gnawing at the bones of existence itself, eager to break through from the dark beyond. In the depths of the abyss, Kai's mind faltered, reaching for Paris, for Provence, for the warm shores of Marseilles—places where hope had once bloomed, fragile as spring wildflowers. But the memories drowned beneath an unending tide of scratching whispers and slithering shadows, their sweetness suffocated by the encroaching dark.

Around him, fates worse than death circled in patient silence, ancient and watchful, their coils tightening at the edges of the void. The vast, unseen shapes writhed in timeless hunger, waiting for their moment to strike.

And so it ended, as it had always meant to end: truth and terror entwined, the cosmos folding under the weight of cruel laughter and hollow eyes. There was no safe harbor, no unbroken line, no frontier left untouched. Beyond that final veil, the horrors waited, vast and eternal, their presence a shadow lingering just out of sight—forever and always.

TRANSCRIBER'S NOTES

Obvious printing errors have been silently corrected where clarity required it. Inconsistencies in hyphenation, spelling, and punctuation remain, reflecting the author's fractured state. Any discrepancies introduced during transcription are unintentional.

The manuscript was discovered with Mr. Garrett H. Jones, found alone, his voice a soft, ceaseless murmur, punctuated by sobs of incoherence. Beside him sat two untouched cups of coffee, their warmth long since faded. Jorah Kai, referenced throughout, eventually reappeared after a time, though no explanation was offered for his absence. Those who knew him best claimed he returned… different. His eyes held shadows that shifted in unseen light, an air of otherworldly knowledge clinging to him like a shroud. His words grew measured, almost rehearsed, as though they were not wholly his own. He was changed, unplaceably yet irrevocably altered.

Mr. Jones, though physically unharmed, remains trapped in a labyrinth of fragmented thoughts. His words spiral endlessly, circling themes too alien and incomprehensible to grasp. Whatever clarity once lived in his mind now teeters on the brink of collapse.

His family, troubled by both his condition and the manuscript's unrelenting weight, made the fateful choice to see it published. And so, it rests in your hands now.

What you have read is not merely a story—it is an echo from the depths, a ripple across the fragile surface of reality itself. Whether it serves as a warning or an invitation, a door or a descent, is a question only you can answer. What lies beyond is neither kind nor forgiving. Choose your steps carefully, for once the veil is touched, it is never whole again.

R.W.

ABOUT THE AUTHORS: ERNEST HEMINGWAY

Born July 21, 1899, in Oak Park, Illinois, and passing on July 2, 1961, in Ketchum, Idaho, Ernest Hemingway remains a towering figure in American literature. Celebrated for his concise prose and the "Iceberg Theory," Hemingway's early work as a reporter for the *Kansas City Star* instilled in him a commitment to brevity, clarity, and vigor. This minimalist style is vividly showcased in masterpieces like *The Old Man and the Sea*, *A Farewell to Arms*, and *For Whom the Bell Tolls*.

Hemingway's life was as adventurous as his writing. From the American Midwest to the bohemian streets of 1920s Paris, where he mingled with Gertrude Stein and F. Scott Fitzgerald as part of the "Lost Generation," his experiences deeply influenced his work. He traveled to Spain to cover the Civil War, shaping *For Whom the Bell Tolls*, and lived in Cuba's fishing villages, inspiring *The Green Hills of Africa*. During World War II, Hemingway spent time in Chongqing, China, observing the resilience of the Chinese people and documenting the effects of war, adding a global dimension to his portrayal of conflict.

Known for his rugged lifestyle, Hemingway explored themes of masculinity, adventure, and the profound connection between people and the natural world. His stoic characters navigate brutal challenges with dignity and resolve, mirroring his own indomitable spirit. Despite personal hardships, including injuries from both world wars, Hemingway remained deeply committed to his craft, capturing the complexities of life, the struggle for meaning, and the quiet courage found in adversity.

ABOUT THE AUTHORS: JORAH KAI

Jorah Kai's life is a tapestry of adventure and creativity, encompassing martial arts, music, technology, travel, food, philosophy, revelry, gaming, and writing. His diverse career began as a festival-headlining DJ/producer, transitioned into a full-time existential detective in a part-time city, and evolved into a gonzo journalist inspired by Hunter S. Thompson—a fellow disciple of Hemingway. In 2014, Kai relocated to cyberpunk Chongqing, where he teaches English and art history while writing and editing for *iChongqing*, part of the *Chongqing Daily News Group*, serving a megacity of 34 million.

When the global pandemic struck in 2020, Kai had a Hemingway-in-Kilimanjaro moment, igniting an urgent writing spree that continues today. He became the first Canadian journalist in China to report for CTV News Canada on COVID-19, earning accolades for his accurate predictions that baffled health experts. Kai has published several nonfiction books, including the international bestseller *Kai's Diary: The Invisible War, Year of the Rat,* and *Aye of the Tiger.* His debut novel, the solarpunk fantasy *Amos the Amazing,* became an international bestseller in children's steampunk fiction, followed by *The Sun Also Rises on Cthulhu,* which adds a literary-horror twist to his repertoire.

Kai's writing is cinematic and immersive, reflecting his rich experiences. He enjoys writing on beaches around the world, gazing into the sea, and relishes being on wheels when not stationary. His imaginative storytelling weaves vivid worlds, offering profound insights into the human condition.

AFTER YOU READ

Thank You for Embarking on This Journey
Thank you for exploring the dark and unsettling
realms of this book. If you enjoyed the experience, please
share it with friends, family, or anyone who might
appreciate its unique blend of cosmic horror and literary
homage.
We also kindly ask you to leave a review on Amazon,
Goodreads, or the platform where you purchased it. Your
feedback is invaluable and helps support the authors in
bringing more stories that challenge the boundaries of
imagination.
Thank you for being part of this journey. Stay
connected to the void.

www.ingramcontent.com/pod-product-compliance
Lightning Source LLC
Chambersburg PA
CBHW032135270626
47172CB00008B/32

* 9 7 8 1 9 5 9 6 0 4 1 9 8 *